She blinked dazedly. Her head felt as though it was taking off and flying away. *Control yourself, girl, and do something*, she told herself.

Simon had left someth
She'd photo-copy that. M
volved would bring her do
copy, Belinda ran through t
the stairs to Production a
which was deserted. Going
the sheet of paper upon t
down into another fit of crying. That was when a hand clapped itself against her mouth and something cold and sharp was placed across her throat.

Her body jerked rigid as tears froze in her eyes. She realized with mounting terror that the hand smelled of man, that a knife lay across her jugular . . .

By the same author

The Devil's Maze
The Elect
The Scar
The Victim
The Offering
Striker
The Block

Non-fiction

Hitler and the Age of Horus

GERALD SUSTER

The Force

PANTHER
Granada Publishing

Panther Books
Granada Publishing Ltd
8 Grafton Street, London W1X 3LA

A Panther Paperback Original 1984

ISBN 0-586-06102-9

Printed and bound in Great Britain by
Collins, Glasgow

Set in Times

Preface

Savage & Markby Ltd

MEMORANDUM

To: HVM Vice Chairman
From: JS Chairman
Subject: Personnel
Date: 12 August 1983

Please keep an eye on the following who are, in my view, the most interesting individuals in the Company:-

BOARD OF DIRECTORS

Peter Jackson – Managing Director.
Stanley Haynes – Financial Director.
Brian Bishop – Creative Director.
Chris Faye – Media Director.
Mike Armstrong – Director of Account Management.

ACCOUNT MANAGEMENT

Roy Price – Account Director.
Tony Westbury – Account Director.
Oliver Dawes – Account Supervisor.
Charles Sutherland – Account Supervisor.
Sid Ingram – Account Executive.
George Webbing – Account Executive.
Sandra Lang – Account Executive.
Martin Bottomley – Graduate Trainee.
Robert Slade – Graduate Trainee.

CREATIVE

Ian Sharpe – Assistant Creative Director.
Ronald Potter – Creative Group Head.

Larry Cunningham – Job Controller.
Simon Burns – Copywriter.
Dennis Wilson – Visualizer.

PRODUCTION
Fred Sayers – Despatch Manager.
Nigel Fulton – Posters.
Bill Perkins – Press Production.
Cliff Mitchell – Photo-Copying.

SECRETARIES
Emily Hyde – secretary to Peter Jackson.
Georgina Mainwaring – secretary to Mike Armstrong.
Fiona Spencer-Wingate – secretary to Charles Sutherland and George Webbing.
Belinda Torrance – secretary to Ronald Potter, Simon Burns and Dennis Wilson.
Harriet Baker – secretary to Oliver Dawes and Sid Ingram.

The problem regarding Nick Peters has been resolved satisfactorily. It is hard to believe that he was once our Managing Director.

JOHN SAVAGE
CHAIRMAN

Prologue

'You're all crazy,' the voice from within the cellar insisted. 'This is criminal insanity. You'll never get away with this. The police'll be here soon.'

On the stairs outside the cellar, the young man's body writhed as doubts invaded his mind. Every passing hour added to his fear that he was going steadily mad.

'Uh . . . ohhh . . .' the prisoner groaned suddenly, 'you're killing me. You're killing me slowly. I'm dying. How can you do this? Murderers . . . do you want this on your conscience?'

God help us, the young man thought. *Now perhaps I know how a lunatic feels*. Footsteps sounded on the steps behind him. He turned to see a girl of roughly his own age.

'Darling, are you all right?' she asked concernedly. He shook his head. 'Yes,' she said, 'that's just how he wants us to feel.' For a few seconds they looked into one another's eyes, then she took his hands and squeezed them gently.

'Water . . .' cried the prisoner. 'Please give me water.'

The young man shuddered.

'I don't know,' he mumbled, 'if I can ever go back in there.'

'I'll get it for him,' she said. 'Come on, you must get some rest.' She assisted him up the stairs to the landing, then went into the kitchen, while he crossed the hall unsteadily and entered the living room. A man and a woman were seated on the Chesterfield. Both regarded him anxiously as he made straight for the crystal decanter and poured himself a large, neat whisky.

'How was he?' asked the woman.

The young man shook his head.

'I know how you feel,' said the other man. He put an arm around the woman and gazed at her tenderly.

The young man sank shakily into a chair and drank some more scotch. The spirit burned as it slid down his gullet before imparting a warm glow to his innards. He relished the sensation but it still did little to assuage his anxiety. *This can't be right*, he reflected as he had done countless times today. *It's all insane. What the hell is happening to me?* His eyes roamed the room restlessly, avoiding those of his companions.

Finally, his lids closed wearily as his head lolled back – but his mind continued to creak on obsessively. How would the nightmare end? With the death of the prisoner, perhaps – that was possible – but in what manner and by what means? Or else there was the prospect of defeat, arrest and life-long suffering in a mental hospital. Which was more likely? He didn't know and didn't really dare think about it further.

Yet he wasn't one of the lucky ones who have complete control over their thoughts. His exhausted brain persisted in grinding out his recent past again and again and again – until he longed to cry out with the pain of it.

Dazed by. shock and fatigue, his mind reeled before its contemplation of a horror that had blighted, scarred and broken lives – and souls, if they exist.

Part I

1

It was a glorious first of September. The sky was clear and a dazzling blue, the morning breeze was cool and fresh and sunshine kissed the passers-by on Kensington High Street. Robert Slade couldn't recall when he'd last felt this good.

Today was a big day for him and he'd dressed to reflect it. His young, lean body was adorned by the well-cut, dark blue pin-stripe suit he'd bought at Austin Reed the day before, along with a pale blue shirt, sober blue tie and discreet shoes of black leather. His right arm swung a Samsonite attaché case. His medium-length, chestnut hair had been attractively barbered and his keen, alert face was graced by a happy smile. Today he'd be starting work and he was thrilled by the prospect. This morning would mark the commencement of his career in advertising.

He was about to become a Graduate Trainee in the Account Management department of Savage & Markby, one of London's top agencies. Landing that job hadn't been easy. Savage & Markby had only two places for which three hundred University men and women had competed. Winning one of them had been exhilarating and now he would receive the first instalment of his prize.

Robert had no doubts about his aims. Short term, he would work furiously hard and learn all he could about the business. Medium term, he'd make the Board by the time he was thirty. Long term? As they'd told him at the second interview, 'the sky's the limit'.

Nor did he harbour any doubts about the nature of the business itself. If any had ever existed, he'd long since reasoned them away. After all, if you believed in a free society – which Robert did very firmly – what was wrong with advertising? Nobody *had* to buy anything because of an advertisement. And without advertising, just about every newspaper and magazine would fold, along with independent television and radio – Robert loved pointing that out to the industry's critics. Advertising kept film directors, actors, photographers and other creative spirits in work and many commercials could be defended on purely aesthetic grounds, or else lauded as examples of sharply observed social satire. 'Anyway,' Robert often said these days, 'I *like* advertisements. Always have done.'

He'd allow nothing to stop him from making a spectacular success of the job. Obviously the training would be hard but he could cope with that. He wondered what sort of work they'd be giving him initially. 'I don't care what it is,' he'd told his girlfriend the night before. 'If they tell me to make the tea, fine, I'll make the tea. Still,' he'd smiled at Vickie, 'here's hoping it'll be a bit more than that.'

The Savage & Markby building was a modern, four-storey block just off the High Street. Robert strode into the foyer, approached the uniformed commissionaire, wished him a courteous good morning and showed him the Savage & Markby letter.

'Account Management, second floor,' the man said promptly and indicated the lift. Robert followed his direction, straightened his tie and pressed the call button. Instantly his hand recoiled smartly as though a wasp had stung it and his arm jerked with pained surprise. It took a couple of seconds before he realized that he'd just suffered a small electric shock.

The lift door slid open silently. Robert stepped inside and pressed the second floor button apprehensively. This time all went smoothly. The lift ascended and stopped, the door slid open oncc again and Robert entered Reception, a large, luxurious room furnished in high tech. Black letters on the white wall facing him proclaimed: 'SAVAGE & MARKBY'. Below these sat a smartly dressed girl with an appealing face, who regarded him over a white, curved desk.

'Good morning,' he smiled. 'I'm Robert Slade, the new Graduate Trainee.'

'Oh, good morning!' she sang back cheerfully, 'we've been expecting you. Do take a seat while I buzz Mike and tell him you're here.' Robert sat down. Moments later, a burly man in his thirties barged into Reception and advanced on Robert.

'Morning, Robert,' he declared briskly and extended his hand.

'Good morning, Mr Armstrong.' Robert rose swiftly and extended his.

'Welcome to Savage & Markby.' They shook hands.

'Thank you.' The clasp was firm.

'Like to come this way . . .' The man led and Robert followed. He'd met Mike Armstrong once before, at his first interview, and the latter's straight and direct questioning had impressed him. Passing through an outer office which contained a very pretty girl, they entered Mike's own, which was unexpectedly spartan. It was as though absolutely everything extraneous to the job in hand had been mercilessly banished in favour of simplicity, single-minded concentration and harsh effort. 'Take a seat.' Mike's voice was flat and hard, with a trace of a Midlands accent. His alert, dark eyes bored momentarily into Robert's. Robert held the strong gaze. 'First day,' Mike remarked with a slight smile. 'How d'you feel about that?'

'Oh, fine, thanks.' Robert smiled back.

'Good, I hope you'll be very happy here.' Mike sat back. 'Thought I'd better fill you in on one or two things before you meet your account team.' Robert leaned forward eagerly. 'As you've probably gathered, I'm head of Account Management. That means I carry the can for everything that happens in our department and represent it on the Board. As such, I'm responsible for the Graduate Training Scheme.' He paused while Robert nodded attentively. 'There is no Graduate Training Scheme. In my view, there's only one way of learning how to do something and that's to do it. So you'll be learning on the job.'

'Fine.'

'I'm putting you on Browning's Beers,' Mike continued. 'It's one of our most important accounts. Your job is to assist the Management team in any way they want. In other words, you're starting out as a gofer.'

'Gofer?' Robert looked puzzled.

'Go for this, go for that,' Mike said matter-of-factly. 'It's an American expression. Anyway, show us you're responsible and don't worry, you'll get all the responsibility you can handle.'

'Fine.' Robert looked enthusiastic.

'One small point. We're almost all of us on first name terms here, so I'm Mike, not Mr Armstrong. The sole exceptions to that are Mr Savage and Mr Markby but you won't be seeing much of them for the present. Finally, something I'd like you to remember.' Mike sat forward again, placed his elbows on the plain and sparsely decorated desk and folded his hands. His large head, craggy face, thick neck and powerful shoulders gave Robert the fleeting impression of a bull about to charge. 'One reason I'm here is to make sure you can do your job properly. If for some reason you can't, whether it's a personal problem or something in the agency that's bugging you, then I want to hear about it. You know where my office is. You can come straight to me. If I'm tied up, see Georgina, my secretary and she'll make sure I see you that day. All right?'

'Fine.'

'Any questions?'

'None I can think of.'

'Okay.' Mike rose and Robert rose with him. 'May I wish you a successful career with us.'

'Thank you.' They shook hands over the desk, then Mike ushered Robert back into the outer office and introduced him to Georgina.

'How d'you do, Robert.' Her manner was gracious, her voice exquisitely soft. Her azure eyes appraised him coolly.

'Robert's on Browning's Beers,' said Mike.

'Oh, so you're chucking him in at the deep end, are you?' she laughed.

'Well, at least he'll have fun today, splashing around in the presentation,' Mike answered. 'Where are they all?'

'Conference Room One.'

'Good, I'll take him to meet the team. And can you dig out the Taplin data summary for me?'

'I already have,' said Georgina. 'It's on your desk. Underneath the Stats M.R.'

'Oh. Good thinking.' Mike turned back to Robert. 'This way.'

The trainee accompanied Mike along a corridor, passing confident, well-groomed men, all of whom seemed in a tearing hurry to get somewhere – and more pretty girls, all of whom walked with a provocative sway of their hips. Mike paid them no attention. Robert's eyes roamed.

'As it happens, Bob,' said Tony Westbury, 'you've joined us on a rather critical day.'

'Stimulating introduction, what?' Charles Sutherland remarked genially.

'Oh, couldn't be better,' added George Webbing.

'Sounds very interesting,' Robert commented politely and sipped his coffee. It was five minutes later and he was engrossed by his surroundings. Mike had gone after introducing him to the team who sat around the table, all of whom had warmly welcomed him to Savage & Markby. It hadn't taken Robert long to work out who was who in the hierarchy.

Tony Westbury, the Account Director, was a big, square-shouldered, rather lumbering individual with a pleasant, open face, a mellow, classless voice and an affable, bland manner. Charles Sutherland, the Account Supervisor, was slim, elegant, debonair and languid. He smoked unfiltered Pall Malls which he lit with a chunky silver Dunhill and lay back in his chair as though mildly bored by the whole proceedings. Yet Charles, like Tony, managed to exude an aura of cool and controlled efficiency, unlike George Webbing, the Account Executive. George was short and stout, his rumpled brown suit didn't quite seem to fit him and his curly, straw-coloured hair was a mess. His face was florid and he kept wiping away droplets of perspiration from his brow with a soiled and crumpled handkerchief. His manner was flustered and he appeared to be having difficulty keeping the mass of papers in front of him in order. He also had a smile which was charming and friendly and frequently directed at Robert.

'Very interesting? Let's hope so,' Tony Westbury continued smoothly. 'The client's arriving in about half an hour. What he'll be seeing and what you'll be seeing is a presentation. Last year, Browning's spent a million with us. This year we want them to up it to two million. Last night,' he smiled ruefully, 'we took them out and entertained them.'

'My head still hurts,' groaned George. 'What *did* they put in those Zombie cocktails?'

'Bit of a bore but it had to be done,' Charles murmured to Robert. 'You know, Northern brewers and all that. They come down to London and they want to see the bright lights. Need a change from all that black pudding and tripe and onions. What d'you do, you give 'em the works. Food with French names, drinks with Hawaiian ones and a spot of classy crumpet doing a strip-tease.' He yawned. 'Odd business, advertising.'

'That second stripper was a bit of all right,' George came in enthusiastically. 'Great pair of knockers.'

'Yes, Colin seemed to like her too,' Tony observed. 'Thought his eyes'd pop out of his head when he saw her. No doubt it makes a nice change from the wife. Anyhow, Bob,' he again addressed Robert, 'you won't need to do much today except watch. Should be a good experience for you.' Tony glanced at his gold Rolex. 'We've got a little bit of time in hand, for once. George, can you take charge of Bob and show him the basics? Meet back here in about twenty-five minutes.'

George conducted Robert back through the corridor, stopping frequently to introduce the trainee to a bewildering variety of people whose names and functions Robert forgot almost immediately afterwards.

'This is where it all happens,' George announced with a flourish of his hand in the direction of a set of offices. 'This is our patch. See that door there? That's where you find Tony. If the door's shut, that means he's busy. If it's open, you can knock and walk right in. Charles's door there is always open.' Robert regarded the small office with its plate glass window looking out onto a gracious square. 'But I wouldn't advise you to waste his time. For the rest of us, it's open plan.' George indicated the window-less space, which had been partitioned into sections of varying size by thin, wooden walls which were shoulder high. 'I'm here, you're there,' Robert's space was half the size, 'and over there it's Janet Ross and Fiona Spencer-Wingate. Janet's Tony's secretary, the rest of us share Fiona.'

'Are you gossiping about me again, George?' a high, affected voice squealed from behind a partition. 'Really! The things a poor working girl has to put up with! I do hope the new trainee's not going to be the same. Come on, let's have a look at him.'

Robert found himself propelled into a work area and stared at critically by two girls. Janet, who was plain but had a plump, sweet face, gave him a friendly greeting and returned to her typing. Fiona, who was tall, willowy and disarmingly attractive, carried on regarding him with expressionless blue eyes. It was as though he was a pair of trousers in a boutique and she was appraising how well they'd been cut.

'You'll do as a boss,' said Fiona. 'He looks a rather intelligent boss,' she added to Janet. 'Robert, isn't it? I only hope you're not *too* intelligent. I'm a bear with very little brain, I'm afraid,' she simpered. 'You won't be too hard on me, will you?'

'I'm sure there's no need,' Robert responded with a winning smile, then George ushered him back to his desk.

'Should be all here,' George declared breezily. 'External phone, internal phone, paper, pencils, everything like that.' He opened a drawer and extracted a bound document. 'Ah, that's what we want right now. The Savage & Markby Account Management Plan for Browning Beers.' He waved it in the air. '*I* worked on putting that together,' he added proudly. 'Every important fact about the beer market is here. This document,' he brandished it again, 'repays *careful study*. In fact,' an idea occurred to him, 'why don't you sit down right now and give it the once over while I just see to a few things? Okay? Lovely! There you go.' He pressed the trainee into his chair. 'Won't be a moment. Fiona!' he called out. 'Anybody asks for me, I'm down in Creative,' and George bustled his way back into the corridor.

Robert lit a cigarette and enjoyed the inhalation. It was all very new but so far everything was going well. He had his office, albeit a small one, and his dishy secretary, albeit a shared one. Major events would be happening today and his colleagues seemed like a nice bunch of people. The only thing which bothered Robert was Tony Westbury calling him 'Bob'. He hated to be called 'Bob', everyone said that he wasn't a 'Bob' and something had to be done in due course. On his first day, though, he could hardly object to anything. He blew out a cloud of smoke, shrugged and turned his attention to the Browning's Beers Account Management Plan. George's flushed, friendly face reappeared over Robert's partition roughly twenty minutes later.

'All ready?' he enquired cheerfully. 'Then let's go. Let's go, go, go. Over the top and into battle. Because that's what it is, you see,' he said as Robert joined him, 'it's a battle which you have to win or else you go under. But you've joined the right regiment, young man, I can tell you. This is a *great company*, you take my word for it. A *great company*. Find the Plan interesting?'

'Very,' said Robert, who'd learned more about the beer market in the last twenty minutes than he'd known for the previous twenty-three years. 'I never realized the extent to which six major brewers dominate the trade and its retail outlets.'

'Right, and Browning's is one of them. Not Number One but one of them. And that's where we come in. We want to establish their Champion Bitter as brand leader in the expanding real ale market. Champion Bitter!' George proclaimed, 'the Champion of beers! Right.' They'd reached the Conference Room. 'This,' George assured him, 'is the big one.'

The client breezed into Conference Room One rubbing his hands with joy.

'God, I had a great cock-stand last night!' he announced gleefully. A startled Robert looked bemusedly at the speaker, a grey-haired, thick-set and bespectacled individual. A tall, skinny man with a thick Zapata moustache had followed him into the room and now hovered anxiously in the background. 'Never better!' the first man continued. 'That second stripper was knockout, lads. Brings on heart trouble just thinking about her,' he grinned. 'Oh, and it was quite some nosh too. *Beautiful* cocktails! Young Tim here,' he jerked his thumb backwards, 'had a whale of a time on those. Don't reckon he's recovered his senses yet, have you, Tim?' Tim smiled amiably. 'Terrific! What joys have you got for me today?'

'Oh, the hits just keep on coming, Colin,' Charles informed him airily. 'We've got the *other* agency reel.'

'The *other* agency reel, eh?' Colin's eyes glowed with pleasure behind his gold-framed spectacles. 'I've heard plenty about *that*.' He guffawed while Robert wondered what on earth they were talking about. 'And it'd better be all it's cracked up to be, I'm warning you. If I don't get a good cock-stand from that, lads, heh heh!, I might just have a think about changing me agency.'

'No chance of that, Colin,' Tony said easily, 'not when you see what we've done for you. We were thinking . . .'

'Eh!' Colin interrupted him. 'Who's this fresh-faced young lad we've got with us today?'

'Bob Slade,' Tony explained. 'He's only just joined us as a trainee. Bob, meet Colin Miller, Group Product Manager, and Tim Rogers, Brand Manager on Champion.' The two men shook hands with Robert and sat down. Seconds later, a woman entered with a trolley bearing coffee and currant biscuits.

Robert watched the ensuing presentation with rapt attention. First, Tony took the floor and spoke quietly and persuasively. Last year, he recalled, a million had been spent on advertising Browning's various beers. Of that, half a million had been expended on Champion Bitter and that was the area on which he wished to concentrate.

'The brutal fact of the matter,' he told them mildly, 'is that Champion's share of the market has nevertheless remained constant. It's still not the brand leader. Our Champion,' he allowed himself a wry smile, 'remains a challenger.

'Where are we going wrong?' he asked earnestly. 'Is it the product?' Colin looked uncomfortable. 'Definitely not. Our research,' he held up a document, 'clearly indicates that Champion is considered to be one of the best mass-produced beers. Is it our advertising? That's more difficult to establish, of course, but sales certainly haven't been slipping. Ah, morning, Chris,' he greeted the slender, dapper figure who'd just slipped into the room. 'The real question is: why hasn't our share increased? We approached that via a Media Study and we think that our data will concern you.

'You've all met Chris Faye, our Media Director. I'll hand you over to him for a few surprises.' Tony retired from the front as unassumingly as he'd arrived there and Chris Faye walked briskly to the stage. Robert studied the Media Director, who looked as though he could equally well run a fashionable art gallery. His dark, curly hair had been teased into place and his eyes were hidden by large, tinted glasses. He wore a speckled, bottle-green suit, a lime shirt and a cravat patterned in white and grey. His slim hands made quick, darting movements as he arranged his papers. When he spoke, his voice was high, clear and cultured, though his manner was straight and to the point. After a few brief introductory pleasantries, he switched on a slide projector which threw a set of figures onto the wall in bold relief.

These figures showed the sales figures and market shares of Champion and its nine leading competitors in the London region over the last year and the year before. They also showed how much the ten brands had spent on advertising over those two years. After making some remarks about general sales trends, Chris Faye pointed out that wherever advertising spending had been increased, so had sales and market share. Wherever it had decreased, so had sales. Champion, he noted, had not increased its budget. Champion's position, he added, had remained the same.

He made the same point when he showed them the figures for the Midlands. The same point was demonstrated by the figures for Yorkshire. He made the same point with the figures for the South, the West, Lancashire and the North West, Scotland, Border and Tyne Tees. He finished by saying that he thought he'd made his point and invited questions. There were none.

'That's very interesting,' Colin Miller observed after a long and thoughtful pause. 'Very interesting indeed.'

'It's the same point, you see,' said Chris, 'made over and over again. I think the moral's obvious.'

'How much are we talking about?' Colin asked slowly and cautiously.

In answer, Chris Faye showed them more figures. These represented, he explained, what should be spent in every region in order to keep pace with the competition. 'Of course, we could get really aggressive and outspend all of them,' he remarked at one point in a rather off-hand way. 'That might put Champion right up top where it belongs. But,' he frowned thoughtfully, 'perhaps we should begin cautiously by only doing that in a couple of regions.' He was, by the end, perfectly open about the fact that his plan entailed the spending of two million pounds next year but, as he pointed out with the aid of more figures, the two leading brewers were already spending more than that and a third was forecast to be joining them.

'Of course, at the end of the day it's up to you,' he concluded affably. 'For all I know, you might want to stick with the present strategy. Of course,' he dropped his voice, 'that'll mean the same results.'

'There's food for thought here, all right,' Colin observed and Tim nodded vigorously.

'That's just as well,' Tony came in, 'because I make it time for lunch.'

Chris shook hands with Colin and Tim, excused himself on the grounds that he had to attend another meeting and left the room. Girls entered and proceeded to serve smoked salmon with a white Loire wine, rare roast beef and tongue with various salads and a claret, and a groaning board of ripe cheeses. Robert, who was sitting next to Colin, felt he ought to make conversation with the client but couldn't think of anything about which to talk to him. Colin solved that problem.

''Ere, lad,' he said suddenly, 'you must get a good cock-stand at your age.' Robert nearly choked on his wine.

'Fine, thanks,' he mumbled.

'I had it great when I was your age,' Colin recalled fondly. 'How many d'you get a day?'

'Sorry?' Robert gaped at him then swiftly composed his features. All the others, he noticed, didn't seem bothered at all.

'How many cock-stands a day?' Colin asked roguishly.

'I don't really know,' Robert answered helplessly. 'I'm afraid I'm not in the habit of counting them.'

'Well, you just wait till you get to be my age,' the client told him. 'A cock-stand is a precious thing.'

'Yes,' said Robert, 'I suppose it is.'

'See, Tim,' Colin triumphantly told his subordinate, 'Robert here agrees with me.' Tim nodded.

Little business was discussed over the meal. Colin frequently assured his hosts that he'd found the Media figures very interesting and they responded by concurring with his opinion. Otherwise, the conversation ranged around drink, food, cars, sport and women, in that order. Coffee was accompanied by brandy and cigars, the girls cleared the table and Tony took the floor once again.

He explained that *assuming* the Savage & Markby

Media Plan was followed next year, there would be two major changes in Creative strategy. One would be the use of sporting heroes, suggesting that Champion was the beer of Champions. Colin and Tim seemed delighted by the idea. Tony then explained that leading sportsmen came expensive and so using them on the *present* budget was quite out of the question.

'The second change,' Tony went on, 'is application of what we call the Brand Recognition Factor. Put plainly, that means it's no damn good making a beautiful advertisement if no one can remember what's being advertised.'

'Hear, hear,' said Colin.

'In other words,' Tony added, 'it's not creative unless it sells.'

'Hear, hear,' said Tim.

'We therefore propose,' Tony went on, 'to add two seconds to the final freeze on the Champion Logo which currently ends each TV ad and to deepen the voice-over.'

'Eh, I'm very pleased to hear you say that, Tony,' Colin came in. 'The agency before yours was always telling us to cut it back. Voss & Venables,' he snorted disgustedly, 'all they wanted was their arty-farty crap.' He swallowed more brandy. 'They couldn't sell beer to a gang of soccer hooligans. It's *branding* that's all important. They *must* remember the *brand*!'

'Exactly,' said Tony, 'and this way they will. Any further questions?'

'Yes.' Colin drained his balloon glass. 'Can I have some more brandy and where's this agency reel?'

Charles replenished Colin's glass from the bottle on the table while Tony pressed a button. A panel in the front wall slid back to reveal a video screen.

'How about now?' Tony suggested. 'I think we're all in the mood for it.' Another button caused blinds to slide down and cover the windows, plunging the room into darkness. The screen came to life to show a full-busted woman who was sucking a man's cock.

'*Phew!*' Colin whistled and leaned forward eagerly. 'Rum stuff!'

Robert had never seen a blue film before and initially watched it with fascination. After sucking the cock, the girl mounted it and fucked it for a time. Then another girl pulled up her skirt to show she wasn't wearing any knickers and masturbated with a vibrator. A third girl had her voluptuous bottom spanked. Colin breathed heavily and called pointedly for more brandy.

But it didn't take Robert long to become weary of the girls' bored expressions and the continual display of organ grinding. There was something about the film's sleaziness which depressed him. Soon he stopped watching the fucking in favour of watching the audience. Colin was perspiring furiously and had both hands in his pockets. Tim was gloating over the display of naked female flesh. Tony, Charles and George looked utterly uninterested, as though they'd seen it all a hundred times before, which, Robert reflected, they probably had. After an act of sodomy and a group orgy, the film ended with a frozen close-up of a cunt, then died away.

'First class!' declared Colin as the blinds slid up and the room was filled with sunshine. 'Absolutely first class! There's no doubt about it, you boys have got the best agency reel in town. *Three* cock-stands,' he informed them proudly, 'and all of 'em were winners.'

'More brandy?' Charles enquired.

'Don't mind if I do,' Colin responded warmly. 'What a time we've had, eh? And I'm not just referring to what you might think, I'm referring to the figures this morning and what we heard from Tony this afternoon.'

'Very interesting indeed,' said Tim.

'Interesting? Riveting!' Colin declared.

'My feelings too,' said Tim.

'D'you have a copy,' Colin asked, 'of the Plan you propose? Oh, and I'll be taking the Media Study too if you have a spare one of those.' Charles passed over a sheaf of documents. 'Those figures, you see,' the client continued, 'they're unanswerable. There's no way the Board can dispute them. So you lads can rest assured that you've convinced me. I'm *totally pro* doing it the way you suggest next year.' He sat back and beamed at them contentedly. Everyone beamed back.

'Sensible,' murmured Tony.

'Furthermore,' said Colin, 'you can minute that.' He turned to George, who'd been taking the minutes and who'd otherwise said next to nothing. 'Go on, George, minute it like I said. I'll be requiring the Board's approval before we sign, of course, but I shouldn't imagine there'll be any problem there.'

After another round of brandies and much hand-shaking, back-slapping and general good fellowship, Colin announced that it was time he caught his plane home and left the room with Tim, escorted by Tony.

'I reckon we can all congratulate ourselves on that one.' George raised his glass. 'Cheers! We've just gone and made ourselves two million.'

'You mean, made the Company two million,' Charles corrected him drily, 'and that's only gross, not net.'

'What's our profit margin?' Robert asked.

'In common with every other agency, Savage & Markby take seventeen and two thirds per cent of every penny spent with it,' Charles answered crisply. 'The net profit on that varies between nothing and three per cent, depending on the skill of the account team. We're currently on two per cent and shooting for three. So it's not that much, you see.'

'They're still spending *two million.*' George swallowed brandy and stuck to his guns. 'The fact is,' he told Robert, 'that Colin Miller's sold on us. And his Board *always* does whatever he recommends. He might strike you as being a bit weird and having his problems but he's very good indeed at his job.'

'Cockstands,' Charles mused. 'Now that's an idea.' He lit a Pall Mall and inhaled deeply. 'CHAMPION GIVES YOU A COCK-STAND,' he chuckled, 'END BREWER'S DROOP WITH CHAMPION BITTER, BEVERAGE OF WORLD-BEATING STUDS . . . and have you ever tried the stuff? Bloody horrible. I don't know how anyone can drink it, what? Give us all another brandy, Robert, there's a good chap.'

Robert left the agency a few brandies after that. His first day had left him feeling wonderfully elated. Certainly advertising had its bizarre aspects but it really did seem like a fun business. He was due to meet Vickie for a drink by the Serpentine and could hardly wait to tell her all about it. He knew what he'd say when she first asked him how it went.

'Fine!' he'd sing out happily, 'just fine, fine, fine.'

2

Peter Jackson was the first to arrive for the Board Meeting. This fact would've surprised no one who knew him, for punctuality was one of the many virtues which had carried Peter, at the age of forty-six, to the Managing Directorship of Savage & Markby.

He was one of the trade's success stories, even though his name wasn't associated with a single famous campaign. There were also no disasters that anyone could recall. That was how Peter operated. He always listened to everyone and then chose the safest option. Clients trusted him. He was a master of the art of delegation. Subordinates respected him. He was a skilful diplomat who could persuade seemingly incompatible temperaments to co-operate. Colleagues liked him.

Peter was perfectly well aware of how the trade regarded him. Once slighted as 'affable but lightweight', he was now 'no high flier' but 'solid', 'dependable', 'delivers the goods', 'able', with some 'really – *surprisingly* able,' and 'still smelling like a rose'. Everyone agreed he was a very nice man. In fact, this wasn't a pose. Peter really had tried to rise without stabbing others in the back and on the whole, he had succeeded.

He'd come up smoothly and steadily on the Account Management side of a variety of agencies, making the Board of Brady & Harding at thirty-eight. Wherever he went the profit was small, but there was always a profit. Perhaps that was why, in a time of recession, with advertising the second fastest item to be cut on any company's budget – the first is charity – Savage & Markby had offered him the recently vacated post of Managing

Director. Peter already had homes in Holland Park, Lyme Regis and Tuscany, a Mercedes, a Saab, a wife, two children and a mistress in a flat he rented. His new salary of sixty thousand plus expenses and stock options would make all the payments a lot easier.

For he'd only joined the Company a couple of weeks ago. The previous MD had been Nick Peters, regarded by some as the best in the trade. Yet something had gone badly wrong for Nick, as Peter understood it. The exact nature of events wasn't clear and anyone who knew wasn't talking, but it seemed that he'd tried to mount some kind of a coup against Savage, failed and been fired. So far, word had it that Nick hadn't yet found another job, though no doubt he would before long.

Although Savage & Markby possessed a formidable reputation, Peter had found the initial going easy. He'd asked Savage & Markby for time to feel his way, they'd been only too happy to oblige and there'd been little for him to do except get to know the Company. That was just what Peter wanted. He had no intention of blundering because of ignorance and, like all good politicians, he was studying just where the power lay.

So when Mike Armstrong strode into the Boardroom, Peter greeted him with a smile and added pleasantries about the weather. Mike might be the Board's most junior member but he was a rising star and not, Peter sensed, a good man to cross. Mike started talking about Browning's Beers. Peter adjusted his glasses, listened attentively and picked an imaginary speck of dust off his immaculate dark grey suit.

'Miller left us twenty minutes ago,' said Mike. 'I've had a word with Tony and it all went okay. He's sold on the idea of two million and reckons he can convince the Browning's Board which, going by past experience, he can.'

'Good work,' said Savage. 'Next item.'

'Forms,' Markby murmured in a puzzled tone of voice.

'Forms?' Savage echoed him.

'Yes, forms,' Mike responded firmly. 'There're too many of them.' The other Directors regarded him quizzically. Mike bit on his pipe stem and warned himself to exercise caution. He felt strongly about the matter but sensed he could spoil his case through excessive impetuosity. 'Take expense forms, for example. I can see the point of an executive signing a chit and getting it counter-signed by his Account Director if he wants to draw out entertainment money. But I can't see the point of his filling out another form, breaking out the VAT and getting it counter-signed by his Account Director in order to give some back.'

'The point? The point is that we want to see what's been spent on what for accounting purposes,' answered Stanley Haynes, the bald Financial Director. Mike sometimes felt that all one could say about Stanley Haynes was that he was the bald Financial Director. He had the sort of English face which is often seen and never remembered. Everyone agreed that Stanley Haynes did his job, then talked about somebody else.

'Receipts should be enough,' Mike returned.

'I don't want my Department wasting time on sorting out and itemizing other people's bits of paper.'

'Oh,' said Mike, 'I thought that was their job.' There was an uncomfortable silence. 'Look, my point is that my people are prevented from doing their jobs and making money for the Company by tasks that aren't theirs and probably aren't necessary.'

'Oh, steady on, Mike,' Markby warned him. 'There's a jolly good reason for every form we use and if there isn't, then I'd like to know about it.' Mike puffed at his pipe and regarded the Vice-Chairman, a tall, distinguished looking gentleman with thick, straight, iron-grey hair and a military moustache. As usual, he wore a three-piece, pin-stripe suit in dark grey. Mike had never really liked him and Markby's approval of his promotion six months ago had been something of a surprise. These days, Markby still irritated Mike with his smooth condescension. It served as a constant reminder of the fact that Hugh Vincent Markby was an Old Etonian and Mike Armstrong the son of a Birmingham lorry driver.

'You seem to be forgetting that I spent ten years in my Department as a humble executive,' Mike pointed out. At the time, though, he'd felt anything but humble. He'd joined Savage & Markby as a despatch boy at sixteen, and his appetite for work and keen, natural intelligence had raised him first to Production, then to Job Controller, and at twenty, what was then for him the dizzy height of Assistant Account Executive. The next ten years saw him slog his way remorselessly up the ladder. He made enemies. He also made money for the Company. He was always as good as his last campaign and sometimes better. One of his strengths was a willingness to take risks in following his gut instincts. So far they'd led him to the Board at thirty-one.

'A hard man', 'a bastard', 'ruthless', 'you love him or you loathe him' – these were some of the things which were said about Mike. Others observed that he had no principles and Mike was the first to agree. In fact, he had some and he adhered to them strongly, though that was recognized only by those who knew him well. He always kept his promises and there was one he'd made to himself. Some years ago he'd sworn that when he made the Board, he'd put an end to all the unnecessary vexations Account Executives suffered.

'In those ten years,' Mike continued steadily, 'I spent far too much time coping with bureaucracy when I should've been doing my job.'

'But my dear fellow,' Markby looked pained, 'surely from this vantage point you can see that every form has a precise purpose?'

'No,' said Mike, 'I'm afraid I can't. What's the purpose, for example, of a requisition form when all that's wanted is a pencil?'

'Oh, dear,' sighed Markby.

'One small point . . .' Peter Jackson intruded tactfully. 'This matter seems a rather vexed question altogether. I was wondering if perhaps a fresh look at it was warranted.'

'Go on,' said Savage.

'Well, what I'm tentatively suggesting is that you turn the issue over to me – assuming, of course, that there are no strong objections – and I can come back with some proposals agreeable to everyone in about a month or so. After all,' he smiled ingratiatingly, 'I don't think anyone's against a little streamlining in the cause of greater efficiency.'

'Yes,' said Savage, 'that's what we'll do. Next item.'

'TV-am,' announced Markby, 'and Honey Crunch.'

Mike sat back and swore silently to himself. Once again, the matter had been delayed. He'd so far failed to abolish a single form. A talk with Peter Jackson was clearly in order now that the man had seized that thorny territory. Could he get what he wanted from the new MD? Mike surveyed Peter and doubted it. Certainly the man was amiable enough but his proposals would probably be amiable too, a tranquillizer which did little and offended no one. Still, it was worth a try . . .

Mike relit his pipe and tried to turn his attention to more important matters. In common with his fellow Directors – except possibly Peter Jackson – he knew what the climax of the Board Meeting would be. Savage & Markby had been holding talks with a top United States soft drinks corporation and word had it that the agency would be pitching for the account. That meant that one of the Directors would be conducting the pitch – and it was rumoured that the client was prepared to spend millions.

It would be a fabulous opportunity for whoever was chosen to make his mark on the trade. Who would be favoured by the Chairman?

Mike glanced at John Savage. After fifteen years with the Company, he still didn't know just what to make of its Chairman and majority stockholder. Savage was murderously efficient, like a finely tuned missile, and if he had feelings, these were never evident. He rarely smiled and he never laughed. He was the sort of man who never seemed to go to the lavatory. One hardly ever saw John Savage except at Board Meetings or when he summoned you to his offices on the top floor. You could go and see him only by appointment and through Markby. No one, except possibly Markby, had ever visited Savage's home – or homes if he had them, which wasn't known. Still, during the time Mike had been with the agency, its billings had soared from six million annually to thirty-one.

'Investigate what rates they'd offer us if we spent a hundred thousand,' the Chairman was telling Chris Faye. 'I think that's our best move here – unless there are any strong objections.'

There was a pause.

'Well, I'm jolly well going to stick my neck out on this one,' Markby said at last. 'I agree with the Chairman.'

'I'll action that today, then,' Chris Faye concurred. Mike respected the Media Director's abilities, tried to like him and didn't quite succeed. The image of slick, public school trendiness which the man projected aroused a mild chemical antipathy in Mike. Chris always appeared to have had it easy and to be doing it easily. He usually went home around six o'clock muttering something about the theatre or an art gallery preview. Yet his grasp of figures was uncanny. He loved figures. Whenever he was questioned, pressurized, criticized or contradicted, he always produced sets of figures in answer – unless his opponent was Savage. Mike had never met anyone so quick to assimilate the significance of a mass of numerical data nor so skilled at summarizing the salient points. According to Tony Westbury, Chris had been superb at the Browning's presentation. The Media Director had appeared as a favour to Mike – numerical wizardry impressed Colin Miller – and that meant Mike now owed him. Chris had to be a strong candidate for the pitch Mike wanted so badly for himself – and the same could be said for Brian Bishop, the Creative Director.

The Creative Director didn't look like one. If it hadn't been for his full, black beard, one would've thought he was a banker. His dark blue, double-breasted suit was sober and discreetly tailored. Far from having an easy-going artistic temperament, he was as prickly as a porcupine. Yet he was an acknowledged adept at his job. It was said that for every frame in a Savage & Markby commercial, Brian could give you a good marketing reason. Mike got on well with him and held him in high respect as the one Director who worked as hard as himself.

'Next item,' the Chairman's voice interrupted Mike's thoughts.

'Overall strategy.' Markby regarded Peter. 'We asked you to have a look at that. Have you arrived at any firm conclusions?'

'I'd say it's a little early in the day for firm conclusions,' Peter demurred. 'The important thing is that our specific tactics are laid down within a strong awareness of their general strategic context. One could, of course, try going against the grain, but I don't think that approach is quite as clever as it seems.' Mike wondered what on earth Peter meant. 'As it happens,' the Managing Director continued, 'I have noticed just a couple of things. First of all, we don't seem to have many women account executives . . .'

'There's Sandra Lang,' Markby pointed out.

'Sandra Lang, certainly,' Peter replied hastily, 'but as far as I'm aware, she's the only one. I was just wondering if this was Company policy.'

'Not at all, not at all,' Markby gave him a thin smile. 'There's no prejudice against women here. We keep hoping to appoint a thoroughly capable female to a senior position. So far,' he shrugged helplessly, 'nobody we've interviewed has been up to it. Does that answer your question?'

'Oh, fully.' Peter took off his glasses and toyed with them. 'Which brings me to my next point, which is Company policy itself. In the past, I've found one thing that's useful and it doesn't seem to exist here – a Strategy Review Board.'

'What,' Mike asked, 'would that do?'

'It would review general strategy account by account,' Peter replied easily, 'and enable us to obtain an overall bird's eye view.'

'I thought we did that here,' Mike objected.

'Oh, we do,' Peter assured him, 'but I'm sure we'd all agree that the Board lacks the time to scrutinize *in depth* the emerging and underlying pattern of each account. Perhaps you disagree with me, but I can't help thinking that this would serve an invaluable function.'

'Presumably,' said Markby, 'the Managing Director would take the chair.'

'That's usually how it's worked in the past, yes.'

'Hmm,' Savage murmured, 'I like the idea. Does anyone have any objections?' Mike did. Mike was opposed to setting up committees on principle, especially committees whose title was broad and whose functions were vague. But Savage clearly favoured the proposal, though for what reasons Mike couldn't fathom. That meant that Markby would favour it too. Stanley Haynes liked committees. Chris and Brian were expressionless. Mike decided that the issue wasn't important enough to warrant a battle he was bound to lose. 'I think there's a consensus in favour,' Savage stated. The opaque panes of his horn-rimmed glasses swivelled to stare directly at Peter. 'We'll discuss the details at ten tomorrow morning. Next item.'

'Kandy,' Markby declared. 'Any of you chaps heard of it?'

'It's an American soft drink,' Brian responded promptly. 'Saw it in the States last year.'

'And we'll be seeing it in the UK next year,' said Markby. 'The Kandy Corporation of Phoenix, Arizona is launching a major invasion of the British market. They expect to do well. In four years, Kandy's share of the US soft drinks market has trebled and only Coke and Pepsi-cola currently outsell it. Children love it, apparently. Anyway, the Kandy people tell us they're prepared to spend . . .'

'Four million pounds on the launch,' said Savage. There was a pause. Chris Faye whistled.

'J. Walter Thompson, Saatchi's and us, that's who it's between,' Markby resumed. 'So our sales pitch will have to be absolutely tip-top. The orchestration of that pitch is naturally a tremendous responsibility.' Peter, Chris and Brian were listening intently.

'Mike,' said Savage, 'you're conducting it.'

'Thank you, I'm honoured by your confidence,' Mike answered as the other three sagged slightly. He meant every word. On New Business, one million was the biggest sum for which he'd ever pitched. Here, his reputation as a future big-shot would be right on the line. If he failed – and given the competition, there was every chance of that – it would be a long time before the next big chance. If he succeeded – and he was sure he would succeed because his being fed on challenge – that would be a giant step towards a Managing Directorship.

'I'm sure you'll do us credit,' Savage told him flatly.

'Let's discuss it further at two o'clock tomorrow. Any other business?'

'No,' said Markby, 'unless . . .' he regarded his fellow Directors and yawned.

'That's all, then.' Savage rose and the Board rose with him. The Chairman's long forefinger flicked a switch on the panel which graced the arm of his chair. That, Mike knew, shut off the microphones which recorded every Board Meeting. Tomorrow, Savage's secretary would type up a complete transcript to be edited by Savage and then summarized and circulated as the Minutes. Meanwhile, the tapes which could play back every word spoken would be stored somewhere in one of Savage's offices.

It was a curious method perhaps, Mike thought, but Savage & Markby wanted it that way.

3

'Strategy Review Board,' Peter Jackson declared enthusiastically. 'Meeting with Savage re that, ten o'clock tomorrow.' Emily Hyde made a note in the weighty appointments book that was bound in red leather. 'Hmm. I still haven't read the Browning's Beers Creative Plan. Can you dig that out for me before I go home?' His secretary nodded. 'The other thing I want is a copy of every internal form the company uses. I'm sure that's something on which we can improve.' Emily made a note on a plain pad.

'Will that be all?' she enquired politely.

'No,' said Peter, 'there's the matter of dinner. Been a while, hasn't it? I think it's time we celebrated our settling in here.' Her lined face lit up with pleasure. 'How about next Wednesday at the Caprice?'

'Oh, it sounds marvellous.' Emily smiled at him and her bony hand briefly touched her greying hair.

'Marvellous, yes, and about time too.' He smiled back. 'I'll look forward to it. Well, I think that's it. We'd both of us better be getting on . . .'

What a gem, Peter thought as the fifty-five year old spinster left his office. Some might say that Emily's dowdy cardigans, plain plaid skirts and flat shoes with woollen stockings did little to advertise her boss's status. The facts remained that she was the best secretary he'd ever encountered, she'd been with him for ten years and her loyalty was absolute. Peter repaid it by insisting she received a very good salary and, he liked to think, treating her well. Twice a year, he took her out to lunch. Once a year, he wined and dined her. He always bought her flowers for her birthday and something small in gold for

Christmas. Once every three weeks, he earnestly enquired how her poetry was going and listened avidly to her reply – she'd had a poem published once and Peter had praised it warmly. In return, Emily was always available for overtime and even prepared to give up her weekends if necessary.

He had no idea why Emily Hyde had never married. She was so well-spoken, well-mannered and genteel that the idea of asking her had seemed like an unwarranted intrusion. She'd never volunteered any information about her love-life or lack of it and Peter sensed she liked to keep her private existence wholly separate from him. That was fine as far as he was concerned. He really didn't want to be burdened with one of those secretaries who pours out her problems along with the tea and imagines her boss is a surrogate uncle.

Peter looked around his spacious office, which was green and pleasant, and picked up his pen. There was nothing for him to sign. He glanced at his IN tray. That was empty too. Emily had taken the contents of the OUT tray. The phone wasn't ringing either.

It was time he made his mark on Savage & Markby. Today's Board Meeting had gone rather well, he felt, though Mike Armstrong had to be watched. He might've lost on Forms but he'd been awarded Kandy, a clear indication that Mike was held in high favour. Still, Peter had taken Forms and hence a hold on administration and would chair the Strategy Review Board, through which he could consolidate his position. Savage had responded well to everything he'd said. Strange how the Chairman's presence had made him feel so tense and anxious, though. Perhaps Savage had that effect on everyone.

Peter fidgeted in his chair. He should be pleased with his progress, he thought, yet for some indefinable reason, he felt vaguely uneasy as though a worm was turning within his intestines. One thing could cure that. He could have a drink. Unfortunately, it was only four thirty.

He'd always enjoyed drinking but unless there was a lunch with a glass of wine or two, he never started before six in the evening and rarely drank to excess. All the same, though, he *did* feel like a drink right now. There was a well-stocked cabinet of booze on the opposite side of the room. One small whisky wouldn't do him any harm. It'd really be rather nice right now. There wasn't anything especially urgent to attend to and, after all, today he'd achieved something. It wasn't as though he made a habit of getting out the bottle every afternoon. This was a once in a lifetime shot. Oh, why not?

So although it was totally contrary to his habits, Peter Jackson toasted his advancement at Savage & Markby with the aid of a large, neat malt whisky.

Downstairs in Creative, Brian Bishop was working. A rough of a full page press advertisement lay before him on his desk and he was marking it furiously with a red felt-tip pen. He put a line through the drawing of a man and wrote: 'Tacky'. He scribbled over the headline and next to it wrote: 'Self-indulgent crap.' He crossed out a line of copy and wrote simply: 'No.' At the bottom he wrote: 'Garbage. See me. B.B.'

Brian had reached his position of Creative Director at the age of thirty-six through his adherence to the principle that the sole purpose of advertising was to sell goods. He had an almost puritanical loathing of superfluous artistry. He was very much a graduate of the USP school of thought – the doctrine that every product has a Unique Selling Proposition which must be identified, isolated and pushed hard. One result was that Savage & Markby commercials weren't especially interesting. Another was that they sold goods.

Brian was a noted departmental administrator too. He'd set up The System, a chain of command reaching from himself to the lowest copywriter and governed by rules relating to time and motion which covered all jobs from the initial Account Management brief to final presentation to the client. For example, no work reached Brian until passed by an Assistant Creative Director, who himself saw nothing that wasn't approved by the relevant Creative Group Head.

So what was this piece of shit doing on his desk? He hadn't seen anything so bad in ages. Had his senior staff taken leave of their senses? Brian inspected the rough and frowned. The only signatures he could see were 'Dennis Wilson' and 'Simon Burns', a visualizer and a copywriter, both very junior. That meant they hadn't had it passed by their superiors. They'd gone directly to him and short-cut The System inexcusably. Brian felt annoyed. He'd have to summon their Group Head, Ronald Potter, and tell him to give them a bollocking. Casting the rejected rough aside, Brian turned his attention to a set of story boards.

These had been prepared by Ian Sharpe, a brilliant but erratic Assistant Creative Director. Brian could tell at a glance that most of it was good but – oh dear, here was an unnecessary witty flourish from Ian. Once again he was having fun on the job. 'Fun on the job?' Brian had told him last time. 'We're not getting paid to have fun on the job.'

He carried on working. Everyone knew how hard he worked. Every morning, he arrived at eight. Every evening, he left at eight. When he had a free lunch hour, he ran around the park. He didn't smoke and he'd given up even moderate social drinking three years ago. The weekends which weren't devoted to Savage & Markby were largely spent asleep at the charming Sussex estate he rarely had time to enjoy. His dedication brought him forty thousand pounds a year, stock options and a big expense account.

It also brought him a marriage in the final, agonizing

throes of breaking up, three children who treated him like a stranger and a duodenal ulcer which was burning his guts out right now.

'How's the new MD strike you?' Georgina Mainwaring asked Mike. It was six o'clock and they were relaxing in a quiet corner pub nearby.

'He's all right.' Mike filled his straight pipe with ready-rubbed black Condor. 'Diplomat. Committee man. Bit of a waffler but I don't think he's a trouble-maker.' He shrugged. 'More of a co-ordinator.'

'In other words, he's no Nick Peters.' Mike's secretary surveyed her boss. Her azure eyes, wavy blonde hair which fell to her shoulders, amused mouth and dimpled chin made hers the prettiest face in the Company. Her shapely figure was enticing too and all the men agreed she had one of the sexiest walks. But, as Mike had recognized within a week of their first meeting, there was more to her than that. Georgina was intelligent, hard working, capable and judging by three years' experience, she was loyal too.

'No, he's no Nick Peters. Mind you, who could be?'

'Yet now,' said Georgina, 'he's become a non-person.'

'Tragic,' Mike agreed. He drank some beer. 'He was a damn good Managing Director and I liked the man too. Shame he went to pieces like that.'

'Has he got a job yet?'

'I don't think so,' Mike sighed regretfully. 'The booze was really getting to him by the end. Gambling too, so I'm told. Pity. He was the one man on the Board capable of facing up to Savage.'

'That,' the girl observed softly, 'is why he's no longer with us.'

'Not quite. He's no longer with us because . . .' Mike checked himself. Even he didn't know anything like the full story. What little he did know couldn't be gossiped about in a public place. '. . . because, by the end, he just wasn't doing his job.'

'Well, in a way, it's a blessing for you, isn't it?' she returned. 'Up until recently, Nick would've got the Kandy pitch. As things stand, it's you.' *And I'm glad it's you*, thought Georgina. *You pretend you're such a bastard but you're decent. You're not a shallow shit like so many of the others. You think you're so tough and underneath I just know you're so vulnerable. Even when you're being awful, I sometimes feel like hugging you.*

'Yes, and I'm very pleasantly surprised about that,' Mike said. 'I've already started thinking about it. When I see Savage tomorrow, I'll be requesting a total free hand in choosing my team.' *God, you look luscious*, he thought. *You're everything I've ever wanted in a woman and I'd like to grab you in my arms right now*. 'I'll also be needing,' he continued, 'every scrap of data on the soft drinks market. You've been to the States recently, love. Did you have a chance to try Kandy at all?'

'Yes, once.' Georgina finished her Martini. 'It's fizzy, slightly sweet and bright pink in colour. Quite refreshing but a little too sickly for my taste, I'm afraid. Mind you,' she laughed, showing dainty white teeth, 'my little niece seemed hooked on the stuff.' *I love your face*, she thought, *when it's like now – so alert and strong and alive*.

'Sounds just what kids'd like,' Mike remarked. 'Well, that's enough of work. Going out tonight?'

'Yes. Some cocktail party in Knightsbridge. It'll probably be a horrible bore but who knows? One might strike lucky. How about you, Mike?'

'I'm going back to the office. Few things to do.' *Some cocktail party* he thought wryly. *It's probably hosted by Rodney and Arabella Pauncefoote-Ffoulkes-Smythe. The sort of occasion where I never fit it. That's her world. She doesn't work for me because she needs the money*. 'After that, I reckon I could do with an early night.' In fact, it would probably be with Sue, though Mike hadn't called her yet. And it would be all right. Sue was all right. No less – and no more.

'You really should go out more, Mike,' Georgina advised him kindly. 'Do you the power of good, you know.' *And I'd rather be out with you*, she thought, *than with weedy Anthony Le Fanu*. 'Well, I must dash. Thanks for the drink. See you tomorrow.'

'Bye, Georgina,' said Mike as she left the pub with her bottom swinging gaily within a tight chocolate brown skirt. There were times when he fancied her so much, it hurt. But even if he had a chance with her – which he doubted – he couldn't take it for the sake of a principle.

Never, never, never screw the payroll.

Hugh Vincent Markby was sipping dry sherry in his office, which was furnished rather like the study of some Victorian grandee. Leather-bound books occupied one wall, there was a fire-place with a marble mantelpiece, a giant mirror and the Vice-Chairman's desk was a massive block of gleaming, dark mahogany topped by objects in green onyx. There was also a gold-framed photograph showing him with his wife and two daughters. A cricket bat stood in one corner. A fishing rod stood in another.

Two doors led in and out of Markby's sanctum. One was the employees' only way to Savage. That meant that anyone who wanted to see the Chairman was obliged first to undergo a preliminary interview with Markby, who frequently denied the petitioner admission. The Vice-Chairman was happy with this arrangement. Nor did he mind watching anxious individuals scurry through his office when summoned by Savage. He enjoyed seeing men squirm.

The other door connected with the outside world via an office which contained a secretary.

Markby drew a salary of one hundred thousand pounds

a year plus a virtually unlimited expense account and preferential stock options. He was in fact the largest minority shareholder, a wise move in view of the fact that Savage & Markby assets included its building. He did very well – and he felt that the world owed him every penny of his living.

For Hugh Vincent Markby was convinced that he should've been a gentleman of leisure, like his ancestors. He'd been brought up to it. He'd believed himself entitled to it. He'd fully expected it to materialize. It was unfortunate for him that a combination of death duties and lavish spending had crippled the estate and enforced its sale. At the end of the day, there was nothing for Markby.

That left him with a choice. He could try to preserve the values of a gentleman by holding fast to a noble code in a harsh and hostile world – like some of his acquaintances – yet that path usually led to a penurious and shabby gentility. Or he could determine that underneath his honourable façade, he'd be more ruthless, clever and cunning than the lower classes he despised, which would bring him the wealth indispensable to a gentleman. Thank God he'd met Savage shortly before the moment of decision. Oh yes, since that far off time, Markby *had* done well.

Finishing his sherry, he consulted the antique grandfather clock. Six-fifteen and he knew just what he felt like. Picking up the white internal phone, Markby dialled 163 and briskly requested the immediate presence of Sandra Lang.

Everyone said that Sandra's face was hard. Pert and attractive, yes, but hard. All softness had been worn away by seven years in advertising. It was a man's world, Sandra knew, and the only way to get on was to out-tough men at their own game, out-clever them at yours and kick them in the balls along the way. Starting as a secretary, she'd clawed her way to Account Executive at eleven thousand per annum. Her accounts were Joy soap powder, Minnie cat food and Toreador contraceptives.

The next step was Account Supervisor. There were rumours of promotion to one in the offing. Sandra was determined to be chosen but knew that the odds were against her. There'd never been a female Account Supervisor at Savage & Markby before. Yet Sandra could see a way of out-streaking the male competition. She could sleep with Markby, who'd been making it plain for some time that he wanted her.

Sandra had considered the matter. Markby might be in his fifties but he wasn't that bad looking. He might be useless in bed – there were rumours that he was – but no woman ever died of that. And he might be a pompous wind-bag – but he could arrange her promotion. It was one way girls can get on – and do – that Sandra had used before. The golden rule was to use the method rarely and only with exactly the right person – and after a feigned show of resistance.

So when Markby rang, Sandra had been expecting his call. He usually called her around six on Monday evenings. She'd been screwed by him for three weeks now and last time he'd mentioned slyly that her chances of promotion were improving every day by leaps and bounds. Brushing down her skirt – he preferred her in a skirt – she rose from her desk and headed upstairs.

For Sandra, it was all pretty much the same as usual. He welcomed her with a wet kiss, gave her a dry sherry, assured her that the Chairman had gone home and listened patiently to her account of her day – he especially relished the gossip. When she'd finished her drink, he rose and ordered her to bend over his office-desk and throw her skirt up over her hips. To please him, she now wore the stockings and suspenders he demanded, along with a pair of white satin knickers, which he lowered slowly.

After fondling her buttocks with his hands for a time, he unzipped his fly and shoved his not quite fully erect member within her. Then he writhed for a bit and she pretended to enjoy it, although that was difficult because she could barely feel him. When at last he came, she echoed his groan of pleasure quite convincingly. Afterwards, he zipped up his fly and, as always, said to her smugly: 'Well, then, sweetie,' his face creased into a leer, 'how about a spot of supper?'

Sally Peters entered her home to see her husband slumped in an arm-chair with a half-empty bottle of whisky beside him. The entire room stank of scotch. Nick himself had glazed eyes, a red face, a wheezing chest and a bulging gut. He wore a stained T-shirt with a grubby pair of jeans. A cigarette smouldered within his slack fingers and dribbled ash onto the carpet.

'Hi!' he grinned mirthlessly. 'Like a drink?'

Sally didn't answer. There was no reply she felt like making. He'd been like this for weeks and nothing she'd tried had worked. Sighing loudly, she took off her coat and went straight into the kitchen, closing the door firmly behind her. But that failed to shut out the sound of scotch splashing into the glass next door. Opening the fridge, she noticed he'd left the orange, apple and tomato juices and the Perrier she'd bought him untouched.

It was virtually impossible to believe that the man next door was the husband to whom she'd been married for twelve years. For ten of them, he'd been the wonderful, dynamic, good-humoured and gloriously assured man she adored. The only thing he'd loved as much as her was advertising, where he'd stormed his way to the top with brilliance and audacity.

Then two years ago, it had begun to go wrong. As he'd told Sally, he found himself more and more in disagreement with Savage and Markby. He started to drink heavily and went gaming more frequently. There was a growing paranoia in his every statement about the Chairman. Soon Savage became an all-encompassing obsession. Nick could hardly talk about anyone or anything else – yet he wouldn't listen to his wife and change his job. The drinking grew worse and he lost larger sums at the tables. Then came the period of his madness.

Sally preferred not to think about that. A shudder ran through her every time she recalled his insane ramblings about evil beings and how he was crusading against them. It was a miracle that the Company kept him as long as it did, but in the end, the inevitable happened and Nick Peters was fired. Thank God it was over.

Yet if living with a manic was agony enough, having a depressive around the house was little better. The degeneration had set in remarkably fast, assisted by chronic alcoholism. Initially, Nick had been inundated with job offers, which had all been withdrawn after one interview. His appearance was enough in itself to make people break promises. Nobody wanted a wreck. His savings were gone too – drunk or gambled away. They could no longer keep the kids at public school, the house was for sale and Sally had had to take a job as a typist.

'*Bastards!*' came an agonized cry from the next room and Sally shivered with fear and revulsion. '*Cunts! Pricks! I hate you!*' he shouted. She lost control and sagged into a chair with tears streaming down her strained, pale face.

'Oh, God,' she sobbed quietly, 'God, please help him find a job . . .'

'*I hate you, Savage!*' Nick Peters screamed. '*You did it to me! You planned it all! Bastard! I'll fucking kill you!*'

4

Savage & Markby Ltd

MEMORANDUM

To: All Staff
cc. Board Directors
From: HVM
Subject: Economy
Date: 4 September 1983

In view of the current harsh realities of the business climate and the increasingly competitive nature of our profession, the Board has resolved to take vital measures in the interest of economy, which measures will be of lasting benefit to all. Staff are therefore kindly requested to co-operate in the direct implementation of the following essential procedures:-

1 – In future, stationery will only be issued against a signed requisition, counter-signed by the appropriate Account, Media or Assistant Creative Director.

2 – All but urgent mail will go by second class post forthwith.

3 – Anyone using the photo-copying facilities will sign the exercise book henceforth provided.

4 – Under all but impossible circumstances, both sides of a piece of paper will be utilized.

5 – Magazines and newspapers may no longer be removed from Reception.

6 – Wherever possible, staff will use public transport when travelling on Company business.

7 – Personal phone-calls are to be discouraged and kept to an absolute minimum.

Thanking you for your understanding and co-operation.

H. V. Markby
VICE-CHAIRMAN

Robert Slade thought that Markby's Memo was the least inspiring communication he'd ever received. It was even more uninteresting than the one Stanley Haynes, the bald Financial Director, had sent yesterday. This had gone on for three long, turgid paragraphs about the importance of security and then concluded by telling everyone to lock their desks before they went home. Robert hoped that the sending of Memos like that wasn't a Company habit.

However, as he was finding out fast, life at Savage & Markby wasn't all brandy and blue films. For a start, there was a great deal to be learned quickly about Browning's Beers. In addition to Champion Bitter, the company also manufactured Star, a keg beer whose once excellent sales had slumped; Golden Eagle, a bright beer which did quite well in the North; Crusader lager, cheap, cheerful and also available in cans; two bottled beers, Browning's Light and Browning's Best Brown, the latter the brand leader in the shrinking brown ale market; and a canned lager called Bremen, which looked imported, was in fact brewed in Britain under licence from Germany and tasted nothing like the original at all. Browning's also had a food division. Mother Miller's Fayre, which served buffet style lunches, was a feature of nearly all their pubs: and three Squire & Lady steak houses, deftly disguised as up-market restaurants, had recently opened and were flourishing in three new towns. Robert was finding all this information fascinating and could hardly wait to get down to the proper business of advertising, but so far the Account team was employing him merely for running messages and answering invoice queries.

The one benefit of this exercise was that it enabled Robert to start today by writing his very first business letter explaining an invoice to the client. He worked on it with his full attention for roughly twenty minutes, tearing up three drafts in the process. Finally, he was satisfied. The letter was short, exact, courteous and to the point, he thought, and it should help him make a good impression on the client. Taking up his handwritten draft and a set of MEAL figures, Robert approached his secretary.

'Morning, Fiona,' he said cheerfully, 'could you please type up this . . .'

'Oh, for heaven's sake!' Fiona cut him short before his first business letter could reach her. 'Look at this.' He looked and saw a huge pile of paper. 'I've got to do this massive document for Charles which'll take me all day and after that, there's George's stuff.' Her cold blue stare might have been directed, not at her boss, but at some grubby little pest. 'What *is* it, anyway?'

'It's a letter to the client,' Robert responded evenly, though he was inwardly shaken by her hostile insubordination.

'*You?* Writing to the client? Well!' She raised her eyebrows. 'What on earth about?'

'Answer to an invoice query,' he replied lamely. 'But it does have to be done,' he added.

'But hardly this minute. Face it, I mean, it's not exactly important, is it? Never mind,' she sighed wearily, 'I'll fit it in when I've got a spare moment.'

Fiona flipped the draft out of his hand and tossed it to one side like a piece of scrap paper. Robert turned away and breathed deeply in an effort to contain both his rising anger and his sinking sense of shame. Glancing down at the MEAL figures in his hand, he realized he should be telling his secretary to photo-copy them for George. It was painfully obvious how Fiona would respond to that. Robert just couldn't face another battery of remarks which informed him of his unimportance. *You bitch*, he thought, *just you wait*. He decided he could manage perfectly well without her and would damn well do his photo-copying himself.

'Quick word, Bob, if you wouldn't mind,' Tony Westbury called out from his office. Robert went in and was motioned to sit down. 'A challenge,' Tony announced, holding up a thick file, 'and it's for you.' Robert instantly forgot Fiona and sat up alertly. 'As you know,' Tony explained, 'we're a marketing agency too. Browning's have a first-class sales organization but they don't know much about marketing. That's where we come in. Here's last year's volume sales figures for Champion.' He passed over a sheaf of documents. 'Here's Stats M.R. Here's the Taplin data. And here,' he held up a densely typed sheet of paper, 'is the Protheroe Marketing Analysis and Summary sheet for Joy soap powder. It's the most advanced marketing tool we have for the summarizing of three separate sources of statistical data. Your job,' said Tony, 'will be to apply the Protheroe Marketing Analysis and Summary technique to Champion Bitter. If you get into trouble with it, see George and he'll sort you out, okay?' Tony smiled. 'Great, thanks for your help, Bob.'

Burdened by a heavy stack of data and the Protheroe – which at first glance looked incomprehensible – Robert made his exit wondering how to stop Tony from calling him 'Bob'. Something had to be done, and soon, but what, when and where?

'Ah, just the man!' George hailed him. 'Pull up a chair right away. Just one or two things you can do for me, if you wouldn't mind . . .' and George reeled off a list of errands which the trainee wrote down.

He also looked disbelievingly at George's clothes. Today the man was wearing a crumpled suit in fawn which was stained with cigarette ash. The jacket was too short, the seat sagged woefully and the trouser bottoms revealed an expanse of hairy, pink ankle. The shirt was screaming blue murder and its collar was strangled by an off-white kipper tie with red spots. The brown shoes, made of some shiny plastic material which vaguely resembled crocodile, were scuffed and down-at-heel. George had dirty, stubby finger-nails, Robert noticed, and this morning he'd cut himself while shaving.

'. . . that's it, then, and good, good, good,' George declared breezily. 'You should chase up that lot in no time at all – here's the poster. You're doing well,' he told his subordinate, 'rest assured you're doing well, but don't let anyone snow you, all right? Show 'em who's boss from the very beginning, eh? Lovely!'

Leaving the marketing data on his desk, Robert strode down the corridor determined to execute what he regarded as a series of missions rather than a bunch of errands. Pretty secretaries passed him by and some smiled at him. He was enjoying being surrounded by sexy girls while he worked, though at times the knowledge that he could look but not touch aroused a gnawing frustration. On reaching the lift, he pressed the call button and once more received a small electric shock.

These happened frequently and at random. You never knew when it was your turn to be jolted. It didn't hurt very much but it startled the system and, Robert was finding, frayed the nerves. People grumbled and said it was something to do with the static in the carpet. Robert had just sworn under his breath when the lift door slid open to reveal a man he hadn't seen before, but who smiled warmly on seeing Robert.

'Hullo, it's Robert Slade, isn't it?' said Peter Jackson. 'Yes, I've seen you around. How're you getting on?'

'Oh, fine, thank you.'

'Glad to hear it. It's always a bit difficult when you're

new, don't you think? I should know,' Peter told him sympathetically, 'I'm new here myself.'

'Oh, what do you do?'

'I'm Managing Director,' said Peter.

'Oh . . .' Robert felt his face flush. 'I hadn't . . .'

'. . . any idea,' Peter completed his sentence genially. 'Of course not. But it's fun finding out who's who, isn't it? Anyway, Peter Jackson's the name, plain Peter to you, and I hope to see more of you in the future. Best of luck and bye for now.'

What a nice man, thought Robert as Peter departed, though he could've kicked himself for asking an idiotic question. Still, how was he to know? Robert resolved to exercise more caution as he stepped out onto the Creative floor. Here the atmosphere was rather different from the slick hustling which pervaded Account Management. Young men shambled around in T-shirts, jeans and boiler suits, looking as though they didn't give a damn, though beneath that one could sense furious activity and harsh effort. And in the distance, there seemed to be some kind of procession. A slim, elegant man in a dark suit was striding towards Robert while shouting and gesticulating petitioners ran to keep up with him. Some bore roughs, some had slogans and some waved chits before his eyes. The man held a gold fountain pen in his hand and it frequently streaked out to sign something.

'Gosh – super – lovely – yes – wonderful, wonderful,' said Charles Sutherland. 'Morning, tight lips,' he addressed an astonished Robert as he passed. 'Keep a straight bat and don't let the side down, what? Ah, what's here? That's no good at all. No, not on. Won't do. Simply not up to scratch. Ah – what have we here – yes – marvellous! – and wonderful, wonderful. Toodle-loo!' he waved as he stepped into the lift and the door began to cut him off from those he'd disappointed. 'And tra-la-la!' He vanished from view.

Robert shook his head bemusedly and set out on his first job. This involved locating Dennis Wilson, visualizer, and Simon Burns, copywriter, which was easy since George had introduced him yesterday and Robert had rather taken to them. However, he had his doubts about the look of their Group Head, Ronald Potter. There he was now and glaring at his two subordinates.

'Don't buck the System!' shouted Ronald Potter as Robert entered the set of offices. 'The – system – is – there – for – *your* – benefit!' he insisted angrily, tapping his pencil on a desk to emphasize every word. He was a short man, with longish, lank and greasy hair, thin lips and 'intellectual' glasses. 'So don't buck it! Ever!'

'But look,' protested Dennis, who was tall, lean and bearded, 'it doesn't make sense to . . .'

'Don't argue!' Ronald Potter shouted him down. 'Do not argue with the System. On *any* account. I won't hear of it. And I shan't tell you again. Don't buck the System!' He stormed out of the office.

'Fuckin' hell,' sighed Dennis.

'Cunt,' muttered Simon, who was pale and clean-shaven with a young and innocent face. They flicked a barrage of V signs at Ronald Potter's departing back.

'Well, that's a great start to the day, ennit?' said Dennis. 'What's next in store? I can hardly wait. Well, well, if it ain't young Robert Slade from Account Management. What's new, sunshine?'

'It's not good news, I'm afraid.' Robert opened up the mechanical of the beer poster he'd been carrying. 'Unfortunately, the client's turned it down.'

'Turned it down?' Simon echoed him disbelievingly. 'He can't've done.'

'Why?' Dennis demanded. 'Just tell me why?'

'Well,' Robert glanced uneasily down at his notes, 'you see how the man in the picture's got a green tie? The client's boss can't stand men in green ties . . .'

'*What?!*' shouted Simon.

'I've never heard such shit in my life,' said Dennis. 'And you went and took it from him? Christ, that's bleeding Account Management for you. Arsehole!'

'Jerk!' yelled Simon.

'Crumb!'

'Creep!'

'But it wasn't me,' Robert protested helplessly. 'I wasn't even at the meeting.'

'Then who was it?' Simon asked.

'George Webbing, of course,' said Dennis. 'Go on. It was 'im, wasn't it?' Robert nodded a reluctant admission. 'Jesus!' Dennis snorted disgustedly, 'George Webbing couldn't sell rosary beads to a nun.'

'He couldn't sell hot soup in the Arctic,' said Simon.

'He couldn't sell water in the Sahara.'

'He couldn't sell umbrellas in the pouring rain. And then *he* sends *you* to take our shit?'

'Well, you're going to take our shit,' snapped Simon. 'Account Management ain't good for much else. Arsehole!'

'Jerk!'

'Crumb!'

'Creep!' Without warning, Dennis and Simon began pelting the trainee with balls of paper from the bin. Robert held up his arms in protest and stumbled backwards in retreat while they booed and hissed him. Belinda Torrance, the group's stunning blonde bombshell of a secretary, collided with Robert as she entered the room, saw the situation, picked up some paper and joined in the barrage, adding her own variation of 'Wanker!' to the jeers. Robert staggered into the corridor feeling very miserable indeed.

His humiliation was provoking an inner rage as he tackled his next job, seeing the Job Controller on Browning's one Larry Cunningham. Larry was scurrying in and out of offices and trying to look inconspicuous. A small, furtive, rabbit-like man, he seemed to be interested in everything except talking to Robert.

'Be with you right away,' he kept calling out before vanishing through a doorway. Robert pursued him fruitlessly for some minutes before finally losing his patience and blocking Larry's path.

'The Light Ale trade press ad,' he said with as much assertiveness as he could muster. 'How's progress on that, Larry?'

'All under control,' Larry instantly assured him. 'No problems at all. Have no fear, the job is in hand.'

'Yes, but what stage has it reached? George is keen to know.'

'Oh, we're right on top of it. Right on top, just tell him that.'

Don't let anyone snow you, George had said.

'Yes, but what's the precise position?' Robert pressed.

'We're moving,' Larry said. 'No doubt about it, we're moving.'

'From where to where?'

'Oh, it's all happening, you take my word.' The Job Controller wiped his nose with the back of his hand.

'*Where's* it all happening?' Robert demanded in exasperation.

There was a pause.

'Good question,' said Larry and consulted his clipboard. 'No, there's nothing here. Not to worry.' With Robert hot on his heels, Larry scuttled into his office, which contained a swelling sea of trannies, mechanicals, roughs and paper, and scratched his head for a time. Robert stood attentively by the door, barring all possibility of escape. Suddenly Larry darted to a drawer and extracted a file, which he opened up and leafed through thoughtfully. 'You're not on Farmfresh Cheese, are you? No, thought not. Hmmm. Ah. Yes. Got it!' He looked triumphantly at Robert. 'It's with Dennis and Simon. If I were you, I'd just pop your head round the door and ask 'em how it's going.'

Not bloody likely, thought Robert. He grunted a curt thanks to Larry and left the office disconsolately. Later, as he continued to chase things which couldn't be caught, he overheard the Controller making his own nervous enquiry about the press ad's progress to Dennis and Simon.

'What're we doing about it?' Dennis retorted. 'Sweet F.A. for today and go away.'

'Righty ho,' said Larry.

The morning remained utterly unsatisfactory. Everyone who Robert had to see was with a client, in a meeting, on a shoot, not to be disturbed or ill at home. That left the joys of duplicating George's MEAL statistics. Robert went downstairs to Production and entered through a door marked: 'Photo-Copying: Cliff Mitchell.'

Cliff turned out to be a glassy-eyed punk with spiky auburn hair. His hands held a Kodak Instamatic with which he was shooting snaps of Belinda Torrance's shapely rear as she photo-copied. The girl didn't seem to mind that at all and kept turning her head to smile for the camera whilst bending over further to elevate her hips. Robert thought that an enchanting sight, but once her duplication was done, Belinda ignored his presence altogether and glided out of the room with a final kiss blown at Cliff.

'Lovely, isn't she?' Cliff commented as Robert signed the new ten pence exercise book provided. Given Cliff's striking appearance, his voice was surprisingly low, flat, sad and rather dreary. 'I must have about fifteen pictures of her. Got lots of the others too. There's plenty of talent cruising round here but Belinda's got the most beautiful bum. God. Imagine that on your face. All round and big and lovely and soft. Can't think of anything better, can you?'

‘On my *face*?’ Robert stopped working the machine and gaped at Cliff. ‘Well, each one to his taste but there’s other things I’d rather do.’

‘Like fucking her, I suppose,’ Cliff said mournfully. ‘How boring. I love a great woman’s bum on my face. And you’d be surprised how they love doing it too, the girls.’

‘I’m very pleased for you.’

‘I used to be into whips and chains and things,’ Cliff continued slowly and unemotionally. ‘And if you’re that way inclined, why not admit it? But being queened beats being beaten any time and hurts less, which is an advantage. It’s a good job, this,’ he went on tonelessly. ‘I get paid to sit here, look at the birds and dream up fantasies about them while you poor bastards give yourselves heart attacks upstairs, downstairs and in my Chairman’s chamber.’

‘Don’t you have to do anything else?’ Robert asked.

‘Oh yeah, sure, fix the machines whenever they break down. That hardly ever happens. I look after them well. They get a good service every evening before I go home. That’s why the Company keeps me. Before me, with whoever they had, everything was always breaking down, spewing out paper and spraying everyone with ink. Keep me here and that don’t happen.’

‘Good.’ Robert nodded pleasantly and picked up his photo-copying. ‘Well, back upstairs to the heart attacks, I suppose,’ he added jovially and turned to go – when something caught his attention.

Along with the studded leather jacket, bondage trousers and violently inscribed T-shirt, Cliff wore an ankh. It was solid and chunky, silver and shiny, and was suspended from his neck by a slim chain of stainless steel. Something about the object – he wasn’t sure what – held Robert’s gaze, then he realized that Cliff was regarding him curiously.

'Just admiring your ankh,' Robert murmured. 'It's very striking.'

'Oh, cheers, mate.' For an instant Cliff looked pleased. 'Yeah, I like it very much indeed myself. And you know why I wear it. Because,' his tone grew even more melancholy, 'the ankh stands for life – and I believe in life.'

Robert wondered if he did believe in life that lunch-time. He went off to the pub with a headache and a chest tightly jammed with frustration. Everyone and everything had pointed out his lack of status, George had briefed him badly and made him look a fool, he'd been unable to sort out anything properly and he couldn't even control his own secretary. Three-quarters of his pint sped down his throat within a minute and he let out a long, heavy sigh of released tension.

'Oh, I wouldn't do *that* if I were you,' quacked an educated but affected and arrogant voice from behind him. Robert tensed up and shot round to face a clean-cut, large young man, who was looking down on him. He was chubby, with thin, fair hair parted faultlessly on the right and, it seemed, polished with brilliantine. Unfortunately, this hadn't stopped specks of dandruff from flaking onto his smart blue suit, done up on the middle button. 'Minus five for that one, I think,' he continued disapprovingly, his expression one of priggish condescension. 'And to think you're on Browning's.'

'Sorry?' Robert regarded him anxiously. Who was this awful man? He looked rather important. And why the ticking off? What offence had he committed? 'I'm new here and . . .'

'I know, you're Robert Slade the new bug. You must be wondering who I am. I am Martin Bottomley. Heah!' he beckoned, 'you can come and sit by me.' Robert didn't especially want to come and sit by him but couldn't see any alternative and so complied. 'Now listen. Lesson

One,' said Martin Bottomley, 'always support the Company. That means, Lesson Two. Support the Company's clients. That means, Lesson Three – a particular example. When you're drinking beer, make sure it's Browning's You see, you just didn't think did you?' he stated patiently. 'You went and ordered Young's – loudly, as I recall. How d'you think that sounds? How d'you think it looks? Frankly, it's letting the side down by not being a team player.

'Take me, for example.' Martin paused for breath and beer. 'Ah! Good. And Champion, of course. Suppose I want cheese with it. I buy Ridley Farmfresh Cheddar – clients of ours. And I eat it with bread and a generous spreading of Rawson's Creamcrest butter, naturally. Very good too – the best, in fact. It's Trafalgar London Gin for me and Tartan Whisky for my scotch-loving friends. As for the ladies – and oh yes, for me there are plenty of ladies – why, it's terribly simple, with delectable gifts like Dewbury Nylons and Chudleigh Chocolates.

'*Now!*' Martin put a heavy hand on Robert's shoulder. 'There are two main reasons for this so pay attention. First: I can empathize with our consumers because I share the mentality. Second: the Company will notice – is noticing – my absolute loyalty and commitment. And that,' he confided patronizingly, 'is *the* way to get on.'

'Very interesting,' said Robert, who was starting to feel slightly sick.

'I should think so too,' Martin returned primly. 'You see, I've never forgotten that when I had my short list interview, Hugh Vincent Markby himself asked me where I wanted to be in twenty years' time. "Where you are," I answered smartly, and it was rather a good reply, I thought. Evidently,' he smiled smugly, 'Savage & Markby thought so too because here I am and rising, you see. How're you managing, by the way? Finding it hard to cope?'

'It's fine,' Robert lied without much conviction.

'Jolly good,' said Martin. 'Well, I must back to work. And make sure you don't stay here too long.' He rose. 'They *see* who's spending time in the pub, you know.'

As Martin Bottomley left, Robert felt utterly dejected. He finished his beer and stared dolefully at the empty glass, wanting Young's Ordinary but wondering whether he had to have Champion. He'd just decided in favour of rebellion as soon as nobody was looking when someone said: 'Let me get that one for you, squire,' and whisked away his glass.

Robert recognized Sid Ingram, who he'd met briefly the day before. Sid was tall but slightly built, with thick dark hair parted in the middle, a bristly moustache and warm brown eyes which repeatedly glanced from side to side. He was standing with a short, florid faced and youngish man who wore a speckled grey suit and was drinking gin with an air of profound despair.

'Go on!' cried Sid, 'what'll you be having?'

'Um . . .' Robert glanced around and saw plenty of people from Savage & Markby. 'A pint of Champion Bitter, please.'

Sid's companion choked on his gin.

'Come *on*,' said Sid, 'you don't have to drink that bleeding muck just because yer working on it.'

'They've got him already,' the other man muttered.

'This is a *free house*, squire,' Sid insisted, 'so why don't you have a nice drop of Young's?' Robert accepted with a mixture of gratitude and relief. 'Reckon you need a good drop of best ale if you've just had a session with Martin bleeding Bottomley. The way he goes on, you'd think he's been here twenty years when the wanker only joined us two months ago.'

'Two months ago . . .' Robert faltered.

'Yeah,' said Sid, 'he's a Graduate Trainee, same as you. Didn't you realize? This gentleman, incidentally, is Oliver Dawes, my Supervisor – here, Olly, meet Robert Slade.'

The despairing gin-drinker extended a slim hand wearily.

'Welcome,' said Oliver Dawes, 'to Living Death Limited.'

'Ha ha!' Robert laughed.

'It's not funny,' said Oliver.

'He means it,' said Sid. 'Cheers!' He grinned happily. 'Not happy in your job, are you, chief?'

'No,' said Oliver Dawes. 'And who could be if he had to supervise the impossible Sandra Lang? She's so neurotic, that girl.' He finished his gin and ordered another. 'And above us all hovers the answer to the question: Was God an Account Director? Yes, he was and he was called Tony Westbury.'

'Oh, he's a good bloke, Tony,' Sid Ingram said.

'Thank you, Sid,' said Tony Westbury, who'd suddenly appeared from nowhere and was flanked by Janet and Fiona. 'Anybody like a drink?'

'Hello, Bob!' Fiona trilled as Tony bought a round for everyone. 'Since *you* didn't seem to want my company at lunch-time, I accepted *Tony's* kind offer to accompany him.'

Robert brooded silently and tried to hide his misery behind a cloak of unassuming modesty while the others chatted animatedly about this and that. Unfortunately, Tony kept calling him 'Bob' and Fiona had taken up the call. It was 'Bob over here' and 'young Bob over there' and Robert was getting to the point where he couldn't stand it. Mutiny finally erupted half way through his third pint.

'. . . and it's all right for some,' Tony Westbury was saying, 'but what's your view of that, Bob?'

'Tony,' Robert spoke gravely, 'd'you mind very much if I ask you not to call me Bob?'

There was silence. Everyone looked first at Robert and then at Tony, to see how he would react. For a few seconds, his face remained affably impassive. One eyebrow lifted slightly in surprise.

'All right, Bobbie,' Tony said blandly, 'Robert it is from now on.' He looked at his gold Rolex. 'Must get back.' And Tony left the pub with Janet.

'Good for you,' said Sid.

'It's no big deal,' replied Robert. 'What's all the fuss about?'

'There comes a time,' Oliver's voice dripped sarcasm, 'when a man has to make a stand.'

'*Well!*' exclaimed Fiona, 'I can't say I understand anything you mean. All I know is that speaking as his,' she jerked her thumb at Robert, 'secretary, I think that sort of thing is *hardly* the way to get on. Coming?' she snapped at her boss then walked away without looking back.

There was an empty hole in Robert's gut as he accepted Oliver's offer of another drink.

The afternoon started badly and got worse. Robert tried to get down to his study of the Protheroe Market Analysis and Summary sheet for Joy soap powder, but beer had fogged his brain to make the mass of figures indecipherable. Then George summoned him, demanded an account of the morning and looked peeved at the lack of results.

'*Push*,' he urged Robert. 'You just have to *push* those lazy bastards in Creative. Well, we'll keep up the pressure. Here's a few more things I hope you won't mind doing for me . . .'

So it was back down to the Production Department for Posters with Nigel Fulton, who wasn't there. ''E's never back 'ere before three,' a smirking despatch boy told Robert. The trainee kicked his heels for five minutes until a beer-breathing, weasel-faced Nigel arrived to survey Robert without interest.

'The Golden Eagle poster? Nah. Nah,' he told the trainee, 'that's not in yet.'

'Oh. But George said it would be here.'
'Well, George said wrong, didn't he?'
'Um – well, *why* isn't it back from the printers?'
'How should I know?' Nigel demanded aggrievedly. 'It's not here 'cos it's not here, that's all I know. *Should've* been here today, of course. And needless to say, if Account Management had moved earlier, like I suggested in my Memo of the twenty-third, we would've had it here by now.'
'But . . . when's it *going* to be here?'
'Could be any time,' Nigel shrugged. 'Later on today. In the morning. Tomorrow afternoon, maybe. Possibly even the day after. Who can tell? Anyway, when's it needed?'
'I'm not sure. But George said it was urgent.'
'Always is with George,' Nigel observed dryly. 'But if he don't even know the date, it can't be that urgent, can it?'
Robert was trying to formulate an answer when Nigel casually picked up a magazine and left the room for the lavatory. The sweat of suppressed indignation was running down Robert's back and soaking into his shirt. It was a real effort to force himself to march briskly into the room marked; 'Despatch: Fred Sayers.'
'Excuse me, this *is* Despatch, isn't it?'
'It is indeed Despatch,' said a man, 'and *I* am the Despatch Manager. Fred Sayers and pleased to meet you. You must be the new trainee.' Fred was very well dressed in an old fashioned grey suit of excellent cloth which had been cared for lovingly. His sparkling white shirt was spotless and wax polish had put the shine on his gleaming black shoes. The maroon silk tie was perfectly knotted. 'May I enquire as to the nature of your business?' Fred drew himself up and Robert noticed that his sleek grey hair had been rigorously brushed straight back. His face was stern and well-preserved – and not unkind.

'Robert Slade, how d'you do. Got a Browning's parcel here from George. He needs it posted off Red Star.'

'Red Star!' exclaimed Fred. 'He would. Did you hear that?' he demanded of the five despatch boys who were sitting around him. 'Did you? Stan, how many times have I told George Webbing to have his Red Star stuff down here by half-past two? How many times?'

'A lot,' said Stan.

'Exactly, a lot.' Fred began to patrol the room. 'Some people never listen. Some people's like that. And haven't I seen 'em come and go! Believe me, I have, haven't I, Kev?'

'Yeah,' said Kev.

'*I*,' Fred told Robert proudly, 'have been associated with Savage & Markby since the Company's foundation.'

'Ah. Fascinating.'

'I know my onions,' Fred continued relentlessly. 'And I know that if you want to get on here, you don't rub old Fred Sayers up the wrong way, do you, Phil?'

'No,' said Phil.

'Correct!' barked Fred. 'But of course,' he added nicely, 'you're new here, Robert, and I wouldn't expect you to know that. Just for once, then, and because you've got a nice face – hasn't he got a nice face, Billy? – I am prepared to *make an exception*. I shall permit the parcel you have brought me to go Red Star. What d'you say to that, then?'

'Thank you,' said Robert.

'That's right,' said Fred, 'and make sure you know the rule for next time. Steve! See to the Executive's parcel!'

Robert left Despatch feeling very small and barely up to Press and Perkins of PR, called so, they'd told him, because he was always so polite. The trainee entered to see a massive, stocky, balding man with a network of tattoos on his powerful arms and shoulders. A roll-up drooped from his fleshy lips and occasionally he held it in a hand that looked capable of breaking bricks.

‘Yeah?’

‘Hullo! Bill Perkins?’ Robert smiled. ‘I’m Robert Slade, the new . . .’

‘I don’t give a bleeding shit who you are,’ said Perkins of P.R. ‘Whadyou want?’

‘Ah – a pull-out of the last Star press ad for the Daily Mirror, please.’

‘Oh, yeah?’ The man gazed at him sullenly. ‘Why?’

‘George Webbing wants it.’

‘Well, George Webbing can fuck off,’ said Perkins of PR. ‘There’s only two left and he’s not having those. Others’ll be wanting ’em. Why, I gave George half a dozen pull-outs only last week – he gone and used ’em as bog paper or something? And you’re his bum boy? You poor bugger.’ He spat out his roll-up. ‘’E’s useless, that man. Used to be down here in Press, see. Wasn’t even up to bleeding graffiti. Thinks because he’s gone upstairs he can have his balls-aching, lah-di-dah airs and graces. Well, not down here, he can’t. And you fucking well tell him that from me. Go on. Hop it – and make sure you tell him what I said.’ Perkins glared at Robert and raised his fist. Robert backed hastily out of the room as the fist crashed down onto the table and sent a pile of metal plates spinning to the floor.

After the battering he’d taken, it became doubly difficult to concentrate on comprehending the Protheroe. Columns of figures blurred before his eyes and failed to convey the slightest meaning. Robert thought of going and asking George for help but felt he couldn’t face him. He’d have to tell George that precious little had been accomplished and George would blame it on him. It was totally unfair since so much that had happened was George’s fault. It was also very depressing to be bossed about by somebody whom nobody appeared to respect. Robert sat gloomily at his desk and stared dully at statistics. He might have done that till it was time to go home if Charles Sutherland hadn't wandered up behind him and said: 'Oh, God! Not the bloody Protheroe!'

'Tony wants me to apply it to Browning's,' Robert explained, 'and I'm having a spot of trouble comprehending it fully.'

'Heaven help you, old fruit,' Charles retorted easily. 'The whole thing's ineluctably tedious and inextricably complicated. I'll send flowers to your grave, but in the meantime, step in here.' Robert entered Charles's office and Charles promptly put his feet up on the desk. 'Allow me to explain, what? The Protheroe means a summary of volume sales and market share, wholesale and retail, free and tied trade.' He yawned. 'You put these figures here, these figures here and these figures here. Here you calculate the sales running over quarterly periods, averaged against last year, in columns like this. The job will take you hours, days or weeks even of blood, sweat and tears – before the great moment when we can see all these figures, previously on many sheets of paper, on one sheet of paper.'

'I see.' Robert *thought* he saw. 'But . . . you must think I'm very dense . . . but how exactly does that help us?'

'It doesn't,' said Charles. 'Not as far as I can see. From Browning's point of view, the entire exercise is completely pointless.' He grinned. Robert didn't return it. He felt as though he was wrestling with a thick, damp fog.

'Then . . . then what's the point?' he queried faintly.

'The point is – from *our* point of view, it might impress the client. After all, we're meant to be wizards at marketing. When it's all done, some poor fool – hopefully not me – will have to stand in front of Browning's and witter on about the Protheroe until they're bored into submission. That's the only point and it might not even work. Still,' he grinned again, 'you're stuck with it, old boy, and sorry about that. There we are.' Charles lit a Pall Mall. 'You can come and see me whenever you get stuck with it. I'm quite a dab hand at those horrible things.'

'Thank you,' said Robert.

'Oh, one other point,' Charles said as Robert rose. 'There's this old friend of mine. Terrible personal tragedy. Gone down in the world. Must help him up. Selling insurance. Little bit desperate. You don't have to buy, of course, but would you be kind enough to see him?'

'Naturally,' Robert answered. 'Should I see him in my office?'

'No, it's not in the office,' Charles informed him swiftly. 'Not on – so I hope you don't object but I've given him your home address, which was on file. He'll be coming round at eight o'clock tonight and that'll be all right, won't it?'

No, thought Robert, *it won't be all right. I don't want work invading my home. I want to keep my private life private and you had no right at all to do what you've done, Charles, and that's all I bloody well need today*. But of course, Charles had helped him and had offered to help more, so he smiled blandly and said: 'Fine.'

That event was the last he remembered at the end of his dreadful working day. Robert left with vast relief at five-thirty. In theory, that was when you went. In practice, no one went then except juniors and secretaries. Robert was past caring. All he wanted to do was go home, have a bath, take a drink and be with Vickie – and forget how ghastly today's experiences had been.

What a day! He'd accomplished next to nothing and all the while had been patronized, ordered, put down, abused, insulted, intimidated and sent packing. He felt tense, anxious, depressed, ignorant and empty. The electric shock he received on calling the lift made him feel close to screaming. But that didn't compare with the jolt he received when the door slid open and displayed the Chairman.

John Savage had been pointed out to the trainee. Tall, middle-aged, square-headed, with thick hair and opaque glasses, the Chairman had been glimpsed going here and going there, always surrounded by a retinue and always steady and purposeful in his every movement. Robert couldn't help feeling slightly awed as he stepped into the lift beside him.

'Good evening, Mr Savage,' he said deferentially.

'Good evening,' Savage responded. Otherwise he gave no sign of recognition. 'Ground floor?'

'Please.'

Savage looked at him. Robert pressed the button. The lift descended and there was silence. Robert tried to think of something to say but couldn't. Savage remained impassive. The lift stopped. Robert stood aside to let Savage pass. As the Chairman did so, he trod heavily on Robert's toe, then strode on as though nothing had happened.

That was virtually the last straw for Robert. Every instinct screamed out: 'Be more careful, you clumsy oaf!' – but John Savage was the Chairman and this was his territory. Robert was only allowed there on condition he submit to training.

His eyes hardened into a fury-filled glare at Savage's back, as though everything today had been the Chairman's fault.

5

Robert lived with his girlfriend in a small flat tucked away in a dingy side-street at the wrong end of Camden Town. Their living space consisted of a tiny entrance hall, a neat bathroom, a well-equipped kitchen and a cosy, colourful living-room where the bed came out of a cupboard. It was the best he and Vickie could afford on their respective salaries of five thousand three hundred and three thousand five hundred a year. Robert had been warned that starting salaries in advertising were low but hoped to win a series of rises before too long: while Vickie worked as an articled clerk and was also studying for her solicitor's exams.

They'd met three years ago, at University, and in their final year had shared a bed-sit, so their current conditions represented an improvement. Although both had been brought up with very much more, neither was interested in living off well-to-do parents. Robert and Vickie were determined to make their own independent way in the world. If that meant hard times initially, they were confident they could cope and no doubt a well-earned affluence would arrive soon enough.

They'd been living together in London for four weeks now, and although they were poor and didn't have a car, they were also young, optimistic, happy and in love. If, in a year or so, it all worked out, they'd agreed to think seriously about marriage. Vickie would carry on working whatever they did. She believed that a woman's intelligence should be exercised on more stimulating goals than a husband and a home, and like Robert, she was fiercely ambitious. Eventually, she knew, she would want to have children but she lacked all desire for them now. Robert and her career were the two most important things in her life. Like him, she'd been thrilled to start work, but again like him, she'd just suffered a very trying day.

'Going through a lease word by word is a bloody boring business,' she told Robert over the chops with a rich, dark sauce she'd made. 'And at times I get this terrible fear about the Law itself. They don't seem to like women very much in the profession.' She frowned and sipped a lager. 'And today I heard that some client of ours wants advice on getting round the sex discrimination laws. I'm not at all happy about that.'

'No,' said Robert, 'I don't think I'd be.' He wore the T-shirt and jeans he'd changed into the instant he arrived home. 'Sounds like we've both had an appalling day.' He'd given Vickie a brief account of his misfortunes – omitting the severest humiliations, which he couldn't bear to tell her – and she'd listened to him with a mixture of sympathy and indignation. The fuss about not being called Bob had astonished her and she'd called it 'stupid'. The Company, she'd added, sounded slightly crazy. 'And my day isn't even over yet,' he continued. 'There's this wretched insurance salesman coming round at eight.'

'*What?!*' exclaimed Vickie. 'Why, for God's sake?'

'Charles asked me to do him a favour for a friend. He'd helped me and I couldn't very well refuse.'

'But I don't feel like seeing anyone, least of all an insurance man. And why does it have to be tonight?'

'Charles arranged it.'

'What?' Her face fell. 'You mean, without asking you first?'

'Um . . . yes,' he admitted.

'You know something,' Vickie said after a pause. 'Just thinking about your day and what you've just said gives me an idea about where you're going wrong. You're not being assertive enough. Why? I'm surprised. I always think of you as assertive.'

'But I *couldn't* be.' Robert lit a cigarette. 'Don't you see? My position's so low and I was so badly briefed that I had nothing at all to assert. It nearly killed me.'

'Well, make sure George briefs you better in future.'

'How?' Robert demanded. 'I'm so green I don't even know the difference between a good brief and a bad . . .' he checked himself. 'Well,' he sighed, 'no point in being negative. I'll just have to find out more. No wonder they call it "on the job" training.'

'I hope,' she remarked acidly, 'that the training doesn't mean regular invasions of our home by your Company.'

'There's no need to be bitchy,' Robert returned sharply. 'Of course the training doesn't mean that. Tonight's just one of those things. Christ, darling, *I* don't want the Company taking over my life.' He spoke with conviction. 'And there's no way it's going to do that.'

Vickie's expression softened.

'I'm sorry,' she said. 'I've had a hard day and I was ratty just then.' She smiled a lovely smile of sensuous lips and healthy white teeth. Warmth glowed in her strong, grey eyes. 'You've had a hard day too, so let's not make it any worse. It's just the working world, I suppose.' She reached out for him and Robert took her hand and squeezed it gently. *Just the working world*, he thought, *and already I've found out how ignorant I am about it.*

'Darling . . .' he said.

The doorbell rang.

'Damn!' Robert snapped. 'I'll go.' He left the flat to open the front door on an unprepossessing individual with a flushed, raddled face and a bloated beer belly.

'Good evening!' The man breathed a cloud of whisky fumes into Robert's face. 'Robert Shlade?'

'Robert Slade, yes.'

'Haughey Life Insurance. Nick Petersh. Pleashed to meet you.' He seized Robert's hand and pumped it up and down. 'Charles Sutherland recommended you.' He swayed slightly. Robert regarded him doubtfully. The name meant nothing. The drink-stained suit, the glazed eyes, the greasy, thinning hair and the trembling hands inspired no confidence at all. And this was a friend of Charles? 'Nishe dishtrict,' Nick Peters continued jovially, 'alwaysh liked Camden Town. Can I come in?'

'Please. Up here,' Robert said reluctantly. He'd already decided what to do – be polite but get shot of the man in the fastest possible time. 'Darling, Nick Peters of Haughey Life,' he announced as the salesman shambled into the room with a beery grin on his face. 'Vickie Strawson. Now, Nick, won't you sit down?' Nick sagged into a seat. 'I don't want to waste your time,' Robert went on briskly. *Or mine*, he thought. 'Charles suggested I see you tonight, but I'm dreadfully sorry, I completely forgot,' he lied, 'that I've already got life insurance. I do apologize for your wasted journey but . . .'

'What Plan d'you have?' Nick interrupted.

'I'm not sure. It's been a long time since I began with it.' Robert swallowed.

'Can you get it out?' Nick requested. 'I'd really love to shee it and perhapsh I can improve your poshishun.' He suppressed a belch.

'I'm afraid it's not here. We've only just moved, you see, and all my documents are still with my parents . . .'

'I don't think it can poshibly beat what we're offering.' He spoke the line as though he read from a script which bored him. 'In our Haughey Life Endowment Policy, payable in instalments of as little as *one pound* a week, you get immediate life cover of *thirty thousand* pounds.'

'So what?' said Robert. 'All that means is that somebody gets thirty thousand when I'm dead. What good is that to me?'

'I wash thinking,' Nick leered at Vickie, 'of your loved ones. For example, if you were to . . .'

'I don't want him dead,' Vickie said sharply, 'and I don't need his thirty thousand, thanks. I've already arranged my own cover.'

'Look, please,' Robert addressed the salesman kindly, 'it's not worth your while trying to convince us. It's a pity you've had to come all this way but . . .'

'The answer's no,' said Vickie. 'Sorry.' She stood up. Robert looked encouragingly at the door. Nick Peters rose wearily to his feet.

'If you change your mind . . .' he began without conviction.

'. . . we'll let you know,' Robert replied hastily. 'It's been a pleasure meeting you and . . .'

'You've just joined Savage & Markby, haven't you?' the man said suddenly, with an unexpected hardness of tone.

'Yes . . . ?'

'I was Managing Director there.'

'Sorry?' Robert gaped at him. Was this some kind of alcoholic fantasy? 'When?'

'Until last April.' He no longer slurred his words. 'That's how I know Charles, you see. I gave him his first job, God help me.'

Robert sensed that Nick was speaking the truth and it stunned him. He couldn't reconcile the wreck he saw with the Managing Directorship of Savage & Markby. How could it possibly have happened? He hardly dared ask and wasn't sure what to say.

'Get out,' said Nick Peters.

'I beg your pardon?'

'Get out. Get out while you still can.' His eyes had acquired an alarming intensity.

'I don't understand.'

'Leave Savage & Markby,' the man urged him fiercely.

'Leave them before they suck the life out of you and eat up your soul. Leave them before,' he spat the words bitterly, 'they make you into me.'

There was silence.

'Well,' Robert said pleasantly and at last, 'I'll certainly bear in mind what you've said. Very interesting.' He beamed with the sudden geniality with which one takes leave of a bore. 'Thanks once again and nice meeting you, Nick, I'll just . . .' he started for the door.

'Don't bother,' Nick shot back disgustedly. 'I'll see my own way out.' He stumbled towards the door, then turned for a final glare at Robert. 'You were made for those bastards,' he snarled, 'and I hope you get what you deserve.' The door slammed and he left.

'Phew!' Robert exclaimed. 'What an awful man! I'm really sorry he got inflicted on you.' Vickie was staring abstractedly into space. 'What's the matter?'

'He's made me feel really uneasy.'

'He was enough to make anyone feel uneasy.'

'I don't mean that. I mean . . . how did he get that way? Is *that* what your Company does to people?'

'No, of course not. He did *that* to himself and that's why he's no longer MD.'

'I hope you're right,' said Vickie. 'But did you hear what he said about the sucking of lives and the eating of souls? It gave me the creeps.'

'Poetic language,' Robert observed drily. 'He was drunk. He's clearly got a grudge against the Company for sacking him.'

'I hope you're right.'

'What d'you mean?'

'Darling . . .' Vickie came and sat beside him on a floor cushion, 'd'you remember when we went to Porlock Hill last month? No, listen. It's important. We got out of the car and there was no one else around. We sat on a rock and had cider together. All around us, there was this fabulous silence except for the birds, and that glorious field of purple flowers . . . and the hills and the moors below us in the distance. There wasn't a cloud in the sky that day and the sun was beating down on our skin. We were happy, so wonderfully happy. We'd got each other. We'd got our degrees, too. The world seemed such a glorious place. We got to talking about how going to work would affect us and both of us felt the same thing. We wanted to succeed, we believed we would succeed, but we would succeed without being corrupted. You said something then which I can't forget. It put what I feel and believe into words. You said that there was something in every human being which is ultimately pure and noble. You swore to preserve it in yourself. D'you still feel that way?'

'Yes,' he answered crisply. 'Yes.'

'I love you,' said Vickie, and kissed him.

'I love you.' He took her in his arms. 'I love you very much indeed.'

'Please,' she whispered, 'don't ever become like that poor, broken man.'

'Never,' said Robert. 'Forget him.' He ran his fingers lightly over Vickie's soft and pretty face, then his fingers played with her long brown hair. She touched his earlobes with cool finger-tips, then drew them tantalizingly down his neck. He couldn't stop himself sliding a hand up her grey pleated skirt to massage the welcoming warmth within. She moaned softly.

'Beast . . .' she whispered.

'Oh, God, I love you,' he breathed. 'Let's fuck.'

6

Savage & Markby Ltd
MEMORANDUM

To: George Webbing
From: Nigel Fulton
cc: Peter Jackson
Charles Sutherland
Paul Adams
Robert Slade
Subject: Browning's Golden Eagle Poster 28
Date: 27 September 1983

It has come to my attention that the Poster Department is being unfairly blamed for late delivery to the sites of 28 – 'It's not your local lemonade'.

As I pointed out in my Memo of 4/9/83, the Account Management Printing Brief of 25/8/83 was not accompanied by appropriate authorization. This delay on Account Management's part resulted, obviously, in a further delay in delivery to the printers. Were it not for the excellent relations which the Poster Department has established with them, the printers would have taken their standard time and the delay caused by Account Management would have been extended further.

I would suggest that in the future, Account Management liaise more closely with Media regarding the booking of the sites and supply me with all relevant documents and authorization on the day originally promised. This would help us avoid an unhappy situation in which my Department is wholly blameless.

Nigel Fulton

Savage & Markby Ltd

MEMORANDUM

To: Nigel Fulton
George Webbing
From: Paul Adams
cc: Peter Jackson
Chris Faye
Tim Dawson
Robert Slade
Subject: Browning's Golden Eagle Poster 28
Date: 27 September 1983

I am in receipt of Nigel's Memo of today and am moved to comment on his mention of Account Management-Media liaison.

Media would and has always welcomed closer liaison between itself, Account Management and the Posters Department. Unhappily, close liaison was not the case here, although Media has discharged its functions fully.

I look forward to closer liaison in the future and an end to others' unfortunate errors.

Paul Adams

Savage & Markby Ltd

MEMORANDUM

To: Nigel Fulton
Paul Adams
From: George Webbing
cc: Peter Jackson
Mike Armstrong
Chris Faye
Tony Westbury
Charles Sutherland
Robert Slade

Subject: Browning's Eagle Poster 28
Date: 27 September 1983

Thank you both for your Memos of today, the nature of which was surprising. One can only be astonished by the eagerness to blame Account Management for the mistakes of other departments. The facts of the matter are as follows:

1 – The Printing Brief was delivered to the Posters Department, and copied to Media, on 25/8/83.

2 – Authorization followed the very next day.

3 – 'It's not your local lemonade' should have returned from the printers to the Posters Department no later than one day after the date originally agreed.

4 – Media was kept continuously informed of our progress, or in this case, lack of it.

5 – There can therefore be no excuse for the Poster Department's lack of efficiency in this instance.

I trust that these points make the situation clear and will be noted for future reference.

George Webbing

Peter Jackson put down the stack of Memos which had arrived by the third, mid-day internal post. He'd enjoyed reading through them and it was now a house rule that he was cc'd on every Memo. The poster squabble might have interesting results, he felt. Essentially, it represented a struggle for mastery at a low level between Account Management, Media and Production. Naturally, if the matter grew to become worthy of the Board's attention, he would support Production. They were directly responsible to him.

Peter wasn't sure why Posters, Press, Despatch, Catering and Photo-Copying reported directly to the Managing

Director. Perhaps it was a compensation for their lack of glamour. Anyhow, he didn't mind at all. Production meant the final product and it was good to have his finger on that particular button.

Early on, he'd gone down to Production and introduced himself around. Everyone seemed pleased to see him and lost no time in telling him their troubles. Peter listened patiently then acted quietly to put things right for them wherever it was possible. Unsurprisingly, this made him popular and he visited again. He became even more popular when he treated the entire Department to a slap-up lunch. Everyone had got so drunk, they'd ended up singing him a chorus of: 'For he's a jolly good fellow.' After that, they were willing to oblige him any time. That could one day be very useful, Peter thought, and in any case, they were a nice crowd.

The Managing Director was pleased with his progress. He'd brought a few accounts with him from Brady & Harding and delegated their daily running to teams which did the job smoothly. Sometimes he lunched with top level clients. Sometimes he lunched with potential clients. Sometimes he lunched with his agency colleagues. Always he lunched long and lunched well.

Some might observe that there was surprisingly little for Peter to do, but Peter would've disagreed vehemently. For a start, there was the Strategy Review Board – basically the Board minus Savage and Markby – which he chaired. The first meeting considered Browning's and demonstrated that there were so many beers, so many actual and possible strategies, so many issues and so many egos, that three months' weekly sessions of an hour each wouldn't be enough to thrash them through. Peter had responded by setting up the Browning's Beers Strategy Sub-Committee, which drew on executive personnel and which he chaired.

Then, Peter could see that Forms was a highly complex

question, raising other concerns which were equally troubled. His solution was the new Administration Committee, which he chaired.

A third area requiring attention, in Peter's view, was the poor relations between lower level Account Management and Creative personnel, which he'd noticed. This had led him to create the Account Management-Creative Liaison Committee, on which juniors sat and which he chaired. In the future, it might serve a major arbitrating role, he hoped. And perhaps a similar committee was required for liaison between Account Management, Media and Posters.

Peter had carried all these measures triumphantly. Savage and Markby were wholly in favour of them and there was an unexpected ally in Stanley Haynes. He'd endorsed Peter's every proposal. In return, Peter invited him to sit on every committee, even when his function wasn't at all relevant. 'Don't mind me,' Stanley Haynes always told the committee, 'I'm just here as an observer.' After that, he sat back contentedly and observed.

Peter was glad to have Stanley Haynes there. The presence of the bald Financial Director added extra seriousness and credibility to his committees. Moreover, Stanley's support on the Board, plus vital Savage and Markby backing, put Peter in a majority and made him invulnerable. All the same, he'd endeavoured to conciliate or neutralize the other three Directors. When Mike Armstrong saw him to protest about Forms, Peter promptly welcomed him to the position of Vice Chairman, Administration Committee. Chris Faye's openly expressed abhorrence of committees had been respected – so the Media Director sat on nothing. Brian Bishop wanted to sit on the Account Management-Creative Liaison Committee – and now did as its Executive President.

This morning had witnessed another victory for Peter.

He'd out-boxed Mike Armstrong in a Board Meeting. Despite a fierce argument in which Mike's temper had threatened to fray, Peter now had full charge of the Account Management Training Scheme. It was unsatisfactory not to have one, Peter argued. Young executives on the job were crying out for extra instruction. This, he thought, could best be done at lunch-time in Conference Room One with beer and sandwiches provided. It would involve a series of talks, with tips and hints, and much sound advice on the secrets of solid presentation. The proposal was carried by six votes to one.

The first session would be next Monday. It would begin with the Managing Director's Opening Remarks and be followed by his Introductory Overview. Then he'd show them a film – everyone liked that – and conclude with Questions. Feeling highly enthusiastic about the prospect, Peter seized a pen and jotted notes upon a pad.

'Open with joke about the Corley Coffee cock-up,' he wrote. 'Then serious. Attendance not compulsory but we shall be keeping an eye out. Then – illustrated case of Lush shampoo's success story . . .'

His hand reached out for the glass at his elbow and raised it to his lips, but the vessel was empty. Almost automatically, he took the whisky bottle and poured generously.

It was a quarter past twelve, mid-day.

'Right,' said Mike, 'this is the team for Kandy.' Georgina prepared to write. 'Assistant Creative Director – Ian Sharpe, and he can pick his people. Senior Media Planner – Craig Anderson plus whoever he wants. Account Management – the Browning's lot, Tony, Charles and George.'

'George?' The secretary regarded him quizzically. 'Are you sure that's really such a very good idea?'

'Why not?' Mike lit his pipe. 'He's got a long way to go but he's trying very hard and in the end he always gets the job done. Browning's seem to like him a lot.'

'Yes,' said Georgina, 'but is he right for Kandy? I can't help wondering how the Americans will react to him.'

Mike considered her statement.

'Hm. Good point. Yes, let's leave him off Kandy and have Sid Ingram instead. Give George another chance later in the year. He deserves it, don't you reckon?'

'I'm not sure just who would agree with you, Mike,' Georgina answered cautiously.

'Oh? Hard to keep my ear to the ground. What're people saying about him?'

'Well, word has it that he's rather inefficient.'

'Oh, really?'

'That poor trainee Robert Slade keeps making a fool of himself on George's account, one's told. Apparently George keeps dropping him in it.'

'He'll learn,' Mike commented flatly. 'And he'll learn more from that than from Peter's fatuous Training Scheme. Jesus!' He shrugged and smiled wryly at Georgina. 'You seem to have taken quite a fancy to young Robert.'

'He's very polite. That helps.'

'I'm glad to hear it. Hope he realizes it takes more than politeness to get things done here.'

'Why not have him on Kandy?' Georgina suggested. 'You could do with a general dogsbody.'

'True,' said Mike, 'but not Robert Slade. He seems all right but he's still too green. We'll have that keen young lad, Martin Bottomley.'

Georgina wrote. Mike found himself looking at her longingly.

'You're going to love this!' cried George as he bustled into the small Conference Room Three and shook hands with Tim Rogers of Browning's. 'Look.' George displayed a mechanical of a poster. It showed a strong-looking shirt-sleeved man of indeterminate age looking pleased and drinking Browning's Best Brown. 'BROWNING'S BEST BROWN,' said the slogan, 'BROWN ALE AT ITS BEST'. 'Now just look at that, Tim,' George urged the Brand Manager. 'Lovely! Isn't it lovely? And see how we've given him a nice maroon tie? Colin'll be pleased about that.' There was a pause while Tim considered the poster. After a time, he frowned slightly. 'You don't look happy,' George said with pained surprise. 'What on earth's the matter?'

'It's . . . well, it's his expression, really.'

'What's wrong with his expression?'

'Well, I don't think there's anything wrong with it but you know how Colin is. I just don't feel he'll like – well – the bloke looks a bit too self-satisfied.'

'Of course he's satisfied,' said George, 'he's drinking Browning's Best Brown.'

'Yes, but I can see Colin saying it's a bit overdone. The man looks smug. Know what I mean? I mean, Colin won't want people going round thinking that Browning's Best Brown is a beer for smug people.'

'Oh, come on, Tim, you can't say he's smug. Look, there's a slight frown here.'

'Sorry, George,' said Tim. 'I can't risk it.'

Savage & Markby Ltd

MEMORANDUM

To: All Staff
cc: Board Directors
From: Peter Jackson
Subject: House
Date: 27 September 1983

Many of you may not be aware of the recent substantial increase in billing on Browning's Beers. This was in response to Savage & Markby proposals which had been thought through most ably and were presented with commendable dash by the account team. A warm word of congratulations is in order, then, for Tony Westbury and his assistants, who enjoyed formidable and telling support from Chris Faye and his Department.

Jane Shelton, who has been an indispensable Girl Friday to everyone fortunate enough to work with her, is leaving us after two years to get married next Friday. I am sure everyone will join with me in wishing Jane and her future husband Brian every possible happiness for the future.

The first Account Management Training Scheme session will take place at one o'clock this coming Monday in Conference Room One. It will feature an in-depth Introduction to the subject, provide essential groundwork and will be accompanied by suitable refreshments. Account Management personnel are most strongly urged to attend but all, including secretaries with executive ambitions, are warmly invited to be present.

Peter Jackson
MANAGING DIRECTOR

Oliver Dawes read through that Memo with an expression of acute distaste, then scrunched it up and tossed it into his bin. He was sick of the Memos with which Board Directors and others assaulted him every day. He couldn't stand it. He couldn't stand much about his job, in fact, and had lost all interest in it several months ago. He found he couldn't care less about the volume sales figures for Joy soap powder in Yorkshire. It all seemed so meaningless and farcical. He'd never really wanted a job in advertising anyway. It was just that a job was needed and advertising had seemed less dull than anything else. Ad men all said that the business was fun. Oliver knew that it wasn't.

All he ultimately cared about was playing the guitar.

His style was classical and anyone who'd heard him play admitted that he could tease the most beautiful and haunting melodies from the instrument he loved. He'd tried for years to obtain concert bookings, make records or publish the music he composed yet, despite his talent, he hadn't succeeded. But it remained one area where he had vowed to go on trying.

So here he was, still at Savage & Markby, a company, he thought, where with the exceptions of boring Brian Bishop and brawling Mike Armstrong, the Board Directors sat on their fat arses and drew their fatter salaries while everyone else sweated their guts out for not very much, thank you.

Some time ago, Oliver had decided on rebellion. For the last two months he'd come to the office at 9.30 with a briefcase and a Jeeves of Belgravia carrier bag which contained a spare jacket. At 9.45, he hung this jacket on his chair, sprinkled his desk with statistics and reports, told his secretary he was going down to Creative and went home. Home was now a small flat he rented nearby, and where he spent his mornings playing the guitar and composing music. At 12.45 he returned without his jacket, sat at his desk in his shirt-sleeves and pretended to be working furiously. All invitations to lunch-time drinks were declined with a curt 'love to, but I'm busy' until 1.20, when he went to the pub and stayed there as long as he decently could. There he spoke of Savage & Markby with such withering sarcasm that nobody really believed him. The afternoon saw him closeted in his office, where he studied musical scores which he kept hidden beneath a fat pile of Company Memoranda. As far as was possible, he avoided seeing anyone. The only visits he couldn't evade were from clients – and Oliver could still turn on the charm for them – from his Account Director, Tony Westbury, who was coming less and less often, and from the two executives he supervised, Sandra Lang and Sid Ingram.

Sandra Lang was a pain, he felt. She was always bothering him with something uninteresting. Not that the hard-faced bitch wasn't capable, but she seemed to resent him intensely, and even appeared to like interrupting his quiet, creative reveries with shrill demands for active support. At least Sid Ingram, honest spiv that he was, had sussed something of the situation and was shouldering nearly all of the work. In return, and provided Sid remained loyal, Oliver would give him a glowing recommendation for promotion. They'd more or less agreed that tacitly.

Oliver glanced at his watch. It was one o'clock. Thank God, only another twenty minutes to go. He amused himself by flipping his door open, enabling everyone who was going to lunch via the corridor to see him at his desk and apparently working with alacrity, enthusiasm and gusto.

The magnificent figure of Belinda Torrance – clad in a white blouse with a plunging neckline, a black pencil skirt slit to the thigh, black seamed stockings and high-heeled patent leather pumps – was having a deeply distracting effect on Simon Burns and Dennis Wilson. Whenever Belinda leaned forward, her firm and voluptuous breasts threatened to burst out of her blouse. Whenever she bent over, her luscious bottom threatened to split the seat of her skirt. Whenever she stood up, she stretched out a long, lissom leg so that her split skirt parted to display succulent thigh and threatened to bare her crutch. Both men, Belinda knew, were writhing with pulsating erections. She loved making men writhe with pulsating erections.

Now she sat with a pocket mirror in her hand whilst brushing her long shock of strawberry blonde curls. Her vain, sensuous face with its baby blue eyes, freckled snub nose and wide, pink mouth stared back at her vacantly from the glass. She'd just turned down a Simon and Dennis invitation for lunch-time drinks. In fact, she liked both of them very much – they were fabulous fun to work with – and quite fancied Dennis. Simon, she thought, had the hangdog face of a young bloke who's married too young and regrets it, and so he didn't really attract her. However, he was vastly preferable to the Group Head, Ronald Potter, who had those awful 'intellectual' glasses and was always shouting 'Don't buck the System!' Ronald Potter pretended that she didn't attract him at all, was snappy and cold whenever he spoke to her and then ogled her from behind his glasses when he thought she wasn't looking. But the real reason Belinda wouldn't be in the pub with Simon and Dennis today was because she had a previous engagement.

Blowing a kiss to Dennis and Simon, Belinda wiggled out into the corridor leaving a groan and a sigh behind her. She took the stairs down to Production and the Lower Projection Room, where she knocked softly three times before going in. She was greeted with a sexy, lop-sided smile as Ian Sharpe popped a champagne cork.

Most people considered Ian to be the outstanding Assistant Creative Director. One reason many liked working with him was because when things became difficult and tedious, he was perfectly willing to cheat. Belinda had laughed at two stories about that. Once, on a TV commercial set, when a cat repeatedly selected any bowl of cat food except Minnie, Ian solved the problem by putting foul-smelling cough mixture into every bowl of cat food except Minnie. And when Star keg beer – 'Creamy head. Deep throat' – repeatedly failed to raise its creamy head on a photographic shoot, Ian gave it head with an aerosol can of frothing shaving cream. It was rumoured that he was the Company cocaine fiend. It was also rumoured that he was the Company stud. Belinda had tried him and decided that so far, in her journey through the Company, he was.

Ian was quite good looking too. Because he kept his lean body fit, strong and hard, the fact that he was balding added to his virility rather than announcing an ageing which diminished it. And although his face was engraved with lines which suggested more years than his thirty-five, it had acquired a maturity which appealed to Belinda. The only thing she didn't like about him physically was his irritating habit of frequently sniffing and blowing his nose.

He was kind to her. He made her laugh. He enjoyed spending plenty of money on her. He fucked her repeatedly and very well and was about to do that again right now. Belinda loved his style. Ian had requisitioned a large working lunch so he could 'put in more time studying soft drinks commercials' in the Lower Projection Room he'd booked – and where he was on no account to be disturbed. The room was furnished with several comfortable sofas with padded cushions and the light had a dimmer switch. As for the champagne he'd just opened, that had been stolen from a crate of Trowbridge, Benson & Mirabel Wines donated by the client for a photographic shoot.

They took a glass of champagne together, giggled, gossiped – then put down their glasses and seized each other's bodies. Jingles from the soft drinks commercials on the video drowned their cries, moans and grunts of animal pleasure. There'd be plenty of time to talk later.

'She's gorgeous,' Simon Burns said over beer and sausages. 'She's the most gorgeous fucking bird in the agency.'

'Yeah,' Dennis Wilson bit into a pie, 'and she's fucking with Ian Sharpe.'

'I can't stand it.' Simon drank more beer. 'What's Ian Sharpe got that I haven't?'

'He's the Assistant Creative Director.' Dennis helped himself to cheese and onion crisps. 'C'mon, let's have another beer and we'll get there too in the end.'

* * *

'Another pheasant pâté sandwich?' Charles Sutherland offered.

'Thanks,' Cliff Mitchell responded. 'Don't mind if I do.'

'And do have the last drop of claret.' Charles poured the last of the half-bottle. 'No point in the stuff if you don't finish the bloody thing, what?'

'Cheers, Charles,' said Cliff.

They were sitting in a basement room which nobody ever used except to store out-dated office furnishings. It was lit by a portable strobe lamp which one of them had brought and the power beam flashed on and off on the two figures who sat in arm-chairs which had once felt the weight of Savage & Markby.

'Here's to life,' Cliff said gloomily and drank. 'See, they throw all this shit at you – parents and teachers – and you just have to unfuck yourself as best you can. So seven thousand a year for doing next to nuffink, surrounded by beautiful women and eating pheasant paté sandwiches in interesting company can't be bad, can it? Still, you don't do too badly yourself.'

'Not so bad. Matter of sussing it, isn't it, what? This stuff helps.' He passed the half-smoked joint back to Cliff.

'Yeah.' He took a shallow drag. 'I've got your stuff here. Lebanese Red.' He handed a plastic-wrapped package to Charles. 'Good but not great, you know, nice, standard stuff. You can get a fairly sensual high from that. And if you don't like it, bring it back for a refund. I can always sell it elsewhere. It's what we've been smoking.'

'Oh, it's fine and many thanks, Cliff.' Charles gave him a twenty pound note. 'I can see I'm in for quite a jolly afternoon on it. Well,' he rose, 'boring meetings never will be the same again. Keep a straight bat, then, and don't let the side down. Toodle-loo.' Charles left. Cliff grasped his ankh.

On reaching the lift, Charles pulled on a rubber glove before pressing the call button. It might look silly but being electrically shocked was sillier, he thought. Arriving at Account Management, he went straight to the lavatory and locked himself in a cubicle. He was there for five minutes, during which time he rolled five joints which looked identical to his Pall Mall cigarettes. On leaving the lavatory, he lit one immediately. It was the only way he could face the dreary prospect of this afternoon.

A group of Assistant Brand Managers on Browning's had been sent on a field trip which included an afternoon at the agency. Charles had been lumbered with the job of occupying them 'in a serious and sober way'. That meant his standard introductory talk on the purpose of advertising and the structure of the agency followed by – for him it was the eighty-sixth occasion – the agency reel. Then he'd take them on a tour of the agency, halting at previously arranged stops where colleagues would talk earnestly and dully about their work, showing Assistant Brand Managers that London advertising wasn't the flashy show it seemed, but a meticulous, purposeful and professional business. A curtain speech at five-thirty, a half of bitter for everyone and only then could Charles make his escape.

He inhaled, sighed and entered Conference Room Two where George Webbing was chatting affably to the five Browning's Assistant Brand Managers, all of whom looked murderously boring.

'How d'you do. How d'you do. How d'you do,' said Charles. 'Hot turds! How d'you do.'

The fourth Assistant Brand Manager stared at Charles in stunned astonishment. Had he heard right? He *couldn't've* done. It had sounded – well, a bit like 'Hot turds!' but the Savage & Markby Account Supervisor couldn't possibly have said that. He'd now sat down at the head of the table and was regarding his guests with solemn gravity.

No, the Assistant Brand Manager shook his head, *I must have heard wrong*.

'Hallo, Robert, having fun with figures? I've got another fun job for you,' said Tony Westbury. 'There's some fellow in Reception – God knows how he got in – who claims he has an appointment with the Chairman. The Chairman says there's no such appointment but he has received a letter and wants the chap seen. Trouble is,' Tony frowned, 'he seems to be a bit of a raving loony and says he'll only talk to the Number One Man. Anyway, we've told him it's you.' Robert's jaw dropped. 'You're our dynamic, whiz-kid leader. Your title is Chairman of the Executive Committee and you're seeing this Dave Wilcox character in Conference Room One with coffee and currant biscuits, okay? Great. Thanks a lot, Robert – yes, see him right now.'

Robert wandered along the corridor blinking dazedly, then drew himself up, straightened his tie, did up his jacket and smartened up his walk into a kingly stride. It was difficult to keep that up when he saw Dave in Reception, for he didn't seem to belong there at all. Dave was tall, thin and spindly, with wild and matted black hair and a thick, bushy beard which lacked a moustache and terminated in ragged whiskers which drooped from his chin. His dark eyes glowed with fanaticism. He wore a black polo neck sweater with black trousers and boots and had thrown a black cloak around his shoulders.

'Greetings,' he proclaimed, 'from the Free Spirit.'

'Good afternoon,' returned Robert, a little uncertainly.

'You're the Number One Man?'

'Robert Slade, Chairman of the Executive Committee,' Robert answered with as much conviction as he could muster. Behind Dave, the Receptionist suppressed a smirk.

'You're a bit young,' Dave murmured suspiciously.

'It's a young Company,' said Robert. 'This way, please.' Feeling perfectly ludicrous, Robert led the caped figure into Conference Room One, where coffee and currant biscuits were waiting. 'Please – do sit down.' Robert took the chair. 'Now, what can I do for you?'

'Question.' Dave glowered at him. 'Will your say on this matter be decisive?'

'I'll listen, of course, to all of my colleagues, but at the end of the day . . .' he left the sentence unfinished and looked knowingly at Dave.

'Good, then you're my man. You're the Chairman. Powerful. Driving. Successful. But – Enslaved. Kept Down. Tied Up. In Bondage. Now I,' said Dave, 'am a Free Spirit. D'you get me?' Robert nodded bemusedly. 'All right. Now let me make myself clear. I have access to certain secret knowledge. That knowledge gives me the most *uncommon* insights. The first thing you have to see is there's a lot more to life than what you first sce because so much is shrouded in mystery which only the initiated can penetrate for the good of humankind who exist in their narrow world guided by unseen forces some of which are malevolent but some of which send teachers who speak the truth no matter what it costs them, like the Free Spirit. With me so far?'

Robert sipped coffee and tried to feign polite interest.

'Okay,' Dave resumed, 'now the Free Spirits go back to five thousand years before Christ when they linked up with the UFOs and located the survivors of Atlantis some of whom later branched out to become the Twelve Lost Tribes of Israel before the Masters of Agarthi focused the inter-stellar ray which enlightened them so founding the United States of America whose Great Seal on the dollar bill of the Eye in the Triangle was the sigil of the Free Spirit in Ancient Egypt. Now I am *not* a crank! And I get *very annoyed* if anyone calls me a crank, okay?' His eyes flashed with abrupt anger.

'Of course,' Robert murmured uneasily. 'But what's the position of Savage & Markby here?'

'Your position?' Dave leaned forward urgently and breathed ether fumes over Robert. 'You're on *our* position. Your building happens to be built on a sacred site known to the Free Spirit long before the Druids and part of the sacred macrocosm reflected in the microcosm permeates the planet with its network of fluidic power-zones which the uninitiated term ley lines before set up by the MIBs who follow up every UFO sighting and subject the witnesses to psychiatric psychic brainwashing all the while ignoring the unseen presence of the Vast Old Ones slumbering beneath the Pacific Ocean amidst the trapezoidal pyramids of lost Lemuria.'

'Hmm,' Robert murmured. 'I wonder what I should tell the Board here.'

'Leave the building,' said Dave.

'Sorry?'

'Leave the building.' Dave sat up. 'Leave it to us. It is ours. It belongs to us. We have the right of its divine inheritance. We – the brethren of the Free Spirit. Because if you don't,' his eyes glowed with visions, 'malevolent forces will arise to devour you. There'll be Madness. Cruelty. Murder. And Despair.'

'Fascinating. You've argued your case very well.' Robert stood up. 'I shall consult with my colleagues and let you know. Where can we contact you?'

'Nowhere!' Dave declared defiantly. 'The Free Spirit blows where it lists. Just remember, I'm not asking. I'm telling. And it's the Truth. I and my exalted Brethren expect this building to be vacated for our occupation by the next Full Moon.'

'I'll bear that in mind,' Robert shook his hand heartily and wished him gone. 'A pleasure meeting you . . . if you'd be kind enough to come this way . . .'

* * *

Afterwards, Robert thought that he'd never in his life had such a mad meeting.

But the order that Tony Westbury gave him, to write a full account of it for the Chairman, was madder still.

Twenty-nine year old Roy Price liked to think he was a great advertisement for advertising. He was handsome, smooth, fit, well-dressed and earned twenty-three thousand as an Account Director on various prestige products, including Slims Cigarettes. He sensed his friends envied his elegant flat in a fashionable area, his Ferrari, his frequent changes of girl and his fast and glossy living. He imagined women saw him as the ideal lover portrayed on the pages of Cosmopolitan magazine. He had vowed to make the Board by the time he was thirty and was coolly optimistic about his chances – or had been until today.

Savage had summoned him. Roy now sat in the secretary's office outside Markby's. The secretary seemed bored by his presence and appeared disinclined to talk to him. Savage and Markby were keeping him waiting and so far he'd suffered through twelve minutes. His girl of last night would barely have recognized the chain-smoking nail biter who was squeezing his thighs together hard because he wanted to go to the bathroom.

Account Directors were generally summoned by Savage to be promoted, have their salaries raised – or be fired. Occasionally one had to go and discuss a particular strategy but Roy had only done that once, about a year ago. The few previous encounters had all raised him. He hoped to God that would be the case again now. There was a sudden tearing hope in his chest that today he'd be appointed to the Board – but no, that was very unlikely. He hadn't had a spectacular success in a while. Salary increase maybe? He'd certainly worked hard and kept things ticking over briskly. Of course, that was far more likely than getting the sack. What had he done to deserve it? Nothing! Well, Slims had been just a little bit disappointing but hardly a major catastrophe . . . No, it couldn't be the sack. The sack would be the worst thing in the world for him right now. Roy was deep in debt. No, it couldn't be. But why wasn't Laura the secretary being friendly as before?

'Mr Markby will see you now,' she told him coldly. Roy stubbed out his cigarette, knocked on the heavy wooden door and went into the Vice-Chairman's office. Markby was writing and didn't seem to notice him. Roy cleared his throat. Markby ignored him. Roy shuffled his feet and wasn't sure what to do. Eventually, Markby looked up.

'The Chairman's a little tied up,' he told Roy. 'I hope you don't mind waiting while I get on with this.' Then he looked away and carried on writing. Roy wasn't sure whether to take a seat or not. He felt foolish standing silently with nothing to do and in front of Markby. Minutes passed. Indignation roused Roy's spirit and he took a seat with a certain defiance. Markby ignored him as though he should've sat down in the first place. Roy's hands were sweating. A buzzer sounded. Markby picked up a black phone.

'Yes,' he said, 'yes, he's here right now,' paused for a reply and smiled. 'Yes. Haha, of course.' Markby replaced the receiver and regarded Roy disdainfully. 'He'll see you now and if I were you, I'd make a clean breast of it. Room Three.'

Roy's knees were trembling as he walked lamely away from Markby. He felt as though the Vice-Chairman had smashed him in the heart. Room Three? He'd never been to Room Three before, thank God, and he dreaded his visit there now. He'd never been to Room One either and only knew of its opulence by hearsay. Room Two – an expensively furnished but austere Chairman's office – was where he'd been called before for discussion, promotion and salary increases. But Room Three – that was where you went to get carpeted. He felt sick.

Markby's office led to a plain corridor with numbered rooms along it. Roy knocked nervously on the door of Room Three. There was no reply. For a frantic instant he hoped that Markby had made a mistake and that the Chairman awaited him kindly in Room Two. Anxiously he knocked again.

'Come in,' came the Chairman's toneless voice.

It was just as he'd heard from those who'd been sacked. The room contained nothing except a green carpet, and a window at the end out of which Savage was staring, with his back to Roy.

'You know why you're here,' the Chairman stated briskly. 'Don't you?' he added. Then he turned and looked over his shoulder at his employee. Roy stared helplessly into the opaque spectacle panes which hid Savage's eyes. 'Or don't you?'

'Slims . . . ?' Roy suggested tentatively.

'Precisely.' Savage turned back to the window. 'Do you recall when we last talked about Slims strategy?'

'It was . . .' Roy faltered, 'roughly this time last year.'

'Yes, this time last year. And you advocated, I remember clearly, a strategy which associated Slims cigarettes with womens' liberation. Do you recall that?'

'Yes . . .' Roy shifted his weight from foot to foot and wondered what to do with his hands. Wherever he put his limbs, he felt awkward.

'And do you recall the views I expressed at the time?'

'Ah . . . as I recall, you said you weren't – well – keen on the idea.'

'Quite so. I wasn't. Even so, as I remember, I nevertheless allowed you to persuade me round to your point of view. Is that your recollection also, Roy?'

'Yes . . .'

'Why d'you think I did that?'

'Because . . .' Roy's brain raced in search of survival, 'because . . . because you agreed with my reasoning?' he suggested hopefully.

'No,' Savage retorted icily, 'I didn't think much of your reasoning at all. No. What I did notice, and it helped persuade me, was a certain fire of conviction you had. I could see it burning in your eyes. So I gave your way a try.'

'It's much appreciated,' said Roy.

'No, it's not,' snapped Savage. 'I regret my decision entirely. The fact is that we've had your campaign done your way. It's come and it's gone and the sole result has been a mild dip in Slims sales figures.'

'It's only a slight dip . . .'

'But you promised a big rise.'

'I'd suggest that . . .'

'We've already tried out your suggestions.'

'It wasn't really me who . . .'

'Came to Room Two and argued it with me? Last year? This time? Have you got amnesia?'

'Please, I . . .'

'We've seen the results,' Savage cut him short. 'And now let me ask you a question. Roy,' the Chairman turned his body to face him, 'do you know how to sell Slims or do I know how to sell Slims?' Roy opened his mouth and strained the muscles on his throat but all that came out was a croak. 'You're demoted,' said Savage and walked out.

Roy stood alone on the carpet in Room Three feeling that Savage had broken his jaw and followed that with a savage beating. It was worse than having the cane at school. At least there you could pretend that it didn't hurt at all and swagger about like a hero. Here, as soon as the news came through, he'd be pitied and sneered at and jeered at. He'd be pointed out to all as the man who'd been demoted. It would be like licking spittle off the office floor. His brain spinning, his feelings a writhing mass of humiliation, shock, anxiety and pain, he stumbled back into Markby's office.

Once again, the Vice-Chairman was writing and paying him no attention. Roy slunk past him but Markby called out just as he reached the other door.

'Oh, one thing, by the way,' said Markby. 'Take a pew.' Roy shuffled forward and sagged into a chair. 'About your demotion.' Roy squirmed inwardly. 'Though your salary will remain the same, your position will now be that of Account Supervisor, with your new office round the other side from Tony Westbury, your Account Director and immediate boss.' Roy gulped at the thought of taking orders from his former equal and rival. Being fired might be like being executed – but this? This was slow torture.

'For your secretary,' Markby resumed evenly, 'you'll now be sharing Maud Bunting with Herbie Tyler, your Executive, and with Martin Bottomley, the trainee. Your accounts in the future will be P & Q Grocery Stores, Jack Rochdale Motors, Lavley Toilet Paper, Bowden's Shoe Polish, Pawson's Hotels, Wheatley's Holiday Coaches and Comfort Sanitary Tampons. All clear?'

Roy nodded dumbly. He knew he had to find another job or die inside – but his debts and obligations consumed all of his twenty-three thousand pound salary – and who would pay that kind of money for a man who'd been demoted?

'That's all.' Markby smiled pityingly. 'Goodnight, Roy.'

For Sandra Lang that evening, it wasn't quite the same as usual. She went into the Vice-Chairman's office wearing the clothes in which he desired her but received neither a wet kiss nor a dry sherry.

'Sit down, please,' Markby told her gravely. 'Sandra,' he sighed regretfully, 'I've greatly enjoyed our liaison. Unfortunately, much as it pains me to say this, all good things must come to an end and I fear the time has come for the parting of the ways. In view of this . . .'

It's the end, thought Sandra, *fine. He's tired of me and that's okay. I'm utterly sick of him*. She tried not to look too relieved and arranged her features into an expression of pained regret. One hand fumbled for a tissue in her bag. She intended to dab an eye at a tactically effective moment. *Now for my payoff*, she thought.

'In view of this,' Markby repeated as though he had a solemn duty to perform, 'let us be perfectly civilized. Work out your eight week period of notice, in consideration of which you will receive a tax free bonus of fifteen hundred pounds – and naturally, first class references will follow.'

Sandra gaped at him in disbelief. The sack? He couldn't be serious . . .

'You seem a little surprised,' he commented, 'in which case I'm surprised at you. You know how these things work.'

'But I thought . . .' she faltered.

'Yes?' he enquired, 'what did you think?' Sandra was silent. 'We can hardly carry on as normal after what we've had between us,' Markby continued in a brisk and businesslike way. 'That'd be far too embarrassing all round. After all, you're a professional woman and it's not as though you became involved with me for any reason other than that you happen to find me attractive. As I say, I've enjoyed knowing you.'

Sandra swallowed and tried to contain her rising anger and her growing outrage at his treatment of her. Her entire being felt dipped in slime and drenched in disgust. She wanted to scream obscene abuse at Markby and tear him bodily from his Vice-Chairman's desk where he sat so smugly as he dictated to you – but that was what he wanted, she felt. He longed to see her crack before his eyes so he could despise her as a weak and hysterical little woman.

'This strikes me,' Sandra bit her lip and fought to hold

her voice steady, 'as being a case of flagrant unfair dismissal.'

'Who said anything about dismissal?' Markby queried and looked pained by the thought. 'I was under the impression that you'd be resigning.'

'Suppose I'm not,' she countered. 'Suppose I have no intention of resigning. You couldn't sack me. I'd sue you for unfair dismissal and . . .'

'And it'd all come out, quite so,' said Markby. 'Your own reputation would be finished if you did that. Who would employ you afterwards? Nor can you refuse to resign,' he continued coldly. 'You have no future here.'

Sandra felt as though she'd been shattered into a hundred jagged pieces and every piece glistened with the spittle of impotent rage and self-loathing. Her frilly knickers, stockings and suspenders clung to her clammy skin and proclaimed her prostitution. She wanted to kill Markby for tempting her into this trap where she writhed in anguish yet had to keep her feelings hidden. But she did have one last card left to play.

'Fifteen hundred's nothing like enough,' she said icily. 'You'll have to pay me a lot more if I'm to go quietly.'

'You think you can damage me?' Markby seemed amused.

'You know I can,' she snapped, 'so if I were you, I'd start thinking about a larger sum. A very much larger sum.'

'Oh, dear,' sighed Markby, 'you won't see reason, will you? Pity.' He opened a desk drawer and extracted a brown paper envelope. 'You leave me no alternative. This envelope contains some photographs I had taken. Twelve pictures of you, in fact. Nothing but you – oh, and this desk.'

'You shit . . .' she breathed.

'So, if you don't go quietly, a number of people will be seeing them. Relatives, friends, colleagues . . .'

'You blackmailing swine!'

'No,' said Markby. 'You're the one who originally demanded money with menaces. I had to protect myself, that's all. You'll get the prints and the negatives on your last day here in two months' time, don't worry. Just work out your notice period while we find a replacement, then take your money and your references and go quietly like a good girl – that's all I'm asking. And to show good faith, I'll make sure you land something better elsewhere – there, what could be fairer than that? After all,' his tone became patronizing, 'I am not without influence in the world of advertising.'

'Perhaps not,' Sandra had risen wearily but now spoke with a frozen dignity, 'but that's all you are. Everything else about you is just a grope and a squirt.'

She had the satisfaction of seeing his calculating eyes sent spinning for a second as his face became empurpled by his secret shame. Then she left the room calmly for the Ladies where she burst into tears and broke down sobbing for the first time in four years.

After he had recovered from Sandra's insult, Markby consoled himself with the thought that the bitch had just forfeited her good references. Well, good riddance. It was time the Company employed another female Account Executive. For the last twelve years, Savage & Markby had always employed a female Account Executive – and an Asian Account Executive and a black Account Executive – and Markby always got her in the end. He glanced fondly at his fishing rod a moment before Savage came through.

'Goodnight, Hugh,' the Chairman said, 'it's been a good day's work.'

Sally Peters entered her home to see her husband slumped in an arm-chair with an empty bottle of whisky beside him. The entire room stank of scotch. Nick himself had glazed eyes, a red face, a wheezing chest and a bulging gut. He wore a stained T-shirt with a grubby pair of jeans. A cigarette smouldered within his slack fingers and dribbled ash onto the carpet.

'Hi!' he grinned mirthlessly. 'Like a drink?'

Sally put down her shopping bag, hung up her coat, came into the living room and stared down despairingly at her husband.

'I wish,' she said, 'that you could see yourself.'

'But I can. I can shee myshelf very clearly. Here I am – reflected in the bottom of thiss glasss.'

'Drowned in it, you mean.'

'What d'you mean?' Nick demanded irritably. 'What'sh with this hostile fucking stupidity? You're ash bad ash the rest.'

Oh, God, please help me control myself, Sally prayed fervently and silently. *He's in one of his aggressive moods. But God damn it, I feel aggressive too. I've worked my arse off today for peanuts and a foul-mouthed drunk.*

'You're slurring your words again,' she sighed.

'Sho? Doesn't matter. Nothing matters.'

'Don't I matter any more? I suppose I don't.'

'Courshe you do. Courshe you do.'

'How?'

'Come here, darling,' he wheezed, 'you know how much I love you.' He gave her a skull-like grin, seized her hand and pulled her violently towards him. 'Give uss a kisss.'

'Nick.' Sally snatched her hand away. 'I can't remember when you last made love to me like you used to.'

'Tonight.' He gazed at her glassily and hiccupped.

'I don't fancy you when you're like this. Don't you realize?'

'Course you fancy me, Shally. You'll stick by me, won't you? And tonight,' he used the phrase which once had so excited her, 'I'm shticking my throbbing cock right up your beautiful sexy cunt.'

Sally winced as though she was a nun who'd just heard a particularly atrocious piece of blasphemy.

'I doubt it,' she retorted acidly, 'there's no way you're up to it.'

He sprang from his seat, grabbed her arms and pressed his lips against hers. Sally kept her mouth tightly closed. The stench of stale beer and whisky made her want to retch. His hips shoved something soft against her pubic bone. Sally stepped back with an expression of disgust and slapped Nick's face hard. He went crazy.

His open hand cracked across her face and sent her body spinning against the wall. She lashed out with a foot aimed at his groin and missed.

'Bitch!' he hissed as he came forward for her, seized her neck within his hands and pressed his thick thumbs against her throat. She kicked out with her legs and beat upon his back with her fists but he seemed oblivious to her struggles and she was choking. She tried to get her hands between their faces so her fingers could gouge his eyes and save her – but his head had pinned hers against the wall as he throttled her.

Sally's eyes bulged, her face went a mottled purple and her nails broke in ripping through his shirt in an attempt to claw his back. He carried on strangling the life out of her as though she was the one who had suffocated him. She wasn't very strong. Her struggles became feebler. Her head lolled. There was a muffled, snapping sound. Blood came out of Sally's mouth as she died. Nick stepped back to contemplate the ruin which was sliding down the wall into a soggy heap upon the carpet.

Afterwards – after his panting had subsided and his adrenalin and surge of triumph had drained away – Nick wept. He stared disbelievingly at the corpse of the wife he had loved, and bawled like a terrified child. He gathered

Sally's body in his arms, applied the kiss of life to her blue lips and begged God to restore her to him. At last it dawned on him that she had gone for good. He broke down into a fit which alternated sobbing and screaming.

He left the house soon after and shambled through the dark, wet streets, gesticulating to himself and muttering. All who passed sensed a violent drunk and avoided his wild and anguished eyes. Finally he saw the blue light for which he'd searched and stumbled inside the police station.

'Good evening,' he mumbled, 'I've just killed my wife. Please arrest me before I kill myself.'

Part II

7

Savage & Markby Ltd

MEMORANDUM

To: All Staff
cc: Board Directors
From: HVM
Subject: Economy
Date: 27 November 1983

The response to my earlier Memos on this subject has been, on the whole, rather disappointing. It is absolutely essential for our continued profitable existence that Staff realize the fundamental importance of the measures which the Board has seen fit to take. 'Take care of the pennies and the pounds will take care of themselves,' is a proverb with much age-old wisdom to commend it. In order, therefore, to curb wasteful extravagance, all Staff will henceforth kindly observe the following procedures:-

1 – Staff are graciously requested to be sparing in their use of stationery requisitions, a matter which will be receiving attention.

2 – All mail will go by second class post forthwith unless accompanied by the new Despatch Brief designed by the Administration Committee and counter-signed by the appropriate Account Supervisor, Creative Group Head or Senior Media Planner.

3 – Whenever photo-copying amounts to more than twenty copies, the new Duplication Brief, designed by the

Administration Committee, must first be counter-signed by the appropriate Account Supervisor, Creative Group Head or Senior Media Planner.

4 – Tracey in reception has been asked to report all instances when newspapers and magazines are improperly removed.

5 – Anyone travelling on Company business may only use taxis if the Expense Form has been approved by the relevant Account Director, Assistant Creative Director or Assistant Media Director.

6 – Personal phone-calls may no longer be made except with the consent of the appropriate Account Supervisor, Creative Group Head or Senior Media Planner.

Thank you all for your understanding and co-operation.

H. V. Markby
VICE-CHAIRMAN

Robert Slade crumpled up that Memo and threw it into the bin. It was a horrible reminder of how much he was hating his job. Every day found him deluged by irritating Memos and grappling with detestable Forms. For example, right now he needed a pencil. For that one needed a Stationery Requisition Form. There weren't any.

So much happened at Savage & Markby which seemed wholly pointless to Robert. One instance was the Account Management Training Scheme, which he'd initially attended with enthusiasm. He thought that Peter Jackson was a very nice man. Yet all he'd actually learned so far was that if you're presenting with the aid of a blackboard, don't stand in front of it. The rest of the time had consisted of Peter's jokes, anecdotes and personal reminiscences with some advice on public speaking which Robert already knew. At least Peter's commercials were quite enjoyable, but what precise point they illustrated, Robert couldn't fathom.

No, things weren't going well. George continued to be ever so friendly and kept telling Robert he was doing so well and then dropped him in the shit. Robert blamed incompetence rather than malice – how could George possibly be malicious? – but it was agony having to take shit for which you were not responsible. For instance, there was the Browning's Best Brown poster, which seemed to have a curse on it. Tim Rogers kept finding faults which he felt might upset Colin Miller and every time George presented it, it was rejected. And every time it was rejected, Robert was lumbered with the task of taking it back to Simon and Dennis, who assaulted him with insults, balls of paper and withering contempt. Robert was starting to feel that if he were properly briefed, he could do George's job better than the Executive – yet George had recently been appointed to the Account Management-Creative Liaison Committee, clearly a mark of favour.

Charles Sutherland was at least giving essential help on the Protheroe in his casual and off-hand way. He hadn't mentioned Nick Peters again and the one time Robert had brought up the name, Charles immediately changed the subject. Yet the Supervisor seemed to have developed a certain fondness for the trainee and proved a skilful teacher of marketing analysis. Last week, Robert had finally completed the Protheroe sheet, a task he'd found ghastly beyond words. 'Well done and spot on,' Charles had said, 'and young Tony's going to love it, what?' Tony Westbury had loved it so much that he'd told Robert to apply the hateful Protheroe region by region – a total of ten more Protheroe Marketing Analysis and Summary sheets. 'Sorry, old fruit,' Charles had told a despairing Robert, 'but I can't help finding it funny.'

Tony was carrying on in his own bland way – a way which Robert was finding increasingly infuriating. Every time Tony saw him sweating over the wretched Protheroe, he beamed affably and said: 'Having fun with figures?' Robert always forced himself to smile and nod – and later cursed himself for a creep. Yet just when he was forming an intense dislike of his Account Director, Tony had invited him to his party. 'Keep it under your hat,' he'd said, 'because I don't want to offend all the people I haven't invited.' Robert had felt complimented and gratified – until the party itself, where he spent all evening being passed from agency wife to agency wife as 'the man who didn't want to be called "Bob".' Vickie had hated the entire affair.

Meanwhile, Fiona was still being a bitch. He dreaded asking her to do things. Every time she reminded him that his work was piddling by comparison to George's and utterly insignificant by contrast to Charles's. She appeared to adore Charles. She seemed unwilling to wipe her shoes on Robert. Whatever he asked for took at least four hours and he despised himself for his failure to master his secretary. Things had been so bad that he'd accepted a favour from Sid Ingram.

'Don't worry, squire,' Sid had told him one lunch-time, 'I had that situation myself when I started. Happens to the best of us. Look, mate, any time you need something done urgent, slip it in with *my* secretary, Harriet. Harriet Baker – she's an angel, that lady. *She'll* look after you – tell her I said so.'

On the rare occasions when something seemed urgent and Fiona didn't think so, Robert had gone shamefacedly to Harriet. She was a tall girl with short, dark hair and a nice smile. She was always working hard but never too busy to fit him in. She struck him as one of the kindest people at Savage & Markby and bright with it. It surprised him that she was just a secretary.

'Robert!' Fiona called out suddenly and sharply. 'The Vice-Chairman wants to see you. Now.'

Robert left for the top floor wondering what on earth it could be about. He'd never been there before and had never had occasion to speak much with the Vice-Chairman. This morning he'd come up in the lift with Markby. Both had said 'Good morning,' and Markby had glanced curiously at Robert's clothes – today a flared sports jacket with cavalry twill trousers and a welcome change from the dull, dark suits so many seemed to wear.

'Ah, morning once again, Robert,' Markby greeted the trainee.

'Good morning, Mr Markby.'

'Take a pew.' Robert sat down. Markby gazed at him and frowned. 'What on earth could've inspired,' he looked at Robert pityingly, 'your dress today? We're not on a country weekend, you know.'

'I'm sorry. I thought this was acceptable.'

'Good Lord!' exclaimed Markby. 'What on earth could've made you think that?'

'Well,' Robert swallowed, 'I've seen others dressed similarly.' *Chris Faye and Ian Sharpe for a start*, he thought.

'Possibly so.' The Vice-Chairman raised an eyebrow. 'But hardly people in your position. Or am I wrong?'

'It . . . seems I've made a mistake,' Robert said.

'Exactly. I suppose you weren't to know. Kindly remember in the future that you are an Account Management trainee. You would be well advised to dress like one. That's all. Good day.' Markby picked up his fountain pen and commenced writing.

Robert went away feeling shamed and angered but impotent to do anything about it. That was the story of his life at the Company. He was desperately unhappy – and that seemed to be the lot of so many others too, judging by their behaviour. Here so much was joyless and laced by a disconcerting element of fear and paranoia.

Why? Robert shrugged hopelessly, stepped out of the lift and slouched wearily towards the Account Management corridor.

'Excuse *me*,' said Stanley Haynes. Robert turned to see the bald Financial Director regarding him crossly. 'Is *that* the way in which you walk down corridors?' He drew himself up to his full height of five feet eight. 'I like to think it isn't but I rather suspect it is. I've been observing and I'm not entirely happy with what I've observed, young man.'

Robert was too astonished to speak.

'I'd buck up my ideas if I were you,' Stanley Haynes continued. 'Now let's see a smart, brisk Executive stride. Go on. One-two, one-two, one-two . . .'

It was a colossal effort for Robert to keep himself from smacking Stanley Haynes in the chops. Yet he allowed the man to march him through the corridor in front of everyone.

'Better,' Stanley Haynes pronounced as Robert reached his desk. 'Much better. And keep it that way.'

Robert sat at his desk as Stanley Haynes departed and found himself trembling with fury. Gradually his rage found form in an idea. No longer caring what the consequences would be, Robert stormed into the office of Georgina Mainwaring.

'Hullo, Robert,' she smiled at him. 'You seem a trifle upset.'

'I am,' he returned tersely. 'Can I see Mike, please?'

'Probably. I don't think he's too busy. Mike!' she called out at the office behind her, the door of which was open. 'Robert'd like to see you.'

'He can come in right away.'

Robert went in to see Mike working at a mass of papers. He'd removed his jacket, loosened his tie and rolled up his shirt sleeves.

'Morning, Robert,' he opened briskly, 'what's the problem?'

'You said I could come and see you whenever . . .'

'Yes,' Mike interrupted. 'Go ahead.'

'I,' Robert spoke slowly in an effort to contain his temper, 'have just been lectured on the way in which I walk down corridors and then forcibly marched through one in front of everyone. I feel extremely insulted.'

'Who did that to you?' Mike asked. *I'd be outraged too*, he thought.

'Stanley Haynes,' said Robert. *God, the man's impossible*, Mike thought. 'I know he's senior to me,' Robert went on, 'but he's got no right to do that. It's not as though I keep bumping into people and knocking things over. It's my own damn business how I walk down corridors.'

'I'll have a word with Stanley,' Mike answered. 'Is that all?'

No, thought Robert, *it's not all by a long way*. But if he took this moment to pour out his troubles, he'd merely come over as a little boy who couldn't take it and was bleating.

'That's all,' he said heavily.

'Well, on behalf of the Company I'd like to apologize for the indignity you've suffered.'

'Thank you.'

'As I say, I'll talk to Stanley.' *More's the pity*, Mike thought. 'Have one at lunch-time and you'll soon get over it.' *What else can I tell the poor bugger?* 'Oh, and Robert,' Mike looked at him kindly, 'don't take it all to heart.'

Robert tried hard to follow Mike's advice that lunch-time, only to have his quiet reflections shattered by the presence in the pub of Martin Bottomley.

'You must've heard the big news by now,' said Martin.

'No?'

'What, you mean you haven't? Dear, dear, we obviously move in very different circles. I,' he gave his fellow-trainee an oily smirk, 'have been promoted to Assistant Account Executive.'

'Congratulations.' Uttering that word nearly choked Robert.

'D'you want to know why?' Robert didn't especially. 'Consider, please!' said Martin. 'I've attracted the attention of the right people. That's very important, you see. Heah, let me give you some advice so you can follow in my footsteps. Nine words, that's all. They say everything. It's not what you know, it's who you know. Think about it, dear boy. And have a cigar!' Martin proudly produced two Slims Panatellas and thrust one at Robert.

'No, thank you.' Robert drew back to avoid taking it. 'I really must be getting back.'

'Have it for later, then.' Martin shoved the cigar into Robert's breast pocket. 'And are you sure you can't stay? You can't possibly be as busy as me – and *I* intend to enjoy another pint of Champion.'

Robert resisted the offer and wandered disconsolately back to the agency, entering via the back door and Production. Ian Sharpe and Belinda Torrance were coming out of the Lower Projection Room and for some reason looked rather furtive. Robert must've stared for too long at Belinda because Ian suddenly whirled on him with a snappy: 'I want a word with you. Right here. Now. Oh, and thanks for your help,' he added mildly to Belinda, 'I'll see you get your overtime.'

'Thanks, Ian.' Belinda walked away with as little wiggle as she could manage, which was still rather more than many girls who try harder.

'This latest Bremen Control Brief regarding trade press advertising,' said Ian. 'What the bloody hell does it mean?'

'I'm not sure,' Robert answered.

'Not sure? But it's in your handwriting.'

'Yes, I took dictation.'

'Oh, I see. From George, presumably.' Ian sniffed and

blew his nose. 'But you don't have a clue what it's about – is that right?'

'Well, you see, I . . .'

'It didn't occur to you, I suppose,' Ian cut in scathingly, 'to ask George to explain it.' Robert had often wondered whether he liked Ian Sharpe or not. Right now, he decided, he disliked him intensely.

'I did exactly that,' he retorted – but his tone was defensive. 'And he did try to explain it.'

'So you should be clear.'

'I should be, I suppose. But I'm afraid I'm still not clear.'

'Nor am I,' said Ian. 'That so-called Brief means precisely nothing at all. I've torn it up so you'd better ask George to do it again. And when he does it again, it's your job to make sure that he's clear and you're clear so I don't get given shit like that ever again – do I make myself clear?'

'All right,' Robert breathed. He went away feeling like inflicting grievous bodily harm on someone – and received another electric shock when he called the lift. The afternoon promised more Protheroe. The evening promised nothing. Vickie would be at some Law Society function and Robert had neglected to fix up an evening with a friend. Not that he felt up to seeing a friend. He could hardly boast of his joys and successes at Savage & Markby. The alternative was to moan about it, be a bore and receive advice. No, tonight he'd go out on one of his once a year, solitary benders.

He'd just stepped into the lift when Cliff Mitchell came past. The solid silver ankh bounced against Cliff's chest, caught the light from the sun's rays streaming in through the window and flashed and shone with a blinding brilliance – raising Robert's spirits as the lift door slid shut smoothly to banish it from view.

8

Meanwhile, in Conference Room One, it was the afternoon of the Kandy pitch. Mike Armstrong chaired a table around which sat three emissaries from the Kandy Corporation and his own team. There was a marked contrast between the two sides, Mike thought. His own team consisted of individuals – Tony Westbury, Charles Sutherland, Sid Ingram and Martin Bottomley from his own Department; Ian Sharpe, Ronald Potter, Dennis Wilson and Simon Burns from Creative; and academic Craig Anderson and sporting Paul Adams from Media. On the other hand, the Kandy men might have been cloned.

They all had that youthful male face one sees too often on those American TV commercials which claim that a product is bought by the successful. They were noticeably clean and scrubbed and of the type that's obviously good at athletics and public speaking. Their hair, teeth, nails and waist-lines were in immaculate condition. They all wore black suits, ties and shoes with white shirts and white handkerchiefs poking out of breast pockets by three eighths of an inch. Their disconcerting sameness of appearance bothered Mike – as did the three cold and dedicated pairs of quietly demented blue eyes which regarded him steadily.

The uncomfortable truth was that so far, things hadn't gone too well. The Kandy Corporation had made it clear that business would precede entertainment, so there was no possibility of a lunch which might oil things beforehand. Mike had offered them coffee and currant biscuits but the three Americans had asked pointedly for Kandy. There wasn't any in the Conference Room.

Everyone agreed that there was a crate of Kandy somewhere in the agency and a frantic search for it had been instituted – but all the Kandy had gone. Sid jokingly suggested that this showed how popular Kandy had already become with the agency and was rewarded by three blank stares. It was an awkward start.

Mike was dreading the next stage. Although he'd argued against it vehemently at the last Board Meeting, he'd been outvoted by four to three and Peter Jackson had carried his motion that the pitch should begin with his Opening Remarks. Mike bit his lip as the Managing Director mounted the platform and prayed that Peter would for once get down to business.

It didn't take long before Mike realized that something was wrong. Peter had opened well with a warm welcome, he'd told an amusing anecdote which made even the Kandy men smile and he'd modestly stressed the importance of what was to be done today. Fine. It was time he sat down. Instead he'd carried on talking and telling more jokes and anecdotes.

The man didn't look well either. His complexion had acquired an unhealthy ruddy glow and there were beads of sweat on his brow.

'With this point,' Peter was saying, 'I must express my full concurrence.' There was a pause. 'I concur. To which point does this bring us? To this point.'

Mike glowered at the Managing Director. This was worse than his wildest nightmares about the pitch. He found himself wishing that this was an Amateur Night and that a hook would drag Peter from the stage.

'*To* this point,' Peter repeated and wished he hadn't had so much at lunch-time. What *was* the point? He couldn't remember. He passed a hot, dry hand across his perspiring forehead. His audience blurred slightly before his vision. Then he gritted his teeth and swore to himself that he would get safely out of this one. 'In fact, to *this* point.

Advertising in this country must be legal, decent, honest and truthful. The British Advertising Standards Authority will not permit anything less. Which brings me to my next point.' And Peter's eyes suddenly lit up because he had suddenly recalled the point. It was that brilliant idea which had struck him at five o'clock yesterday. '*This* point,' he spoke with renewed confidence.

Mike's jaw sagged as Peter produced a bottle of Kandy from his brief-case and held it up triumphantly.

'Legal,' said Peter. He whipped a bottle-opener out of his pocket and flipped off the bottle top. 'Decent.' He poured the pink liquid into a glass and gazed at it approvingly. 'Honest.' He drank a glass of Kandy with evident relish and smacked his lips with satisfaction. 'And truthful.' He put down the glass as though he'd enjoyed using it and stared gravely at the Kandy trio. 'Also,' he added, 'successful. Very successful. And *that*,' he punched the air, 'is *the* point.'

There was a pause. The Kandy men looked at one another and then broke into a brief burst of applause.

'Thank you,' said Peter. 'And now, forgive me if I leave you in the eminently capable hands of Mike Armstrong, Director of Account Management.' He smiled a final farewell, made his way to the door unscathed, closed it smartly behind him, lurched his way to the lavatory and threw up his lunch and his glass of Kandy.

'Thank you, Peter,' Mike had said on the Managing Director's departure. 'From that illuminating point, I suggest we proceed directly to brass tacks.' He wished to God that Peter hadn't been there. Yet, and to Mike's amazement, it seemed as though Peter's gambit had come off – unless the Kandy men had been so bemused by it, they'd clapped as a courtesy to a bizarre and foreign presentation custom. That was a horribly plausible explanation too. One just couldn't tell what Chuck Davey,

Stuart Simms and Cal Lowry, Vice-Presidents, might be thinking.

One simply had to soldier on hard. Mike had spent weeks analysing every aspect of the proposed campaign and now gave it everything he had. He started by presenting a break-down of the soft drinks market into sectors and segments of socio-economic classes and age groupings, supplementing this with research surveys on taste, and then drawing conclusions about the target audience.

'C1, C2 and D kids between five and fifteen are our primary target,' he stated. 'So, in a nutshell, they have to want it and their Mums must be happy to buy it for them. A third vital factor is what we see as being Kandy's Unique Selling Proposition – in common with your United States agency. American advertising stresses Kandy's secret and unique taste-tickling ingredient. In other words, it tastes better to kids than anything else. Three major marketing conclusions, then. Here's how we advanced from there.'

Mike handed over to Tony Westbury, who explained that the agency saw not only the primary target of kids but also a secondary target – their mothers. The former would be wooed by a strategy conceptualized as 'It tastes so good.' The latter would be won by the message that kids' love of Kandy made for happy family occasions.

Craig Anderson explained the proposed Media Plan. Kids would be reached via TV commercials at their peak viewing time and also by comics. Mothers would be given a nice television commercial to go with their favourite soap operas and there'd be a supplementary press campaign in top-selling, down-market, womens' magazines. Although, in Mike's opinion, Craig was nothing like as slick as Chris Faye, his thoughtful and typically English professorial manner seemed to have gone down well.

Ian Sharpe then took the floor and showed the potential clients two projected slides and two sets of story boards.

He put verve and drive into his delivery. He demonstrated how the press ads reinforced the TV messages and finished with a flourish by pointing out ingenious 'subliminal but legal' links between the mother and the child campaigns.

'That's it,' Mike announced. 'Any questions?' The Kandy men looked hard at one another.

'The press advertisement aimed at C1, C2 and D mothers,' said Chuck Davey. 'It shows a happy family. But does that particular happy family reflect the concept of a happy family throughout the United Kingdom?'

'Or is the concept of a happy family subjected,' Stuart Simms said, 'to regional variation?'

'There's regional variation of that concept, of course,' Mike answered directly. 'What we've shown you is the overall theme. Obviously it would be varied according to locality. It all depends on how many regions you want to tackle initially – we've suggested London, the Midlands, TV Southern and Granada.'

'Thank you,' said Cal Lowry. 'And now, will you excuse me for just one moment? Where exactly did you say the bathroom was?'

'Good idea,' said Stuart Simms.

'Me too,' said Chuck Davey.

Everyone sat in silence while the Kandy men excused themselves. Nobody wanted to venture an opinion as to how it had gone. Everybody felt that the team had done its job to the very best of its ability – but that didn't matter if the pitch wasn't good enough. There was a brooding tension in the room when Stuart Simms and Chuck Davey returned.

'Cal's making a call,' Chuck explained. 'He'll be through in a few short moments. Meanwhile,' his face lit up, 'could Stu and me have just a little of what your totally fascinating Managing Director left in that Kandy bottle?' Martin Bottomley served them two small glasses. 'Why, thank you. It's all been extraordinarily interesting.'

'You don't play baseball here, Mike,' Stuart remarked. 'I guess you're all too busy playing cricket. But if you did play baseball, we'd all know exactly the position for you. Pitcher.'

'And that's an all-American compliment,' said Chuck.

'Thank you,' Mike answered, 'I'm honoured,' just as Cal came back into the room and sat down between his colleagues.

'I've been talking to the President,' he announced. 'Mike – we liked your style and the style of your team and the illuminating panache of your Managing Director. You're the last people we've seen. You're the last people we will be seeing. The UK Kandy launch will be tried your way.'

Around ten o'clock that evening, Mike was walking along Piccadilly feeling a mixture of exhaustion and elation. If what the Kandy men said was true, he'd landed a four million pound account for the Company. That meant he'd be big news in the trade.

Dinner had still been a strain. It hadn't been easy making pleasant conversation with what seemed like three complete aliens. Mike liked Americans generally but the Kandy trio was something else. Whatever was said, they always responded with exactly the right nothing and no real human contact was made. However, Tony and Charles had coped with them well and all three Kandy men praised the dinner.

Despite the advice of Charles to choose the Connaught Hotel restaurant as the best in England, Mike had decided that was laying it on too much and opted for Wheeler's Braganza. The party consisted of himself, the Kandy men, Tony, Craig, Ian, Charles and – as a special gesture of thanks to Mike's own department – Martin Bottomley, who'd got on surprisingly well with Chuck Davey. Tomorrow Mike would treat the other juniors on the team –

though hardly as lavishly as tonight. The menu, which Charles had chosen, went from oysters to lobster – both of which the Americans pronounced 'better than our Pacific and almost on a par with our Atlantic' – and everyone chose his own dessert. Charles intrigued the Kandy men by persistently referring to his raspberries and cream as 'pudding'. After coffee, the meal ended with general expressions of goodwill, declarations of mutual interest and promises of a signed contract worth four million gross.

'Well, thanks, Mike,' said Cal Lowry, 'for a truly memorable meal. We'll be flying back first thing in the morning and our President will be in touch with your Chairman by the day after.'

On that note it had concluded and it was time to go home – for night-clubbing with the Kandy trio would be, Mike sensed, a horrendous mistake. So he'd shaken hands and escorted his guests to a taxi, muttered something about getting a taxi for himself, thanked his team heartily, slipped into a Soho side-street and started walking. Mike liked walking. It was a fine night and he would walk home.

Home meant his flat in Notting Hill, which was only a couple of miles away. The night air, which was crisp and clear, would help him arrange his thoughts. So here he was – all being well – with the greatest triumph of his business career. Strange how he didn't feel that ecstatic about it. Perhaps all the work for it had drained him more than he realized. Well, at least he could feel proud of his team, right down to Martin Bottomley.

Mike wasn't sure what to make of Martin. His gut instincts told him that the trainee he'd had promoted was a public school prig. His reason advised him to curb his prejudice against someone whose background and manner were so different. His observation showed him that the lad was willing and undertook every job with seriousness and dedication. He also listened alertly to every word Mike spoke, which was flattering.

Mike wished he could slough off all the tension of today. Perhaps he should stop off somewhere and enjoy a solitary celebratory drink. After all, he'd been deliberately careful earlier. Just two glasses of that superb white wine Charles had chosen and an Irish coffee had passed his lips. A brandy now would be just right. Where? That was a problem. Mike disliked the atmosphere of so many pubs. It would have to be the one he could just about tolerate in Mayfair's Shepherds Market. He rather liked that area, anyway. Class and rough trade rubbed shoulders there and spawned entertaining flash and stylish sleaze. One brandy there, then a good walk home, a shower and bed alone sounded like a welcoming prospect.

On reaching the pub and going inside, Mike ordered a brandy, looked for somewhere to sit and saw – to his surprise – a lonely and miserable Robert Slade, who was drinking beer. Mike wasn't yet sure what to make of young Robert. His gut instincts told him the trainee was good. Reason and observation raised doubts. Take today, when Robert had complained about Stanley Haynes. Yes, Stanley had been insufferable. Tomorrow Mike would tell him that. And yes, Robert had been right to complain. But he'd complained with a certain air of desperation. That didn't augur well.

Robert recognized Mike and gazed at him with slightly drunken eyes as the latter went up to him.

'Hallo, Mike,' he said, then smiled with a curious mixture of natural charm and bitterness. 'I can see there's no escaping Savage & Markby.'

'Seems like it.' Mike sat down opposite. 'I didn't expect to see you here either. Sorry, I'm not interrupting anything, am I? Can I get you a drink? You sure? All right.' He sipped his brandy. 'I'll twist your arm for one of these in a while.' He forced a smile as Robert nodded mechanically. 'Sorry it's been a bad day for you.'

'Thank you.' Now Robert forced a smile. 'I'll survive.'

'That's how I felt when I was in your shoes,' said Mike. 'Why pretend? It can be bloody horrible. Still,' this time the smile was genuine, 'I'm still here.'

'Trouble is,' Robert drank, 'I want to do much more than merely survive.'

'Don't we all? But sometimes it can take a while.'

'True.' Robert stared into space, then remembered himself. 'How did the pitch go?'

'Went well, thanks.'

'It was for a soft drink, wasn't it?'

'Kandy,' Mike said.

'Kandy?'

'Yes, why?'

'It's pink, isn't it?'

'Pink soft drink that's swept America, yes.'

'Oh.' Robert frowned. 'I'm not sure if I should tell you . . .'

'Tell me what? If it's bothering you, spit it out.'

'Well, my girlfriend told me only the other day,' Robert said thoughtfully. 'Vickie's an articled clerk with a firm of solicitors. The firm has a branch in Hong Kong. And a woman is using that branch to sue the Hong Kong division of the Kandy Corporation because her six year old daughter died of cancer after drinking five bottles a day for six months.'

'What?' Mike regarded Robert with a mixture of surprise and suspicion. 'Are you sure it's Kandy? But that's ridiculous. I don't see how Kandy causes cancer. Lots of things cause cancer. I think it's a very dubious argument trying to link up disease and a soft drink. How's the woman going to prove her case?'

'Two reports, I was told. One from Switzerland and one from Sweden, both sponsored by their respective governments, supply Vickie's firm with pretty powerful ammunition.'

'Well, what did these reports say?' Mike demanded anxiously.

'Kandy's appeal,' said Robert, 'is apparently based on its secret and unique taste-tickling ingredient. According to Swiss and Swedish chemists, when this ingredient was discovered, extracted and fed to rats, most of them died of cancer.'

'That *can't* be right,' Mike replied heavily. 'There has to be some mistake here. You sure all this isn't just rumour?'

'I don't think Gough, Trumper and Mawdesley (Solicitors) deal in rumour.'

'I'll check that out.' Mike shifted his weight uncomfortably. A walk and bed no longer seemed so inviting. 'Join me in another?' He tipped his empty glass.

'Very kind, but no, thanks. I think I've had more than my fair share tonight – and Vickie should be home by the time I get back.' Robert rose, clearly eager to get away. His behaviour outside the office struck Mike as being much more forceful. 'I'd appreciate it if you could let me know whether what I've told you is true. I'd find it unbearable, you know, pushing Kandy if it is true. Anyway, see you tomorrow and,' at last it was a genuine smile, 'thanks for seeing me earlier today.'

After Robert left, Mike sat miserably over his brandy. The desire to go home had gone. If he could've had a wish, it would've been for the Swiss and the Swedish Kandy reports. All sense of victory had left him. Where there should have been exhilaration in his being, there was just an empty hole.

9

It was two days later. Mike sat impatiently in the office of Markby's secretary and puffed furiously at his pipe. He was very disturbed. Since his perplexing encounter with Robert, he'd devoted every atom of his intelligence and resourcefulness to the obtaining of more information on Kandy. It had involved phone-calls to Embassies and to friends in journalism and the calling in of favours owed in order to have documents fast. The result confirmed Mike's worst fears. Robert had been right. There *were* reports sponsored by the Swiss and Swedish governments, which indicated that a link between cancer and Kandy existed – and they strongly urged the banning of the product. And the Kandy Corporation *was* being sued in Hong Kong. That was why, at his own request, Mike was sitting outside the Vice-Chairman's office and biting hard on his pipe-stem.

He was invited into Markby's office after a delay of only two minutes.

'Ah, good morning, Mike,' Markby said pleasantly, 'do take a pew.' Then he scrutinized Mike and added quizzically: 'You seem a little flustered.'

'With reason,' Mike returned. 'I need to see the Chairman.'

'Oh? What about?'

'Kandy.'

'Whatever for?' asked Markby. 'He knows how wonderfully well you've done. The President of Kandy has been in touch with us and the lawyers'll be busy drawing up the contracts. This is all splendid stuff, Mike. I can't understand why there should be any problem.'

'It's the nature of the product itself.'

'Oh?'

'There's some medical evidence,' Mike stated, 'which has disturbed me. I'm referring to the Swiss Schenck Report and the Swedish Johanssen Report, both government-sponsored and both cause for considerable concern.'

'Nothing else?'

'Nothing else?' Mike echoed incredulously. 'I think that's quite enough.'

'Oh, that's all right, then,' Markby murmured casually. 'The Chairman will see you now. Room One.'

Plagued by a mixture of bewilderment and unease, Mike made his way to Room One. He'd only been there once before, when Savage had appointed him to the Board, and he'd never forgotten the disquieting sense of irrational envy the environment aroused in him. He knocked and was invited to enter. The large room hadn't changed since his last visit. Savage sat at his massive teak desk, with a Monet on the wall behind him. His fingers hovered over a panel of buttons before him. At their command, panels would slide open to reveal videos, slide projectors, calculators, computers and screens. The grey carpet was so thick that one seemed to sink deeper into it with each step one took. Yet there was nothing specific to which one could point as arousing a strong reaction. It was much more a question of the room's atmosphere. Every time one breathed in, one inhaled the perfume of power.

'Morning, Mike, congratulations on Kandy. Do sit down.' Mike lowered himself into a vast arm-chair. The seat gave beneath his weight and he sank several inches, leaving him looking up at the Chairman. 'I knew we weren't wrong to pick you for the pitch.'

'Thank you, I'm honoured by the compliment. But I'm not honoured by what we intend to do with Kandy.'

'Very understandable.' Savage nodded once. 'You're referring, I take it, to the Schenck and Johanssen Reports? If you're the man I take you for, I imagine they gave you pause for thought.'

'You could say that.'

'I just have. So I'm glad you've come to see me because there's no real cause for concern.'

'No cause for concern?' Mike retorted disbelievingly. 'Sorry, I'm afraid I'm not with you.'

'What *is* your concern?' Savage queried.

'I don't want to be involved in selling a product which is likely to give kids cancer,' Mike said firmly. 'I would've thought that was obvious.'

'They're not British reports, are they?' said Savage.

'No, but being Swiss and . . .'

'Is there an American study?'

'No, but the Swedish . . .'

'Have curious statistical methods,' stated Savage. 'The same is true of the Swiss. And until such time as the British Government sees fit to study Kandy, we must take its standards as our own.'

'Just a moment,' Mike protested.

'In a moment,' Savage shot back. 'You haven't thought this through as clearly as one would like. Look at your past career. You used to be on Slims cigarettes – and cigarettes are alleged to cause cancer. You've worked on Trafalgar London Gin, Claymore Whisky and Browning's Beers – successfully – and look at the figures for alcoholism. A long time ago, you were Supervisor on Tom Spivey Leisure – and who would deny that betting and gaming have led very many to financial ruin? So it's really rather surprising to find you objecting to Kandy. Why? This is a free society, Mike. Nobody *has* to smoke, drink, bet – or drink Kandy.'

'I don't think you're quite comprehending my point,' Mike returned, somewhat uncomfortably. 'We're going all out to sell Kandy to kids, who're easily influenced. We're going all out to sell it to their Mums, who can be persuaded to do most things for their kids. Giving kids Kandy is all very well. Giving kids cancer just isn't.'

'The evidence for that,' Savage answered, 'is fragmentary. If the product was anything like as harmful as you suggest, I'm quite sure the American Government would've banned it by now. So – that's enough of that. What d'you see as being the next step?'

'I'm afraid I can't share what comes over as being a view tinged by complacency,' said Mike. 'I will not be involved in Kandy. I simply can't do it and I don't quite see how anyone else can.'

'What d'you see as being the next step?' Savage repeated as though he hadn't heard.

There was a long and uncomfortable pause. Mike sighed heavily.

'I resign from the Kandy account,' he said.

'Resignation not accepted,' said Savage.

'You're not reading me right,' Mike responded forcefully. 'I've done my bit, unfortunately, and that's it. I will no longer be involved in it.'

'Yes, you will,' said Savage, 'you're just the man for it.'

'Mr Savage.' Mike took a deep breath and gazed steadfastly at the panes of the Chairman's glasses. 'I've very much enjoyed working here at Savage & Markby. But if you insist that I ride rough-shod over my conscience, you leave me no alternative except to resign from the Company altogether.'

'No,' Savage told Mike with total confidence, 'you can't do that.'

'I just have.'

'I didn't hear you. What you propose strikes me as being misguidedly hot-headed. And very, very unwise. It would be a terrible mistake on your part. An inexcusable error of judgement which reminds me, somehow, of Nick Peters.'

He used to be brilliant, Mike thought and swallowed.

He'd supported Mike's climb all the way up the ladder. Then he'd started to clash with Savage and along with that came the drinking. He'd progressed steadily through drunkenness to what had struck Mike as sheer lunacy. He'd sworn that the Chairman wasn't human – he was an enemy alien who had to be destroyed – or some alcoholic nonsense like that. And recently Mike had read in the papers that the poor, broken bastard had killed his own wife and was now confined in a prison hospital for the criminally insane.

And it had all started when Nick fell out with Savage.

'Be reasonable,' the Chairman urged. 'You have everything to stay for. Why spoil it?'

'Are you honestly telling me,' Mike demanded in a final effort to make Savage see reason, 'that you're perfectly happy about Kandy?'

'Yes. Perfectly.'

'I just can't share one atom of your happiness.'

'Well, it's not happiness really, is it, Mike?' Savage returned easily. 'It's business. And you're here to do business. This weak and emotional talk of petulant resignation is altogether unworthy of you and not what I would expect from a potential Managing Director.' Mike couldn't help sitting up at the mention of that title – and could've kicked himself instantly afterwards. 'It's allowable once in a while, of course. I accept that you work under considerable strain. But you're on the Board because you can handle that. Go now, then, and think about everything I've said. I'm sure you won't disappoint us.'

Savage stood up. Mike had to follow.

'Mike,' Savage extended his hand, 'I regard you as potentially our most valuable asset.'

'Thank you,' Mike muttered as his hand was shaken. Suddenly he felt strangely dazed, confused and weak, as though he was sickening for something.

* * *

'Mike,' Georgina sipped her dry martini, 'are you *sure* you're all right?'

'Of course I'm all right,' he snapped irritably. In fact, he wasn't. A headache had hit him shortly after leaving Savage's office and was threatening to split his skull apart. It made clear thinking virtually impossible and he had accomplished uncharacteristically little this morning. He couldn't think about anything except Kandy and his argument with Savage – and he had no idea at all about what to do. Georgina's suggestion of a quick lunch-time drink had seemed a welcome relief from the vacuum of indecision.

'I hope you're all right. You don't look too well. And I've got what might be bad news, I'm afraid.'

Oh, God, he thought, *not more*.

'I'm resigning,' said Georgina.

'Why?' Mike asked faintly.

'Well, I had an aunt who died recently and left me her house and . . . quite a lot of money, really.'

'I'm very pleased for you,' Mike responded dully. He'd never been left a penny in his life. 'But I always thought you didn't really need the money you earn here. I was under the impression that you worked here for the fun of it.'

'That's just it,' said Georgina, 'it's not fun any more. Oh, it's not you,' she assured him hastily. 'If you were running everything, I'd be happy to stay for years and years. But you're not, you see, and . . .' she faltered and frowned unhappily. 'How can I put it? Well, frankly, I've finally decided that I don't like this Company, to be perfectly honest. It was all terribly good fun at first, but now . . . I want to get out before I'm sucked in.'

Mike's pipe went out.

'How d'you mean?' His head throbbed.

'I've been here three years,' Georgina said soberly. 'Three years seems about the limit. Once anyone's been here three years, they seem committed to a life sentence – haven't you noticed? I know it's weird and I don't pretend to understand it, but I feel there's something rather, well, *sinister* about Savage & Markby. So many people go through their time here as though it were Purgatory. They're all aspiring to a Heaven which they believe awaits them in the end whilst enduring the pains of Hell here and now – but nobody ever seems to arrive at Salvation. Maybe I see it in these terms because I'm a lapsed Catholic, but still. Some rise to the top and are then ground down – take Nick Peters, who was destroyed altogether. There seems to be so much suffering. Roy Price is acting as though he's been castrated.

'And look what happens to those who try to leave when they've been here too long,' Georgina continued earnestly. 'Tom Kingsley left two years ago and is still without a job. Larry Belling left last year and I'm told he's now a waiter. Sheila Scott went six months ago. Yesterday I heard she'd had a nervous breakdown. I don't like it. I'm going while I can – with luck, unscathed.'

'Are you suggesting,' Mike struggled against quicksands of depression, 'that the Company might have some kind of malign psychological influence over its employees?'

'Yes,' said Georgina, 'and because I'm leaving, I can jolly well say what I like. John Savage gives me the creeps. Want me to shut up? I'm sorry if I'm compromising your sense of loyalty.'

'No, go on. I just don't know what to make of him.'

'Precisely. Did you know he's a multi-millionaire? I didn't think you did. He doesn't need to work. Why does he bother with Savage & Markby? I mean, I worked it out one night. He can't make *that* much money from the Company – not by the standards of the super-rich, anyway.'

'How,' Mike's voice was strangled, 'did you find that out?'

'One meets people,' Georgina replied vaguely. 'One hears things. Savage is known to a number of highly placed people I . . . well, meet at parties from time to time and so on.'

'What else do you learn about him from,' he couldn't resist a drop of sarcasm, 'your highly informed social circle?'

'Nothing,' said Georgina. 'Absolutely nothing. Not even where he comes from. That's the trouble, you see. Everything about him adds up to nothing.'

10

Savage & Markby Ltd

MEMORANDUM

To: All Staff
cc: Board Directors
From: JS
Subject: Morale
Date: 30 November 1983

In the harsh realities of the current economic climate, only a Company with a strong corporate spirit can hope to survive and prosper. It will therefore be of lasting benefit to all staff to implement the following procedure:-

At 9.30 A.M. tomorrow morning, Friday 1 December, all members of staff will stand by their desks and proceed with enthusiasm to sing the new Company Song.

THE COMPANY SONG

(To be sung to the tune of the S & M Joy Soap Powder jingle.)

ALL:
Here we are at S & M
Ready for another day.
Here there is no us and them.
Advertising! Great! Hooray!

CHORUS

Let's give three cheers for our Corporation!
Divided we fall but in union we trust.
Blessing and thanks to our organization.
Savage & Markby look after us.

ACCOUNT MANAGEMENT:-
Selling concepts to the client,
Co-ordinating the campaign,
Alert, dynamic, sharp, reliant.
Our presentations win the game.

CHORUS

CREATIVE:-
Radiant sparks of divine fire
Inspiring pictures, plays and poems
And word and image tune our lyre –
Selling the product to numberless homes.

CHORUS

MEDIA:-
We in Media buy the spaces,
We in Media buy the time.
We in Media play our aces,
Devoting our brains to figures sublime.

CHORUS

ACCOUNTS:-
Never forget your friends in accounting
Whose attention to detail can never relax.
Our vigilant brains are bent to surmounting
The mazes of billing and back-alleys of tax.

CHORUS

PRODUCTION:-
We've got pride in our humble stations.
Let's hear it now – we've got our patch:
Refreshments, Posters, Duplication,
Press Production and Despatch.

CHORUS

SECRETARIES:-
What excitement! Here comes our rhyme!
And here is a secret – we've got the suss.

All of our bosses may be in the big time
But none of our bosses can do without us.

ALL:-
Let's give three cheers for our Corporation!
Divided we fall but in union we trust.
Blessing and thanks to our organization.
Savage & Markby look after us.
Savage & Markby look after us.

Thank you.

John Savage
CHAIRMAN

Robert gaped disbelievingly at the Memo that morning.

'What *is* this?' he demanded incredulously. 'Some kind of a joke?'

'Hmm.' George scratched his head and looked unhappy.

'Sing-song, what?' Charles called out from his office. 'Sounds terribly good fun.'

'Of course it's a joke,' Tony Westbury came in. 'Look. That's nothing at all like the Chairman's signature.'

'Thank God for that!' breathed Robert.

'Joke is it, what?' Charles sounded disappointed. 'Pity. Always used to enjoy Assembly at school.'

'You don't mean,' Tony looked amused, 'that you lot took this idiotic prank seriously, do you?' He chuckled. 'My, my, I've got a right lot here. Though I wonder,' he frowned, 'just *who* the joker is. The Chairman will be wondering too.'

Robert was wondering about that as well. The mysterious author had somehow pin-pointed the imbecility of so much at Savage & Markby. The real horror lay in the fact that the Chairman might conceivably have sent that Memo.

'Well, back to work,' Tony said cheerfully. 'How's the Protheroe going, Robert? Having fun with figures?'

Harriet Baker had originally felt like taking the Memorandum to the Ladies and using it there for unmentionable purposes. She'd taken it seriously, gazed at it furiously and suppressed her rising inner urge to scream. When Sid Ingram finally persuaded her that it was definitely a joke – Tony Westbury had told him – she'd read the Song through again and fallen about in a fit of hysterical giggles. For Harriet definitely wasn't happy in her job.

She'd left a Polytechnic with a degree in Business Studies eighteen months ago. Her ambition was to become a successful advertising executive. Six months of sixty-seven job applications ended with her still being unemployed. At last, she lowered her sights, and realized that like so many ambitious girls she knew, she'd have to start off as a secretary. Five agencies out of five had offered her that job – and the Vice-Chairman of Savage & Markby had made a promise which decided Harriet.

'From what you've said,' the distinguished-looking man had told her, 'you clearly have executive ambitions.' Harriet had nodded excitedly, delighted that Markby himself should choose to interrupt her interview with his secretary. 'In that case,' a slight smile, 'you've come to the right place. If you discharge your secretarial duties satisfactorily for six months, I see no reason why we can't then offer you a place that's better suited to a girl with your – ah – qualifications.'

Then, Harriet could've kissed him. Now, she could've wrung his neck. Six months had passed some time ago. Six months in which everybody praised her work – especially Sid. She thought Sid was wonderful. He told everyone about her abilities and treated her like an intelligent woman. Oliver Dawes – who neglected to boss Sid and Harriet along with neglecting everything else –

nevertheless was pretty nice to her and never found fault. Yet after six months, Harriet was still a secretary. Two more months passed before she'd gone to see Markby to remind him of his promise. The Vice-Chairman waxed lyrical in praise of her abilities – it was music to her ears – and then informed her regretfully that he 'couldn't see his way to a promotion at the present time.' However, there was 'every likelihood of promotion in the not too distant future'. She'd be well advised to work even harder.

Harriet worked even harder. Four more months passed and nothing happened. She decided to go and see Markby again but the Vice-Chairman sent word that he was too busy to see her and passed her on to Peter Jackson.

Peter, who was obviously a very nice man, listened sympathetically to her and promised that he'd do everything he could to improve her position. A day later, Harriet's salary was raised by three hundred pounds a year and she was promoted from Secretary to Senior Secretary.

The nature of her work remained exactly the same and she found it horribly mechanical and desperately boring. Basically, she did photo-copying, ran messages, answered the telephone, served coffee, took dictation and typed out what others had written. Right now, she was typing a letter for Robert Slade, who seemed so nice and polite and hard done by – and whose own secretary was that bossy and affected cow, Fiona. Harriet helped Robert partly because Sid had asked her and partly because she felt a bit sorry for the trainee and liked what she'd seen of him so far. She couldn't help wishing, though, that he'd stick up for himself more often.

'Good morning, Harriet. I say, you *do* look ever so lovely today.' She winced inwardly as Martin Bottomley poked his shining, dandruff-ridden scalp and chubby face over her partition. 'Oh, *yes*. We *do* look feminine.'

'Thank you,' she responded mechanically and carried on typing.

'You know,' he quacked – and why *wouldn't* he go away? – 'you look so charmingly serious when you're typing. That's something I personally find intriguing.' He leered at her but she went on with her work. 'Heard the latest?' Harriet gritted her teeth. Whenever Martin said that, she always had. 'Apparently that Memo which we all thought was from the Chairman has turned out to be a joke.'

Harriet looked up into Martin's mud-brown eyes and suddenly saw a way of getting back at him for three months of unwanted, unencouraged, unpleasant and generally harassing attempts at sexual flirtation.

'Who told you that?' she queried.

'Herbie Tyler.'

'Oh, Herbie. I see. Funny. Because what I've heard is that Tony Westbury says the signature's genuine.'

'Genuine?' Martin frowned. 'Golly! Are you *sure*? This puts a completely different complexion upon the matter altogether. Hmm.' He frowned harder. 'Excuse *me*, my dear girl, but *I* intend to get to the bottom of this.'

As he strode away purposefully, Harriet reflected that at least he'd be out of her hair for a time. Anyway, it was some sort of revenge on Savage & Markby.

'Is this the way you keep your accounts?' Stanley Haynes demanded crossly. 'I like to think it isn't but I rather suspect it is.' He pursed his thin lips.

'Oh, no way!' cried Sid Ingram. 'No way. Honest. I mean, I don't deny we may have made one or two slips here and there. Happens all the time, guv. No point in denying that, is there?'

'No,' said Stanley, 'so don't. I have observed quite a number of curious slips, in point of fact. Take The Tom Spivey Leisure Group, Item TS 139 – FX1548P – U89 – one bottle of gin charged to the Client on 8/10/83. What's that doing here?'

'Oh – for the photographer,' Sid replied quickly. 'He got through the shoot in record time and we wanted to keep him happy.' In fact, the bottle of gin was for Oliver Dawes but Sid couldn't give away his chief. 'Know what I mean?' he added.

'No.' Stanley scratched his ear. 'You can't charge that to the Client. He's queried it. In my view, he's right and so we'll have to pay. So your decision has cost the agency money. Congratulations.' Sid reddened. 'Now the next item I've observed. SM237481 – FX9681R – V7 – 20/10/83 – one bottle of gin and this time charged to the agency.'

'Ah, I'm glad you asked that.' Of course that item was Oliver Dawes again but he still couldn't give away his chief. Oliver might do next to nothing but he was nice to Sid and had just written a Memo to Tony Westbury urging Sid's promotion. You didn't shop your friends – that was one thing Sid believed in. Another was getting on, and by covering for Oliver, he was getting on in some quarters – like Kandy, for instance – even though he was doing badly with Accounts. 'Knew you'd be asking me about that one, guv'nor.' He tried to look comfortable and lit a cigarette. 'That's explained easily enough. Somebody – can't remember who – was asked to bring a bottle of gin up to a meeting in order to demonstrate a packaging point. Unfortunately, the bottle got broken on the way there – so we thought we'd better own up to that one.' He smiled broadly, exposing the white front teeth of which he was so proud. 'Nobody's fault, really. Just one of those things.' He took his cigarette between his thumb and top two fingers as he exhaled a nervous puff of smoke. 'Happens, doesn't it?'

'Too often,' Stanley commented coldly. 'And I put it to you that this bottle of gin wasn't broken at all. I put it to you that somebody drank it.'

'Nah,' Sid said with a wrinkling of his nose and a fierce shake of his head, 'nah.'

'Nah?' Stanley queried. 'What does "nah" mean? I would remind you that the word is "No". But I'm wondering if perhaps it should be "Yes". I like to think it isn't but I rather suspect it is. Take the next item I've observed, for instance, from which perhaps a similar conclusion can be drawn . . .'

Sid listened dispiritedly. he wondered whether his dad and his grandad had ever had it this bad. All right, so they were East Enders and life was hard then but they'd lived by their wits and always had enough for the booze and the betting and the birds. And now here was Sid with his prestige job in a glamorous world with its touch of class way above street trading – and with not much more than bugger all to show for it. He was grossly overworked doing Oliver's job as well as his own and rarely got home before eight-thirty. For that he was paid eleven thousand a year, much of which went in taxes, on the mortgage and in fares to the little house in respectable Ewell, Surrey, upon which his wife had insisted. There was little left over for the good time Sid craved. He knew his forbears couldn't've stood it. He sometimes wondered how he could.

'. . . and I'd listen closely if I were you,' Stanley Haynes was saying.

'Oh, I'm listening,' Sid assured him. ''Course I'm listening. You're the guv'nor.'

'I'm not the "guv'nor", if you don't mind,' Stanley returned irritably, 'I'm the Financial Director. And I give you due warning that after this item there are fifteen more items which I intend to bring out into the open.'

Sid suppressed an insensate desire to pelt Stanley Haynes with rotten tomatoes. There had to be an easier way of getting a good living.

'"Nearer and nearer crept the slobbering Thing,"' read Dennis Wilson. '"A slimy tentacle snaked out to touch the erect nipples of the trembling girl's soft breasts with its loathesome and lustful embrace as blood poured in rivulets from the man it had so obscenely killed."' He looked up from the badly typed, beer-stained manuscript. 'What *is* this shit?' he demanded.

'Fuck you,' said Simon, 'it's my novel.'

'I know that. But who wants to read this sort of crap?'

'I do,' Simon shot back. 'I read horror all the time. So do lots of people. You don't – so you know nothing.'

'I do read horror,' Dennis countered. 'I used to read it a lot and these days I read it now and again. So I reckon I know. And *this*,' he held up the sagging manuscript, 'is the sort of thing I've read ten thousand times before and don't ever want to read again. And anyway,' added Dennis, 'it's terrible.'

'You're such an ignorant bleeder,' Simon retorted. 'What you've just said is what a lot of stupid cunts said about James Herbert when he started. Look at him now. He's Number One in this country and rich with it. Where did he start? Advertising, same as me.'

'Yeah,' said Dennis, 'but he can write and you can't.'

'Simon!' Ronald Potter called out from his office. 'A word.' Simon rose heavily and went in to his Group Head, who surveyed him frostily through his 'intellectual' glasses, which had often tempted Simon into trying to rip them off. 'This slogan you conceived on this rough here. "Champion – Beer of Champions All Over". That's not bad as it stands. But, when I was looking at it, I saw an attempted erasure on this rough. I looked more closely – and what did I see? You'd written something on the rough in pencil and then tried to rub it out. "Champion Gets You Drunker Quicker", you wrote. I suppose you think that's funny.'

'It was just a sudden impulse,' Simon mumbled. God, how long would he have to endure this? How long would it be before his novel was completed, accepted by the publishers and soared to instant bestseller status, showering him in money in the process – like his idol, James Herbert? How long before he could give up the copywriting job he loathed and work freely? For when that happened – and he knew it would happen – then at last he could call himself a happy man. What a joy it'd be to see his wife's face as buses went by advertising his books! Chris was always slagging off his writing, and he was aching to amaze the nagging cow.

'A sudden impulse?' Ronald Potter's reedy voice jerked Simon back to reality. 'We don't have time to indulge sudden impulses here. We've had one silly joke with that Memo already this morning. You're not here to amuse yourself, you know. You don't seem to realize you're part of The System. I detect,' he adjusted his glasses, 'a distinct impulse on your part to try and buck The System.

'Well,' he took a deep breath. 'Don't buck the System!' Ronald Potter shouted. 'Ever! The System exists for *your* benefit. The System will look after you so long as you don't buck it. You do your bit and The System will do its bit for you. So don't buck The System! I've told you before. Don't buck The System! I don't want to tell you again. Don't buck The System! And do this rough again!'

'The usual?' Dennis murmured as Simon slouched miserably out of Ronald's office.

'The usual,' said Simon.

'You know something? He might just be right. And if he is right,' Dennis mused, 'I reckon I shall shoot myself. C'mon,' he flicked ash off his roll-up, 'let's get back to fucking Joy Soap Powder.'

Peter Jackson sipped his third pre-lunch whisky and contemplated his situation with considerable pleasure. All continued to go well and he felt he'd scored a particular personal triumph at the Kandy pitch. Unquestionably it was his own inspired gambit with the Kandy bottle which had got the meeting off to such a flying start. It was in matters like that, Peter thought, that experience really counted.

He couldn't recall when he'd last felt so happy in his job. His initial anxieties about the Chairman had turned out to be groundless. Every day bore witness to the steady progress of the Managing Director. Take the Browning's Beers Strategy Sub-Committee, for instance. The first meeting demonstrated that there were so many beers, so many actual and possible strategies, so many issues and so many egos, that three months' weekly sessions of an hour each wouldn't be enough to thrash them through. Peter's solution had been to set up Browning's Beers Tactical Sub-Committees for Champion, Star, Golden Eagle, Crusader, Light, Best Brown and Bremen, all of which he chaired.

The Strategy Review Board was currently considering Joy Soap Powder and although quite a number of sessions had already been expended and would be expended on it, much positive cross-fertilization was coming out of these sessions, enabling vital conclusions to be drawn at an appropriate point in the future. Mike Armstrong had stopped turning up to the Administration Committee, but things seemed to be going more smoothly without him, and the Account Management-Creative Liaison Committee was in cracking form, along with the Account Management-Media-Production Liaison Committee recently set up and which he chaired.

Obviously, all Committees and Sub-Committees had to produce interim Reports outlining their progress. And in order to maintain an essential inter-departmental balance, it would clearly be necessary to have a Reports Committee, which would scrutinize Reports impartially and which he'd chair.

Account Management Training was also flourishing and it was gratifying to see the sessions so well attended. Peter had had a brilliant idea for the next step. Each Executive would now have to present the advertising strategy of an imaginary product to his fellow Executives, who'd pretend to be potential clients. After every presentation, everyone could participate in an analysis of what they'd seen, which would be extremely helpful to the presentation skills of one and all. It would be voluntary for Account Supervisors and above but everybody below that level would have to do his bit – which meant a minimum of twelve presentations followed by discussion at the rate of one a week. Splendid. Peter beamed. This one would run and run.

Still, all this organizing was undeniably strenuous work. That was why, Peter admitted to himself, he took a drink in the office every now and again. There was no harm in that, surely, and anyhow, he was finding that the odd one here and there inspired his best ideas. Dear old Emily seemed unduly concerned by the fact. She'd even mentioned that his predecessor had ended up an alcoholic. Yes, what had happened to Nick was a terrible story – but how on earth did that example apply to Peter?

'Your office,' Emily had suggested tentatively. 'You don't think there's something curious about its atmosphere by any chance, do you?'

'No?' Peter had stared at her in startled surprise. 'No, not at all. What on earth could've made you say that, Emily?'

'It was only a suggestion.'

Peter shook his head, shrugged, drank some more whisky and turned his attention back to the Memo he was writing. Today, some clown had sent one purporting to be from Savage and instructing all Staff to sing a Company Song. One glance at the signature had assured Peter it was just a childish prank – although a *good* Company Song might be just the thing for celebratory occasions, he thought. But that could wait for later. For the present, he wanted to restore the credibility of genuine Company Memoranda. There *was* a need for a good Memo on Morale and who better to write it than the Managing Director? And in order to convey the sense of togetherness so essential to a Company's health, a striking metaphor was required.

What? Peter sought for it and found it. Of course. A ship. A ship with a crew. A ship captained by himself with Savage and Markby as the Admiralty. He seized his pen eagerly and wrote for ten minutes. The result struck just the right note, he felt, and he beamed broadly as he gave it to Emily, who for some reason was looking worried.

Why the worry? Peter didn't understand. Personal problems, perhaps? Well, the fact remained that there was work to be done. Pouring himself his last whisky before lunch, Peter addressed himself to planning the Future Planning Committee.

'Peter, are you sure you want this Memo sent?' Emily Hyde had felt like saying – but no, it wasn't her place to say so. Presumably he knew what he was doing, though he had been acting rather strangely recently. It was really rather worrying, she felt.

Emily Hyde liked Peter Jackson. She didn't especially like her job. In point of fact, it bored her to tears and she would much rather have stayed at home – where she lived alone – and written poetry. However, she couldn't afford to do that and in any case, she had been brought up with a very firm sense of Duty. As long as her boss was pleased, all was well – though she couldn't suppress her own treasonable thoughts. Although Peter made her job as pleasant and easy as he could, she couldn't help finding him – well, frankly rather insubstantial. He never actually said or did anything Emily deemed truly important, the sort of thing she tried so hard to capture in her poetry. And right now – well, to be perfectly honest, for there was no point ultimately in pretending, he appeared to be Managing Director of Much Ado About Nothing. His drinking appeared to be spiralling out of control. Very well, men drank quite a lot on the whole and Emily wasn't averse to a tipple herself – but Peter was going way over the top. One result was the Memorandum in front of her – but then it wasn't her job to reason why, so she shrugged and sighed and typed and sent the following:-

Savage & Markby Ltd

MEMORANDUM

To: All Staff
cc: Board Directors
From: Peter Jackson
Subject: Morale
Date: 30 November 1983

As we tack into the stormy winds and gales which sweep the swelling seas of Winter, the time has come for a few pointers from the old sea salt boxing the compass at the helm. I am confident that we have a tight ship and am moved to congratulate our matchless crew on the diligence with which all superfluous ballast has been thrown overboard whilst the sails of the S.S. Savage & Markby have been trimmed to the wind. We now approach our ports of call in a ship-shape and seaworthy vessel.

However, we need all hands on deck if we are to weigh anchor and round the Horn without being wrecked upon its rocks or becalmed in the Doldrums. Whilst there is no objection to splicing the main brace between 1300 and 1400 hours, all gunners are expected to keep their powder dry. The Company expects that each man will do his duty and the skipper pacing the quarterdeck will not be turning a blind eye. Many a vessel has gone down to Davey

Jones's locker on account of a jolly Jack Tar who should've been clapped in irons.

Let us hoist our flag with pride, then, scrub the decks spick and span and set sail upon our voyage with stirring spirits.

Heave ho, my hearties!

Peter Jackson
MANAGING DIRECTOR

Robert Slade stared disbelievingly at the Memo that afternoon. It was obviously another joke. It *had* to be a joke – and as such, he found it very funny. But suppose it wasn't? He stared around him wildly in search of another opinion but there was nobody in the immediate vicinity except Fiona. If Peter's effusions were meant to be taken seriously, then Robert had to be living in a world run and inhabited by madmen.

'Robert, a quick word, if you wouldn't mind,' Tony Westbury beckoned to him. 'Seen the joker's second Memo? Mind you, it's a passable imitation of Peter Jackson's signature.' Tony frowned. 'Nobody knows who the hell the joker is, but when it's known, he'll be walking the plank.' He smiled at his own humour. 'Still having fun with figures?'

'Yes,' said Robert – and proudly presented Tony with the completed Protheroe Marketing Analysis and Summary sheets. The loathsome and detestable documents had nearly killed him but at last the task was finished.

'Hmm.' Tony looked through the sheets carefully for a few minutes. 'Good work. Very impressive.' He leafed over to the Appendix Charles had advised Robert to present and which contained a list of statements which Charles termed Intelligent Remarks and Clever Points. 'Well done. You *have* mastered the basics of marketing. Yes, this'll be a big help to George.'

'George?' Robert looked puzzled. What had George got to do with it?

'Oh, yes. George'll be presenting it to the Client tomorrow.'

Robert felt sick. So far, the client seemed barely aware of his own existence. He'd sweated for hours, days and weeks in the hope that the client would eventually perceive his marketing excellence – and now George would be taking all the credit. George, who claimed that the Protheroe was 'laughably easy' but ran away whenever Robert needed help with it. George, who didn't seem to have a clue about the Protheroe and had done nothing whatsoever to bring it into being. Something rose in Robert's throat once more and threatened to choke him.

'But many thanks indeed for all the work you've done,' said Tony, 'and make sure you brief George properly.'

'Oh, yes,' Robert returned blandly, 'I will.'

George wasn't happy either that day. Earlier that afternoon, he'd pitched the brown ale poster once again. He'd gone in to see Tim convinced that this time he simply couldn't miss. The man in the picture didn't look smug at all. Yet Tim had thought that Colin might feel there was still something not quite right about the expression.

'You know what I can hear him saying?' Tim had reflected, '"Eh, Tim, lad, don't he look a miserable sod?"'

'Miserable? he's not miserable at all.'

'But he looks so serious.'

''Course he looks serious,' said George. 'He's the sort of man who takes his brown ale seriously and that's why he makes it Browning's. Just look at it again. Great beer! Great slogan! And what a lovely man! Great picture altogether! Colin'll love it.'

'No, he won't,' said Tim. 'He won't have anyone drinking Browning's Best Brown and looking miserable. Sorry, George, I can't risk it.'

That meant another job for Robert. George was damned if he was going to be lumbered with facing the wrath of Dennis and Simon if he could avoid it. So Robert could try and explain what George sensed Tim thought Colin felt might be a better way of redoing the poster. That'd keep him out of mischief.

It wasn't that George disliked Robert. He disliked virtually nobody. The trainee seemed a decent sort of bloke – polite, helpful, a trier just like George and bright with it. That was just the trouble. Robert might be too bright for comfort. One solid victory would raise him to Assistant Account Executive, which would give him more scope, and from there it was only a hop, a step and a jump to full Account Executive. From there he could overtake George, even though he was five years younger. That had happened before.

George hated being passed over for promotion and also lived in dread of getting the sack. He worked as hard as he could to the best of his ability. He took pride in his career, his trade and his Company. He longed with all his heart to be really successful and then provide really well for the wife he loved and the two children he adored. And so there was nothing personal in his attitude: it was just that, for George's own protection, Robert had to be kept down.

However, right now he needed the trainee's help urgently. Tony had just told him that tomorrow he'd be presenting the Protheroe to Colin, Tim and two other visiting Brand Managers. George didn't have a clue about the Protheroe. Just one glance at it made his head whirl with terror. He'd kept well away whenever Robert was working on it whilst assuring one and all that he was familiar with its every aspect. Now he was for the high jump unless he learned about it fast. His hands were sweating at the thought of tomorrow's presentation as he approached Robert's desk with a happy smile.

'Hallo there, Robert! Heard you really impressed Tony. Like I always say, talent will out. Let's have a look at the Protheroe, then, eh?' Robert passed over eleven densely typed pages of figures. George's heart sank into his scuffed shoes. 'Lovely! Ah, yes, it's all coming back.' He stared dully at the incomprehensible sets of statistics. 'Er – where's the Appendix?'

'Appendix?' Robert looked baffled.

'Yeah, Tony said something about there being an Appendix where you'd sort of summarized . . . the summary,' he concluded lamely. 'You know.'

'Oh, those notes,' Robert replied vaguely. 'Spilled my coffee on those, I'm afraid, but not to worry, I can remember it all. The first point,' he continued glibly, 'is how the Protheroe makes possible a trilateral differential association.'

''Course it does.' George wiped sweat off his face with the back of his hand. 'But will the client understand that? How can one put it to him?'

'It can't really be put any other way,' Robert replied regretfully. 'Standard marketing term which leads directly to the next point. With the aid of the Protheroe, we can predict a confluence within the sales nexus in any given monthly period and pro rata it according to regional variation. Are you with me?'

'It's familiar ground,' George answered faintly. He was starting to feel horribly tired.

'Good. Because,' Robert spoke with verve and enthusiasm, 'that's vital to an understanding of the third and wholly essential point, that by calculating the appropriate running rate and averaging it out against the relevant tied trade percentage share, we can arrive at a thorough comprehension of our margins above the line, below the line and – most important of all – on the bottom line.'

'Well done,' said George and screamed inwardly. 'I can see you've developed a very good grasp of it. But just tell me how,' his eyes narrowed, 'you would put that in the form of a concrete example.'

'Simple. Take the national volume sales running rate for October, November, December, for example. Now – if Champion could match that running rate for January, February, March, there'd be an overall sales increase – indicated here – of thirteen per cent.'

'Good one.' George thought that point just about comprehensible. 'You've passed. Trilateral differential association, eh? Who'd've thought you'd've mastered that?' He attempted a breezy laugh and coughed a wheezing chuckle. 'And you understand the confluence within the sales nexus. Quite right, it's essential.' He attempted a winning smile and achieved a sickly grin. 'Well, tell Fiona to get that lot copied for everyone who'll be at the meeting tomorrow. Oh – and – er – you can have a souvenir copy for yourself too. Quite a day it's been, eh?'

Robert agreed with George, and as soon as his immediate boss had gone, he strolled jauntily to the lift and went down happily to Photo-Copying. His good cheer vanished when he entered to see a furious Cliff Mitchell who wasn't wearing his ankh.

Mike Armstrong was sitting at his desk with his head in his hands and refusing to see anyone. He wanted to go home as soon as he could, for once, but tonight he had to attend Sandra Lang's leaving party. Mike had nothing against Sandra. She did her job reasonably well. Unfortunately, she didn't seem to like Mike and whenever he was around, clammed up and shied away from him. That was a pity because Mike sensed she was unhappy with certain aspects of her job and would've been happy to hear any serious complaints. Even so, she was coming along quite nicely and in his view was second in line for promotion to Account Supervisor. Her abrupt and tersely written letter of resignation had come as a surprise to him. He'd called her into his office but she'd refused to discuss her reasons, claiming they were personal. As far as Mike could see, there was some form of tragedy involved. The last eight weeks had seen her looking suicidal – yet he had no idea how to reach her.

And there were bigger problems too. Like Kandy. Like everything Georgina had said. And like his proposed resignation. Mike could see no alternative other than resigning from the Kandy account and if he couldn't do that, then – very, very reluctantly – resigning from the agency. Given his reputation and the Kandy triumph – even though the latter threatened to throttle him – finding another job would surely be easy. Yet here was a Memo which Markby had sent him and which, for once, provoked profound thought.

Savage & Markby Ltd.

MEMORANDUM

To: Mike Armstrong
cc: JS
From: HVM
Subject: Company History
Date: 30 November 1983

The ensuing biographical details may conceivably be of interest to you:-

1 – Daniel Gray. Joined the Company 1960. Managing Director 1972. Resigned 1978. Nervous breakdown 1978. Divorced 1980. Admitted to Colney Hatch Mental Hospital 1981. Discharged 1982. Unemployed.

2 – William Saunders. Joined Company 1977 as Director of Account Management. Left 1982 to become Managing Director of Marks, Goodwin, Harper. Fired January 1983. Unemployed.

3 – Quentin Taylor. Joined Company 1967. Creative Director 1975. Resigned 1978. Committed suicide 1980.

4 – Ed Andrews. Joined Company 1970. Media Director 1977. Emigrated to USA 1979. Killed in bar brawl, New York 1981.

5 – Maurice Foster. Joined as Account Director 1975. Left to run own business 1978. Declared bankrupt 1980. Hospitalized for alcoholism 1982. Abode unknown.

6 – Derek Johnstone. Joined Company 1976. Assistant Creative Director 1979. Resigned 1981. Currently employed as mini-cab driver.

7 – Harry Chamberlain. Joined as Senior Media Planner 1976. Left to become Media Director at Brady & Harding 1980. Fired 1981. Currently employed by Department of Health and Social Security as a clerical officer.

Further details can be supplied on request.

Thank you for your understanding and co-operation.

H. V. Markby
VICE-CHAIRMAN

'And then,' said Robert, who was telling Vickie about his day but who, for some reason, had omitted to mention the Protheroe, 'something happened which outraged me. You remember I told you about that weird guy Cliff in Photo-Copying?'

'The one with the nice ankh?'

'That's him.' Robert lit a cigarette. 'He looked ready to kill somebody today and I can't say I blame him. He was *ordered* to remove his ankh.'

'What? How incredibly petty! Who ordered that?'

'Fred Sayers, who's Cliff's immediate superior. But the unbelievable thing is that the order apparently came from the Chairman himself. Have you ever heard anything so contemptibly small-minded? I mean, the Chairman of a big Company getting uptight because some poor bloke in Photo-Copying is wearing an ankh?'

'That's despicable,' said Vickie. She paused for a moment. 'Didn't you say Cliff wore it because he believed in life? I thought so. I can't help wondering,' she said slowly, 'if it's something to do with that.'

'How d'you mean?'

'Well, looked at in that way, don't you find it just a little bit sinister?'

'Sinister? How?'

'Oh, it's just a thought.' Vickie shrugged and dismissed it. 'Like to hear about my day?'

It was Sandra Lang's last day at Savage & Markby. She hadn't wanted to attend the leaving party which Oliver Dawes had organized for her and which would be charged to Trafalgar London Gin. Oliver had meant well but Sandra felt she couldn't stand the smarmy speeches in her honour, the giant card on which so many of her colleagues had tried to be funny and failed, the leaving gift of The Good Housekeeping Cook Book and the false and strained bonhomie.

She hadn't found another job. Nine attempts had terminated with the companies saying they would keep her name on file but were sorry in this instance. A tenth had offered her a post as Assistant Account Executive, which she'd declined. Not that she'd performed well at her interviews. She'd been too depressed inwardly to project herself properly. Markby was once again welshing on his promises. Markby wasn't pulling any of his strings.

Sandra hated him so much she'd actively considered going to the newspapers. The trouble was that the story made her look almost as dirty as him – and wouldn't her mother love that! The bitch had never forgiven Sandra for announcing that a husband and children didn't interest her at all but a career did. Mother lost no opportunity of reminding her darling daughter that in making that choice, she was failing as a woman. And now Sandra felt she'd failed in a man's world too.

For the last eight weeks she'd slid helplessly into a swamp of anxiety and depression. In everything she did, there was an infinite weariness and disgust. She had difficulty in breathing, palpitations in her heart, twinges in her guts and continual cold sweats up her spine. She found herself dozing during the day and started up and cried at night. There was no relief. Getting drunk always made her feel so horribly ill – and ever since Markby, the very idea of sex had disgusted her. She'd been to the doctor who'd prescribed Valium and the pills did no good at all. She'd neglected her job and lost all of her social confidence. It was hard to put her thoughts together, harder still to express them. Tonight her face looked harder than ever, as if she would never feel much ever again. She was a failure in a sordid and disgusting world and that was all. It was with that thought that she slipped out of her leaving party just as Peter Jackson spoke up.

'A toast!' he cried out, 'I'd like to propose another toast!'

'Speech! Speech!' somebody shouted and the guests gradually went quiet as Peter mounted the platform. Nobody noticed that Sandra had gone.

'Thank you.' Peter smiled at his audience. Yet for once he didn't feel like smiling at his audience. The reaction to his Memo on Morale had stunned him. Incredibly enough, everyone had taken it as a joke at Peter's expense by the author of the Company Song. 'What did you think of my Memo on Morale?' he'd asked and been answered by gales and storms of laughter at his supposed broad-mindedness and wit. It'd all been so embarrassing that Peter had been forced to play along with the staff and attribute his Memo to the Company Song man too. He'd lost count of how many times this evening he'd smiled wryly and said he didn't mind a joke against himself provided it was a good one. It was therefore essential, he felt, to make his mark on the staff once again. What a dull bunch they could be! Not one of them could see the pointed cleverness of his nautical metaphors. A more solemn tone was therefore the order of the day.

'Ladies and gentlemen,' he began. 'I wonder if I could just add a few words. We're all having great fun here but I hope I may be allowed to sound a serious note.' His expression became grave as he lowered his voice. 'Underneath all the perfectly understandable frivolity, it's nevertheless always a sad occasion when somebody leaves us . . .'

Sandra had left for the Savage & Markby offices on the top floor. As she'd expected, the area was deserted, though the door which led to Laura, the top S & M secretary, was locked. She stood in the lobby, looked from the locked door to the lift and then to the windowless walls all around her and extracted a spray can of red paint and a Stanley knife from her bag.

'I trust that Sandra would agree with my view that her time at Savage & Markby has, on the whole, been a happy one,' Peter continued. 'And I'm sure all of us would agree that we shall be very sorry indeed to lose her.'

Sandra stepped back to survey her work. All four walls had now been sprayed with blood-red slogans. There was: MARKBY PROMISED PROMOTION TO SANDRA, MARKBY FUCKED SANDRA, SANDRA HAD TO WEAR STOCKINGS AND SUSPENDERS WHEN MARKBY FUCKED HER, MARKBY CAN'T GET A PROPER HARD ON, MARKBY TOOK PHOTOS, MARKBY IS A BLACKMAILING SWINE, MARKBY FIRED SANDRA and GOODBYE SANDRA.

* * *

'. . . we hope, of course,' Peter went on, 'that in the future, Sandra will come back and see us. I shall certainly look forward to that – but in the meantime,' he raised his glass, 'I trust all of you will join with me in wishing Sandra well wherever she goes.'

Sandra scattered the photos Markby had sent her that afternoon over the floor. Then, her expression one of total desolation, she eased the short, keen blade out of the Stanley knife and drew the razor-sharp edge in one vicious stroke across the veins of her left wrist. Blood spurted out of the severed vessels and she screamed, but no one heard her. As she sank slowly to the floor, her blood-soaked left hand grasped the hilt of the Stanley knife and tore open the veins of her right wrist. She cried out once more and slumped onto the stained carpet. Blood came pumping out of her veins to surround her sob-racked body in a sticky sea of gore.

Sandra Lang died cursing Markby as the top floor lights went out.

11

At 10.30 P.M. that evening, a uniformed security guard checked every room in the building, made sure that everyone had gone home and, as was his habit, took the lift to the top floor to make sure all was well. The beam of his torch showed him that a great deal wasn't. After he had finished vomiting, he telephoned a particular number, spoke for a time and listened very respectfully to the reply.

Shortly after midnight, four burly men arrived bearing a box intended for industrial transportation but big enough to contain a human body and a bag of tools which included a large can of paint stripper and a Stanley knife, which last is useful for taking up carpets.

At 8.00 A.M., Laura Jensen received a phone-call at her home from Markby. He'd be spending all day with the Chairman, he told her, and she could have the day off.

At 9.00 A.M., the same security guard as previously conducted a plasterer, a painter and a carpet-layer to the top floor. All carried the tools of their trade and, soon after, a number of carpets arrived. The top floor was declared out of bounds for the purposes of redecoration.

Seven days later, the River Police found the headless body of a woman with slashed wrists in the Thames at Wapping. There was no proof of identity and no one came forward to claim the body.

A head was found some months later.

Part III

12

At 9.30 the following morning, Oliver Dawes entered the Account Management section of Savage & Markby just in time to see Martin Bottomley astonish all by standing to attention at his desk and singing the Company Song. Martin was only persuaded with difficulty to stop singing and it took even longer to convince him that the song was a joke. Oliver, who watched the entire proceedings, wept tears of mirth, for he was the song's author.

Yet another Stanley Haynes Memo on Security had driven Oliver to write the Company Song in his office the day before yesterday, and the fear, consternation and amusement it had aroused had given him many hours of enjoyment. There was no way that anyone could discover that he was the man responsible. He'd typed it out himself, photo-copied it when Cliff was out to lunch and slipped the copies into internal envelopes to be popped in the internal post when nobody was looking. This morning's climax had been unexpectedly glorious and after Martin had been restrained and disillusioned, Oliver laughed all the way to his office.

He stopped laughing when he couldn't get in. That was strange, for he couldn't recall locking his office – and then he noticed a pile of musical scores dumped on the floor by the door. All his high spirits drained away. What the hell had happened? He looked around frantically for Sid and Harriet but they weren't there. What there was, however, included a Memo on Harriet's desk. Oliver picked it up, started reading – and suddenly felt horribly hot.

Savage & Markby Ltd

MEMORANDUM

To: All Staff
cc: Board Directors
From: JS
Subject: Oliver Dawes
Date: 1 December 1983

Oliver Dawes is the author of two puerile Memoranda purporting to have come from Peter Jackson and JS. This juvenile behaviour is hardly surprising in one who, for the past four months, has neglected his responsibilities, let down his subordinates, wasted Company time and shirked his work.

Savage & Markby is not a Company for sniggering schoolboys. Oliver Dawes has therefore been sacked without compensation and his departure takes effect from today.

John Savage
CHAIRMAN

Oliver's hands were trembling as he put the Memo down. His ears burned. He couldn't prevent his face from flushing furiously. Taking a deep breath, he tried to think things through clearly.

All right, so he'd been sacked – and insulted publicly into the bargain. Both hurt, especially the insult. However, he'd known underneath it all that his departure from the Company would have to come some time. What to do now? He was conscious of a rising indignation. No doubt the Chairman was congratulating himself on the speed and venom of his riposte. Savage wouldn't be expecting Oliver to counter-punch. There was no way Oliver would take this lying down. No compensation? He'd soon see about that. He had nothing to lose. He'd storm up to the top floor, force an entrance, insult Markby, abuse Savage and create such a bloody racket, they'd pay him handsomely to go away.

How on earth had Savage found out about him, though? Did he have a network of Company spies? That'd be typical of the Chairman, not that it mattered any more. Spies were irrelevant now. Oliver would soon show Savage that a dull dinosaur of a corporation stood no chance against a courageous and anarchic individual will. He took off his tie, threw the symbol of Company servitude onto the floor, spat on it and then, picking up his musical scores, he marched jauntily into the corridor. Everyone he passed shrank away from him as though he was a leper and every time that happened, Oliver yelled: 'Arse-hole!', which gave him a clear path to the lift.

He stepped boldly inside the car and the door slid shut behind him. There was a grim smile on his face as he pressed the button for the top floor. An electric shock wiped away that smile, zapping him harder than any he could recall. He reeled back against the walls of the car, swore loudly and kicked the lift, which hadn't moved. A little notice above the buttons informed Oliver that the top floor was closed for today owing to redecoration.

'Bugger that,' said Oliver, 'and bugger this fucking lift.' A little apprehensively, he tried the button again. This time he screamed as the electric current jarred his body and flung him against a corner, sheets of music slipping from his nerveless fingers. It took half a minute before he felt able to stand upright. Once again, the lift hadn't moved.

'Shit,' he breathed. The shocks had robbed him of his appetite for a confrontation with Savage & Markby. He muttered a curse on the elevator system. Damn! Why weren't there any stairs to the top floor, anyhow? Well, he'd change his plans. He'd leave the lift for Peter Jackson's office, and create havoc there. Oliver pressed the 'Open Doors' button gingerly – and the shock jolted his nervous system, tore a shriek from his throat and sent him spinning to the floor, where he crouched dazedly and sobbed.

His benumbed brain tried to grasp what was happening. The lift still remained stationary. It didn't seem possible but he couldn't go up and he couldn't get out. Could it be that Savage had deliberately wired the lift for this occasion? No, that couldn't be right. How could the Chairman know that Oliver would be taking the lift at this moment?

His hand hovered nervously over the buttons. He dreaded the thought of pressing another. His being revolted against the idea of being trapped like this. All that mattered right now was getting out. His skin was sweating with fear and confusion. Perhaps he should try for the Ground floor. Once he was out of this horrible cage, he could return to Account Management via the stairs. All his desire for a row had departed, but at least he could collect his cards. His finger stabbed the Ground floor button tentatively.

This time the current streaked through his arm to the shoulder, sending him staggering backwards, whimpering like a wounded animal. His self-control deserted him entirely and he broke down and wept with fear, pain and frustration. It was only after tears had flowed down his face that his bewildered mind grasped the fact that the last shock had in fact been the mildest of the four, even though his previous sufferings had amplified its effect. Was there a message in that? Was there any way out? Well, there was the Basement with its back entrance.

Did he dare press the Basement button? He didn't want to. Yet the alternative was remaining a prisoner in this hateful, confined space. Perhaps that would be the best policy, though. Loads of people in the building would be wanting the lift and when it didn't come or the doors didn't open, they'd complain. Help would be found and Oliver would be released. Yes, that's what he'd do.

Five minutes passed and nothing happened. Oliver started to feel he might go mad if his incarceration persisted much longer. He plucked up enough spirit to beat against the doors with his fists and kick them with his feet but made no impression at all upon the shining steel surface.

'Fuck you, Savage! Savage, you bastard!' he screamed but since he could hear no sounds from without, it seemed most unlikely that anyone had heard him. 'Please!' he wailed as more tears trickled down his cheeks, '*please* let me out . . .' His only answer came from the light, which abruptly began to flicker on and off.

Another minute of that and Oliver knew he'd go crazy. In an agony of desperation, he stabbed the Basement button. To his overwhelming relief, there was no shock. The lift commenced a smooth descent. The release of tension drew sob after sob from Oliver, who buried his face in his hands.

The lift stopped and the door slid open. Oliver leapt forward, tripped over a metal box which someone had carelessly left in what turned out to be just the right spot to catch his shin, and fell flat on his face on the cold stone floor, where he lay moaning.

After a time, he became conscious of people sniggering. A small group of despatch boys and catering girls stood by the exit, chewing gum and regarding him with a mixture of amusement and contempt. He looked back at the entrance which led to the stairs. A burly man he hadn't seen before leaned in the doorway, blocking all access.

'You're the wanker what's been sacked, ain't you?' he said. ''Ere's yer cards.' He tossed a brown paper envelope at Oliver. Oliver picked it up wearily and rose heavily to his feet. He was painfully conscious of his tear-streaked face.

'Little boy's been crying,' said a girl and everybody giggled.

'This ain't no place for little boys,' said one of the messengers and spat a piece of gum at Oliver's shoes.

There was nothing for it but to shamble past the sea of grinning faces. Oliver's own burned with ignominy, shame and utter humiliation as he staggered into the pouring rain outside.

'Who's laughing now?' said a girl and snickered.

Peter Jackson stared apprehensively at the Oliver Dawes memo and fiddled nervously with his glasses. This really was very bad news. Not only had Oliver been fired – and the firing, though probably deserved, had been done far too abruptly, publicly and vindictively for Peter's taste – but the nautical Memo of which the Managing Director had once been so proud was here again attributed to Dawes and dismissed by the Chairman as 'puerile'.

He blushed and squirmed in his seat. Evidently his use of naval metaphors had not been a good idea at all. How could he have been so self-deluded as to write it in the first place? Was it the drink? Admittedly both his wife and his mistress had taken to lecturing him about the booze but Peter felt that this was wholly unjust. If he was really drinking that heavily, he'd be waking up each morning with a murderous hangover, yet he hadn't suffered from one in months. Every day he arose brimming over with energy and went off to work possessed by a glorious exhilaration. And up until yesterday, his career at the Company had been going splendidly – proof, if proof were needed, that he was doing nearly everything right.

He would simply have to be more careful in the future. After all, everyone made the occasional mistake. It was best to look on the bright side because once again he'd been lucky. Nobody knew that Peter was the real author of the Memo on Morale, apart from Emily with whom he'd have a cautionary word. He would go along with the Chairman and the Company and blame the wretched document on Oliver Dawes.

Morale would be boosted by some other means. One good idea which occurred to him was to set up a Recreation Committee. This could organize Company bridge and backgammon tournaments and play tennis, squash and ping-pong against other agencies. Yes, that was clearly something worth developing and meanwhile he should congratulate himself on a fortunate escape.

With his office clock showing one minute past ten, Peter heaved a sigh of relief and reached into his desk drawer for the Scotch bottle.

'With the aid of the Protheroe,' George Webbing told his audience in Conference Room One, 'we can predict a confluence within the sales nexus in any given monthly period and pro rata it according to regional variation. Not only that. By calculating the appropriate running rate and averaging it out against the relevant tied trade percentage share, we can arrive at a thorough comprehension of our margins above the line, below the line and – most important of all – on the bottom line.' He beamed triumphantly at Colin Miller, who was listening intently but whose expression had become progressively more fixed.

''Ere, Tony,' Colin said, 'what's he on about?'

'George,' Tony's face gave nothing away, 'd'you think that perhaps you could spell it out a little more?'

Charles had both hands over his mouth and was trying to control a series of spasms in his chest, though so far no one had noticed them.

'I reckon George *should* spell it out a little more,' the Browning's Group Product Manager insisted. 'Because I don't reckon I'm stupid but by gum, I'm finding all of this a bit hard to follow. How about you lads?' he glanced pointedly at his subordinates. 'Is it striking you the same way?'

'Very much so,' said Tim Rogers of Champion and Best Brown.

'Hard to follow,' added David Poyning of Crusader and Bremen.

'Complex,' pronounced Roger Scott of Light, Star and Golden Eagle.

'Well, that's real marketing for you,' said George. 'I found it all a bit hard to grasp myself at first. But it does repay careful study and I'll give you a concrete example. Take the national volume sales running rate for October through December. Now – if Champion could match that rate for January through March, there'd be an overall sales increase – shown here by the Protheroe – of no less than thirteen per cent. See?' He grinned confidently but the expression sagged into a grimace during the long and uncomfortable pause which ensued.

'Well, I'm buggered if I know how that helps me,' Colin said at last. 'George, all you told us just then is that if we sold as much beer in January through March as we do in October through December, then we'd be selling more beer. I know that. I don't need fancy figure farting to tell me that.' He leaned forward aggressively. Tony looked uncomfortable. 'What the blazes are you on about anyway? What the bloody hell is this "trilateral differential association" stuff?'

'Er . . . that's what leads on automatically to the confluence within the sales nexus, of course.' George attempted another confident grin which began soupily, failed to find any meat and ended in cheese. 'And that leads on . . .'

'Stop,' said Colin. 'Just stop it right there. I've never heard such blithering lunacy in me life.' He looked at his men. 'Have you?'

'Never,' said Tim.

'Colin's right,' said David.

'As ever,' added Roger.

'*What* did you say this was, Tony?' Colin demanded with annoyance. 'We'd be learning more watching blue films. At least we'd be getting a cock-stand from those. What's the ruddy point of this blooming crap?'

'It has its uses,' Tony returned uneasily. *This is an absolute fucking disaster*, he thought.

'Such as?' Colin queried sharply.

'Over to you, Charles,' Tony said quickly. 'And George, you can sit down for now.' George stepped down miserably from the platform. The Browning's men assaulted him with four hostile stares and he shrank into his seat, where Tony transfixed him with a withering glance.

'Well, Charles?' The client's eyes glittered behind his glasses. 'Perhaps you can explain it to us.'

'In point of fact, the man we really want isn't here,' Charles answered smartly. *There's no way Tony's dumping this disaster on me*, he thought. 'Young Robert Slade was the chap who put it all together for us . . .'

'Who?'

'The trainee,' Tony explained. *You slippery sod, Charles*, he thought. *Saved your own skin, as usual – but at least you've given me another one I hadn't considered*. 'The Protheroe was young Slade's idea, in fact,' Tony continued smoothly. 'He worked extremely hard on it and with such enormous enthusiasm that we decided to give him a chance. He should really have presented it himself, I suppose, but we felt he was a mite too inexperienced. So that's why,' he looked back at Charles, 'Charles here will . . .'

'I want this Robert Slade here right now, if you don't mind,' Colin interrupted. 'If he's the man who's ultimately responsible, I reckon he owes me and my chums an explanation for what's been inflicted on us.' Colin's men exchanged knowing glances. They knew when their boss was going out for blood. 'No, Tony, I won't have any arguments, just get me Robert Slade . . .'

Charles looked immensely thoughtful as Tony reached reluctantly for the internal phone.

'Always said he wouldn't last here.' Fred Sayers, Despatch Manager, crumpled the Chairman's Memo re Oliver Dawes into a ball and tossed it to Steve, who caught it and dropped it into a bin. 'That's him in there,' said Fred.

'Yeah, he didn't half look crumpled when he crawled out into the rain,' Stan recalled gleefully. 'Face red as a beetroot, hanging his head with the shame of it, falling over and crying his eyes out before he slunk away.'

'Bloody disgrace, he was,' Phil commented.

'Disgrace is just the right word for it,' Fred declared. 'Oliver Dawes tried to make fun of The Chairman,' he pronounced the title reverently. 'Now you boys mark my words. If you have a laugh at The Chairman's expense, he'll have a much bigger laugh at yours and it'll cost you more than you ever imagined. That's why I gave you a break to see Dawes's departure.' In fact, the order had come from the Chairman himself but Fred saw no reason to disclose that. 'There's a real lesson to be learned there. And I hope you learned it thoroughly.' He began to patrol the despatch room while his messengers sat around him in attitudes which varied from respect to ill-concealed but impotent boredom and resentment. 'When you've seen Executives rise and fall and come and go for as long as I have, you acquire a rare feel for these things. A rare feel,' he savoured the phrase. 'See, I've been with Savage & Markby for a *very long time*. How long, Phil?'

'Since the Company's foundation,' Phil replied sullenly.

'That's right, sonny,' Fred looked down at him. 'I was here before you were even thought of. Don't forget that.' He straightened the red silk tie which hung from his crisp white collar, then resumed his pacing of the room. 'And Kev, tell me why I'm still here and paid a good salary.'

''Cos you know your job,' answered Kev, whose cheeks were red and raw from acne but whose eyes smouldered with ambition.

'Exactly,' Fred responded approvingly. 'Good. Why, I can recall when Mike Armstrong was in Despatch and taking orders from me. I gave Mike his first step up the ladder. *I* made his career.'

'So how come,' said Billy, whose mouth was a smirk, 'that he's gone up there and you're still down here?'

'Billy thinks he's being clever,' Fred observed acidly. 'Don't he think he's being clever? What a right little clever-dick we've got ourselves here. Now you boys just listen to *me*.' He extracted a Capstan Full Strength from a silver cigarette case and lit it with a silver Ronson. 'I'm not saying a word against Mike Armstrong. He's a fine fella and a shining example to you all. If *you* show willing, slog your guts out, treat people right and don't forget your friends, provided you've got a bit of nouse up top,' he tapped his skull, 'then *you* might be able to follow in Mike's footsteps. And the best of British luck to you! So why haven't I? I'll tell you exactly why. Because, in one sense, I'm cleverer than him.'

'You?' breathed Phil.

'Cleverer than Mike Armstrong?' Kev queried disbelievingly.

'I know my onions,' Fred insisted proudly. 'Look at it this way. All right, so young Mike earns rather more than I do. That's okay.' He shrugged. 'I don't begrudge him that. But the price he pays for that is devoting not just his days but his evenings and sometimes his weekends to the Company. Now *I* reckon there's more to life than just work. What are my main interests in life? Go on. You tell me.'

'The wife and kids,' sighed Steve.

'Right – and what else?'

'Boxing,' said Stan.

'Exactly – and what else?'

'Classical music,' said Kev.

'Correct!' barked Fred. 'And I want time to enjoy 'em. So,' he looked wise, 'that's why *I* am a Despatch Manager. I can do the job standing on me head, I get paid well and I can go home at the end of the day, forget about it all and enjoy my pleasures. *I* would advise *any* young man to do as I have done and become A Despatch Manager. You get a lot of power that way too,' Fred confided. '*I* have the ear of the Managing Director. *I* sit at the table of The Chairman himself at every Christmas party. And if I don't like the attitude of some stuck-up little Executive – well!' Fred preened himself, 'I know a way to bugger up his deliveries so it looks like nobody's fault but his own – you've seen me do it. So – bad manners and a poor attitude to me may cost an Executive his job. And there you have it.' Fred gazed importantly at his boys. 'I've said it before and I shall say it again. It's a grand life as A Despatch Manager.' He paused to let his words sink in, then glanced at his silver Certina. 'Right, time we were moving. Stan, Phil, Steve, take the mid-morning post. Billy, you're on sorting. Kev, you're with the van and off to Euston station. Well, don't just sit there looking like a bunch of idiots. Jump to it!'

After they'd gone, Fred extinguished his Capstan, coughed violently, lit another almost immediately and tried to ignore the gnawing pains in his chest. He'd given the youngsters a piece of true wisdom, he felt – or at least he felt that whenever he didn't think too hard, which was most of the time.

Occasionally the doubts came, and with them the pains, though Fred refused to believe there was any connection. And much of the time he couldn't see why he should have any doubts at all. When everything was said and done, he had a comfortable life. Once upon a time, of course, when he was young and foolish and just out of the Army, he'd indulged in all kinds of grand and ridiculous dreams about how his life was going to work out and how he would be somebody special. How silly he'd been to believe that for a moment and thank God he'd had that interview with Mr Savage!

It had happened such a long time ago that Fred couldn't really recall what was said – but certainly everything he was today he owed to the Chairman and to that interview. So these feelings from which he sometimes suffered – that an iron clamp was crushing his chest, that his life had ended long ago and that he'd sold his soul for a mess of mediocre pottage – were nonsense and should be ignored.

He ought to be truly thankful for his lot. Yet on the rare occasions when he was on his own and couldn't avoid thinking, he somehow wasn't. Funny, that.

Robert entered Conference Room One to see George slumped in an attitude of total dejection, Charles chain smoking and Tony having difficulty in remaining unflappably impassive – along with four clients who regarded him with frozen hostility.

'Ah, so here's the culprit,' Colin Miller muttered.

'Robert,' Tony said after a perfunctory introduction to the two Brand Managers the trainee hadn't met, 'would you mind stepping up over there and explaining why you believe the Protheroe is so important?'

'Certainly.' Robert strode to the front. This was the moment for which he'd been waiting. Yesterday, something within him had snapped. That was why his explanation of the Protheroe to George had been so deliberately atrocious. It was nothing personal – Robert had just had enough of being sat on and wanted to kick back. He knew that George would cock up the presentation. As he'd visualized it, Tony wouldn't want to risk his own credibility by following on from failure, so either Charles would rescue the situation or Robert would be called in to carry the can. He'd been hoping and waiting for that call all morning. He saw his opportunity before him now. But what he hadn't expected was that his reception would be quite so blatantly antagonistic.

'We were hoping,' Colin's thin voice dripped sarcasm, 'that you could tell us about "trilateral differential association".'

'Of course.' Robert ordered himself to stay calm. 'All that complex marketing term means is that on the Protheroe, three sources of data are combined to our advantage.'

'What advantage?' Colin demanded suspiciously.

'*At a glance* we can see how volume sales figures relate to our market share. In other words, if our goal is to increase Champion's market share – on which I think we're agreed – it's no good merely selling more beer if everyone else is doing the same thing. That way we won't achieve our goal.'

There was a long pause.

'That sounds like sense, I'll give you that,' Colin commented. 'Go on, young man.'

'Secondly,' Robert pressed his advantage, 'we can see from the Protheroe precisely where to make our greatest advertising efforts. For example, take the figures in Section A, columns 8, 9 and 10. If less beer is being sold by everyone in Tyne Tees due to the recession *but* Champion's market share is nevertheless increasing, there'd be no point in Browning's spending more money with us to promote Champion up there. The product's doing its job without us.'

'First proper piece of sense I've heard today,' Colin observed. 'Hear that, lads?' Everyone nodded. George now looked even more unhappy, Charles looked quizzical and Tony appeared slightly apprehensive. 'So what're you suggesting?'

'Well – take the Midlands – and we can see the picture clearly on page seven – columns 8, 9 and 10 – TV Central. Here, last year, more beer generally *was* sold. Yet Champion's market share remained the same, percentage wise. The moral is obvious. We attack this area. And we can see that *at a glance*.'

'You know something?' said Colin. 'That really is genuinely interesting. Hit the Midlands. That's what Chris Faye advised, as I recall. Mind you, that's always been my own opinion.'

'And mine,' Tony came in swiftly. 'Fascinating, isn't it, to see it confirmed by the much maligned Protheroe?'

'You've got a point, Tony,' Colin replied thoughtfully. 'Lads,' he glanced at his men, 'you lot may well have to eat your words. I sensed there was something here from the very start.'

'Exactly,' George came in hastily. 'It's the technical terms which . . .' Everyone stared at him frostily. 'You know.' Everyone looked away and back to Robert. George gulped and fidgeted in his seat.

'I tell you something, Tony,' Colin announced. 'This young man here,' he pointed at Robert, 'ain't quite the green little innocent he looks. He's got a future on Browning's, I can see that. Come on, then, lad, give us some more.'

'With pleasure, Colin.' Robert smiled warmly at his attentive audience. 'The next point's even more interesting. Take our ultimate strategy of winning the championship for Champion. Now look at page seven – columns 3, 5 and 13. We can tell – *at a glance* . . .'

The presentation continued smoothly.

'I think you were clever,' Vickie commented later. 'Oh, yes,' she continued listlessly, 'very clever.'

'So what's wrong?' Robert drank some wine.

'Nothing.' She shook her head.

'Oh, for heaven's sake,' he said exasperatedly, 'if you think there's something wrong, for God's sake say so. Frankly I'm deeply disappointed in your attitude. There was George keeping me down and Browning's ignoring me. At one stroke and after a very difficult challenge, the clients are impressed, Tony's very pleased, Charles is delighted and George is utterly discredited.'

'Yes, George.' Vickie drank. 'What you did to him was pretty dirty.'

'All right, so it was dirty,' Robert retorted sharply. 'He was playing dirty with me. What else could I have done? He was driving me crazy. And why should he take one atom of credit for my work?' He lit a cigarette irritably. 'It's not a vicarage tea-party out there, you know. It's a fucking jungle.'

'I know,' Vickie sighed, 'and maybe you couldn't've done anything else. I just think it's a pity that the only way to get ahead in your Company is to shaft some poor sod. It's perhaps even more of a pity that your biggest triumph so far has consisted of conning people into believing that the Protheroe is worthwhile when you've told me all along that it isn't.'

'Well,' Robert shrugged, 'I guess that's advertising.'

'Is it?' Vickie queried. 'Or is it Savage & Markby?'

'There you go again!' he burst out bitterly. 'I finally get somewhere and you have to knock it. Thanks a million. You've really made me feel good.'

'Yesterday,' she countered crisply, 'and for days and weeks before that, you said that the Company was making you feel so bad. It's a very sudden change of tune.'

'I was losing then and at last I'm winning now. Okay? Satisfied? What I feel isn't exactly abnormal.'

There was a moody silence. Vickie lit a cigarette. Both drank and stared into space.

'So who's giving this party tonight?' she asked at last.

'Martin Bottomley.'

'*Him?*' She looked astonished. 'I thought you couldn't stand him.'

'I can't,' Robert admitted. 'The man's a creep. Frankly, I'm astounded he invited me. He really is appalling.'

'So why the hell are we going?'

'Because,' Robert sighed patiently, 'one really should show up at these agency things.'

'God, you really bored her, you did,' Chris Burns snapped at her husband Simon seconds after Linda Giles had excused herself for the loo at Martin Bottomley's party. 'I've never seen a woman look so bored. I s'pose you thought you were being all flash and impressing her. Will you ever grow up?'

'Just having a chat,' Simon protested. 'No harm in that.'

'With most men, no, there wouldn't be,' she returned acidly, 'but with you there's no stopping you once you've got a skirt in sight. Nobody'd think I was your wife the way you carry on. Can't you be polite for a change? Look, you've made me drop ash on the carpet. What a gentleman!'

'It's okay, Chris, I'll get you an ash-tray.'

'Not that one, stupid,' she retorted with cutting asperity. 'Look at it. It's choking with fag ends. I don't want that. Get me another one that's clean. And get me another drink while you're at it.' She shoved her glass into his hand. 'And be quick about it, too. You've been neglecting me all evening.'

Hardly surprising, Simon thought as he plodded away obediently. Was there no escape from Chris's nagging? How could he have been so stupid as to have married her in the first place? Simon sighed heavily. He knew the answer to that one and so did she. Back in his Technical College days in Hastings his main aim in life had been to get laid, an aim he'd pursued frantically and without success. And then he'd met Chris. She'd seemed a right little goer then and taken him further than he'd ever been before. She'd dressed so sexily too – a bitter contrast to the drab blue blouse and boring red trouser suit she was wearing now. She had lovely long brown hair then too – but had had it cropped within three weeks of the wedding.

Why had he married her? She'd let him do everything except fuck her. She'd explained she would only do that with a man to whom she was engaged. He'd fallen for it, proposed – and she'd accepted, told their families and slept with him. He should've got out after that, Simon reflected, but it was so wonderful and he'd been so unsuccessful previously that he didn't dare leave her. She'd listened to him too in those days and given him what sounded like brilliant advice. She'd read his short stories, declared the utmost respect for his literary talent – no girl had ever said that before – and urged him to turn his skills to profit by working for an advertising agency, preferably one in London. He could work at his fiction in his spare time, she'd said, until the day came when he'd have his best seller.

So Simon applied for a vast number of jobs, landed a few interviews, took copywriting tests and, to his delighted astonishment, was offered a job at Savage & Markby. He was married three weeks later and a month after that, he and Chris were proud possessors of a new, mortgaged flat on a housing estate in Sudbury.

He'd worked at Savage & Markby for eighteen months now, while Chris was a secretary with a small Sudbury Town business. Initially, Simon had loved all the glamour of London advertising. It was incredible having so many pretty girls around while you worked. But they were also a constant reminder that what you'd originally thought of as the hot little number you'd wed was really rather ordinary – and got more ordinary and duller by the day. Meanwhile you sighed and groaned your guts out for the delectable dollies just out of your reach. It was torture. And whenever you went to a party where you had a chance to make your mark on the sort of girl you wanted, your wife came along going 'nag nag nag', made you look about two inches tall, put a collar round your neck, clipped on a lead and dragged you away.

No, life didn't amount to much at present. At work he was teased by the presence of forbidden fruit and bullied by that miserable and uncreative arse-hole, Ronald Potter. At home he was nagged into drilling holes, putting up shelves, taking out rubbish, painting walls, drying dishes, washing the car, hoovering and wheeling his wife's supermarket trolley when he should've been writing – which activity Chris now condemned as feeble and unproductive self-indulgence.

Well, he'd show them all. Then they could all just crawl, even Dennis. Simon had much affection for his colleague and cherished their relationship as the one bright spot in an otherwise dismal existence but even good old Dennis totally lacked the perceptual faculties essential to a true appreciation of Simon's genius. Still, there he was now and – trust him – snogging in a corner with some sexy bird. God, how Simon envied the unmarried!

And thank God for *Tentacles*, which was nearing completion. There he could escape into a world of his own creation and enjoy the surging inspiration in his brain. Yes, *Tentacles* would soon make his fortune, showering him in money, love, fame and adulation. Then there'd be no stopping him. Then they could all see the man he truly was. Then they could all gape at his success – and meanwhile all the birds would be queuing up at his door. Then he could pay off his sniping shrew of a spouse and tell her to go to hell.

Where was the dreary old cow, anyway? Typical. Here was Simon standing in the centre of the room with two glasses of wine in one hand and a clean ash-tray in the other and the bitch had vanished. What was he supposed to do – stand there like a stuffed dummy till Madam chose to come back? No way. Fiona Spencer-Wingate had just swept in and was looking gorgeous in tight jeans and a skimpy sweater. Simon fancied Fiona so madly she was even appearing in his dreams.

'Hello there, Fiona, you're looking lovely tonight.' He strolled up to her with a broad smile on his face.

'Simon!' His wife's shrill voice sliced through his hopes. Fiona's charming smile became a supercilious smirk as Chris interposed herself, snatched her wine glass and tipped ash in the tray Simon held. 'Can't leave you for a moment, can I?' she snapped. 'You're just like a little boy – and hold that ash-tray higher.' She turned to an amused Fiona. 'Does he behave himself at work?' she asked.

'Oh, yes,' Fiona trilled as Simon blushed scarlet, 'I can see how well you've trained him.'

'Darling,' said Vickie, 'd'you think this party's any good?'

'No, it's awful,' Robert answered. It was, he couldn't deny it. 'The house' which Martin had claimed to be 'in Hampstead' was in fact a flat in Gospel Oak. Martin shared it with two old schoolfriends who seemed just like him. The directions had been bad and Robert and Vickie had had another squabble on the way. When at last they'd located the place, they'd been greeted by a sweaty Martin in a sickly cream shirt with a light-up bow-tie of green plastic and he'd loftily informed them that they were late.

They'd gone inside to experience a hot, crowded and noisy room packed with people talking loudly about themselves and littered with leaky plastic cups of nasty red plonk with cigarette ends floating in some of them. There was nothing to eat except soggy crisps and stale peanuts, the music consisted of old Rod Stewart hits and Martin kept stressing the importance of 'rocking all night long' because 'some very important people will be arriving later.'

Robert stared around despairingly. Admittedly there'd been some joy in the congratulations many had offered him for 'that superb presentation I'm told you pulled off.' He'd glowed with pride while Vickie tried to look supportive but after that first rush of excitement, there seemed nothing more to say and nobody worth talking to.

He'd tried to make a number of conversations and introduce Vickie to his working colleagues. At least here – in contrast to Tony Westbury's party – he wasn't dwarfed by a plethora of seniors. Nevertheless, it was proving very difficult to have a fun time. Who was there, really, with whom he felt something in common outside work?

He'd introduced Vickie to Janet Ross, Tony's secretary, and as usual the girl had been as sweet as she was dull. Roy Price,, the most senior individual present, had talked to them for ten minutes and said nothing. Everyone was expecting the presence of George Webbing, the current agency laughing-stock, but he hadn't showed up – which Robert thought hardly surprising. Dennis Wilson seemed dedicated to the seduction of the girl he'd brought and unwilling to tolerate any interruption. Robert had hoped for some joy from Sid Ingram and his extremely attractive wife Gloria, but this proved yet another disappointment.

There was nothing remarkable or interesting about Sid that evening. He hovered anxiously by his wife and uttered elementary pleasantries when he spoke at all. It was as though Gloria had put him on silence so she could be the star turn. She talked solely about herself. Her job was Production Manager at some glossy magazine, it seemed, and she lost no time in telling Robert and Vickie that she earned more than Sid. A detailed analysis of her job's every aspect drove Vickie away but Robert stayed – partly because he was too polite to break off abruptly and partly because Gloria was so lovely to watch.

She was tall, with long, straight jet-black hair, a pert oval face with high cheek-bones and a slim, tilted chin.

Her enticing figure was enhanced by a backless dress which displayed superb shoulders and stopped short at her slim, curving calves. What she actually said was very much less than enthralling but Robert didn't really mind. He found himself laughing heartily with Gloria at something which was only mildly funny. Sid continued to stand nervously on the side-lines. His eyes didn't leave Gloria for a moment.

Somewhat surprised at Sid's subdued state yet applauding the appearance of the wife he had chosen, Robert decided not to provoke either Sid's or Vickie's jealousy and reluctantly excused himself to go in search of Vickie.

'In a way, I find advertising absurd,' she was telling little Herbie Tyler. 'It makes me suspicious if a product's pushed too much. They're spending all this money to tell me I should like it when I'd rather see it spent on improving the product itself.'

'You're quite right.' Herbie gazed at her appreciatively. 'There's no way at all that advertising can be defended. It's waste – but that's an essential part of the capitalist system. The fact remains that I have fun and get paid well. And that,' he looked cocky, 'is what it's all about.'

'But advertising *can* be defended,' Robert broke in. 'There's nothing immoral about it at all. Take the most common criticism, for example . . .'

'Robert!' Fiona swanned up to them. 'Simply super to see you. Hello, Herbie,' she added off-handedly. 'I've been hearing *all* about how well you did this morning, Robert,' she simpered. 'And who's this?' she glanced at Vickie. 'Won't you introduce me?'

'I'm Vickie,' Vickie said. 'Who're you?'

'Fiona Spencer-Wingate, his secretary,' she gushed, 'and he makes it all so hard for poor little me. He's *such* a hard man, you see – and only beginning his rise. Robert,' she continued reproachfully, 'you never told me about Vickie.'

'Too busy doing your photo-copying, I expect,' Vickie cut across sharply. 'Excuse me.'

Harriet Baker smiled and waved at Robert as she fought her way through the crush for more bad wine. Having secured a plastic cup of the sour, crimson liquid, she thought of going and talking to him. Unfortunately he was with the stupid and spiteful Fiona – and there was another pretty girl who'd earlier had her arm round Robert. Though it was nice to see that Robert evidently had an attractive girlfriend, Harriet decided there was no point in intruding herself. The bitter truth was that she felt she couldn't compete.

It was the worst party Harriet had attended in a year of miserable social occasions. They were all trying so desperately hard to enjoy themselves and weren't succeeding. Harriet wondered why she had bothered to come at all. At the time of decision, it had seemed preferable to watching television on her own while all her flat-mates were out with their blokes. Yet she was having a really lousy time.

The host had slobbered all over her and she'd spent much of the evening evading his advances. Vaguely hoping that she might meet someone who would change her life, Harriet had talked with – or rather, listened to – a number of reasonably attractive men and played the classic woman's conversational gambit of encouraging them to talk about themselves. They had – and at interminable length. Harriet was prepared to put up with that provided in the end she was given her turn. So far – and it was par for the course – the scoreboard showed Men 6 – Harriet 0.

Three men, including Roy Price, had been so utterly engrossed in themselves that they'd gone the moment she'd started talking. One had eagerly asked her questions – Harriet's spirits had soared – only to interrupt her every answer with: 'How interesting you should say that because

. . .' and six meaty paragraphs about himself had followed. One had opened her up – then put her down the instant she confessed to being just a secretary. And the last one had assured her what a pleasure it was to meet an intelligent woman and run away the instant she lived up to her billing.

God, what bloody fucking pigs men can be, Harriet thought. Her last lover had gone off with someone else four months ago after lying to her for half a year. Harriet felt she knew what the trouble was. It was her intelligence and her refusal meekly to accept the subordinate role prescribed for women by society. Not that she considered herself to be an ardent feminist. She wanted equality, that was all, and she just didn't seem to be getting it.

Again, men were so stereotyped in their sexual preferences, Harriet thought, and it was her misfortune not to conform to the fashionable image which advertising blasted into every home. It wasn't that she felt herself to be unattractive – and every man she'd had had praised her legs. Her women friends told her she had a great personality, but whenever she turned it on, she turned men off. She only had to challenge male views for them to put her down and run away. Men were such cowards – she'd seen that in business. They trod on those below them and licked the arse of the next guy up.

So why did she bother with the male sex at all? she often wondered. They brought her so much pain and only rarely gave her pleasure. The main trouble was that she couldn't stop herself liking some and desiring many. Reason meant nothing when a man's look lit her up. She despised herself for her easy susceptibility but couldn't help adoring the feel of a good man entwined within her limbs.

But where were the good men? Hardly at Martin Bottomley's party. She'd been approached by a few drips and by one or two who treated her with that dreadful cold courtesy that's so utterly sexless. However sexually desperate she became, Harriet would not degrade herself by sleeping with a wimp. The feminists were right and masturbation was preferable. What to do? She did feel randy and it had been a long time, yet – Roy Price came over as a mangy hangdog on the prowl; Dennis Wilson and Robert Slade were otherwise engaged; Simon's wife was giving him yet another tongue-lashing; and lovely Sid Ingram was being horribly quiet in the presence of flashy wifely tits and ass.

'My dear Harriet,' a drunken Martin ogled her. 'Positively glowing with sex appeal, I see. Oh, you wicked, wicked woman,' he waggled a finger at her, 'you played a practical joke upon me only yesterday. Yet I,' Martin swayed against a shelf and caught himself, 'have far too excellent a sense of humour to be offended by the mirth at my expense.' His piggy eyes narrowed. 'Oooh, that *was* naughty of you, you delightful, impetuous thing. And you do look so ravishingly pretty tonight.'

'Thank you,' said Harriet, 'and if you'll just excuse me . . .'

'On no account.' Martin barred her escape. 'I am reliably informed that it's your birthday today.'

'Yes, but . . .'

'No "buts". I have a little gift for you. Heah, come with me.' Harriet found herself conducted, propelled and shoved into a bleak bedroom. 'Theah!' He handed her a badly wrapped package. 'A token of my esteem.'

'Thank you, but you really shouldn't've . . .'

'Open Sesame!' Martin cried 'and witness the delights of Aladdin's Cave!'

Harriet reluctantly complied with his request and unwrapped the package while he watched her reactions eagerly.

'Oh . . .' she murmured and for a moment her brain was paralysed by contemplation of his birthday gifts. For these consisted of two bottles of Kandy, a packet of

Dewbury Nylons, a box of Chudleigh chocolates, a tin of P & Q Stores Own Brand Tomato Soup, an invitation to a free test drive of a Ford Escort at Jack Rochdale Motors, an Economy Giant Size pack of Comfort Sanitary Tampons – and a return trip for two to Southend on a Wheatley's Holiday Coach along with a voucher for two nights in a double room at that resort's Pawson's Hotel.

'Lots of fun, eh?' Martin gave her a lecherous grin. 'And I was thinking we should make our start tomorrow. Meet at Victoria at eight-thirty tomorrow morning and off for a weekend of passion and romance!'

'Martin, I'm afraid that . . .'

'Allow me to declare my unbridled passion for you!' He seized Harriet in his arms and pressed his fleshy lips against her mouth. She relaxed for the moment when she hoped his grip would slacken and as it did, tore herself away and rushed from the room.

'So *that* was a party?' Vickie shouted above the roar of the Northern Line back to Camden Town.

'Okay, okay!' Robert shouted back. 'It was terrible.'

'Glad you think so!' Vickie yelled. 'Yet that awful jerk Martin had the nerve to be offended when we left!'

'I know!' he bellowed back over the clash and clatter.

'Are all advertising parties like that?!'

He didn't answer. They'd both had far too much to drink because there'd been precious little else to do and now Vickie was in one of her aggressive moods.

'Well?' she demanded as the train came to a halt in Camden Town station and the doors opened noisily. 'I spoke to you just then.'

'How should I know? We've only been to two.' They walked disconsolately to the escalator.

'And it's difficult to tell which one was worse,' she remarked scathingly. 'Your Company seems staffed by a bunch of berks.'

'That's enough now.' They ascended to the ticket barrier. 'Quit taking the piss out of my work.' Robert was feeling increasingly fed up. Vickie had been more or less like this since he'd told her of his triumph. All right, she had a point in that part of what he'd done was sneaky and underhand – but he'd won. It felt good to be a winner and he didn't appreciate her attitude.

'You know what I think,' she said as they handed in their tickets. 'I think advertising people are perfectly hateful.'

'And so're you when you're like this,' he snapped. 'Nor am I impressed with your legal colleagues. Bunch of over-privileged pompous farts.'

'Oh, fuck off,' said Vickie as they commenced their walk back home.

'Fuck off yourself.'

'And fuck you right back,' Vickie returned. 'Just go and get buggered by your precious fucking Company.'

13

The sudden sacking of Oliver Dawes, which nearly everyone loudly agreed to be richly deserved, had a number of repercussions. The most immediate was a universal tendency among the executives to insist that every cock-up which came to light was somehow the fault of Oliver Dawes. Minds were stretched to the outermost limits of ingenuity to find some way of implicating Oliver Dawes in any and every mistake. A lingering fart in the Lower Projection Room would've been blamed on Oliver Dawes.

The position of Account Supervisor which Oliver had made vacant by his abrupt departure was left that way. At a Board Meeting, Markby argued against Mike that since Oliver had supervised no one and nothing yet his accounts had nevertheless ticked over, then the expense of a Supervisor wasn't warranted. Mike insisted that Sid Ingram would be just the man for that necessary position. Eventually the matter was resolved by a Peter Jackson compromise by which Sid was promoted to the newly created position of Account Manager – below Supervisor but above Executive – and received a salary increase of one thousand pounds a year. He also continued to work on Kandy and so rarely arrived home now before nine in the evening.

Herbie Tyler became the Executive on Sandra Lang's accounts. This left no one to help Roy Price in Piddling – the agency nick-name for his cluster of small-spending clients – and so he was given an Assistant Account Executive in the shape of Martin Bottomley. Roy grew more sheepish by the day.

Nobody showed interest in discussing Sandra Lang. It

was vaguely hoped she'd found greater happiness elsewhere.

'. . . and if you could get hold of Patrick Spence at Rawson's around four forty-five this afternoon, I'd appreciate it,' Mike said mechanically. He struck a match to light his pipe but the flame shrank and died before it reached the tobacco. 'Thanks, Georgina.' But his secretary remained seated and continued to stare at him. 'That's all,' he added.

'Mike,' she ignored the hint, 'is something wrong?'

'Not at all,' he returned automatically but his tone was wholly unconvincing. Markby's Memo on Company History and the events of the ensuing four days had left him badly unsettled. He'd spoken to a number of his contacts in the trade about a Directorship at another agency and they'd all responded similarly. Although Savage & Markby was respected by everyone in the industry, there was a curious reluctance to hire its personnel. Apparently there'd been too many cases of disappointed expectations and many had concluded that Savage & Markby people should stick with their own Company.

Yes, there was a slim possibility that Mike might get in somewhere if he brought some big accounts with him – but Mike knew from experience that there was precious little chance of that. Savage and Markby themselves always made a point of knowing the key people at every client company and – contrary to the general nature of the business – the agency had hardly ever lost an account. Some thought that fact strange, if not positively uncanny.

A second possibility was for Mike to join the Board of some minor agency. However, the thought of changing from million pound multi-media campaigns to the sort which involved five weeks of provincial radio spots backed up by the odd poster was exceptionally unappealing. The only temptation towards that course of action had been supplied by Savage & Markby's blatant attempt to frighten him. That was almost enough in itself to provoke Mike into daring them to do their worst. Yet although rashness was perhaps Mike's greatest business fault, he had learned the rudiments of caution in his climb and knew the futility of defying a tank when one's only weapon is a pea-shooter. Those predecessors who'd antagonized Savage had all come to very sticky ends and Mike couldn't deny that the fact worried him intensely.

'It's just,' said Georgina, 'that you haven't been looking well recently. It may not be my place but I can't help saying that you're coming over like a man who's being eaten up by something.'

'Do I?' He smiled bitterly as he finally got his pipe going. 'Cancer, probably.'

'That's not funny.'

No, thought Mike, *it's not. And nor's Kandy, for that matter*.

'All right, there is something,' he admitted, 'and I'm not sure how to put it to you.' He frowned and considered the matter while she waited patiently. In fact he longed desperately to unburden himself to someone. On Saturday night, he'd nearly opened up and told Julie – a girl he'd met and seduced recently. Somehow, though, the idea of talking seriously to her simply hadn't seemed right. He couldn't believe that she would understand his predicament. In the end and whatever her many charms, Julie really was just a pretty face – like far too many of his women.

'Georgina,' he said at last and hesitantly, 'I gather you enjoy a pretty comfortable existence. Now suppose you had to do something to preserve it when the alternative might be losing it altogether. Just how ruthless would you be prepared to be?'

'Oh, pretty ruthless,' she answered immediately, which

surprised Mike. 'I value everything I've got and I'd hate to lose it.'

Same here, he thought.

'So where would you draw the line?' he asked.

'Strange question,' she mused. 'Can you give me a concrete example?'

'Well, suppose you felt that the action which made the difference between continuing success and possible ruin would be a permanent stain on your integrity. Would you do it?'

'No. No, then I wouldn't,' Georgina answered thoughtfully. 'Even though it would be hard. But I happen to believe that we all have a soul and that a stain on one's integrity is a stain on one's soul and can never be eradicated. And you can't measure that in terms of material comfort. I could live without wealth, I think, but I don't feel I could carry on without a basic sense of worth.'

Easy for you to say that, he reflected. *You've got no idea what it's like to be struggling at the bottom of a heap.*

'Mike,' she continued, 'why can't you tell me what this is all about?'

Because we're so different, he answered silently. *You've had it all given to you on a plate and I've had to fight for every penny. You can afford to have the scruples I want for myself.*

'It's just something I'm trying to work out,' Mike evaded her question. *And if I told you I was considering a policy of to hell with it and carry on with Kandy, you'd look down on me, wouldn't you?* he thought. 'Suppose,' he resumed, 'that someone was trying to force you to – well – stain your soul, as you put it, and threatening to spoil your cushy life if you didn't go along with him.' *And* why *is Savage doing that to me?* he mused bewilderedly. *I don't understand*. 'What would you do then?'

'Oh.' Georgina gazed at him steadily. 'Now I'm beginning to see.' Her next statement surprised him. 'Why, I'd pretend to play along with him until I saw a way of turning the tables.'

'I see,' said Mike. 'That's very interesting.' *And by God*, he thought, *she's an angel and she's right*. 'That's very sound policy indeed,' he said. 'Clever, too. Thank you very much, Georgina. That's really helped a lot.'

'I'm glad.' She was regarding him curiously. 'Is that what was bothering you?'

'Yes. And thanks again.' Georgina rose. 'Oh, just one other thing,' Mike added with a puzzled expression she hadn't seen on his face before. 'What would you think of a man who forced another to stain his own integrity?'

'I'd say,' she replied instantly, 'that he was loathsome, detestable and utterly evil.'

'Hmmm.' Mike nodded slowly. 'I must think about that.'

'Mike . . .' Her azure eyes begged him to unburden himself to her but he felt incapable of doing so. 'You can talk to me, you know.'

'I just have.' He forced a tight smile. 'Well, thanks again. Better get back to work.'

Yet it was shortly after that when an event occurred which would horrify the agency. It had its beginnings in a difference of opinion between Belinda Torrance and Ian Sharpe in the Lower Projection Room.

'You're exploiting me,' Belinda was saying.

'Me?' Ian was all baffled innocence.

'Yeah, you. I am a victim,' Belinda told him self-righteously, 'of your selfish male exploitation of women.'

'How d'you mean?' he asked gently. *What the bloody hell's brought this on?* he thought.

'I've been reading,' she announced proudly. 'Bet you didn't think I had a mind. Typical man. When it comes to women, you can only think of one thing. The fact is that I came across a completely fascinating thing in *She*. It really made me think. It was an interview with Maureen Darbon who writes books and is really clever. And what she said is that most men just want women for their bodies and as soon as they've had them, they throw 'em away and go after the next one and that's exploitation and women shouldn't put up with it.'

'You're quite right,' said Ian. 'But you don't think that of me, surely?'

'Oh yes, I do,' Belinda retorted accusingly. 'My body's all you're interested in. I tell you, Maureen Darbon really has changed the way I look at things. She's what I call a philosopher. She gets you thinking. And I think it's disgusting the way you exploit me. We go out to dinner and what do you want afterwards? My body. We wake up in the morning and what do you want before breakfast? My body. We come here at one and what do you want before we've even had lunch? My body. I know what you are. You're sex mad.'

'And isn't it lovely?' Ian tried a winning smile.

'There you go again with more male bullshit! You'll say anything so long as you can screw.' *Too true*, thought Ian. *And I thought it was true of you. What's made you act like this, all of a sudden? It can't be just Maureen Darbon*. 'I want,' Belinda said, 'a man who respects me for my mind.'

'But I do,' he insisted.

'Oh, yeah, like hell you do. When do we ever talk?'

'Let's talk now. I'm listening.'

'No, you're not,' she returned, 'you're just pretending.'

Dead right, he thought. *But let's have a go at convincing her I'm serious and with luck this squall will blow itself out*.

'I think you have a most interesting mind,' he said.

'Oh yeah? Well, prove it.'

'Prove what?'

'That you think I've got an interesting mind.'

'Sure. But how?'

'See, you're not interested,' she told him bitterly. 'Though I do know one way you can convince me.'

'What's that? I'm happy to try.'

'We can spend this lunch-time just talking,' said Belinda. 'And the evening, too. No sex.'

'Fine,' he said easily. *Sod that for a laugh*, he thought. *I'll give her ten minutes to talk herself out and maybe she'll be back to normal.* 'Talk to me.'

'All right. Just give me some more champagne.' Ian complied, then sat back attentively. 'You see,' she began, 'I reckon I've been sort of radicalized. I remember how my elder sister always used to say – you know, Lorraine, the one I told you about who always had trouble with her bunions and who was going to marry Chas before he went off to Australia which was why she got that job at Sainsbury's where Simon the manager was always going on about his pork pies and – *you're not listening!*' she screamed, 'and I've had enough!'

Her hand seized the glass by her side and hurled it at him. Ian ducked and the object shattered against the wall behind him.

'That's it, Ian,' Belinda snarled. 'Get stuffed!' He shook his head in bewilderment as she ran sobbing from the room.

At the same time, Larry Cunningham, Job Controller, was trying to restore order to his chaotic office. Everyone who passed saw him picking up roughs, Memos, posters and transparencies and putting them in piles.

'My God!' cried George Webbing, 'he's doing something for a change.'

'What d'you mean, George?' Larry looked hurt. 'You wouldn't believe the load I have to bear. All right for you Account Executives to swagger out to lunch. We workers are lumbered with your photo-copying.'

* * *

Simultaneously, Fiona Spencer-Wingate was herself preparing for a photo-copying trip before lunch. The superlative Charles Sutherland had given her some stuff to duplicate but told her to wait until he checked something prior to lunch-time.

Fiona adored Charles. He treated her with the off-handed casualness she inwardly believed she deserved. Charles, she thought, was so unbelievably stylish and a totally super boss. But where was he? Fiona decided to hang on for five minutes. If he didn't turn up, and that wouldn't be unusual, she'd try and delight him by doing his photo-copying anyway – anything to persuade him that she was an excellent secretary.

She waited and asked a few people who passed if they knew where Charles was. Nobody did.

'Much stronger stuff, what?' Charles took a deep drag and passed the joint back to Cliff, who was garishly illuminated by the flicker of the strobe light in the basement room they'd made their own. 'Rather more satisfying altogether. I'll have an ounce of that, if you've got it. Where's it from, old fruit?'

'Venezuela,' Cliff responded. 'Very sensual.' His hand reached automatically for his ankh, only to make the painful discovery once again that it was no longer there. 'Yeah, I've got an ounce here. Want me to weigh it out for you?'

'No, why be boring?' He handed over ninety pounds. 'Neither of us deal in half-measures.' Cliff passed over a polythene bag of grass. Charles beamed. 'Wonderful, wonderful.'

'Spiffing,' Cliff mocked his accent.

'Oh, absolutely corking.'

'Wizard.'

'And top hole, old boy. And now,' his eyes rolled upwards in mock despair, 'it's time I joined Joe Harbinson for a Ridley Farmfresh Cheddar luncheon – frightfully exciting, what? Underneath Joe's abominably dull exterior lurks an even more atrociously tedious interior. Well,' he took a final puff from the joint stub, then extinguished it, 'just keep a straight bat and don't let the side down.'

'Oh, he's not gone already, has he?' Sid Ingram complained to Nigel Fulton's assistant, Will. 'Jesus effing Christ, it's not even one o'clock yet and I've got something here that's important. You're not telling me that Nigel's scarpered?'

'Fink he's in the toilet,' Will observed listlessly. 'Might be back here before lunch but lunch is where I'm going. See ya.'

'Bleedin' ridiculous,' Sid muttered as Will wandered out of Posters, which was next to Photo-Copying. 'Inefficient cunts.' But he decided to wait for just five minutes.

Belinda ran back to her office, which was deserted, and gazed around wildly. Her agitated state of mind might have been due to Maureen Darbon's opinions or Ian Sharpe's behaviour – or to the little blue pill Dennis had given her an hour ago and which made everything happen so fast and with such alarming intensity. She couldn't keep her mind from buzzing with ideas. She couldn't keep her body still. She couldn't control her emotions. She didn't know what she wanted – but the row with Ian now seemed horribly upsetting and she burst into tears once more.

She felt that she hadn't really meant what she'd said and hadn't said what she really meant and didn't mean whatever she'd meant to mean – or something like that, for it was so hard to work out what meant what when your mind was spinning.

God, how she wished she hadn't taken that pill! Dennis would be in for a piece of her mind. What'd he called it? Ampheta-something . . . ampheta-mean, that was it. And it felt like being on a roller-coaster at the fun fair. She blinked dazedly. Her head felt as though it was taking off and flying away. *Control yourself, girl, and do something*, she told herself.

Simon had left something on top of his typewriter. She'd photo-copy that. Maybe the mental exercise involved would bring her down to earth. Snatching up the copy, Belinda ran through the Creative corridor and down the stairs to Production and the Photo-Copying Room, which was deserted. Going up to the machine, she placed the sheet of paper upon the glass surface, then broke down into another fit of crying. That was when a hand clapped itself against her mouth and something cold and sharp was placed across her throat.

Her body jerked rigid as tears froze in her eyes. She realized with mounting terror that the hand smelled of man, that a knife lay across her jugular, that behind her he was panting heavily and that something hard was pressed firmly against her rear.

'Raise your skirt,' he hissed.

Belinda suppressed the urge to scream out her shock. She knew that voice. This couldn't be happening. But the blade across her throat was real enough and she slowly complied with his command.

'Lower your knickers,' he breathed, 'and put your thighs apart.' She obeyed. 'That's good.' Drool dripped onto the back of her blouse. 'Very, very good. Now take my cock and shove it up your slit, you whore, you cunt, you snooty bitch.'

Belinda took his member in her hand. It was long, hot, stiff and spindly.

'That's right,' he whispered fiercely, 'you fondle that just the way you like it, you fucking prostitute.' Sweat oozed from the palm which gagged her mouth and he slobbered onto the back of her neck.

Belinda's fist smacked into his genitals, but she couldn't

see her target, her aim was misguided and there was little strength behind the blow. He emitted a strangled cry, ripped the knife across her throat and stepped back.

Belinda choked and fell, with blood spurting in a fountain from her torn jugular as she landed in a crumpled heap by the machine. She saw the face of her murderer and tried to scream again but all that came out was a stream of sticky crimson which bubbled from her lips in a babyish gurgle.

14

Fiona Spencer-Wingate took Charles Sutherland's letters and documents down to the Photo-Copying Room at exactly one minute past one. Entering with the gaiety of that last, easy task before lunch, she froze the instant she saw the blood-soaked corpse of Belinda, dropped everything, clapped her hands over her mouth and emitted scream after piercing scream as she reeled backwards into the Production corridor.

Her last sight before she fainted remained emblazoned on her mind long after. Larry Cunningham was scurrying anxiously towards her, a tight-lipped Ian Sharpe had just barged through the double doors, a glassy-eyed Cliff Mitchell lolled against a wall with one hand in a pocket and Sid Ingram slammed the door of the Posters Department and snarled: 'Cunts!'

Savage and Markby were enjoying a working lunch in the Chairman's Room One, where they'd just finished discussing Robert Slade.

'I'll action that this afternoon,' said Markby, then helped himself to more dressed crab. It was delicious, yet as usual, the Chairman had left most of it untouched and contented himself with half a glass of white wine. 'Meanwhile, I'm sending out a Memo on the new forms Peter's Administration Committee has devised. We're implementing all of them – and they're all extremely complicated.'

'Yes,' murmured Savage, 'that should have just the right sort of demoralizing effect.'

'That's my intention.' Markby sipped wine and marvelled

at Savage. It was incredible how little he knew the man, even after twenty-seven years of acting as his deputy. He knew nothing of Savage's past before that. The Chairman had never volunteered any information and Markby had never felt himself in a position to ask for it. He was acquainted with a number of people who dealt with Savage in other contexts – merchant banking, commodities, the fringes of politics and other areas where enquiry was discouraged – and they knew little more. The only facts about which everyone was certain were that Savage was very rich, very powerful, very intelligent and very secretive.

Markby no longer wondered why Savage devoted so much of his brain power and two days a week to the Company he'd founded when the sums involved were small compared to his personal wealth. These days, he thought he knew the answer to that. For Savage, the Company was a game which proved his theory about modern humanity and about which he'd written a fascinating, privately printed book. His work at the agency fulfilled his intellectual passion for experimenting on human beings with reward and punishment stimuli and observing the results. Markby had grasped the essence of that game quite a while ago and his own skills were a constant source of pleasure to the Chairman.

'The lifts,' Markby queried. 'What about the lifts?'

'I'm stepping the shocks up to one every three minutes.' Savage twiddled a knob on his panel. 'That should have interesting results.'

'Oh, absolutely,' Markby responded as the internal phone rang. The Chairman looked at the Vice-Chairman, who answered it.

'Markby . . . yes? . . . *what?*' His face paled as he cupped the mouthpiece and regarded Savage anxiously. 'There's been a murder,' he stated hoarsely. 'Belinda Torrance. The police are here . . .'

'Ah,' said Savage and took the receiver with nothing more on his face than a flicker of mild interest.

Whoever did kill Belinda Torrance, it wasn't Martin Bottomley, for he was drinking Champion Bitter in The Half Moon with Robert Slade and trying to find out more about Harriet Baker's feelings for him.

'Simply can't understand the damn girl at all,' he quacked. 'Why, Pawson's Hotels are renowned for their high standards of comfort – but what happens? I offer her a free weekend with *me*, which I thought would be a most delightful prospect, and she runs away. Mind you,' he added accusingly, 'you ran away yourself soon after.'

'Vickie was tired,' Robert explained. 'Anyway, I'm sorry to hear about Harriet. It doesn't quite square with what I've been told about her true feelings for you.'

'Oh?' Martin sat up. 'What've you heard?' he queried anxiously.

'Here, let me get you another pint.'

'My round, I think.' Martin strode away to the bar and Robert lit a cigarette. *Martin's hooked*, he thought, and prepared to be inventive.

Robert sometimes thought of himself as the original Mr I-Can-Be-Pushed-So-Far-But-No-Further. Hence his behaviour to George over the Protheroe and thank God for it. Today Tim Rogers had called him directly, by-passing George. Yes, life definitely felt better when one was winning. Yesterday he and Vickie had apologized to one another for Saturday night's row, made up and made love several times. He'd woken up today actually looking forward to the week at Savage & Markby. Perhaps the working world was just a matter of playing it right, as Charles seemed to do. And it was definitely true that one victory aroused an insensate appetite for another.

That was why he'd suggested a lunch-time drink to Martin because, he'd told his senior colleague, he needed some advice. A flattered Martin had been only too pleased to pontificate on the correct mode of sorting out some minor problem, after which he'd requested Robert's opinion 'on a personal matter'.

Robert would have brought up Harriet even if Martin hadn't. It was essential to his strategy. He'd noticed Harriet's enforced departure to the bedroom on Saturday and her frantic flight from the party a mere few minutes later. He'd also observed how remarkably quickly Martin became affected by drink.

'Heah!' Martin dumped two mugs on the table. 'Cheahs! Now, what was this about Harriet's feelings?'

'Well,' Robert tried to look uncomfortable, 'I'm not really sure if I should pass on a confidence. I mean, Harriet's a very nice girl but for all I know – and for all she knows – you're just out for a quick lay.'

'Certainly not,' Martin responded indignantly. 'Why, you misunderstand my position entirely. Oh yes, she is what I'd call a very fine filly but I do have feelings for her, y'know.'

'Really? She wonders about that, I was told. I mean,' Robert leaned forward with a concerned frown on his face, 'I don't know if I can tell you more until you tell me how you see her as a person.' Martin swallowed beer. He was drinking very quickly, just as Robert had intended. 'Good heavens, we've both of us knocked back our drinks already, just about. Let me get you another.'

'We ought to be getting back, really, oughtn't we?'

'All right.' Robert shrugged. 'If you insist.'

'Trouble is,' Martin looked unhappy, 'we can't talk there and it is rather important. Oh, God damn it, I could do with another.' Robert went away and returned with two more pints and two double whiskies.

'Tartan,' he explained, 'and it really helps when one's trying to talk properly. Cheers!' He hoped his own head would hold out. 'So tell me how you see Harriet.'

'You shouldn't, y'know,' Martin sipped whisky. 'Not good for one at lunch-time. Still, it's excusable once in a while. Well, then. My views on Harriet. Now attend please, because it's important. Firstly, like ever so many of these Women's Lib types, what Harriet's really looking for is a man and a child. I think I'm being rather perceptive heah, so listen carefully. Harriet is the sort of person who . . .'

Robert paid little attention to Martin's words. Instead, he concentrated on convincing the speaker that he was being listened to with rapt attention. His face constantly changed its expression, from concern to avid enthusiasm to encouragement to weighty consideration. His body swayed slightly with every telling point that Martin made. He murmured things like 'hmm', 'go on,' 'right', 'exactly', and 'that's my own impression'. By the time the monologue had ended, their glasses were empty again.

'Well, it's obvious that you understand her pretty well, better than she thinks and I'd love to tell you how she sees it. Unfortunately,' he paused and tried to look regretful, 'I really must be getting back.'

'Absolutely not!' cried Martin. 'You're not leaving without telling me everything. Hic! Heah, you shall have another, I insist.'

'All right,' Robert agreed with feigned reluctance. 'Same again, please.'

'Shame it shall be!' Martin declared and walked unsteadily to the bar.

Shame – exactly, thought Robert.

By ten minutes past three, everyone in the Company knew about the murder except Peter Jackson, who was still out to lunch, and Robert and Martin, who re-entered the building with the latter singing the Company Song. Robert smiled grimly to himself as he guided his perspiring, florid-faced and staggering companion into the lift.

He'd given Martin some soft soap about how Harriet really liked him but was put off by a pushy approach and there'd been yet more drinks in celebration. Now Martin was completely plastered. He would spend the afternoon making a fool of himself and, as Robert had planned, he would be discredited. Yet nothing could have prepared Robert for the curious twist of fate which enabled him to bring his plan to perfection. For when the lift stopped, its door slid open to reveal Markby, two men in raincoats and three uniformed policemen.

Martin saw them, hiccupped, stepped across the lift threshold, tripped and sprawled at the feet of the Vice-Chairman. Gasping an apology, he groaned, tried to raise himself and vomited over Markby's shoes.

Markby's face puckered with acute distaste. He gazed stonily first at the prone form on the floor and then at Robert.

'Have you been with him?' he demanded frostily.

'Yes,' Robert admitted frankly. 'He seemed very upset about something and I was trying to talk him into coming back this afternoon. Unfortunately, I couldn't stop him . . .' he gazed sadly at the spluttering figure who had struggled to all fours.

'Get him out of my sight,' ordered Markby.

Detective Inspector Geale and Detective Sergeant Dexter had set up a temporary headquarters in the Lower Projection Room, where they were helping themselves liberally to the chicken legs and beef sandwiches originally ordered by Ian Sharpe.

'The Chairman seemed to think it might be someone with a grudge against the agency,' said Dexter, a bloated man with a raddled face. 'Oliver Dawes was the name he mentioned and I've sent some of ours to see him right now. Here,' he passed over the one glass of champagne.

'Unlikely,' returned Geale, a gaunt man with thinning,

greasy hair. He took the glass Dexter had offered him, consulted his notebook then drank deeply. 'Stan Broadhurst and Billy Knight were lounging by the back entrance between 12.40 and 1.10 – despatch boys skiving off. Well, they saw nobody come by. We've talked with the commissioner at the front entrance and it's the same story. People left the building but no one entered. What does that mean to you?'

'It means,' Dexter chewed chicken thoughtfully, 'that in all probability, the killer's a member of the Company.'

'That's the way I see it.' Geale poured more champagne. 'We can narrow it down still further. We'll have to get it checked, of course, but those white blobs on the dead girl's face looked rather like semen to me.' Dexter nodded. 'Type who jerks off afterwards. So we know it's a man. As for Belinda Torrance, she was last seen alive around two minutes to one.' He glanced once more at his notes. 'Seven people saw her walking down a corridor in Creative and every single one said she looked agitated.'

'Wonder what caused that.'

'We'll soon find out. Anyhow, no one saw her go through the Production corridor or enter Photo-Copying. When that hysterical Fiona bird saw her at one minute past one, Belinda Torrance was dead. So she was murdered between 12.58 and 1.01. Where would you go from there? Mmm, these sandwiches are good.'

'Lovely,' said Dexter. 'I'd start with whoever was in the vicinity at the time. That means, for instance, Sid Ingram, who claims he was waiting in Posters.'

'And who the Fiona bird described as looking "murderously angry" and swearing about cunts.'

'That's worth pursuing,' Dexter commented and took the champagne glass from Geale. 'Then there's Ian Sharpe who says the deceased was acting wildly and irrationally minutes earlier in this very room.'

'Where he said he'd been on his own but had lunch enough for two.'

'Where's the other glass, if any?' Dexter queried.

In answer, Geale glanced pointedly at a patch of moisture by the wall several feet away and the fragment of glass embedded in the carpet.

'Somebody's tried to clear up,' said Dexter.

'She might've been so angry with Mr Sharpe over something that she chucked it at him and it broke. He cleared it up because he didn't want people to know about that. The Torrance girl wasn't even his secretary.'

'He was knocking her off,' Dexter observed and attacked the sandwiches again. 'That's my bet.'

'Yes, we want another talk with him.' Geale retrieved the champagne glass. 'And with Larry Cunningham. Furtive little bastard, that one.'

'Him? He could punch an egg with all his strength and it still wouldn't break.'

'I don't know,' Geale said. 'The quiet ones are often the worst, you take my word for it. Yes, we'll put a bit of heat on little Larry and see what happens.'

'And put some heat on Cliff Mitchell too. Didn't like the look of him. Smalltime delinquent if ever I saw one.'

'Seems he was always snapping Belinda with his camera. Here,' Geale passed over a stack of photos. 'Looks like he had a thing about her bum.'

'Oh, one of those.' Dexter looked through the snaps with growing interest. 'Mmm, don't blame him, it's a bloody nice bum, the dirty bastard. What's his alibi?'

'He says,' Geale's tone was scathing, 'that he was sitting in an empty basement room and reading a comic.'

'What, in the dark on his own? Where is this room?'

'The boys're down there now.' There were two smart raps at the door. 'Probably them. Yeah?' The door opened and Police Constable Norden came through. He was a young man with close-cropped blond hair, alert blue eyes, a flat nose, a mean mouth and a hard face, who radiated cockiness. 'Find anything?'

'Oh, yes sir, we gave it a very thorough search and I spotted a loose brick which, when taken away, revealed a hiding place where we found these,' he passed over a stash of sado-masochistic pornography, 'and this,' he displayed a thick slab of cannabis resin.

'Enough there to smoke out the Company,' Geale muttered. 'Naturally you've arrested him?'

''Course we have,' grinned Norden.

At four o'clock, Robert was told that Markby wanted to see him and so left his desk for the top floor feeling apprehensive though not fearful. In common with everyone else, he'd been horrified by the news of Belinda's murder and had also had a brief interview with the police which seemed to clear both himself and Martin. Martin had then been sent home in disgrace on the Vice-Chairman's instructions. Markby probably wanted to see Robert now for a more detailed explanation. Robert had it ready – an amplification of what he'd said at the time and to the police and intended to make himself look like a concerned Company man.

'Mr Markby will see you right away,' Laura told him, which was a good start. The Vice-Chairman's look of approval when he entered was an even better tonic.

'Ah, come in, Robert,' he beamed. It was a total contrast to the last visit. 'Sit you down. Dreadful business, this unpleasantness. And to think one could be murdered in *our* Company!' Markby looked genuinely disturbed.

'Terrible,' Robert agreed.

'And damaging to our image.' Robert nodded sadly. 'Makes it hard to concentrate on mundane things like work, doesn't it? Still,' Markby sighed, 'we have to carry on as best we can, I suppose.' He fixed Robert with his hard hazel eyes. 'We've kept an eye on your progress.

We're pleased with the way you're coming along. Your endeavours have been recognized in consequence of which your salary is being raised by five hundred pounds per annum . . .'

'Thank you,' breathed Robert.

'And you are being promoted to Senior Assistant Account Executive.'

'Thank you.' He forgot Belinda's death entirely in a glorious rush of joy. Perhaps old Markby wasn't so bad after all.

'Savage & Markby expects decent behaviour from its executives, of course,' Markby continued. 'One simply can't carry on here like a drunken oaf. We're on show every minute of the day, aren't we?'

'Exactly.'

'Quite so. And speaking of your working day, it's been noticed that you spend too much time photo-copying. That's your secretary's job, surely?'

'Oh, it's quite all right,' Robert hastened to assure him. 'I don't mind. Fiona works very hard doing much more important work for Charles and George and really, it's not a problem.'

'Quite frankly, it sounds like one to me,' Markby returned crisply. He added proposals to which Robert agreed and which made the new Senior Assistant Account Executive still more cheerful. 'One final thing. I've discussed all this with Mike and you'll be seeing him next. You're replacing Martin Bottomley on Kandy.'

'How d'you feel about that, Robert?' Mike asked ten minutes later.

'Fine.'

'Fine?' Mike frowned. 'In view of the evidence that the product could be dangerous to health? It was you who told me that, as I recall. And you added that you'd find working on Kandy "unbearable".'

'Yes,' said Robert. 'At that stage I still hadn't thought things through properly. Until there's a British study which condemns Kandy, I'm happy to push it.' In fact, he wasn't quite as happy with the situation as he pretended but his sudden success was flowing through his veins like some intoxicating drug, mingling with the alcohol he'd absorbed and drowning all cries of conscience. 'Perhaps that's your attitude too.'

'I can see,' Mike ignored Robert's comment, 'that you're becoming very well adjusted to this Company.' *And you're hardly the naive idealist I took you for*, he thought. *That surprises me*. 'So the ethics of selling Kandy don't bother you at all?'

'No,' Robert shook his head. 'If it's good enough for the Company, it's good enough for me.'

Mike felt sick with depression.

'He's sticking to his story.'

'I don't believe him for a moment,' Geale said thoughtfully. He jabbed his knife into the yolk of his fried egg and yellow fluid spurted into the grease surrounding his bacon. It was seven o'clock in the evening and he was having supper in the canteen with Dexter. 'It's the most ridiculous story I've ever heard. Goes to a basement room in his lunch-hour, sits on his own with a strobe light and contemplates the meaning of life or something – how can he sit there and be so ridiculous? Is he still saying he's never seen the porn before in his life and we went and planted the drugs?'

'That's right,' said Dexter. 'What he needs is a good hiding.' He sawed into a sausage.

'Not yet. Later, maybe.' He sipped from a mug of strong tea. 'Let's not be too hasty. We've got a drugs conviction that's virtually certain, we know Cliff Mitchell's a pervert and he's a likely looking candidate for murder too – but we've got him in the cells where we want him. But let's not neglect the others in the meantime.'

'Ian Sharpe – he's a dirty bastard.' Sticking his fork into a piece of bacon fat, Dexter used it to mop up the remains of his egg yolk. 'Plain as paint he was shafting Belinda Torrance and they went and had a tiff.'

'These flash places.' Geale guffawed as he scooped up the last of his baked beans. 'Always the same.'

'So Sharpe had a motive for being angry with the girl,' Dexter observed as he attacked the fried bread he'd saved till last. 'Keeps sniffing too – though he hasn't got a cold. Might be using cocaine. That's the favourite drug of many well-paid creative people. Maybe he had some and went barmy on it.'

'Unlikely.' Geale laid down his knife and fork. 'Sharpe's the type who screws women not the type who cuts their throats. Same's true of Ingram by my reckoning. There's a shyster if ever I saw one but cutting up girls ain't in his line.'

'And Larry Cunningham?' Dexter produced his pipe and proceeded to fill it with St Bruno Ready Rubbed. 'Personally, I'm still not satisfied with him. Claims he went down to Production just in time to see the Wingate girl fainting. I can't believe it's him but it still sounds too pat. Better keep an eye on him.' He struck a match. 'That just about wraps up our leading suspects.'

'Not quite.' Geale sat back as Dexter started puffing. 'Mitchell's a dealer. Where did he do his deals? I reckon it was in the basement room. What I can't help asking myself is: with whom was he dealing?'

'Promotion,' Vickie said over her celebration dinner with Robert, 'great. Salary rise – wonderful. Getting ahead – fine. Fighting dirty? Maybe it's essential. Success? Yes, yes and yes. But getting these things through conning kids and their mothers into contracting cancer – no, no and no.' She gazed at him over the restaurant table. 'How can you do it?'

'What about you?' Robert shot back. 'Where's your great moral stance these days? What're you working on? Legal ways in which companies can cheat women out of economic equality, that's what you told me. So you're hardly in any position to pronounce on ethics.'

'I know, I know,' Vickie swallowed wine. 'And it's making me feel terrible.'

'What good's that?'

'At least I've still got some conscience,' she retorted. 'You seem to have abolished yours altogether. You've changed and it worries me. It's as though the Company's taking you over.'

'D'you mean,' he returned coldly, 'like the Law's taking over you?'

There was silence while Robert and Vickie picked gloomily at their food. Robert wondered if love and success were compatible.

15

The murder of Belinda and the ensuing police investigation infested the corridors and offices of Savage & Markby with a thick, dark fog of fear and suspicion. One man who walked freely within the Company was a sexual murderer. Many women instinctively shied away from men and all tried to avoid being alone with one. Secretaries scrutinized their bosses and made them feel acutely uncomfortable. No one wanted to visit the Photo-Copying room, where there was now a uniformed security guard. Each day abounded in gossip and rumour. The arrest of Cliff Mitchell was the talk of the agency. Some recalled Cliff's bizarre sexual preferences and assured others that the police were merely using the drugs charge so they could hold Cliff for questioning and find positive proof that he was the murderer.

However, one or two suspected Martin Bottomley. Why had he become so disgustingly drunk? Could it have been due to remorse? And although most were familiar with Robert Slade's story of lunch-time drinks, which exonerated Martin, nearly everyone was pleased about the latter's fall from grace. For Martin returned to the agency to find himself fired from Joy and Kandy, regraded as the Junior Assistant Account Executive, confined to Piddling and generally shunned.

Robert's promotion to Senior Assistant Account Executive was generally popular – though George Webbing and Martin Bottomley remained notably silent – and a day later, he was appointed to the Account Management-Creative Liaison Committee, where Peter Jackson hoped he would supply 'a fresh viewpoint from a unique angle'.

'You *have* done well,' Fiona Spencer-Wingate gushed. 'I'm so terribly proud of my boss. Got any work for me?'

'Yes.' Robert passed over the Protheroe. 'I need a perfect copy, without one single mistake.'

Fiona slaved over her figure typing for nearly two days, smiled at Robert, wiggled her bottom at him, mentioned that she had nothing fixed for Friday night when she'd be *so* bored – and finally produced a perfect Protheroe.

'Thank you,' said Robert. 'And as from Monday, you're no longer my secretary.'

'*What?*'

'Yes, I've spoken with Markby and you're being replaced by Harriet Baker – I'll be sharing her with Sid Ingram. I gather,' Robert was enjoying this, 'that Maud Bunting is coming for George and Charles and you're going to Bottomley and Price in Piddling. You're quite a good secretary when you bother to try,' he stared coldly into her crumpled face, the eyes of which blazed venom. 'What a pity I've only just discovered that.' He gave her a tight smile. 'That's all – oh, and get me Harriet.'

'You're my secretary from Monday onwards,' Robert told Harriet ten minutes later. 'You were so kind and helpful whenever I was in a jam that when Markby offered me a choice, I asked for you. I hope that's okay.'

'Oh, yes. I'm very pleased.' She was – and glad too that Robert had risen.

'You're obviously much too intelligent to remain a secretary.' Harriet warmed to him even more. 'Sid tells me you want to be an Executive. Well, unfortunately that's not up to me, but I can give you some minor executive tasks, if you're willing.' She nodded eagerly. 'You'd be a sort of Assistant Senior Assistant Account Executive,' he smiled.

'Where's Fiona going?' she asked.

'Posted to Piddling.'

'Ha ha!' Harriet couldn't help laughing. 'Bet she's

delighted with that. Anything I can do for you in the meantime?'

Robert glanced at the perfectly typed Protheroe.

'I suppose,' he said, 'that you're understandably reluctant to do photo-copying . . .'

'Oh, what the hell!' Harriet exclaimed. 'There's a security guard down there. Here, I'll do that right away.'

'That reminds me of a time, ha ha!' said Peter Jackson, 'when I was presented with a photograph of washing proudly displayed as an advertisement for Kiss soap flakes. And I said: "Why did you leave a grey smudge on the washing?" The photographer replied: "I must shoot what I see." Ha ha! "The time will come," I told him, "when you see what you shoot." Ha ha! that shook him. Hasn't been heard of since.'

'Ha ha ha!' laughed Roy Price. 'That's a great story. And I love the way you tell it.' He was accompanying the Managing Director from the Reports Committee meeting, which had just ended, to the latter's office.

'Oh, I'm glad you appreciate its point.' Peter stopped as he reached his door. 'Well, Roy, it's been a profitable meeting, I think and I'm looking forward to the next one. Tell me,' he looked thoughtful, 'if there were to be a Co-ordination, Ratification and Implementation Committee – CRIC, for short – to co-ordinate, ratify and implement all decisions taken in committee generally, would you be interested in serving on it?'

'Very interested indeed,' said Roy. 'It's an absolutely terrific idea. I'm very flattered to be considered for it.'

'Excellent,' said Peter, 'you're just the man we need. Well, I'll have a word with the Board regarding that one. Bye for now.' He gave Roy a final smile, stepped inside his office, closed the door very firmly behind him and made straight for the whisky bottle.

Roy Price should definitely be given another chance, Peter reflected as the scotch slid down his gullet. Savage and Markby had been a little too hard on the man. However, Peter could see for himself that Roy was trying with every ounce of his abilities to prove that he was worth reconsidering. He took a keen and active part in every Committee to which Peter appointed him and was always a staunch supporter of the Managing Director's every proposal.

Committee work was really helping Peter to get to know the Company at every level. Ronald Potter was performing particularly well at meetings and addressed the work with seriousness and dedication. George Webbing had yet to master the finer points of committee work but showed a commendable enthusiasm, which boded well for the future.

The one problem for Peter was that he now spent so much time in committee that on occasion he neglected his clients – though Markby was always happy to stand in for him, which was kind. Moreover, he no longer had enough time for appropriate solitary reflection in his office. Those periods were essential to him. So many of his best ideas were born then. One was coming to birth at this very moment, as he poured himself another scotch.

He could have more time for these moments if he exercised his noted skills of delegation. The Vice-Chairman could become Chairmen of the more junior committees. This would leave Peter with much more time for much more essential work, though he'd retain overall control by creating a Board of Chairmen of these committees, and naturally he'd be in the chair.

'Brilliant, Peter,' he murmured to himself, then he raised his glass and drank his own health.

He was unaware that he was being watched with interest on a television screen.

* * *

There were thirty screens in Room Four, where Savage often went to sit alone. These thirty screens and a chair with a panel of switches and buttons were all the room contained. Every screen showed a different part of the agency.

Savage watched Markby playing strokes with his cricket bat. He saw Mike Armstrong talking tersely on the phone. Chris Faye was at his calculations, Brian Bishop was writing on a rough and Stanley Haynes was going through the accounts of Sid Ingram, who looked very unhappy. Fred Sayers was displaying his boxing skills to the despatch boys. In Creative, Ian Sharpe was at his desk and finding it hard to concentrate, Ronald Potter was shouting at Simon Burns and Dennis Wilson was idly picking his nose.

In the second floor lavatories, George Webbing was leaving without washing his hands while Fiona Spencer-Wingate was having a quiet cry. In the Ground Floor ones, Fanny Martin was applying lipstick while Nigel Fulton had entered with a pile of magazines. Charles Sutherland was in the lift and had just removed his rubber glove – a move which amused Savage and aroused a certain small respect in him. In the Lower Projection Room, Tony Westbury was proudly presenting a TV commercial to a client. Soon the man would merit advancement.

Much depended on what eventually became of Peter Jackson who'd just sat down and was furiously scribbling notes, pausing occasionally to drink from the glass at his elbow. Savage smiled faintly. Peter was acting according to plan.

Savage's attention wandered to the screen which showed the Photo-Copying room, where Harriet Baker was handing over her Duplication Form to the security guard. The murder which had taken place there wasn't part of the Chairman's plan at all but the event could be accommodated.

Savage knew who the murderer was. He'd watched the slaughter on television. And it would be interesting, he thought, to see how long it would take the police to charge the true culprit.

Harriet came out of Photo-Copying, glanced anxiously down the Production corridor and saw something which made her stop and look again – and harder. Was it Sandra Lang who'd gone into Press just then? Harriet had always liked the woman and Sandra had given her plenty of encouragement – but what was she doing here and carrying transparencies? Had she come back for a visit? Harriet frowned and, her curiosity aroused, followed the figure into Press.

'Yeah?' said Perkins of PR.

Harriet looked at him and blinked.

'Excuse me,' she said, astounded by the fact that the only person in the room was Perkins, 'but didn't Sandra Lang come in here just now?'

'You must be joking,' said Perkins. 'She's left the Company. Happened ages ago. Don't they tell you anything upstairs?'

'But . . .' Harriet faltered, 'but a woman *did* come in here just now.'

'Yeah,' said Perkins, 'you. What of it?'

'No, I mean just now, before I did.'

'Eh? What're you rabbiting on about?'

'Are you saying,' Harriet gaped at him, 'that a woman didn't come in here just before I did.'

'What's it sound like, darlin'?' asked Perkins.

'Oh, Christ.' Harriet shook her head. 'I must be seeing things.'

The murderer lay on his bed after work and sighed as he caressed his stiff, spindly member. When he recalled the ripping of the knife across Belinda's throat and the sudden spurt of rich, red blood, he came to orgasm. Afterwards, when he was clearing up, there was a certain sense of self-disgust but he remained glad he'd given in to the feeling which had been growing in him year after year. He had dared and now he would have his reward.

Belinda was only the beginning.

16

'It was incredible,' said Ian Sharpe. 'My girl goes and gets killed by some twisted pervert and the police treat me as though I might've done it. Christ, how can they seriously think that? Me kill a woman? The only person I'd like to kill is whoever did Belinda.' He sniffed and drank some wine.

'I'm really sorry,' said Mike. 'You knew her well, didn't you?'

'Yes, I was fucking her,' Ian admitted. 'I can't say there was anything serious between us but she was a good, kind-hearted, fun-loving girl and I was fond of her. So I'm more cut up by it than most.' He poured more wine for the two of them. 'You always said: "Never screw the payroll,"' he remarked bitterly. 'Now I see you had a point.' He sniffed. 'Poor old Belinda – she had so much going for her.'

'I just hope they catch the bastard soon.'

'Quite.' Ian took a deep breath. 'Anyway, enough of that. It's too depressing. And I'm sure you didn't invite me to a wine bar in order to talk about that.'

'No.' Mike's pipe was burning furiously. 'I asked you to come because I feel you ought to know something. You're the Assistant Creative Director on Kandy. How d'you feel about this?' And Mike told him everything he'd discovered about the hazards of the product. 'Well, what's your reaction?'

Ian was silent for a time as he pondered what he'd just heard.

'Sorry, Mike,' he said at last, 'I can't carry on with it. I don't condemn what you're doing but I must nevertheless regretfully resign from the account.'

'I tried that,' said Mike. 'They wouldn't let me.'

'How d'you mean?'

'Savage simply refused to accept my resignation.'

'Well,' Ian sighed and drank deeply, 'in that case I shall be forced into resigning from the agency.'

'Savage told me I couldn't do that either.'

'Are you serious?'

'Perfectly.' Mike told him about Markby's data on those who'd left the Company. 'So unless they make an exception for you, it looks like we're in the same position.'

'You look worried.'

'Wouldn't you be?'

'So what're you suggesting?' Ian enquired concernedly.

'Oh.' Mike knocked out the ash of his pipe. 'I was hoping to leave that to Creative.'

'Don't buck the System!' shouted Ronald Potter. 'And it's not as though I've never said that to you before. You should know by now – but what happens whenever my back's turned? There's you and that other joker and you're trying to buck the System. You *can't* buck the System. It'll beat you in the end.'

No, it won't, thought Simon, though he had to admit he was groggy and on the ropes. The Kandy TV script was going badly, his wife wanted bookshelves put up this evening and Ronald Potter was shouting at him now. But Simon would be coming off the ropes and throwing dazzling combination punches any day now. *Tentacles* was finished and with a publisher – the same firm which had first published James Herbert. It wouldn't be long before the big offer came, then the massive US deal followed by a publicity tour with plenty of television exposure – and all the joys of fame, fortune and fucking would be his.

'So don't buck the System!' Ronald Potter dragged him back to his miserable present. 'I've told you before.

Don't buck the System! I'm not telling you again. The System is for you and the rewards will be yours if you won't and you don't buck the System!'

'Good grief! What on earth's the matter?' George Webbing enquired of his new secretary, Maud Bunting. 'You look as though you've just seen a ghost.'

'Yes . . .' Maud was staring sightlessly and straight ahead. 'I went down to duplicate these letters and Sandra Lang was walking down the corridor.'

'Well, there's nothing strange about that,' George declared. 'She's come back to say hello again. Can't tear herself away from us, that's what it is.'

'The trouble is, it didn't look like that.'

'How d'you mean?'

'It didn't look as though she was just visiting. She was carrying a brief-case and looking purposeful. That doesn't make sense if she's left. It made me feel rather creepy and weird.'

'Oh, I know what's happened,' George told her genially. 'After she left Savage & Markby, she died of grief and now she's come back to haunt us.'

'Oooh!' Maud shuddered. 'Don't, George. You're giving me the chills.'

'You know, I saw a ghost once,' George reminisced. 'At least, I thought I did. I was lying in bed in this old room. Woke up suddenly in the middle of the night with this terrible feeling that something was wrong. I stared into the darkness and . . .' He lowered his voice and Maud craned forward to hear. 'There was this shadowy shape by the door. A black shadowy shape, rather like a shrouded human figure. I was terrified. I pulled the covers over my head and lay beneath them, quivering and shaking till morning came and revealed the bizarre explanation.'

'What was it?' demanded a wide-eyed Maud.

'My dressing-gown. I'd hung it up on the door-hook,

you see. Anyway,' he beamed smugly, 'where did you say you saw Sandra Lang? I think I'll go and have a chat with her.'

Fiona Spencer-Wingate had a high opinion of her own powers of detection. After all, she always won at *Cluedo*. One of her many fantasies consisted of seeing herself as a brilliant and sexy woman detective solving murders at country houses. Savage & Markby wasn't exactly a country house but it would do for her purposes. She intended to fulfil her fantasy and name the murderer before the police had worked it out. She would be the woman who'd solve the crime the press had celebrated and they'd put her picture in the papers and show her on TV. After that, she could spit at people like Robert Slade.

She was in a very fortunate position, being the person who discovered the body – though she never wanted to see a sight as ghastly as Belinda's corpse ever again. Ideally, one would only be called in to detect once the body was removed by whoever was responsible for that sort of thing. Still, she'd witnessed the prime suspects just before blacking out. Which one of them was the guilty culprit?

Fiona had a method of detection which some might find curious. 'I follow my nose,' said the detective she played in her fantasy. And Fiona's nose was telling her that the man to watch was Sid Ingram. She couldn't have given a reason for her suspicion – but her nose led her and that was enough. The facts were that he'd been in the vicinity, she clearly recalled demonic rage on his face and he'd been screaming obscene abuse of women. That was enough.

And that was why, during the lunch hour, Fiona slipped into Sid's office when no one was looking and went quickly through his drawers. In the first five, there was nothing except papers. Fiona gasped as she opened the sixth.

Lying on a document was a short, sharp knife, its keen blade soiled with crimson wetness. Fiona picked it up by the handle and sniffed. Yes, it was definitely blood.

'Me?' Sid exclaimed. 'No, no, 'course it wasn't me. Not on that, it wasn't. No, that one was Oliver Dawes.'

'I detect,' said Stanley Haynes, 'a distinct tendency in you which tempts me towards certain conclusions. Before, it was never anybody's fault. These days, it's always the fault of Oliver Dawes. I sometimes wonder if you're trying to put the blame for your mistakes onto him. I like to think you're not doing that but I rather suspect you are. Take the next item, for example . . .'

I can't stand it, Sid thought and gritted his strong white teeth. Oliver Dawes had in fact been responsible for every single one of the irregularities Stanley's observation had discerned. He'd left absolutely everything with which he'd been at all concerned in a hopeless mess. Sid was genuinely trying to sort it all out and Stanley's insinuations that it was his fault were insufferable. Unfortunately, Oliver Dawes had by now been blamed for so many things that Stanley simply refused to buy that story, even if it was true.

In any case, Sid felt that his sessions with Stanley were a complete waste of time. Thirty unpleasant minutes passed and at the end, ninety-six pounds and forty-three and one half pence had been exactly accounted for. What was the point of it? Didn't the bald Financial Director have anything better to do? Sid had important work to be getting on with – didn't Stanley realize that? Last night he hadn't got home before nine-thirty. Once again, Gloria hadn't been there.

Once upon a time, she'd been the pride of Stepney. She'd been courted by aspiring rock stars and boxers and criminals, and had looked down her nose at Sid. Yet instead of getting married, she'd gone away to University, same way as Sid, and they'd dated occasionally during the vacations. Sometimes he wrote to her at Lancaster from Durham but she never replied. However, when Sid returned to London and landed a job at Savage & Markby as a Graduate Trainee, Gloria responded to him better.

Before, she'd seemed excited by men whose every day was uncertain. Now she put them down as hucksters and praised security and respectability. Sid redoubled his efforts to interest her and shortly after he was promoted to Assistant Account Executive, she allowed him to seduce her. That had been quite an experience for Sid. It wasn't the act in itself – he'd been screwing around regularly since he was fourteen – it was Gloria. Not only did he possess the girl he'd dreamed of, she possessed him with an erotic fury more explosive than any he'd encountered.

She became an obsession. He didn't want to do anything except be with her, watch her, listen to her – and touch her and suck her and fuck her. He proposed marriage and she accepted – on condition they could live somewhere respectable and far away from the East End. Sid agreed, and on his wedding day, he strode from the aisle like a king who's just married an empress.

It was unfortunate that the jobs they did were so demanding. Sid was often home late and feeling too exhausted to do anything except slump into a chair, eat dinner, watch TV and go to bed. Gloria was frequently back even later. The trouble was that she never looked tired out at all. Sid had his suspicions and they pained him deeply. Whenever he went to parties with Gloria, she always flirted with other men and danced with them too, yet she made a scene about his immaturity if he so much as spoke a word of protest. And if he started to flirt himself, there was all hell to pay later.

Gloria had a dreadful temper. When it erupted, which was increasingly often, she swore like a drunken fish-wife, threw crockery and even attacked her husband with stinging slaps, hair pulling and finger-nails across his face. He dreaded her tantrums. He would do almost anything to avoid them. Every time one erupted, it destroyed another portion of his once great love for her. He wished she wouldn't drink so much – alcohol always encouraged her outbursts – but there was nothing he could do to prevent her.

So what was his life about? A hard time at work and a hard time at home with little opportunity for release. It was hardly surprising that at last, this very evening, he was going all out to break the rules.

'. . . and that sort of thing,' Stanley Haynes was saying, 'will not and cannot be tolerated.'

'I don't know just how much more I can take,' Harriet Baker sighed over a Bloody Mary. 'I mean, Robert's being really good to me and you're very good to me but I'm still just a secretary and going nowhere. There are days when I absolutely hate the Company.'

'I feel the same way myself sometimes,' said Sid, who was sitting with her in Trader Vic's after work. 'Strictly between ourselves, I'm not happy about the way the Company treats its people. You shouldn't be a secretary after all the time you've spent here, 'specially after that promise made to you by Markby.' He drank some Planter's Punch. 'And I should've replaced Olly as Account Supervisor instead of being given some stupid newly created title like Account Manager, which means nothing.'

'Why's it so awful?' Harriet asked.

'God knows.' Sid stubbed out his cigarette. 'I sometimes wonder if it's being done deliberately. Still, at least we've escaped from the bloody place this evening. I was thinking we could go on to dinner at The New York Cafe. How d'you fancy that?'

'Sounds great.' Harriet smiled.

'Good, I was hoping you'd say that.' He flashed her a warm grin. 'Meanwhile, let's have another round of these,' he suggested as his hand came to rest on Harriet's thigh and she snuggled closer to him.

Oliver Dawes was walking by the canal at Little Venice that evening and taking stock of his life. Much of it was bad. There was the humiliating departure from Savage & Markby, his failure to find another job, the drain on his savings and, to cap it all, the visit from the police the other day. They'd had the nerve to question him as though he might've killed Belinda Torrance. Fortunately, Oliver could prove that he was nowhere near the agency at the time of the murder but that had taken a most uncomfortable hour. He couldn't help suspecting that his name had been suggested to the police by Savage. God, what a bastard he was! Oliver would get even with him some day. But for the present, that could wait – for something good had happened which made all his problems shrink into insignificance.

Yesterday, he'd auditioned for a concert tour. Today, he'd been told that he was on the tour and that if he performed well, there was the possibility of a record contract. Oliver looked fondly at the fingers which had caressed the strings of his guitar and plucked the sounds which were at last receiving recognition.

Not that the money was anything much. And not that he cared about that. Nothing mattered so long as he could practise his art. He'd go on social security if the worst came to the worst. He'd survive. He'd win through.

As he walked towards the Harrow Road, the sounds he played reverberated within his skull and his left hand ran over an imaginary guitar. In a mere ten days he would be playing before the public. All those years of struggle, of bitterness and disillusionment hadn't been in vain after all. Oliver felt like smiling at the three men who were approaching. One of them was smiling slightly at him. Oliver grinned back amiably.

He stopped grinning when a steel-capped boot thudded into his testicles. Uttering a strangled gasp as the agony spread upwards through his guts, Oliver pitched forward onto the pavement. Someone grabbed him from behind and hauled him to his feet as though he was a rag doll. Still doubled up with the pain in his genitals, his mind one raging sea of fear, Oliver found himself shoved down steps into the deserted pedestrian subway and slammed against the tiled wall. One man held him fast. The second gripped his left wrist and held his hand steady. The third produced a length of lead piping.

Oliver emitted a piercing screech as the metal bar smashed against his hand and crunched the bones. He was conscious of nothing but the blinding pain which was greater than any he believed possible. Again the pipe whipped down and went *crunch* on his hand, shattering it into fragments of splintered bone. The victim writhed in speechless torment as the object struck a third time and pulverized his fingers into a throbbing pulp.

Oliver slid down the wall, moaning. The broken pulpy paw which had once been a hand would never again make music.

Just before he blacked out from the excruciating pain, he heard someone say: 'Who's laughing now?'

17

The man sat upon a lavatory seat, breathing heavily and squeezing his throbbing penis. It was in these private, sacred moments that he became most aware of the invisible forces which surrounded him and which he had invited to permeate his being. Below him, there seethed and festered the power which drove him on to the fulfilment of his lust. Above him was the force which had for so long oppressed his spirit, until that glorious moment when he had rebelled against its restraints. All around him was a thick fog of fear and frustration. Soon it would be darkened further by the spilling of a woman's blood.

'It's very kind of you to bring this in, Miss Spencer-Wingate.' Dexter regarded the package Fiona had placed upon his desk. 'Found in Sid Ingram's desk drawer, you say?'

'Yes,' Fiona told him proudly. 'I suppose he hid it there because it's such an obvious place, he didn't think anyone would bother to look. But I followed my nose, you see. I may be a bear of very little brain but I do believe in following my nose and here we are.'

'Open it up,' said Geale.

Dexter unwrapped the silver foil to reveal the short, sharp kitchen knife encrusted with crimson.

'I'd get finger-prints off that, if I were you,' said Fiona. 'And you'll probably find that the dried blood matches that of the deceased.'

Dexter and Geale pondered the knife in silence for a time then looked quizzically at one another.

'Are you thinking what I'm thinking?' asked Dexter.

'Yeah.' Fiona watched eagerly as Geale picked the knife up by the handle and sniffed the blade. 'Tomato ketchup,' he said disgustedly.

'If you don't mind,' Larry Cunningham said, 'I am going to be assertive.' Sid glowered at him. 'Um – if that's okay with you.'

'No,' said Sid, 'it's not.'

'Righty ho,' said Larry.

'There's nothing right about it,' Sid snapped. 'You promised me that the mechanical of the children's Kandy press ad would be here first thing this morning. It wasn't. You said it would be here an hour later. That was two hours ago. I've never known such inefficiency.' He restrained the urge to grab the Job Controller and shake him till his skull rattled. Last night with Harriet had been so wonderful that it had been an agony to drag himself out of her bed and go back to Gloria – who once again wasn't there. For the first time in a long time, Sid had felt really happy – but then it was back to the home he disliked, to the wife who gave him grief when she finally turned up at half-past one and to a job which made him want to scream. 'You're useless!' he shouted.

'Steady on,' Larry pleaded, 'look, I've got it here. On my desk. Came in five minutes ago and . . .'

'A-bout time!' Sid snatched up the mock-advertisement from the shambolic pile on Larry's desk and knocked over the Controller's brief-case. 'Sorry, squire,' he murmured casually as the case crashed to the floor and spewed out its contents – papers, memos, documents, files, transparencies and a paperback book entitled *Jack The Ripper*.

There was silence as Sid looked from *Jack The Ripper* to Larry Cunningham and from Larry Cunningham back to *Jack The Ripper*.

'Funny taste in reading you've got,' he commented.

'Oh – er – it's for the tube,' Larry answered with a nervous little laugh. 'I mean, it's topical, isn't it?'

'Muhammed Ali the greatest boxer of all time?' exclaimed Fred Sayers. 'Never. Joe Louis would've killed him. You see, Ali never knew what to do when a man had a good left jab. Ken Norton, Jimmy Young and our own 'Enery Cooper – beautiful, educated left hand, he had – they all gave him trouble.'

'Yes, but Jack Johnson had Louis right when he called him: "a mechanical fighter who won't know what to do when his plan of battle is upset",' Robert retorted. 'Look at the first Schmeling fight – and the one with Billy Conn. Louis couldn't've coped with Ali's speed of hand and foot, or with his tactical skills.' These days he was getting on very well with Fred, partly because he was always polite to the older man but mainly because they'd discovered a mutual passion for boxing. Classical music, Fred's other interest, was one of Robert's pleasures too, yet Robert tended to avoid that subject because the Despatch Manager clearly knew far more about it than he did. However, when it came to boxing, Robert would argue with anyone. 'Let's not forget,' he added, 'that Ali took a punch better. Louis was knocked down many more times.'

'Now, just a moment, Robert.' Fred lit a cigarette. 'You and me, we know our boxing. And I have respect for your opinion. *But* – and I'm warning you, what I'm about to say is a killer . . .'

'Express Delivery,' interrupted the British Telecom messenger who'd just walked in through the door. Fred signed the receipt and took the Jiffy bag.

'Damn, just when I was getting warmed up,' Fred remarked as the messenger left. 'Sorry, Robert, I'll have to handle this straight away – it's for The Chairman. He'll be wanting it immediately, he always does.' He glanced around the room but there were no despatch boys available. 'Double damn. Everyone's on the job or else skiving off.' He clicked his tongue with irritation. 'Nothing for it but to take it up myself.'

'Well, I'm going back upstairs right now,' said Robert. 'Seems pointless for both of us to make the journey. Give it to me and I'll get my secretary to deliver it.'

'That's very kind of you.' Fred regarded him appreciatively. 'You're right, there is no point in the two of us going up there. Just make sure The Chairman has it without delay.' He passed over the Jiffy bag. 'And be careful with it, won't you? It's been badly sealed and the top's coming apart. Thanks a lot, then – and we'll continue with our boxing next time.'

Robert went out to the lift, pressed the call button and received a mild electric shock. He swore automatically. It might be his imagination but they seemed to be occurring more often. Was there anything he could do about it? He could wear a glove, he supposed, but that seemed rather silly . . .

Stepping inside the lift, he felt the package and wondered what was inside and travelling to the Chairman. It seemed like books. He regarded the badly sealed bag and was strongly tempted to prise it open just to satisfy a mounting curiosity. After all, no one would know. And it would be fascinating to see just what sort of books Savage read.

On reaching the Account Management floor, he went straight to the lavatory and locked himself in a cubicle, where he carefully eased open the envelope. The contents comprised a compliments slip from Simpkin, Chatsoworth (Printers) Ltd, and two identical books bound in black leather. Both had been stamped in gold with the same title: *The Company Spirit*. John Savage.

Robert opened the book his Chairman had authored, flicked through a few pages, stopped, frowned and began to read with growing amazement and unease.

* * *

'So I spent nearly an hour in the loo, quite unable to believe my eyes,' Robert told Vickie later. 'I felt completely dazed and rather horrified. I knew that if the books went on to Savage, no one would believe what I'd read. So I slipped down to Photo-Copying, duplicated certain passages, repacked the Jiffy bag and had Harriet deliver it.'

'But what *is* this book?' Vickie demanded impatiently.

'Listen to this.' He looked down at his stack of photocopied pages. '"The Company, not the nation or the family, is the prime unit of the modern age. In Law, this is acknowledged, in that the Company is a separate legal person."' Vickie nodded. '"But,"' Robert continued to read, '"the Company is also a unique spiritual entity,"'

'What does he mean by that?'

'"Psychologists",' Robert read, '"have been compelled by the facts to treat of crowd behaviour as though a crowd was more than simply a group of individuals. Philosophers of fascist persuasion have perceived the State as an organism, a living being of greater value than the sum of individuals who comprise it. These examples convey the essence of the idea, though it is worth noting that in the modern era of multi-national corporations, many of whose budgets far exceed those of small nations, the age of the nation-state is dead. Today, the Company is the one entity capable of being greater than the sum of its parts".'

'I don't like the sound of that at all,' she commented. 'But I've heard things like it before.'

'Wait, there's more to come. "To employ a metaphor: one might say that a Company's body consists of its assets, its premises and its people while its character is shaped by the nature of its work, the relations with other companies into which it enters and the personalities of its employees. The head of a Company sometimes chooses to leave it at that, in which case the Company is merely a place of work and such spirit as there is develops haphazardly. Such leadership lacks all foresight and creativity and demonstrates a failure to grasp this essential truth: *though the Company partakes of and manifests itself in individuals, the individual qua individual is of no importance at all*. The growth and development of a healthy company spirit requires intelligent guidance. *For the strongest spirit is created by the subsuming of individual wills within the Company's identity*."'

'That's horrible,' said Vickie. 'But thank God it's easier said than done.'

'Is it? Listen. "Human beings, like all mammals, seek pleasure and endeavour to avoid pain. Human action is motivated by a desire for reward or a fear of punishment. Through the intelligent application of reward and punishment stimuli, a human being can be conditioned into virtually any required pattern of behaviour.

'"It is vital to bear this in mind when considering the following question: how is the individual human will to be broken into the ethos of the Company?

'"This is a particularly complex problem since if a Company is to prosper economically, it must recruit individuals of high intelligence, great ability and much strength of character. Such individuals are likely to resist the diminishing of their identities.

'"The first method is that of reward. The individual must be shown that obedience to the Company results in monetary gain, status, material comfort and the approval of superiors.

'"The second method is that of punishment. The individual must perceive that a failure to conform will result in humiliation, the disapproval of his superiors, peers and inferiors, demotion and even the loss of his place within the Company.

'"An essential tactic here is the deliberate use of frustration, which is invaluable for sapping the individual will and convincing each employee that he is impotent in the face of the Company Spirit. There are a number of ways in which this can be done:-

'"(1) Through the employment of mediocrities and time-servers who frustrate the able.

'"(2) Through the use of injustice. The strong can be frustrated through calculated promotion of the weak.

'"(3) Through inequality. It is frustrating for a man to know he is superior in ability to his boss and yet have to take orders from him.

'"(4) Through bureaucracy. It is frustrating to have to conform to complex and pointless procedures.

'"(5) Through sexuality. It is distinctly advantageous to employ seductive females whilst forbidding sexual advances, for this creates a continuous state of tension in an individual and renders him yet more open to manipulation.

'"(6) Through an onslaught on individual integrity. All qualities of character which keep an individual separate from the Company must be identified and destroyed. Examples: a pacifist should be made to sell armaments; a socialist must work for the Conservative party; a teetotaller must encourage others to drink alcohol . . ."'

'And an idealist should be made to sell cancer to kids,' Vickie completed the sentence. 'I don't know if I can take any more of this.'

'All right, I'll just give you the conclusion. "One looks forward to the day when employees will live in homes provided by the Company with wives chosen for them by the Company and their every action dictated to them by the Company spirit. There will be one way of life, one state of being and one mode of acting, all to the greater glory of the Company, as the ignorant many are wisely directed by the appointed few."'

'Ugh!' Vickie lit a cigarette. 'That confirms every horrible suspicion I've ever had about your company. Only . . .' she paused momentarily, 'only I had no idea just how intensely evil, how callously deliberate everything was.'

'You can see why I was so shattered when I read it?'

'Yes.'

'Well, that's it,' said Robert. 'I'm leaving Savage & Markby.'

'Thank God,' Vickie breathed, then took him in her arms and hugged him. 'Thank God. If you'd gone on the way you were going, there's no way we would've lasted.'

'I know.' He kissed her. 'Tomorrow I resign.'

'Oh,' Vickie drew back, 'd'you think that's the best way to play it?'

'I've got to get out.'

'But where will you go?'

'I'll get another job.'

'Yes.' She looked thoughtful. 'But I really wouldn't leave Savage & Markby until you've landed it. Let's face it, we need the money. So use them and don't let them use you.'

'Hmm.' He frowned. 'That's a very good point. But I'll start looking for another job first thing tomorrow. Christ!' he shook his head ruefully, 'to think I was becoming so corrupted I was prepared to work happily on Kandy. Thank heavens I've woken up in time. I was turning into a sleepwalker, just like the other zombies there. You must've found me unbearable.' He kissed her again. 'Let's go away this weekend.'

'The country?' Vickie suggested eagerly.

'Definitely – and somewhere wild and unspoiled. I'm in need of some natural sanity.'

Some miles away, a man was sharpening a steel knife. Every time he drew the shining blade through the sharpener, there was a hiss as he sucked saliva through his teeth.

18

The following morning saw Cliff Mitchell surprise a number of people by nonchalantly turning up to work. He'd been released on bail, he explained, pending the jury trial on drugs charges for which he'd asked and which, he insisted, would find him Not Guilty. A few believed in his innocence, though these did not include the dozen people who scored dope from him on a regular basis – though they sincerely hoped he'd get off. Others shunned him and one or two were sure that he was the murderer.

'I can't understand it,' he told the despatch boys who'd come to visit him in Photo-Copying. 'I've never hurt a woman in my life. I used to get my kicks out of them hurting me, I admit that. But the police have got it all completely cock-eyed. I reckon they're really stupid.'

'Stupid?' queried Geale who'd just slouched into the room with Dexter. 'We'll see just who's stupid.'

'Good morning once again,' Dexter smiled at Cliff. 'You're on a murder charge.'

Hugh Vincent Markby heard about the arrest of Cliff when he was taking morning coffee in his office. The news came as a great relief to him. He found the idea of a sexual murder at Savage & Markby almost too appalling to contemplate. It was a dreadful advertisement for the Company, he felt, though at least the police had moved with laudable speed and caught the culprit – for Markby had no doubt that Cliff was guilty. He'd never liked him and would've been happy if Cliff was hanged. As it was, the youth would be caged and, with luck, for life. That was something – but it really was a pity that the trial couldn't be conducted in secret. The publicity would do the firm no good at all.

There was also the matter of the drugs charge. Cliff had been accused of possession of a large quantity of cannabis resin with intent to supply. To whom did he intend to supply it? The obvious inference was that Savage & Markby employees were buying and imbibing illegal narcotic substances. Which ones? Markby intended to conduct a secret and thorough investigation of the question and at its conclusion, heads would roll.

All the same, it was worrying to learn that the Company had harboured not only a particularly disgusting murderer but also a group of drug-taking degenerates. No, Markby wasn't happy with the recent turn of events. Take the case of Peter Jackson, for instance. The Vice-Chairman could see how the affable and bureaucratic Managing Director fitted perfectly into Savage's scheme and frustrated everyone with his sprawling and growing empire of committees. He could understand how he himself could benefit by it, for while Peter administered, chaired and co-ordinated, Markby was quietly insinuating himself into the good graces of the clients Peter had brought from Brady & Harding. If the Managing Director went, his accounts would stay. Yet wasn't Peter nevertheless going completely over the top?

The man had originally struck Markby as being a clever, cautious and adroit politician. Now he was behaving like an industrious lunatic and the drinking was totally out of control. Was Peter heading for an alcoholic psychosis? That had been the fate of Nick Peters too and was too much of a coincidence for comfort. Had Savage deliberately planned that and if so, why? Somehow it didn't quite fit in with the views expressed in *The Company Spirit*, a copy of which had been presented to Markby yesterday.

The Vice-Chairman had greatly enjoyed the book, though most of it covered familiar ground. Provided that he remained the Chairman's deputy, Markby was perfectly happy to try and bring about a totalitarian control over the lives of the Company's individuals. The exercise brought him great intellectual and emotional satisfaction in addition to the wealth, comfort and status he craved. There was a joy in attaining complete control of another's life. Which was why there was cause for considerable concern when things seemed to be slipping *out of control*.

Should he discuss his fears with Savage? As usual, the Chairman appeared unaffected by the events he observed with such detached interest. What went on in that computer he called a brain? What did Savage do when he wasn't at Savage & Markby? Twice in his life, Markby had been to the Chairman's Belgravia house – it was in a street so quiet that even one's own footsteps seemed muffled – and there had been given dinner and general conversation about the Company. The only new fact he'd learned was that Savage liked severely geometric abstract painting – otherwise the Chairman had given nothing away.

The trouble was that if Markby proceeded to discuss his apprehensions, he'd be tempted into voicing his gravest concern of all – and that would never do. Savage would think that his deputy had gone off his head altogether and perhaps cast around for a replacement. The Vice-Chairman wiped droplets of perspiration from his brow and then attended to the sweat which had congealed in his moustache. For he'd heard that Sandra Lang had been seen in the building.

Maud Bunting and Harriet Baker – both as sensible as he supposed a female could be – claimed that they'd glimpsed Sandra walking through a corridor. There was no motive for lying that Markby could discern, since both girls believed that the former executive was still alive and well. They knew nothing of the measures he'd taken in consultation with Savage to ensure the absence of scandal – and the Chairman had found the matter highly amusing. A headless Sandra Lang was now lying in the Thames somewhere and so couldn't possibly have been seen in the agency.

Markby wished he could stop sweating whenever he thought of the bitch. Naturally she was dead and ghosts do not exist.

But how come two people had seen her?

'I know your type,' Geale said contemptuously. 'So I wouldn't try denying it if I were you.'

'This is ridiculous,' Cliff protested. 'We've been through all this before.' He wondered if he was going mad. This couldn't be happening – the bare, white walls, the harsh, yellow light, the stench of sweat and stale cigarette butts and the accusation of sexual murder. 'I tell you, you've got it all wrong.'

'Where were you at the time?'

'I've already told you hundreds of times. I was enjoying a bit of peace and quiet in the basement room.' Cliff wondered how long he could hold out without naming Charles. Originally, there'd been no problem. Charles couldn't help him over the drug bust and there was no way he'd shop somebody he liked to the pigs. But now, he might have to do it, for Charles was the only one who could confirm his alibi. There might be no alternative – but he wasn't giving up without making life as difficult for the police as he could. 'It's nice in that room,' he continued dully. 'You can do a good bit of reading down there.'

'Yeah, and I know what you read.' Geale leaned forward across the table. Cliff could smell stewed tea on his breath. '*Punished In Silk*,' he spat the title with disgust, '*The Enslavement of Anton, Beneath Her Bottom, Petticoat Power* and *The Secretary Tames The Boss*. You revolt me. I feel sick just looking at you.'

Makes two of us, Cliff thought. *You let me go and then arrested me again just to be nasty*.

'You don't understand, do you?' said Cliff. 'That's proof that I'm not into doing women. I'm into women doing me.'

'You're a pervert,' snapped Geale, 'and a wanker. That's why you have to get back at women, 'cos they don't want you and face it, who would? What did you do with the knife?'

'What knife?'

'Clever bastard, aren't you?'

'This is crazy,' said Cliff.

'Crazy, that's right. That's what you are. And if you don't confess to what you've done, I'm going to drive you even crazier. Far as I'm concerned, you're just dirt,' snarled Geale and stormed out of the room. Moments later, Dexter ambled in with two steaming mugs of black coffee.

'You poor sod,' he told Cliff sympathetically. 'He's really in one of his moods today. Surprising you didn't get a hiding, really.' Cliff swallowed. 'Didn't know how you liked your coffee so I put one sugar in it.' The accused drank gratefully. 'So let's talk this through calmly, shall we? And don't think I don't understand. These girls today, they really lead you on, don't they?'

'Which is more than I can say of you,' Cliff retorted. 'We're not going through all that again, are we? You blokes really know how to waste other people's time. Before you ask me, here's the answer. I was sitting in the basement room at the time.'

'Ah.' Dexter nodded as though Cliff hadn't said that before. 'Don't suppose there's anyone who could confirm that, is there?'

'No,' said Cliff, 'I was on my own.'

There was a knock at the door. A woman police constable entered and held a whispered consultation with Dexter, who looked surprised and promptly rose.

'Enjoy your coffee,' he told Cliff. 'We've just found proof that you're a liar.'

'Let's get this right, sir,' Dexter said to Charles Sutherland a few minutes later. 'You allege that you were having a chat in the basement room with the accused from five to one till just past one.'

'Absolutely,' Charles returned. 'It's why he couldn't possibly have committed the crime with which he's been charged. That's why I'm here, officer. I came the instant I heard the news about Mr Mitchell's arrest.'

'I see.' Dexter nodded. 'The one thing I don't see is why he hasn't mentioned you. He claims he was there on his own.'

'Well, let's face it, officer,' Charles answered easily, 'we were both skiving off for a few minutes. I suppose he thought that if that came to light, I'd be in trouble or something.'

'Skiving off's not a crime, though, is it, sir?' Dexter scratched his head. 'Sorry, sir, I'm finding it hard to make sense of all this.'

'Oh? What's the problem?' But Dexter had risen and was leaving the room. Moments later, Geale came in and introduced himself.

'What my colleague and I find hard to understand,' he told Charles, 'is what you – a twenty-seven year old man and an Account Supervisor – were doing in a darkened basement room with the photo-copying boy.'

'Having a chat,' said Charles. 'I'd have a chat with anyone I liked. Mr Mitchell's quite an interesting chap.'

'Public school, aren't you?' asked Geale.

'Yes, what's that got to do with it?'

'I've been told that people get up to funny things at those places,' Geale remarked casually. 'All those boys together. Gives some people a taste for boys even years after.'

'Now look here,' snapped Charles, 'just what the devil are you insinuating?'

'Don't give me any of that self-righteous indignation,' Geale sneered. 'I've met your sort before. Are you seriously expecting me to believe that you found the conversation of an eighteen year old machine-watcher so fascinating and riveting that you accompanied him to a darkened room in order to hear more of it?'

'Yes,' said Charles

'Don't make me laugh,' said Geale.

'I'm not prepared to be insulted like this,' Charles told him angrily. 'I came here to do my bit as a concerned and law-abiding citizen. Well, quite frankly, your attitude disappoints me greatly and I'm leaving.'

'We haven't finished yet.'

'I have,' said Charles. 'Are you preferring any charges against me?'

'Not yet,' Geale answered, 'not yet.'

'Then unless you arrest me, I believe I'm within my legal rights to walk out of here any time I choose.' He rose. 'Good day.' Charles took two strides towards the door but Geale had risen also and blocked his exit.

'Sit down,' ordered the policeman.

'I would leave,' Charles replied with quiet dignity, 'but you bar my path illegally.'

'I said, sit down. Oops! Sorry,' Geale murmured as Charles reeled back into his seat, doubled up and clutching his groin. 'Old war wound. Makes my knee jerk sometimes. Haven't hurt you, have I? My, my, you public schoolboys are a right bunch of softies. To resume,' he sat down opposite Charles who was still clutching his testicles through his trousers, 'what were you doing in the dark with the boy?'

'This,' Mike told the men in Conference Room One, 'will be the last time we meet before the New Year. By then, I want everything sewn up on Kandy apart from the final details of the presentation. What's the status of the TV commercials, Ian?' But although Mike looked alert while Ian Sharpe talked, he was only listening with half an ear. The fact remained that he felt crippled by his uncharacteristic indecisiveness. Ian had agreed that their position regarding Kandy was intolerable yet had come up with nothing better than Georgina's idea of playing along with the situation whilst looking for another job and waiting for a moment when the tables could be turned. That was all very well but no jobs had come up and Mike couldn't see a way of turning the tables. What did the phrase mean, anyway? What was he supposed to do? How the hell did one even begin to get at Savage?

Should he tell the other members of the team about the true nature of Kandy? Mike felt he could predict their respective reactions. Tony Westbury, Ronald Potter and Paul Adams wouldn't be bothered in the least. Craig Anderson and Sid Ingram would be made to feel thoroughly guilty and uncomfortable but they'd eventually go along with it. Dennis Wilson and Simon Burns would probably experience a certain cynical glee – and that might be the case with Charles Sutherland too, though one could never tell what he really thought. Where was the man, anyway? Missing an important meeting like this was inexcusable.

So what would be gained by talking to his team about his own reaction to Kandy? Precious little. There'd just be a slump in morale and Savage would accuse him of deliberate subversion. One result was that Mike would probably be fired from the account and replaced by Chris Faye. That was absolutely fine – but he'd probably be fired from the Company too and, given what had happened to those who had left, that was hardly an appealing prospect.

Ian Sharpe, Mike knew, was in exactly the same dilemma. What was it that Savage was trying to do to the pair of them? And what was his motive? How could Mike strike back? – or was that kind of talk merely immature and idealistic nonsense? Take Robert Slade, for instance, who was sitting at the end of the table and looking bright. He'd given up his ideals pretty fast when offered the prospect of advancement. There was something pretty nauseating about that – or was Robert the potentially dazzling success whilst Mike's fate was to fail on account of useless and lingering ideals?

'Thank you, Ian,' Mike said as the Assistant Creative Director finished his report. 'Good to know it's all under control. How about the Media side, Craig?'

Robert looked alert while Craig Anderson talked but was only listening with half an ear. How could the men around him acquiesce to being a part of the vileness revealed in Savage's *The Company Spirit*? They had no idea what was happening to them. All right, Mike Armstrong was fundamentally decent but that decency was being calculatingly corrupted and the Account Management Director seemed unable to cope with it. Tony Westbury was fitting in perfectly – did the man have a soul at all? Charles Sutherland was out for himself, Robert reasoned, but how long would that last – and where was he, anyway? Sid Ingram looked tired and fed up – a victim of the frustration employed deliberately by the Chairman. Craig Anderson should've been a University professor – but the rewards of commerce had tempted him into planning the best method of selling cancer. Paul Adams hardly seemed human at all – a programmed zombie just like Ronald Potter. Ian Sharpe? Robert couldn't work him out – but he saw a future of degeneration and miserable conformity for the would-be anarchists, Dennis and Simon.

Well, Robert would be out of this sickening stew soon. A dozen job applications had gone off before lunch, all written on Savage & Markby paper and posted at the

Company's expense. Meanwhile, though, there was this mad desire to tear the corporation apart. Just before this meeting, he made more photo-copies of the extracts from *The Company Spirit* – he was risking running out of tales for the hateful Duplication Forms. On the day he left the Company, Robert would distribute the truth about it to every other employee. Who knew what might happen when the staff realized what was being done to them? Robert had had the odd fantasy about a sudden lynching of Savage.

'. . . if you've got that, Robert,' Mike Armstrong was saying.

'Sorry?'

'I asked,' Mike shot Robert the annoyed glance he always gave people who caused him to repeat himself, 'for the set of Account Management Press Briefs to Creative.'

'Oh, of course. My apologies.' Robert fumbled in his brief-case, pulled out the requisite documents – and accidentally flipped *The Company Spirit* sheets he'd duplicated onto the floor. He darted for them instantly but his haste upset his case, the contents of which spilled out onto *The Company Spirit* photo-copies and were joined an instant later by the Account Management Press Briefs his agitated hands knocked off the table. Sid Ingram swooped instantly onto the pile of paper and tried to help Robert by sorting them into some sort of order as the Company's Senior Assistant Account Executive knelt beside him on the floor and tried frantically to retrieve his papers.

'Don't worry, squire,' Sid said reassuringly, 'I think I've got what's needed.' Robert flushed furiously as Sid handed a pile of papers to Mike. 'Should be all there.'

'Seems to be.' Mike flipped through the sheets Sid had passed him, mentally criticized Robert for his unprofessional clumsiness, wondered why he'd looked so flustered just then – and froze as he came to a page headed *The Company Spirit*. What was this? "All qualities of character which keep an individual separate from the Company must be identified and destroyed," Mike read silently and his eyes widened in astonishment. 'This looks rather interesting,' he commented to Robert, who blushed again. 'I'll keep it by me, if you don't mind, and we'll have a chat about it afterwards.'

Robert nodded awkwardly as Mike's eyes seemed to drill through his own to the back of his skull.

19

Shortly before Christmas, a man lay on a bed with a sharp knife in one hand and a stiff, spindly penis in the other. When he came to orgasm, he cut his own thigh, dipped his finger in the blood, mixed it with the semen he'd spilled and licked up the resulting cocktail.

'Georgina,' he crooned softly, 'soon you will be mine.'

Yet life at Savage & Markby was gradually returning to normal now that Cliff Mitchell had been arrested, charged with Murder and remanded in custody. Once again, women could feel safe in the Company corridors and offices – though the progress of the case against Cliff was naturally the talk of the agency. It was learned, for example, that the accused was being represented by Milton, Goddard, Fletcher (Solicitors), who had always acted for the wealthy Sutherland family, that this firm had briefed Sir Reginald Barham QC to conduct the case for the Defence and that Charles Sutherland or his family would apparently be footing the bill. Charles's reasons for this were a mystery to most – and then people heard that the Account Supervisor was suing the Metropolitan Police for Assault Occasioning Actual Bodily Harm.

Yet more was revealed when Cliff's lawyers challenged the Director of Public Prosecutions at first instance and fought the committal before a magistrate on the grounds that there was no case to answer. The consequent hearing took several days, was fully reported in the press and occasioned a plague of absenteeism from the office, particularly when Charles was cross-examined as a witness. He claimed that he and Cliff had been chatting innocently in the basement room where Cliff, for his own reasons, was sometimes to be found. It was put to him by the Prosecution that he was there for the purpose of enjoying illegal sexual relations with Cliff, which Charles denied. Charles also denied visiting Cliff for the purpose of purchasing illegal narcotic drugs. He furthermore denied the suggestion that he shared the accused's passion for sado-masochistic pornography, which passion had prompted his acquaintanceship with the accused. However, despite these denials, Charles returned to the office on the following day to find himself transferred to the post of Supervisor on Piddling whilst a jubilant Roy Price replaced him on every account except – on Mike's insistence – Kandy.

The hearing dragged on. The Prosecution claimed that the murder of Belinda Torrance had been committed with the short, sharp kitchen knife which Fiona Spencer-Wingate had found in Sid Ingram's desk and which, when examined, turned out to have the finger-prints of not only Fiona and Sid, but Cliff. Sid had to go into the witness box and explain that he and Cliff had shared the knife while spreading tomato ketchup on the fish-paste sandwiches they'd shared one lunch-time when they'd had a friendly chat. He then returned to the agency and was put on Slims cigarettes, the extra work on which made it difficult to get home before ten at night.

Cliff's collection of pornography and photos of Belinda were exhibited in court. It was probably on account of this that the magistrate ruled there was a case to answer and committed Cliff Mitchell for trial by jury at the Old Bailey. Many members of staff went away convinced that the accused was guilty. Meanwhile, the photo-copying machine broke down continuously, refused to respond to treatment by every single one of Cliff's successors, and attacked its users with a spewing of paper and a squirting of ink.

However, despite the unpleasantness of December, the Savage & Markby Annual Christmas Party went ahead on the 20th as planned. It was held at the spanking new Regal, the flag-ship of Pawson's Hotels, and all who attended agreed that it was better than last year. The Company sat down to lettuce in tomato ketchup and salad cream in which the odd prawn could be discerned, rubber turkey with all the tasteless trimmings and a heavy and sodden Christmas Pudding with lukewarm custard. There were three glasses of Trowbridge, Benson & Mirabel red Vin de Table for every employee, though one could of course buy more drink if one thought that allowance insufficient.

After dinner, there were speeches, with prizes and presentations. The Trophy for the Most Efficient Department was collected by Chris Faye on behalf of Media, whose members all received a ten pound voucher for P & Q Grocery Stores. Tony Westbury received the gold cup Savage had donated for Outstanding Individual Executive Achievement and the raffle was won by Stanley Haynes.

Afterwards, there was music and dancing and a good time was allegedly had by all, though there was the odd incident that's inevitable at these affairs. Simon Burns pinched the bottom of Fiona Spencer-Wingate and had his face slapped, Perkins of PR got drunk and punched Martin Bottomley – but otherwise everyone behaved. Peter Jackson was moved to interrupt the dancing and make a second speech, in which he observed how gratifying it was in the Season of Goodwill to witness everyone looking so happy. He felt in his heart of hearts, he declared, that Savage & Markby was not just a company: it was a community, and he earnestly hoped that all present would go home tonight with a song of gladness upon their lips.

Robert did not go home with a song of gladness upon his lips. After leaving the party, he did not even go home.

As arranged, he walked around the block and took a taxi to an address just off the King's Road, where he was admitted by Ian Sharpe and conducted into the stylish living room of Ian's flat. Mike Armstrong and Georgina Mainwaring were sitting together on the sofa and sipping wine. On the table in front of Ian was a mirror, a razor blade, an aluminium tube and a phial of white crystals.

'Enjoy the party?' asked Mike.

'It was ghastly,' said Robert and everyone murmured assent.

'Well, here's a way of cheering oneself up,' said Ian, who was chopping the crystals. 'I know Mike doesn't but perhaps you and Georgina would like to join me?'

'I like it occasionally,' Georgina replied while Robert nodded happily.

'I like it but I can't afford it,' he said. 'But I really could do with some after tonight. I found myself just sitting there and thinking: what the hell am I *doing* here?'

'Aren't you wondering what the hell you're doing *here*?' Mike queried affably.

When Mike had first spoken to Robert about the photo-copies of *The Company Spirit*, Robert had fully expected to be fired. Instead, Mike had become increasingly quiet and thoughtful and had asked for more.

'It's worse than I thought in my wildest nightmares,' he'd muttered. 'Look, Robert, don't say anything about this to anybody just yet – it's very difficult to know who can be trusted, but I think we're on the same side here. There're just one or two people who should be in on this.' Which was why Robert was now at Ian's flat with Mike and Georgina.

'We know why we're here,' Robert said. 'We can't stand Savage & Markby. We believe that its philosophy is evil. We loathe the way in which Savage experiments on us as though we were rats. That's why we're on Kandy – so our integrity will be corrupted. We don't like it, we resent being shat upon . . .'

'And we'd like to do something back,' finished Mike.

'One quick point,' Georgina came in as Ian arranged the cocaine into three long lines. 'I'm here because I believe in the existence of evil and in the necessity of resisting it. But, you see, I've got nothing to lose. I'm leaving the Company the day after tomorrow. Financially, I've got no worries. I can afford a battle in whatever form it takes – but what about you? Quite frankly, I'm not sure if it's worth risking your careers and your potential for what might be a lost cause.'

'The individual's not a lost cause,' said Mike.

'No,' she answered, 'but don't ruin yourself.'

'I don't think that'll be the case,' Mike stated thoughtfully. 'Something happened to me today which I've saved till now. Jones, Moran, Bathurst have offered me the Managing Directorship at the same salary I've got here.'

'Mike!' Georgina exclaimed. 'That's wonderful! Congratulations.' She accepted Ian's invitation and sniffed a line of cocaine. 'So there really is something to celebrate tonight.'

'Certainly congratulations.' Ian sniffed his line. 'But please excuse my ignorance – I've never heard of Jones, Moran, Bathurst.'

'Nobody in London has,' Mike answered. 'They're a Birmingham firm. One of the major Midlands agencies and profitable with it. There's no glamour involved in going there but it's back to my roots, I suppose,' he continued, rather as though, Robert thought, he was trying to convince himself. 'Anyhow, it'll be better than Savage & Markby where they try to turn you into a programmed zombie. So I'm now pretty well placed for a turning of the tables. How about you, Ian?'

'I've made my own arrangements,' Ian returned enigmatically. 'I wouldn't care to say anything more than that for the present – except that I'm keen on hitting back at

Savage.' He passed the mirror to Robert. 'How about you?'

'I've landed an interview at Wilde & Latchford,' Robert told them, then sniffed up his line. There was a general chorus of congratulations. 'Obviously I might not get the job but then I'll try again somewhere else. The fact is that I can't stand the Company much longer, I think Savage is totally evil and I want to strike back.'

'We all do,' Ian observed and poured red wine for everyone. 'We all want to hit Savage & Markby without getting hit. The question is – how?'

'Well, if everybody's agreed on that basic principle, I've got an idea,' Mike announced. 'I warn you, this may sound too extreme and at times I wonder at myself for considering it seriously. For all I know, you won't want to have anything to do with it . . .'

'Mike,' said Georgina, 'cut the waffling and get on with it.'

Robert strode jauntily into work at noon the following day and set about his first task with enthusiasm. Last night's meeting had gone well and everyone had agreed that Mike's idea, though bizarre, was excellent – though afterwards Vickie had advised Robert to be very careful indeed. Then this morning Robert had rung Savage & Markby with some excuse about a doctor's appointment and gone off to his interview at Wilde & Latchford. There he'd had three interviews, the last being with Mr Latchford himself and departed feeling that he'd given a very good account of himself.

For Robert definitely wanted to stay in advertising. The higher one rose, the more exciting the work became – what he needed was a decent employer and Mr Latchford had struck him as being precisely that. The most difficult question to field and one in which Harry Latchford had shown particular interest, was why Robert wanted to leave Savage & Markby after so short a time. Robert had handled it by being as honest as he could. He explained that he was unhappy about working on Kandy, given the Swiss and Swedish reports, that Savage & Markby frowned upon resigning from an account on grounds of conscience and that given that, he didn't feel he had a satisfactory future there. Latchford had listened with sympathetic attention and at one point had asked where his acquaintance Mike Armstrong stood on the matter. Robert replied that he didn't know. Latchford carried on asking questions and continued to appear quite pleased with Robert's answers.

There is always a joy in feeling one has shone at an interview but even that feeling was perhaps insufficient to explain why Robert addressed himself to the job in hand with such alacrity and high spirits. After all, the task in itself would have struck an observer as being mundane in the extreme, consisting as it did of filling out a Job Control Brief on Kandy.

There was nothing unusual about what he wrote. The budget consisted of ten thousand pounds to be charged to the client for revisions on Kandy TV commercial K2 – GR1549Q – on which Ian Sharpe was the Assistant Creative Director. After Robert had filled out the form, he went to see Georgina, who immediately ushered him into Mike's office where the Director of Account Management authorized the expense with his signature. Robert then took the brief down to Larry Cunningham, who filed it in the normal way, and later undertook the routine procedure of sending a photo-copy to Accounts.

Nobody thought of asking Robert why he was smiling so much that day.

'I almost wish I could be there when it happens,' Georgina remarked to Mike that evening, when she'd invited him to dinner at the house she'd inherited. Everything about the home – the Regency exterior, the William Morris wall-paper, the Hepplewhite furniture, the Adam fireplace, even the Edwardian silver dining-service – was touched by artistry and grace. 'Still, I shouldn't be complaining that it's my last day at the agency tomorrow.'

'I'll miss you,' murmured Mike, then tried the home-made fish soup. 'Mmm. Delicious.'

'Thanks, it's a recipe of my late aunt.' She offered him a freshly baked brown roll. 'I'll miss you, Mike. It's been great working for you – which is partly why I'm so glad you've found yourself another job. You deserve something better than Savage & Markby. God, I can barely believe that the Chairman's so obscenely frightful.'

'Have you found out anything more about him?' Mike asked while his eyes cast a lingering and longing look at Georgina. Tonight she was wearing a simple, backless dress in black, which discreetly exposed her delectable cleavage.

'I've made every possible enquiry,' she answered soberly. 'I've even gone to see my uncle – you know, the one who's a Junior Minister. It's always the same story. Absolutely zilch is known about John Savage prior to 1955 and no one's got a clue where his wealth came from.'

'One could look up his birth certificate, I suppose,' said Mike. 'At least that'd tell us something.'

'That's been done,' she replied, 'for a variety of reasons. No such certificate exists – so he probably wasn't born in this country at all. That's quite a relief, really, in a way, don't you think?'

'How d'you mean?'

'Well,' Georgina poured more wine for both of them, 'there's something about him – and certainly about his philosophy – that's awfully un-English, if you see what I mean.'

'I think so.' Mike gazed appreciatively into her azure eyes.

'You will be careful, Mike, won't you?' she said with concern.

'Of course I'll be careful. And anyway, what can he do to me?'

'I don't know.' She sipped her wine and stretched out a leg which brushed against Mike's. 'Sorry.' She withdrew it but only by an inch. 'I just have this feeling that if you tangle with Savage, you could find yourself in terrible danger. One could die, even – or maybe I'm being unjust to him. Anyway, there are worse things than dying.'

'There are?' He suppressed the desire to rise and kiss her soft lips. 'What's worse than death?'

'I think quite a number of things are.' She frowned. 'It may sound terrible to say this, but I'd be more comfortable seeing a dead body than a broken spirit. God, what a morbid conversation we seem to be having! How was the soup?'

'Absolutely delicious, thanks.'

'There's more.'

'I'd love more but I'd better not. I want to have room for the next course.'

'Wait until you see it. It may be so dreadful, you won't want it.' She rose.

'Highly unlikely,' said Mike as she came round to him with her skirt swishing about her knees and took his bowl. Their eyes locked. Mike stood up slowly, still staring intently at Georgina, took her in his arms and overcome by his desire, kissed her. Her lips parted to admit his tongue, her hand put the bowl back upon the table, her arms wound themselves around him and she pressed her hips against his throbbing and rampaging hardness.

Robert sat uneasily in Laura's office the following morning and wondered why on earth the Vice-Chairman had summoned him. It couldn't be his dress – today a dark grey suit. It couldn't be for praise – he'd had more than his fair share of that recently. Since he'd so far been kept waiting ten minutes, that probably meant trouble – but what had he done that was wrong? Well, a couple of things if the truth was known – but how could it be?

'Mr Markby will see you now,' said Laura, just as he was lighting a second cigarette. Robert occasionally wondered if Laura was actually a woman at all. She always remained so completely impersonal that she might've been a robot. Stubbing out his cigarette, Robert rose and entered the Vice-Chairman's office.

The first thing he noticed was that Markby's attention was devoted not to his visitor but to something he was writing. The second thing was the absence of a chair.

'Come here,' Markby murmured without looking up. Robert had no alternative other than crossing the room and standing awkwardly in front of Markby's desk like a schoolboy in disgrace before the Headmaster.

'I gather you've had an interview with Wilde & Latchford,' Markby said softly. Robert couldn't help the sudden widening of his eyes, twitching of his face or churning of anxiety within his guts. In God's name, how did Markby know? 'Weren't you aware,' Markby suddenly looked at him contemptuously, 'that Wilde & Latchford is owned by the Chairman?'

Robert's jaw dropped as his shoulders slumped. He felt like a balloon that had suddenly lost its lifting margin of gas and sagged in a sad, crumpling heap.

'Here's a copy of the letter of rejection you'll be receiving from them.' Markby handed over a brief note which Robert had to take. 'The fact is that your job is here. It's here until we decide otherwise. So go away,' the Vice-Chairman sighed condescendingly, 'and don't be such a silly little boy in the future.'

'We have reached,' the Chairman declared later in Room One, 'a fairly critical point in the Company's evolution. I think it's time we identified those individuals who are obstinately refusing to conform to our ethos and took steps to deal with their recalcitrance.'

'Quite so.' Markby sipped from his china cup of Lapsang Souchong tea – served, as always without milk or sugar – and sat up attentively. He had always enjoyed these sessions of deciding other people's destinies.

'So in your opinion, which members of staff require our attention?'

'Ian Sharpe,' Markby responded immediately. 'He's motivated by self rather than the Company and has been getting away with too much for too long.'

'Interesting.' Savage smiled faintly. 'Interesting that he's your first choice. One wonders why. Oh, you're quite right, of course. Originally I had hoped we could lead him in gently but it appears he's rather too independent-minded.'

'I don't think he'll bend.' Markby nibbled at a cucumber sandwich. 'Those who won't bend must be broken.'

'Precisely,' said Savage. 'Get me every item of data on Sharpe. This one will have to be managed with some subtlety. Who else?'

'Mike Armstrong?' Markby suggested hopefully.

'Not yet,' returned Savage. 'I intend to keep watching him. A number of alternatives are possible here. We've got him scared and it's always curious to witness which way a scared cat jumps. I'm rather hoping that Kandy will make him more amenable and then – who knows? He might be a candidate for the Managing Directorship.'

'I presume that Nigel Fulton and others of his ilk can stay,' Markby said. 'They appear to be causing just the right amount of dissatisfaction.'

'Exactly. And Fred Sayers continues to merit being left alone along with people like him. They're submissive, they do their jobs and they show everyone that the Company takes good care of you.'

'What about Roy Price?' Markby enquired. 'It was obvious he was trying to recover his position through being a sycophant of Peter Jackson's. There he was, sitting hopefully on all those committees and following Peter around like a shorn little lamb – and sure enough, there was Peter recommending Roy. But I'm surprised you went along with that.'

'It was appropriate,' said Savage. 'It was time we had Charles Sutherland standing in the corner with his trousers round his ankles so Roy had to be moved. He's had a big boost going back to important accounts. He feels he's rising once again.'

'I don't quite see the reasoning behind that one, I'm afraid. Surely you're not suggesting that Roy should climb back to Account Director?'

'Certainly not,' Savage answered crisply. 'The first mistake he makes, he'll be sent back to Piddling. That should do the trick. Anyone else?'

'Robert Slade,' said Markby. 'To be perfectly candid, I'm astounded at your leniency. His approach to Wilde & Latchford was an act of brazen disloyalty. I gave him a caning just now as you instructed but I can't help feeling he requires further public punishment. Underneath that modest manner which he sometimes puts on, there's a genuine sense of self-esteem which needs to be crushed.'

'No,' answered Savage, 'leave Robert Slade alone. I have other plans for him.'

It was twenty-five minutes past five on Friday evening, five minutes before Georgina's time at Savage & Markby would expire. After that, there'd be a leaving party and the usual speeches, cards and presents. Georgina was quite looking forward to that. She liked quite a number of people at the Company and although she doubted if she'd see many of them again, it would be nice to part with them on good terms. As a joke she'd insisted on doing one last secretarial task for Mike – the photo-copying of some data on the UK soft drinks market.

Last night had been glorious. She'd been dying for Mike to make a pass at her and thank God he'd overcome his inhibitions. They hadn't bothered to go on to the next course which Georgina had lovingly prepared. Instead they'd fucked on the floor like animals. No man had ever taken her so completely. No man had ever given her so much of himself. She'd laughed out loud when she'd finally wandered naked into the kitchen and discovered that the crown roast of lamb had been burned to an unappetizing crisp. It didn't matter. There was a prepared barbecued chicken in the fridge and they'd wolfed that down with champagne before retiring to her bedroom. She'd always imagined that Mike possessed raw power in his loins and he hadn't disappointed her – but he proceeded to exceed all her expectations by changing his sexual style and making love to her with an exquisite gentleness which kept her coming again and again. He spent the night with his arms around her and they fucked twice before work in the morning. Georgina had gone through her last day at the agency glowing from within.

Oh heavens, am I in love? she thought as the lift arrived to take her for her last trip down to Photo-Copying. Shrugging gaily, she stepped inside the car accompanied by Larry Cunningham, who was carrying a pile of roughs he'd just exhibited.

The door slid shut as Mike came charging into the lobby with a piece of paper crying: 'I forgot to give you this!' – and Larry grinned as he produced the sharp, steel knife.

'Georgina!' Mike yelled as the fluorescent light flashed on Larry's blade a split-second before the lift door cut it off from view. 'Georgina!' He hurled himself against the door, bruised his shoulder without budging it, pressed the call button frantically and received a small electric shock. 'Shit!' he screamed. 'Georgina!'

Nobody else was in the vicinity. Mike's head whirled with panic. His fists clenched and his mouth opened to emit a hoarse cry of anguish. He raced for the stairs with his heart pounding furiously.

'The lift!' he yelled in agony. 'He's trying to kill her in the lift!'

John Savage sat calmly in Room Four and watched a woman struggle for her life against a drooling man. The thought occurred to him that his screens showed him matters of far greater interest than British television – and there was Mike Armstrong hammering vainly at the steel elevator door on the first floor. No, he wouldn't be able to help the girl in any way – though it was curious to witness just how desperately she was fighting. The blade had sliced through her blouse and torn the skin between her breasts. Blood was pouring into the thin fabric, staining her blue skirt and dripping onto the lift floor.

The Chairman continued to watch Georgina bleed as she battled for her life. A slight frown marred his normally impassive features, as though what he witnessed was slightly more intriguing than usual.

'The bastard's killing her!' Mike bawled as he ran into the lobby of Creative on the ground floor. 'Help! Please somebody help! The fucker's jammed the lift . . . !' but his agonized cry was fast breaking into a sob. Hardly aware of his surroundings, conscious only of the fact that one he loved was trapped in a box with an armed maniac, he beat upon the elevator door with his fists, making no impression. '*God!*' he screamed.

The lift door slid open smoothly.

Georgina lay in a blood-soaked heap in the corner of the car. Her blouse was a sopping mess of wet crimson. Her face was just a gory mask.

And yet she was breathing! Georgina was sobbing! And

Larry Cunningham lay sprawled upon the floor of the lift, his hands clutching the hilt of the knife, the blade of which lay buried between his ribs. In common with Georgina, there was sticky blood all over him but unlike the girl, he wasn't moving.

Mike leapt into the lift and seized Georgina in his arms. He didn't care about the gore which spilled onto his suit as he clutched her to him. He didn't care about anything except the fact that Georgina was alive and crying out her relief upon his shoulder.

20

Savage & Markby Ltd

MEMORANDUM

To: All Staff
cc Board Directors
From: Peter Jackson
Subject: House
Date: 12 January 1984

Many of you may not be aware that today, 12 January 1984, marks the twenty-seventh anniversary of the foundation of Savage & Markby. Since that time, and for some of us 1957 must seem like a very long time ago, the Company has gone from strength to strength. Last year saw our billings increase from thirty-one million pounds annually to thirty-seven million.

1983 was therefore our most successful year to date, though it was, in some respects, a year fraught with difficulty. Nevertheless, we have emerged triumphantly into 1984 and I, for one, have only one regret: that I did not join the Company earlier on in my career.

To match or exceed our economic performance of last year is a most demanding, though exciting, challenge. I am confident, however, that all of us have the determination and ability to meet it. Let us go forth together, therefore, and fight the good fight amidst the harsh realities of the current economic climate, sustained in competition by the joyful spirit of co-operation which, I am glad to say, exists between us.

A warm thank you to you all.

Peter Jackson.
MANAGING DIRECTOR

The Managing Director contemplated his copy of the Memo which had just been sent out and nodded sagely. In his opinion, it struck precisely the right note. There was no point in emulating the practice of those firms which always denied the existence of problems. It was a far superior policy to admit that despite the great successes of the preceding year, there had been difficulties and this admission, Peter felt, would go down well with the staff.

He himself had not been spared his share of tribulation. A series of bitter quarrels had finally forced him to leave his wife and move in with Candida, his mistress. Unfortunately, that was not working out as satisfactorily as he'd hoped and there had been a disconcerting number of rows just recently. In order to escape the resulting emotional upset, he'd started coming to the office on Saturdays and even Sundays, though in any case that was probably a necessary practice for the present if he was to stay on top of the growing burden of administration.

He was increasingly troubled by feelings of emotional isolation. Candida had taken to increasingly barbed criticism of his drinking and even went so far as attacking his approach to his job. The woman simply didn't understand the nature of his work. It was so demanding and since Christmas he'd been fighting feelings of exhaustion. The only way in which he could maintain the high level of energy he needed in order to perform successfully was by drinking and he expected a woman to be sympathetic. Accusations of alcoholism angered him intensely.

He suspected that the verbal assaults of his wife and his mistress were a jealous and typically feminine reaction to a man who, in truth, was married to his work. At the exalted level of business at which he operated, it couldn't be any other way. There was so much to be done. In a moment, when he'd finished his second morning drink, he'd have to write a Memo which ordered all account teams to bring their Account Management Plans up to date for 1984, and these would then have to be examined in depth by the Future Planning Committee and in all probability, revised as a result. Then in an hour, he would have to go and chair the Board of Chairmen. It would be nice to have a friendly chát with Emily before what was bound to be an engrossing but demanding meeting, but unfortunately she'd left the Company three days ago. It was something to do with having to look after an ailing elder sister – Peter couldn't quite remember the details.

His new secretary, Lucinda, was efficient enough but it wasn't quite the same and he'd had neither the time nor the inclination to get to know her yet. That could wait until he felt less tired. Peter decided to have another scotch – that might put some energy back into him. Spots exploded before his bloodshot eyes as he poured the whisky and perspiration mounted on his forehead. There was a sudden ringing in his ears as he drank and he wished that whoever it was would stop muttering. A minute passed before he realized that the mutterer was himself.

Perhaps he was in need of a good, long rest – but who else was capable of doing his job for him? Moreover, his fellow Directors were, he suspected, jealous of his success and might take advantage of his absence to diminish his influence. He would simply have to grit his teeth and battle his way through this difficult time. Peter drank to that, blinked, tried to focus his eyes and glanced down at the pad in front of him, on which he'd been doodling idly – and signing his name over and over and over again.

'Peter Jackson,' he mumbled, 'Peter Jackson, Peter Jackson, Peter Jackson, Peter Jackson . . .'

The internal phone rang, its shrill scream startling him

and jerking him upright. His brain fumbled its way towards clarity as his hand picked up the receiver.

'Peter Jackson . . .' he mumbled again.

'Morning, Peter,' came Savage's voice. 'I wonder if you could step up to Room One for a moment. It's to discuss your promotion.'

Mike Armstrong stared moodily at the calendar on his wall. The Kandy film was done and the second of February, the date on which it would be shown, wasn't far away but at times he wondered if he could last that long. At least he had a job to go to, which was more than could be said of Robert Slade. The latter's humiliation after the Wilde & Latchford interview still troubled Mike. It was as though nowhere was free from Savage's scrutiny.

The fate of Cliff Mitchell also disturbed Mike. Six months imprisonment for possession of cannabis with intent to supply seemed a very stiff sentence, even if it was Cliff's third offence. Obviously the police had dropped the murder charge but Mike was still left with the uncomfortable feeling that unpleasant fates kept overtaking every person who in some way rebelled against Savage & Markby.

Take Georgina, for example. Why, of all people, did the revolting Larry Cunningham have to pick on her? Although she was recovering from the shock, she still had nightmares from which she awoke screaming. *Thank God I've moved in with her*, he thought.

Yet that thought was succeeded by the horrible suspicion that somehow, Savage knew.

21

'How about,' Simon Burns suggested sullenly, 'BROWNING'S BEST BROWN – YOU CAN'T DO BETTER . . . ?'

'Nah,' Dennis shook his head, 'you can do better than that.'

'Jesus effing Christ!' snapped Simon, 'what the hell do they want from us – blood? I tell you, I'm going to kill that bleeding George Webbing. It's his fucking job to sell our work to the client. What's the result? The wanker couldn't sell tea to Alcoholics Anonymous.'

'Easy,' Dennis warned him, 'I'm as pissed off as you but let's take it easy.'

'Easy? *Shit!*' Simon exploded. 'How can I take it easy? We've spent hour after hour, day after day, week after week and month after month trying to get the face right on this stupid bloody poster. Every time it gets sent back because George can't persuade his arse-hole of a client that it's what his stinking boss wants. Finally we get it right by going back to exactly what we had in the first bloody place. Then what happens? That tit of a client tells George that all of a sudden, he don't reckon his boss'll be happy with the slogan. He wants something more exciting than: BROWNING'S BEST BROWN – BROWN ALE AT ITS BEST – even though he's been happy with that all the way along the line. You know something? I'd like to take a bottle of Browning's Best Brown, dip it in sulphuric acid and shove it right up the client's arse-hole.'

'Did I hear you right just then?' demanded an outraged Ronald Potter, who'd just entered the room. 'Correct me if I'm wrong,' he adjusted his 'intellectual' glasses, 'but it seems I just heard you insulting one of the Company's clients in language unworthy of a Company employee. Don't bother to deny it! I know what my ears tell me and it seems,' Ronald Potter leaned over Simon's desk and breathed instant coffee fumes in his face, 'that you're up to your old tricks again. I won't have it! I tell you, I won't have it! Imagine if a client had been walking by just then . . .'

That's all you're fit for imagining, Simon thought bitterly. *You're about as creative as a factory foreman. You make me want to puke*. His Group Head wasn't the only element in Simon's life which made him sick to his very soul. Last night his wife had demanded that he make love to her. 'You haven't done that in ages,' she shrilled. It was hardly surprising since her behaviour had put him off her entirely – but he'd tried to do his marital duty – and all it seemed like was an unavoidable duty – and he'd failed. She'd called him a queer, kicked him out of bed, driven him from the bedroom with ridicule and abuse and locked the door on him. Simon had spent a miserable night on the sofa – and in the morning, the post had brought back his manuscript. *Tentacles* had been rejected without a word of explanation.

'You don't seem to understand the way things work here,' Ronald Potter was saying. 'There's a System and everyone is expected to conform. You seem to think that you're cleverer than the System. You seem to think that you can get away with bucking it. Well . . . *don't buck the System!*' Ronald Potter shouted. 'If you buck the System, the System will buck you harder. Don't try and fight it, 'cos you'll lose. Don't try and out-clever it, 'cos it'll make you look stupid. Don't buck the System! How many times do I have to tell you? Don't buck the System! You should know by now. Don't buck the System . . . ugh . . .'

His voice trailed away because Simon's hand had snaked out and whisked his 'intellectual' glasses from his nose. Ronald Potter was left squinting ineffectually at his subordinate as his hands gesticulated feebly and his mouth opened, closed, opened again and emitted a bewildered croak at the instant when Simon snapped his spectacles in two.

'This . . . you . . . no . . . can't . . .' the Group Head floundered in a state of twittering ineptitude. Simon's right fist shot out and punched Ronald Potter squarely on the nose. Ronald staggered backwards, lost his balance and fell sprawling to the floor, blood trickling from one nostril.

Simon rose, went over to his immediate boss who was on his back and in a state of shock and stupefaction, and spat down into his face.

'Don't buck the System?' Simon yelled at him. 'Bollocks! I just have.'

Robert Slade was working at his desk – or rather, he was pretending to be working at his desk, for the fact was that he couldn't concentrate on sales figures for Golden Eagle Bright Beer. His campaign to secure another job had so far come to nothing and yet, since his humiliation at the hands of Markby, that somehow didn't matter. What mattered most in his working life was his part in the subversive Kandy plan, which would exact some sort of vengeance on the Company which had endeavoured to subvert his individuality.

Vickie was worried by his attitude, he knew, yet she couldn't help applauding his manner of rebellion. Aside from her anxiety about his future, their relationship was back to the glory it had been. Whenever Robert thought about how he'd been tempted to give up Vickie for the sake of advancement at the agency, there was a hot flush of shame and anger up his spine. Savage & Markby would pay for that and pay dearly.

Yet that thought, from which he derived a grim satisfaction, nevertheless failed to assist his solution to the problem of how he was to approach his working days. Ambitious as he was and had been – and would be in another company – he had lost interest in the work he did for Savage & Markby. Each day it became more difficult to act the role of a dynamic and dedicated Senior Assistant Account Executive. Right now, he was meant to be analysing the data in front of him with a view to drawing up a report for the Golden Eagle Tactical Sub-Committee, to which he'd recently been appointed, and he couldn't see the point of the exercise at all.

Perhaps he could fritter away some time by getting a coffee from the machine just up the corridor. With luck, the dratted thing would be working properly today and wouldn't be spewing out cold soup with sugar. The coffee was really very little better – but at least it was something to do. He rose wearily, entered the main corridor and approached the automatic vendor – which was when he noticed the woman up ahead.

She seemed vaguely familiar, though he couldn't see her face, and walked with a provocative sway of her hips beneath her flowing skirt. He followed her towards the vending machine, hoping that she'd turn her head, but that hope was in vain. Abandoning his half-hearted desire for bad coffee, Robert walked faster, hoping to overtake her and get a glimpse of her features – but the woman was striding fairly briskly herself and passed through the double doors to the stairs before he came anywhere near her.

Robert was seized by an insensate curiosity regarding the girl's identity. The issue seemed much more interesting than the papers on his desk, so he barged through the double doors and descended the stairs as though he had just recalled an essential mission which necessitated his immediate presence in Media, Creative or Production.

Her high heels tapped an inviting beat upon the flights

of steps she went down with her skirt switching enticingly. She still hadn't looked back by the time she reached Production and entered that department's corridor. Robert strode along behind her, tormented by the temptation to break into a run. Her appeal transcended that of a girl who was merely attractive and walking ahead of him. It was hard for him to formulate his thoughts, harder still to put them into words – but it was as though she embodied the lure which had drawn him to Savage & Markby in the first place. He suppressed a sigh as she entered the Lower Projection Room – but could not repress the gasp which erupted from his chest at the gesture she made to him seconds before she vanished within.

For without warning, the woman flipped up her skirt to display stockings, suspenders, white thighs and a round, plump bottom swathed in white silk knickers.

Robert stopped as though he'd been kicked in the stomach. He tried to swallow but his mouth was dry. His heart was thumping furiously. His legs seemed to have escaped his brain's conscious control as he found himself once again moving steadily towards the door the woman had just closed behind her.

Was hers the brazen invitation it had seemed? What else could it be? Should he accept it? His feet left him no choice. His erection throbbed with an almost painful intensity. What about Vickie? Yet every atom of his being sang with one pulsating and electric desire. He grasped the door-handle dazedly, turned it to enter hungrily – and recoiled back into the corridor as though she'd spat directly into his face.

A faintness came over him. He shook and trembled as he stumbled away and towards the lavatories, overwhelmed by his sudden sickness of soul. Bile churned in his stomach and surged up his gullet. Cold sweat broke out all over his body as he resisted the almost overpowering urge to vomit in the corridor. His skin crawled as though he had come into contact with a poison which could destroy his entire being.

For as he'd entered the room, he'd finally recalled that the hair and the walk belonged to Sandra Lang. It was unexpected, but not impossible, that she would come back and visit the agency. It was extremely improbable, though not utterly inconceivable, that she might seek to entice Robert into sudden sexual relations.

But there was nothing on earth which could explain the weeds entwined within her fringe, and the vacant eye-sockets, lipless grin – and the naked bones which protruded from her blouse as her skeletal fingers invited him towards her.

22

On 2 February 1984, the day of the Kandy presentation, Harriet Baker found herself much in sympathy with Simon Burns, who'd walked out nearly three weeks ago. Her career wasn't moving at all. Even though her bosses continued to appreciate her, the grim fact remained that she was still just a secretary.

She'd also had a row with Sid last night. The strain of life at Savage & Markby seemed to be getting to him as well and recently he'd become paranoid in case his wife found out about their affair. This made him nervous, irritable – and impelled his annoying habit of looking around furtively whenever he and Harriet were in the street together. Yesterday evening, she'd felt driven to comment that he was acting like a novice burglar with his first bag of swag – and he'd exploded. They'd parted before dinner and after angry words and this morning had passed without their speaking to one another.

Harriet's anger at the way in which her life was going had just provoked her into seeing Laura in an attempt to obtain another interview with Markby and remind him of his promise. However, Laura had curtly informed Harriet that the Vice-Chairman was 'extremely busy' and couldn't see her until the last Monday of the month. Harriet was seething with indignation as she left Laura's office. The electric shock she received on pressing the lift call button made her swear aloud.

Feeling that she couldn't bear the thought of waiting three more weeks before confronting Markby, Harriet resolved to go and see Peter Jackson, who at least had displayed sympathy and done something – however small

– on her behalf. The instant the lift stopped on the Account Management floor, she strode out into the corridor, rapped hard on the door of Lucinda, Peter's new secretary, and went inside.

'Hallo,' said Lucinda, who was drinking coffee and idly turning the pages of a magazine.

'Hello, I'd like to see Peter, please.'

'Oh,' said Lucinda, 'I'm afraid he's not in.'

'When will he be back?' Harriet asked impatiently.

'I don't know.'

'But you're his secretary.'

'Not after today, I'm not,' Lucinda returned. 'They're transferring me to Mike Armstrong.'

'But . . .' Harriet faltered, 'but what's happening to Peter?'

'Search me. I haven't seen him in ages. Apparently he's working on some high level project.' She shrugged. 'Sorry I can't help. Who are you, by the way?'

'Never mind,' Harriet retorted through gritted teeth. 'Forget it.' She turned and strode out of Lucinda's office suppressing an almost irresistible urge to scream.

Markby thought of Harriet when a client he was lunching at Simpson's In The Strand momentarily excused himself. According to the Vice-Chairman's calculations, the girl would shortly be desperate enough to take the bait of possible promotion in exchange for the use of her body – and then he'd have her hooked. She was no beauty but her long legs really were most attractive and would be seductively enhanced by black stockings and suspenders. This time, though, he'd have to exercise a little more caution. He didn't want a repetition of the Sandra Lang affair – and he was finding the impossible tales about the suicide's reappearance increasingly disturbing; inhibiting, almost. Once again, Markby ordered himself to remain rational and ignore what had to be bogus reports. Obviously there was a perfectly reasonable explanation – yet he couldn't entirely repress a gnawing, inner anxiety.

'Coffee?' he enquired as his guest returned to the table. 'And perhaps you'd care to join me in a brandy?'

'Good idea,' replied the Managing Director of Pearl Toothpaste, a half-million pound account. 'Yes, as I was saying, we're actually rather pleased with the way in which the advertising side is going.'

'Oh, I'm glad to hear it.'

'I don't mind telling you,' the client continued, 'that in my view, it's been a very good move leaving Brady & Harding and joining Peter at your agency and I'm delighted I allowed him to persuade me.' The coffee and balloon glasses of brandy arrived. 'How is Peter, by the way? I haven't seen him in a while.'

'No, he hasn't been too well recently, I'm afraid,' said Markby.

'I'm sorry to hear it. Nothing serious, I hope?'

'Tired out from overwork, really.' Markby sipped cognac and looked sympathetic if somewhat regretful. 'We rather feel that he's in need of a rest.'

John Savage sat silently in Room Four, the opaque panes of his spectacles fixed upon the closed-circuit television screens. On Screen 9, the Kandy account team was assembling in Conference Room One and Mike Armstrong looked curiously jubilant. This was certainly an unexpected development and one to be watched with interest, Savage thought. Could it be that Mike had suddenly and finally decided to knuckle under?

Certainly the Chairman had no complaints about the way Kandy had been handled so far. A week ago, Mike had presented the advertising to Savage and Markby in Room One and it was excellent. The Chairman knew winners when he saw them and in his mind there was no doubt that the Kandy Corporation would be pleased and that provided the client moved on the sales side with the efficiency so far displayed, the launch would be sensationally successful.

Much credit to Mike Armstrong, then, for the man was showing intriguing resilience despite the strains of Kandy and the misfortunes of Georgina – with whom, Savage gathered, Mike was now cohabiting.

He surveyed his thirty-one screens through the thick panes of his spectacles. It seemed like a normal day at the agency – except that Harriet Baker was crying in the Ladies on Screen 22. Perhaps she was cracking in response to the punishment stimuli which had been deliberately applied to her. Possibly one should ease the strain – except that Savage still detected an independence of spirit in Harriet which remained to be crushed.

Other than the events in Conference Room One, there was little to divert the attention. On Screen 6, Brian Bishop was working. On Screen 8, Stanley Haynes was lecturing Sid Ingram. On the newly installed Screen 31, Peter Jackson was performing according to plan. And on Screen 23, the Upper Projection Box which looked out onto Conference Room One, a cheerful Robert Slade was handing over the Kandy reel to the projectionist.

Savage's hand reached out for the panel of sound control knobs.

'Thank you, Robert,' Mike said as the assistant returned to the conference table. 'Well, I think that since all of us are here . . .' he looked around then frowned. 'Where's Sid?' he asked Tony Westbury.

'I'm not sure. He's usually on time.'

'He should be here,' Mike commented. 'We'll just have to start without him.' Pressing a button on his chair-arm, he gazed steadily at Chuck Davey, Stuart Simms and Cal Lowry, who were dressed as identically as on the previous occasion and whose faces had come to resemble one another even more. 'I should like to begin,' Mike told them, 'by proposing a toast.'

Girls entered and the faces of the Kandy men relaxed into whole-hearted approval as all were served a glass of chilled Kandy with ice.

'To Kandy,' said Mike.

'To Kandy,' said everyone and drank.

'Another time,' Sid Ingram pleaded. 'I've got this Kandy meeting right now and I'm already late for it.'

'As far as I'm concerned,' Stanley Haynes retorted crossly, 'your meeting is not as important as this one here. You don't have to present anything, do you? You'll just be sitting there and enjoying it, won't you?'

'No, but . . .'

'But me no buts,' Stanley Haynes interrupted him. 'Next item: MIN313 – FXP437R – X19 – five pounds and fifty pence charged to the agency for a taxi fare . . .'

Sid, who was feeling wretched on account of last night's row with Harriet, ground his teeth and curled his toes with anger and impatience.

'So having made our TV commercials,' Mike was saying, 'we decided to use consumer research before presenting them to you.' The Kandy men were listening attentively. 'The relevant Report is in front of you. As you can see from it, in a random sampling of one thousand Londoners and one thousand Birminghamites, an average of 81% liked them as advertisements – while an average of 87% said they now wanted to try Kandy. To split these figures up a little more . . .'

'Now look here,' said Stanley Haynes. 'I intend to get to the bottom of this. Are you seriously expecting me to believe that once again Oliver Dawes is the villain of the piece? Always put the blame on somebody else – that's your attitude all over, isn't it? I like to think it isn't but I rather suspect it is. Don't think I haven't had my eye on you for a while,' he continued remorselessly. 'I've been observing you and I'm not happy with what I've observed, young man. It's your whole attitude that's wrong. Why, it's even revealed in the way you walk down corridors . . .'

'You know what makes these sessions so uniquely unbearable?' Sid abruptly interjected.

'I beg your pardon?' The Financial Director frowned irritably, annoyed and perplexed by the manner of interruption.

'You fart all the time,' said Sid. 'You can't stop farting silently and stinking the place out and I can't stand it.'

'Now you listen to me!' Stanley shouted as he rose to his feet and quivered with fury.

'No, you listen to me!' Sid shouted back and jumped enragedly to his feet. 'I've had enough of you shitting on me and farting while you're at it. You know something, sunshine? You stink from arse-hole to breakfast-time. Your own mother don't want to come near you . . .'

'Get out!' screamed Stanley. 'You're fired!'

'Fuck off, scum-bag,' Sid snarled back and strode from the office.

'*Sacked!*' Stanley's voice screeched behind him. '*And you'll pay for it!*'

'Thank you, Craig,' Mike rose as the Assistant Media Director returned to his seat. 'So that's when and where everything will be shown – and now let's move to what we'll be showing.' He sensed that the presentation was going exceptionally well. The Kandy trio looked impressed while the agency team radiated confidence. 'The last time you were here with us,' Mike recalled, 'our Managing Director made, I felt, a most illuminating point. He said that Kandy was legal, decent, honest and truthful. And successful. Very successful. This point has played a substantial part in guiding our advertising strategy, with results which we think you will find interesting.' He signalled to the projectionist. 'Gentlemen, I give you the Savage & Markby television commercial for Kandy.'

The blinds slid downwards to shut out all light from the windows. The room was drowned in darkness, then a rectangle of light appeared on the screen at the room's end.

OPEN TO:

Savage & Markby Ltd
KANDY
'HAPPY TEA-TIME'
K1c

CUT TO:

Average interior but with large table. A rowdy group of boys and girls, KIDS aged 7-15, are not eating the bread and jam, biscuits and cake which MUM has provided for their tea. Although their faces are innocent and laughing, KIDS will be KIDS, and they're shouting and pushing and shoving one another.

Cheerful pop music with an early Sixties flavour.

CUT TO:

MUM looking at KIDS from doorway, though they haven't yet noticed her. It's clear that although she loves them, they've been tiring her out. But . . .

MUM enters with a forced smile and bottles of Kandy.

FEMALE SINGERS (OFF-SCREEN)
Kandy's here!

KIDS see Mum and Kandy, stop fighting instantly and are overjoyed.

FEMALE SINGERS (O.S.)
Yeah, Kandy's here!

The sun shines in through the windows, lighting up the happy faces of KIDS as they reach out eagerly for bottles of Kandy.

FEMALE SINGERS (O.S.)
And everybody's hap-py!

This time, MUM's smile is genuine as KIDS start eating, opening bottles and pouring Kandy with glee.

SEXY GIRL WEENY BOPPER
(JOGGING TO THE MUSIC) It tastes so good!

SWEET LITTLE GIRL
It tickles!

STURDY BOY
I just think it's great.

FEMALE SINGERS (O.S.)
Everybody's happy when it's Kandy.
Kandy, Kandy, Kandy's here to stay.

As KIDS drink with joy, STURDY BOY smiles up at his MUM as he passes her a glass of Kandy. KIDS look at MUM with adoration.

FEMALE SINGERS (O.S.)
Why does she give them Kandy?
Cos Kandy is so dandy . . .

MUM
(SMILES) It's been proved it gives them cancer
(SINGS) *And I want these stupid brats out of the way.*

Music stops.

SEXY GIRL WEENY BOPPER
(LASCIVIOUSLY) Cancer – the drink for the chick who doesn't give a fuck.

CUT TO:

Close-up of a bottle of Kandy.

SMALL BOY'S VOICE (O.S.)
Can I have some more please, Mum?

Sounds of KIDS coughing, retching and spewing.

CUT TO:

BLACKOUT

23

The blinds slid up to flood the room with light and expose the ashen faces of the viewers. There was a stunned silence.

'That's all,' Mike said calmly and stood up. So did Ian. 'Thought you'd find it interesting. Cheers.' He walked out.

'Bye,' said Ian and followed him.

'What's the meaning of this?' demanded a bewildered Chuck Davey.

'What's going on?' rasped Stuart Simms.

'I demand an explanation,' Cal Lowry spoke icily, 'for what strikes us as being a most outrageous insult.'

The agency men looked completely dumbfounded and shrank further into their chairs. Each one was hoping desperately that someone else would speak up with words which would somehow save them.

'Robert, get Chris Faye,' Tony tried to murmur coolly, but he couldn't keep his voice from quavering. Robert, who'd stayed put on the insistence of Mike and Ian, left the room just as a speaker crackled from somewhere within it.

'This is Savage speaking,' came a clear and steady voice, 'to apologize profusely for this unprecedented and calculated act of sabotage. It is quite inexcusable and I shall be dealing immediately with the offenders. There is no need to remain agitated. A full account of this outrage will be presented to you shortly.'

Mike, who was packing up his things in his office, was startled by the crackle of the hidden speaker.

'Savage here,' snapped the voice. 'I want to see you in Room One now.'

'Good,' Mike returned, 'because I want to see you.' He closed his brief-case. 'But you can wait until I've made a phone-call.' Picking up the internal receiver, he dialled Ian Sharpe's number. 'Mike here. I'm going up to see Savage. You coming too?'

'I've just had orders to see him,' Ian's voice shook slightly as he replied. 'Shit, I had no idea this place was bugged – and there's no way I'm seeing Savage. I've got nothing to say to him.'

'So where're you going?'

'I'm just going.' Again the voice trembled. 'In a while, I'll be in touch and for the present, good luck. If I were you I'd . . .'

Mike heard a speaker crackle in Ian's office. He could just make out the words of Savage: 'If you don't come up, then I'll come and find you . . .'

Ian's line went dead.

'Martin, will you *please* let me out of here,' Harriet Baker demanded angrily. 'I came in because you said it was urgent but you've no right to keep me here.'

'I have every right,' Martin Bottomley returned self-righteously, 'to insist upon an explanation of your conduct with Sid Ingram. Well?' he quacked. 'What d'you have to say for yourself?'

'It's none of your bloody business,' she shot back furiously. 'Now let me out of here.'

'Until I am given the explanation to which I, as a suitor, am entitled,' he continued to bar the door from the Lower Projection Room, 'heah is where we shall stay.'

Harriet rushed at Martin in a fierce attempt to force him aside but he merely pushed her back and held her at arm's length. Harriet emitted a squeal of rage, her hand darted to the back pocket of her trousers, she pulled out the flick-knife she'd carried since the first murder and – *knik!* – the naked blade was bared.

'Let me out!' she yelled and waved the knife before his face. 'You're driving me CRA-ZY!!!'

'How *dare* you threaten me with an offensive weapon!' he spluttered. 'Give that to me at once!'

'Let me out!'

He seized her arm.

'Let me *out!*'

She kicked and struggled.

'*Let me out!*'

He pulled her towards him.

'*Let me OUT!*'

Blinded by her fury, Harriet struck with all her strength. She gasped as the blade pierced the flesh of Martin's soft belly and slid through his intestines. He screamed in shock and pain, blood spurted onto Harriet's clothes, she cried out and pulled back the red, glistening blade and Martin slid groaning to the floor.

Her mind was blasted by horror. As she ran crying into the corridors and up the stairs, she was conscious of little other than the overwhelming urge to destroy.

Robert saw her running wild as he emerged from a vain search for Chris Faye. For a few seconds he stopped in total astonishment, then pursued the knife-wielding, blood-spattered figure up the steps.

Mike burst into Markby's office without being invited and strode through it, ignoring the Vice-Chairman.

'I've never liked you,' Markby murmured as his eyes spat malice. 'Goodbye.'

When he reached Room One, Mike went in without knocking and took a seat without asking.

'Yes?' he queried with a direct stare into Savage's spectacles.

'You,' the Chairman stated simply, 'will be broken bit by bit.'

'Any other threats while you're at it?' It was hard for Mike to hold the Chairman's gaze. It was as though the man exuded some intensely malefic force which came over one in waves of nausea and weakness. He swallowed, shook his head and fought a sudden onrush of dizziness.

'Yes,' said Savage, 'this one will be a great pleasure.'

Markby pondered the manner of Mike Armstrong's certain destruction until he reached the lift, when he forced his mind to return to the problem of pacifying the Kandy men. It was clear that Mike and Ian had made their own version of the Kandy commercial at the expense of the client and then edited it into the real commercial. So much for the explanation, Markby reflected grimly as he entered the lift and commenced his descent. But how was he to mollify the men in Conference Room One? Comforting phrases sped through his head as the door opened and he stepped out – to recoil when he saw the blood-stained clothes of Harriet.

She uttered a howl of demented anger. Her blade sliced through the air and slashed Markby's face from ear to chin. Markby shrieked out and fell to the floor, his hands covering a visage which was rapidly turning into a wet, crimson mask.

Harriet sprang into the lift and the door closed behind her just as Robert ran into the lobby.

'You're evil,' Mike affirmed through clenched teeth. 'I hate everything for which you stand. That's why I did it – but I don't suppose you'd understand that.'

'Of course I understand it,' Savage answered matter-of-factly. 'It's why your life will be ruined and you will be broken.'

'You're not human.'

'Goodbye,' said Savage.

'Go to hell,' snarled Mike – then both looked away in surprise as a door slammed in the outside passage and a gore-spattered madwoman stormed into the room and flung herself at Savage with her knife poised to slash and stab.

Human instinct made Mike leap up, catch her arm a second before the blade reached Savage's face and pull Harriet's wrist back sharply. The knife dropped from her sticky fingers but her knee thudded into Mike's groin. Mike grunted, doubled up and sank to his knees groaning.

Harriet shrieked again and hurled herself at Savage.

The Chairman was sitting upright. He'd opened a drawer and pulled out a small black pistol which he was aiming directly at Harriet. The instant that her wet, outstretched fingers touched his head, Savage squeezed the trigger.

The roar of the gun shook the room as its bullet smacked into Harriet's forehead, drilled a neat red hole and pulverized the brains behind the bone. Harriet gaped as the impact threw her backwards with brains spilling out of her skull, stood perfectly still for a fraction of a second, then crumpled to the floor, watched by an expressionless Savage. Harriet Baker died as Robert ran into the room, saw her corpse and swayed in stunned stupefaction.

'That . . .' Mike gasped, for he was almost too stunned to speak, '. . . that was murder.'

'No,' said Savage, 'she shot herself.'

'You *killed* her! I saw you!'

'No,' said Savage, 'she shot herself.'

'Your gun . . .' Mike staggered to his feet.

'What gun?' Savage removed his glasses and his dark, dead, alien eyes bored into Mike. Mike was possessed by an urge to vomit and looked away. 'D'you mean the gun with which she shot herself?' asked Savage. 'It's over there.'

Mike looked – and his eyes widened dazedly. Harriet lay in a heap, blood oozing down her face. Her right hand clutched a small, black pistol.

'Goodbye, Mike,' said Savage.

'I know what my own eyes showed me,' Mike shook his head in an anguish of bewilderment. 'I'm going straight to the police.'

'That's a waste of time,' said Savage, 'I'll be calling them myself in a moment or two.'

'You won't get away with this,' Mike insisted. 'You'll be put behind bars.'

'Why?' Savage asked. 'Because she shot herself?'

'Come on, Robert,' Mike urged him. 'Let's get out of this hell.'

'Robert is staying for a bit,' Savage stated.

'I think you'll find he's coming with me.' Mike regarded Robert who was looking dazedly into Savage's eyes. 'Come on.'

'Later,' Robert muttered.

Mike looked speechlessly around the room then stumbled from it on legs that shook and with a brain that was benumbed.

'We haven't much time,' the Chairman told Robert as though nothing unusual had happened. 'So sit down.' Robert obeyed, apparently oblivious of the bloody corpse on the carpet by his feet. Savage continued to gaze at him steadily. 'It's been interesting watching you struggle and you've done well. In my view, you have great potential. Robert, there is an *excellent* future for you here at Savage & Markby, though you will have to make certain changes. Oh, and you did see how she shot herself, didn't you?' Robert's head bobbed like a string-puppet. 'And naturally you'll assist me in dealing with it.' The head bobbed again. 'Exactly. As for these changes, there's your home life, for example. The girl you live with is really rather unsatisfactory.'

Robert struggled vainly against the fog which had enveloped his intellect, leaving him prey to a pressure which threatened to squeeze out all human awareness. A poison seeped into his being with every breath he took, insinuating itself into his emotions and corrupting his very soul. Once again, his head nodded in answer to something which Savage had said. The Chairman calmly replaced his glasses. The blur before Robert's eyes cleared slightly – and he discerned the small black pistol upon the Chairman's desk.

The sight gave his reeling mind a further pounding. Before, he had seen it in Harriet's hand. He could no longer be sure of anything. Perhaps Savage was right after all and he should . . .

Never! Driven by a desperation to save his own spirit, burning with the knowledge that the man before him incarnated evil, driven onward by the fear that he was losing all his true self – Robert threw himself at the Chairman, snatched up the gun and fired.

The bullet struck Savage squarely in the midriff. Blood spurted onto his desk. His mouth opened in surprise and his body sagged back into the chair, where it slumped and remained still with the head lolling limply.

The pistol slipped from Robert's nerveless fingers. He stepped fearfully away, blasted by the sight of the Chairman dead before him. His brain whirled and span. He staggered around the office without knowing what to say or what to think or what to do. His rubbery legs tottered towards the door. For a moment, he leaned on it to support himself from falling, then he tottered the few more steps towards the passage.

'Where are you going?' Savage asked quietly.

Part IV

24

Vickie arrived home at six-fifteen that day, after a relatively easy time at work. It was just as well, she reflected, that she felt brimming over with energy, for the evening was likely to be a demanding one.

Robert had told her everything about the secret plan for Kandy. Vickie approved whole-heartedly of the action itself but was worried about Robert's involvement. He hadn't yet found another job and if his part in the proceedings got out in the trade, that would be the finish of his career in advertising – and he could forget good references for future jobs. She had urged him to take the advice of Mike and Ian, who had promised to cover for him, and appear a totally innocent party.

Vickie was worried about how it had gone today. In any event, they were invited to dinner with Mike and Georgina with Ian as the other guest. Vickie was looking forward to meeting Robert's fellow rebels of conscience, though there was a slight itch of resentment. It was all very well to rebel openly if you had inherited pots of money, like Georgina, or had very well-paid jobs to go to, like Mike and, it seemed, Ian. But how was Robert going to survive now? Vickie decided to have a glass of wine while waiting for Robert's arrival.

He came in around fifteen minutes later with a small smile on his face and an abstracted look in his eyes.

'How'd it go?' she asked anxiously.

'Fine.' He stood nonchalantly in the doorway. 'I've been promoted.'

'What?'

'Yes,' he replied easily, 'and my salary's now been

raised by two thousand a year. I'm a full Account Executive as from tomorrow on Joy, Browning's and Kandy.'

'*Kandy!*' she gasped, then: 'You're not being serious?'

'Of course I am,' he answered.

'Darling, you're different somehow,' Vickie stammered. 'What's happened?'

'Oh, just a little talk with Savage. You know, I think the two of us had it completely wrong. He's the most extraordinarily intelligent man I've ever met. And rather nice with it.'

'*What are you saying?*' Vickie burst out.

'Do stop being so tiresome,' said Robert. 'I don't see the need for all this hysteria. I'll just get my things and go, if you don't mind.'

She gaped at him wordlessly as Robert took a bag from the cupboard and started packing pairs of underpants and socks, ties and shirts.

'Hmm, my red pair of socks is missing,' he muttered. 'You've probably lost it in the wash. Always happening.'

'*Robert!*' Vickie screamed.

'Must you?' asked Robert. 'I'm trying to pack my things.'

'You're mad!'

'You know, the Chairman's *so* illuminating,' he told her thoughtfully.

She sprang at him, brought her arm round in a wide, swiftly drawn arc and slapped his face so hard her fingers burned in her panic-stricken attempt to shock sense into him. His head rocked back on his shoulders but his face did not change its bland expression as his open palm smacked her face so hard she reeled back against the cupboard and cracked the back of her skull against the wood.

'Calm down,' said Robert. Vickie's eyes rolled as he coolly zipped up his bag. 'If you follow, I'll hit you again and harder. We're finished. I never want to see you again. I hate everything for which you stand. Goodbye.'

He left the flat quietly. Vickie began to writhe and wail.

At roughly the same time, Peter Jackson was slouched in a chair and enjoying the last of the day's first whisky bottle. He sang a little ditty to himself as he poured and prepared once more to toast his own promotion. For Peter was now Administrative President as a result of a most illuminating talk with the Chairman.

It was all so much better than before. His salary had gone up by ten thousand. He'd been relieved of all duties other than the crucially important one – for which every atom of his ability was needed – of authoring The Jackson Report with Full Recommendations on the entire administrative structure of Savage & Markby.

In view of his increased importance, Peter had been moved to the top floor itself and given an entirely separate set of rooms from those of Savage and Markby. A lift sped directly from his suite to the ground floor and a separate entrance. It was almost like being at home – for Peter's exceptionally luxurious environment consisted of a hall, an outer office, an inner office, a living room, a dining room, and a double bedroom and a bathroom and a kitchen.

To Peter, the arrangement had seemed the solution to all his problems. The evening after his talk with the Chairman, he packed some bags, left his mistress, accepted Savage's suggestion that he move into his suite for the time being and proceeded to enjoy the first bottle from the many crates of scotch provided.

He'd finally achieved, Peter decided, absolute success in life. Materially, he had everything he desired. There was a housekeeper in the small flat next door and she was nice and motherly and brought him delicious food whenever he wanted it. Apparently Doris had been in Mr Savage's employ for sixteen years and she said he paid well. Peter was flattered by the generosity of Savage and delighted in Doris's homely attentions.

If he wanted sex, there was Davina, the divinely sexy secretary they'd given him. She said that she was upper class and convent-educated but she wore the most lust-provoking clothes he'd ever seen in an office. On her second day, he made a drunken pass at her and she succumbed, proving herself to be the most sensational sexual turn-on Peter had encountered in years. She was the answer to his every fantasy. She provoked him into telling her his every secret lustful thought, sighed lecherously at his every word and did everything he wanted with wilful abandon.

He was starting to believe that life was currently too good to be true. The Chairman had urged him to take his time with the Jackson Report, so all the pressure had finally abated. The domestic side of things was also much improved. Doris and Davina repeatedly told him how important he was, how vital his work was and how essential his abilities obviously were to the continued health of the organization. Doris doted on him adoringly. Davina said he was the greatest lover, finest intelligence and dearest man she'd ever met. And what made it all so completely delightful was that neither woman had the slightest objection to his drinking. On the contrary, they brought him drinks quite happily and assured him that when he drank, he was even more fascinating than when he was sober.

Davina was easily the best girl Peter had met in his life. When he talked, she listened avidly. When he asked her to talk, she talked well and about him. When he wanted her to go away, she went away and when he needed her to be close, she was close. The only problem she had was agoraphobia, which made her terrified to go out. Naturally Peter was understanding and sympathetic. What was the point of going out, anyway?

He felt he'd reached the summit of every man's ambition. He could do absolutely anything he wanted. And anything he didn't want to do, he didn't have to do. For instance, the outside world was becoming an increasing nuisance. Sometimes he simply didn't feel up to dealing with it. He therefore gave up the use of the phone and left the fending off process to Davina. This wasn't to say that he did no work. Many hours were spent on The Jackson Report. Peter felt it should open with diagrams and devoted much of his energy to constructing a schema. Days passed when his only tools were paper, a ruler and pencils. On other days, he didn't feel like it and so read and wrote Company Memoranda. The Administrative President often felt moved to comment to all staff on every Memo he received. He wasn't to know that Davina's instructions were secretly to shred every scrap of paper he gave her.

There were other days during which he idled. He'd become a firm believer in the importance of inspiration before proceeding fully with a project and so saw no harm in inviting it by having a rest, reading a thriller, watching TV, listening to music, making conversation, enjoying sex or drinking all day. His promotion made it obvious that his methods worked when it came to success in life. Twice a week Savage came for an appointment – a great honour, this – and Peter always had something new to show him. Savage invariably studied the notes or diagram with minute care, then expressed his enormous satisfaction with what he termed Peter's 'unique abilities which are quite indispensable'.

Peter finished his drink, rose and stumbled in the direction of the whisky crates. Today there'd been more good news. Markby had come to see him just before lunch, and after praising his ideas had slyly insinuated that it was perfectly all right for any man on the top floor to install a woman as resident. When Peter now thought about that conversation, his cup of joy overflowed. He would ask the exquisitely wicked Davina to move in with him. As it was she was coming round within the hour but sneaking her out in the morning for a witnessed return ten minutes later had been a deadly nuisance.

Savage & Markby is wonderful, he thought as he took a bottle of Tartan from the crate, screwed off the top and drank directly from the bottle. He coughed twice as the scotch slid down his gullet but the overall sensation felt good. Well, that was work all wrapped up for the day except . . . Peter's glazed eye fell upon a pile of letters and documents which lay on his desk.

Damn! This was Peter's only real complaint about his situation and the problem would be analysed fully with appropriate remedies suggested in The Jackson Report. He accepted that certain letters and documents required the signature of the Administrative President before nine o'clock the following morning so they could be actioned instantly. However, it annoyed him intensely that these urgent matters never arrived on his desk before five-thirty. By then, he always had many more important issues to think about and was hardly in any sort of mood to go through the small print. Nor could his series of signatures wait until the morning, for these days he was rarely up before eleven.

'Oh, damn,' Peter muttered as he held up the pile of documents before the bloated, raddled face he never saw – for his suite contained no mirrors and a barber came each mid-day. 'Get through this lot. How boring,' he sighed to himself and scrawled a drunken signature on page after page.

Good, it was done. As he tossed the pile onto Davina's desk, Peter remained blissfully unaware that he'd just signed away fifty thousand of his salary.

Peter Jackson was a very happy man.

'I must say,' said Markby, 'it's frightfully kind of you to come and see me. That really is very much appreciated.'

He sat up in the magnificent bed on which he reposed in a private hospital suite. His hand touched his angry, red facial scar gingerly. 'Not that this is anything much to a military man like myself but thank you again.'

'Not at all, Hugh,' said Savage, 'I've been gravely concerned.'

'Very kind indeed,' purred Markby.

'I came as soon as I could.' Savage sat impassively by the bed-side. 'Unfortunately, I was delayed by a series of unforeseen problems.'

'Ohh,' Markby sighed heavily, 'not more?'

'Yes, and all of them fascinating. But I do understand if your injuries have left you not quite up to hearing about them.'

'Of course I'm up to it,' Markby returned instantly. 'It'll take more than today to bowl me out, I can tell you. Just retired hurt for an instant, that's all that's wrong with me. The wound's not severe. Just a mild case of shock, they say, that's all. I'm over it now.' He smiled tightly then grimaced. 'Ow!' He sniffed. 'It only hurts when I smile.'

'I doubt if I'd find that a problem,' said Savage. Markby registered amusement but controlled the urge to smile. 'You can have the scar seen to by plastic surgery, anyway.'

'That's a thought,' Markby muttered. 'I assume that maniac of a girl was duly caught.'

'Not in time. She came into my office and blew her brains out.'

'*What?!*'

'Even I was amazed. Robert Slade, who'd followed her there, could barely believe it. Mike Armstrong, whom I'd summoned, proved to be off his head entirely. He actually accused me of shooting the girl.'

'I don't understand.' Markby groaned and shook his head. 'Forgive my stupidity – are you saying that Harriet Baker, after slashing my face, *shot herself in front of you?*'

'Yes. Robert is my witness.'

'Oh, God.' Markby's head sagged. 'How can you remain so calm? Is the Company going insane?'

'There might be an element of that,' said Savage. 'I can see a number of possible explanations.'

Markby was silent.

'Thinking?' Savage queried.

'I am almost,' Markby said, 'too overwhelmed to think.'

'Oh? You disappoint me.'

'Our image!' Markby burst out. 'It's ruined beyond redemption. One murder, one slaying and now one suicide in the Chairman's office! That's quite aside from the Kandy disaster . . .'

'Calm yourself,' said Savage. 'You pride yourself on that.'

'I know,' sighed Markby, 'but this is all completely mad.'

'There's morc madness yet,' Savage stated. 'Sid Ingram was grossly insulting to Stanley and walked out. Before Harriet assaulted you, she stabbed Martin Bottomley. Fortunately, the wound's not fatal. He's recovering here, a few floors down. But that's awkward too. And Kandy could not be rescued from disaster. Chris Faye was away from the agency. Brian Bishop and Tony Westbury did their absolute best but it wasn't enough and we've definitely lost Kandy. After that, I had to cope with the police.'

Yet you don't look tired at all, thought Markby. *Why is it that you never do?*

'They were tiresome,' Savage continued in a bored voice. 'As I told you, Mike appears to have gone round the bend altogether and is telling lies hysterically, rather like Nick Peters. He really should be charged with wasting police time – and of course we'll be suing him for the profits of the Kandy account which his outrage cost us. Personally, I feel that he's earned himself something extra after my time with the police he sent.'

'He needs to be destroyed,' said Markby.

'And will be.'

'But the police were presumably no problem?'

'Certainly not,' Savage responded. 'Even they couldn't miss the gun in the demented girl's hand. Clear case of suicide.'

'The publicity . . .' Markby breathed heavily. 'We could end up losing every account . . .'

'We'll lose some. It will take a while to recover.'

'Disaster,' muttered Markby.

'Yes, but temporary,' Savage replied. 'Anyway, what d'you think's at the root of it?'

'It's possible that this outbreak of . . . well, I can only call it collective insanity – was the result of being perhaps a little too hard on some.'

'You mean, they just snapped?'

'People do.' Markby touched his wound and winced at the memory of its infliction.

'You're probably right,' said Savage. 'And it'd be a wise move for the present to reduce levels of stress. Of course, there is another explanation.'

'Oh?'

'Yes, perhaps there's something in the story that the site on which our building stands was once used for Druid rituals. You may recall Robert Slade's report of his meeting last September with a man who argued something very like that.'

'You're not serious?' Markby gasped. 'The man Slade saw was a complete lunatic.'

'Even lunatics have their insights. Perhaps the suicide of Sandra Lang triggered off some force which possessed the more unstable of our employees. All too little is known about these matters.'

'Quite frankly, you stagger me,' commented Markby, who'd shuddered at the mention of Sandra's name.

'Do I?' Savage shrugged. 'Once one's done a little

travelling, things which once seemed strange become commonplace.'

'You mean, you accept the reality of the – ah – supernatural?'

'I don't like the term. Let's say simply that there are certain classes of event which few can explain and the existence of which is denied by many.'

'Do you believe,' Markby asked anxiously, 'in ghosts?'

'Yes.'

'Yes? Why?'

'The evidence for their existence, studied impartially, is overwhelming. You look concerned. What's on your mind?'

'Some people,' Markby gulped, 'claim to have seen Sandra Lang in the building.'

'Oh, yes, I'm familiar with those reports. They're probably true.'

'*What are you saying?*'

'That the ghost of Sandra Lang has returned,' Savage answered matter-of-factly. 'That could be awkward for some. If I were you, I'd organize a discreet exorcism. That usually works.'

'I'm just flabbergasted, quite frankly,' Markby sighed. 'This is all completely beyond me. You're treating a stupendous violation of the natural order as though it was merely an administrative problem.'

'Yes, that's exactly what it is,' said Savage. 'Dear me, you are being dull today.'

'Well, I don't pretend to have your understanding of these matters.' Markby shook his head and tried to fend off its ache of unreality. 'But I'll bow to your wisdom and bring in an . . . an *exorcist*, was it? Quietly one night.' He searched for a line which might recover his position. 'In the meantime, our next major action is obvious.'

'And what's that?'

'Leave the building, of course. Sell it or lease it and find another site.'

'No,' said Savage, 'I like it there. It's very interesting.'

'It's a damn sight too interesting for me, I can tell you. For heaven's sake, we can't carry on like this. It's insane.'

'Today has been,' the Chairman admitted, 'but now you and I shall proceed to restore sanity. Leaving the building is out of the question, so forget that. What we have to do is pull the Company together again and I may have to devote more time to it. Our billings are obviously going to take quite a tumble. Still, it's a superb opportunity to trim our fat. That'll restore common sense soon enough.'

Markby writhed inwardly. Anything irrational disturbed him deeply and Savage's impassive acceptance of the supernatural had astonished and perplexed him.

'The restructuring of Savage & Markby,' said Savage. 'Start from the top. Your move.'

The Vice-Chairman passed a weary hand across his furrowed and perspiring brow. At least he was back to a familiar game and could shut out every other concern for the present. Yet he hadn't felt so uneasy in the Chairman's presence for a very long time indeed. For nearly three decades he had enjoyed everything he'd always wanted. He'd virtually forgotten that talk in which he'd acceded to Savage's bizarre request. Of course what Markby had done was no more than complying with the irrational whim of an intellectual giant. He'd never really taken the action seriously, though there were times – like tonight – when his mind was invaded by intensely horrible doubts. *Control yourself!* he commanded his thoughts and forced his attention back to mundane matters.

'Peter Jackson.' Markby licked his dry lips. 'What's going to happen to him?'

'Isn't it obvious? And he's perfectly happy about it. The attention of adoring women, sexual pleasure, a playpen and a bottle to suck – what more does any man want?'

'That,' Markby swallowed, 'leaves the Managing Directorship vacant.'

'What's your proposal?'

'How about,' Markby sought for a solution sufficiently ingenious to please the Chairman, 'a Joint Managing Directorship shared between Brian Bishop and Chris Faye? They'd be at each other's throats until they dropped.'

'You mean, kill two birds with one stone?' Savage nodded approvingly. 'At any other time, that'd be exactly the thing to do – but there's an urgent need to pull the Company together and restore credibility and confidence with our clients. That's why I'm promoting Brian Bishop to the position, though he'll still continue as Creative Director too. He'll do well, wear himself out utterly and shortly be ripe for plucking. Meanwhile, Chris can seethe until we're ready for him. Next item: Stanley Haynes – and I expect something good from you.'

'Why, leave him where he is,' said Markby. 'He's with us in spirit and he does his job.'

'Precisely. I commend your succinct brevity. Though I think it's about time Stanley started amalgamating, winding down and abolishing most of Peter's committees. Next item: Mike Armstrong's replacement on the Board.'

'Tony Westbury,' Markby answered without the slightest hesitation.

'Quite so.' Savage smiled slightly. 'Oh, I *am* glad you're back on the ball. Yes, it was a good move to tempt him from Brady & Harding and there's a lot more juice left in that orange. Who goes up to Account Director?'

'Trevor Crosby?'

'No, Charles Sutherland. He's worn the dunce's cap for long enough. The man gets more interesting with every step he takes towards us,' Savage reflected. 'We'll let him fly for a bit before we clip his wings.'

'And Roy Price?' Markby queried. 'What about him? The other day I noticed that the profit on all his accounts had fallen by half a per cent.'

'Then it's back to Piddling for Roy.'

'That'll give him a nervous breakdown.'

'Exactly,' said Savage, 'after which we'll take good care of him. George Webbing could do with a spell in Piddling too. He remains much too sloppy.'

'Why not,' Markby suggested, 'brief Stanley to observe him?'

'Good idea.'

'Which means we need an Executive on Browning's.'

'Slade,' said Savage.

'Slade?' Markby looked astonished.

'Yes. Oh, he helped with the sabotage of this afternoon all right. I managed to get all the details out of him. It was a most satisfactory meeting altogether. Eventually, I persuaded him to see reason and he's now one of ours. There's quite a future here for young Robert.'

'I'm afraid your strategy's beyond me,' said Markby.

'How disappointing. You simply refuse to perceive his potential.'

'He's fought against us.'

'And he's lost,' said Savage. 'Now he'll be fighting for us. Next item: who replaces Ian Sharpe as Assistant Creative Director?'

'It has to be Ronald Potter,' Markby insisted. 'Completely loyal and utterly reliable.'

'My thoughts exactly. I'll have to have a talk with him soon. And Dennis Wilson can move up to Group Head.'

'Dennis Wilson? But the man's an anarchist,' Markby protested. 'Frankly, it wouldn't surprise me if he took drugs.'

'How closely have you been watching him?' Savage retorted. 'Yes, it'll be interesting to have a word with Dennis. As for Simon Burns and Sid Ingram . . .'

'The rebels,' Markby muttered.

'I have something in store for them which may amuse you.' Savage explained and Markby listened, initially with incredulity and then with growing admiration. 'Meanwhile there's one more promotion,' the Chairman continued. 'I wonder if you can guess it.'

'If George is off to Piddling, then you must mean Martin.' Savage nodded. 'Promotion, Bottomley,' Markby chuckled. 'Junior Assistant Account Executive to *Seenyah* Assistant Account Executive.'

'Precisely,' said Savage, 'and he'll be under Robert Slade. Other vacancies can be filled from outside the agency. Given the current recession, low salaries for new blood and fresh spirits will hardly be a problem – Hugh, why did you shiver just then?'

'Your choice of expression,' Markby answered uneasily.

'How amusing,' Savage remarked. 'You're not suffering from any regrets, are you? It's a little bit late for that. Do I have to remind you of what you signed almost twenty-eight years ago?'

'No,' Markby sighed, 'I remember what I signed.'

'And as I recall,' said Savage, 'it was in your own blood.'

25

It was eight o'clock in the evening when the gleaming black Mercedes limousine with its smoked glass windows pulled up outside a sedate Belgravia mansion. The grey-uniformed chauffeur stepped out and opened the door for Savage, who nodded curtly and went inside his home, where he lived alone.

His first action on arriving within the spartan, tasteful and discreetly expensive interior was to draw the cork from a bottle of vintage Burgundy and then leave the wine to breathe. Sitting down by the white telephone, he proceeded to make a number of calls to persons he addressed as Films, Transportation and Connections. In each case, Savage spoke briefly and issued instructions.

Ten minutes later, he went into a room which contained two abstract paintings by Mondrian, a table, a panel of buttons and a large chess board, the ivory figures of which were engaged in a game. Savage moved his Queen's Pawn forward one square, then pressed a button. Seconds later, his opponent responded, for he played against a computer and the answering move was shown on a small screen. Savage moved his antagonist's surviving knight as indicated and contemplated the board as if unimpressed.

'Mate within a dozen moves,' he murmured and returned to the main living room. There he poured himself a glass of red wine, sat down and watched independent television with ferocious concentration, paying particular attention to the advertisements. At midnight, he switched off the TV, finished the last of his one glass of wine and retired upstairs for the two hours sleep he normally took.

Perhaps the problems of today had robbed him of his appetite. In any event, he did not eat.

It was eight o'clock in the evening when Robert Slade poured himself a glass of red table wine and took stock of his surroundings. The comfortable flat in the Barbican, which was owned by the Company and which would cost him a mere twenty-five pounds a week, had every modern convenience. Robert gazed approvingly around the room. This home and the acceleration of his career at Savage & Markby would make him the pride of his parents and the envy of his friends. From now on, there'd be no stopping him. Thank the Lord for the wisdom of the Chairman!

He tried to recall the details of his talk with Savage, and the events which had led up to it and those actions which had followed, but a fog of confusion engulfed his faculties every time he made the attempt. It was no use exhausting himself in a futile battle through the haze his memory had become, he decided. Tomorrow everything would be clearer and for the present it was best simply to relax. Television was always good for that and these days he found the advertisements so engrossing, which is why he chose to watch independent television.

He had just seen a way in which the current Champion Bitter commercial could be improved when there was a short, sharp ring of the doorbell.

It was eight o'clock in the evening when Clarissa Markby said goodnight to her husband and left his hospital suite. Hugh would continue to rest in bed until some time tomorrow, he'd told her, for he still felt too weak to be moved. Clarissa thought that this course of action was thoroughly sensible. She wasn't to know that a mere thirty minutes after her departure, Markby rose from his bed, dressed and discharged himself.

Leaving the hospital, he stepped inside the Company

limousine he'd ordered. Markby had once defined good taste as being able to afford a Rolls or a Bentley but instead buying an Alvis or an Armstrong-Siddeley, and so his chauffeur-driven vehicle was a 1957 model of the latter. The Vice-Chairman enjoyed his ride, just as he secretly revelled in his many other pleasures: visits to his tailor in Dover Street and his bootmaker in Jermyn Street: lunching at the Connaught, dining at the Savoy and taking port by the upstairs window at Boodles. Tonight, however, the car took him to The Empress, where he was joined soon after by Teresa Greenwood and they proceeded to enjoy caviar accompanied by vodka and champagne and followed by a rare chateaubriand with which they drank a fine old claret.

Teresa, who was twenty-five and strikingly attractive, worked as an Assistant Account Executive at Wilde & Latchford. Much of the conversation was about her career, about her admiration for Savage & Markby advertising and about her impassioned ambition to make Account Executive soon. She'd had two interviews at Savage & Markby and the Vice-Chairman had met her on the second occasion. Over coffee and liqueurs, Markby told her he could 'probably' persuade his colleagues to give her a job as a full Account Executive with the Company and perhaps she'd like the evening to end with a 'personally conducted tour' of the premises where she might very well be working. Teresa accepted his invitation and did not remove her leg when Markby's knee brushed against hers.

A few minutes before midnight, the Armstrong-Siddeley halted at the back of the Savage & Markby building. Markby led Teresa to a scruffy yellow door marked PRIVATE, produced a key, opened up and ushered the girl into a narrow lobby with a lift. This whisked them up to the top floor, where the door slid open on Laura's empty office. Markby produced another key and unlocked his own.

The Vice-Chairman had the use of a flat on another section of the top floor but it was being occupied by Peter Jackson at present and in any case, he wouldn't have taken Teresa there. Nowadays he was virtually impotent except within the confines of his office. He hadn't made love to his wife in a year. He needed the surroundings of his inner sanctum, the spicy stimuli of skirts with frilly knickers, stockings and suspenders, the exhilarating sensation of power when the girl bent obediently over his desk and submitted to his baring of her buttocks, the intoxicating joy of his corruption of innocence and sometimes even the thrill of knowing that another woman was concealed behind his giant two-way mirror and taking photographs of the girl he debauched. Oh yes, Savage had always been most accommodating when it came to Markby's pleasures.

However, there was no hidden photographer tonight. That pleasure would come later. For the present, the relish of strange and unfamiliar flesh would be enough for his jaded appetite. And as he talked to Teresa afterwards about landing the job and the things he wanted her to do for him, he would gain her assent with the aid of a vibrator.

Markby opened the door and switched on the light but nothing happened. He frowned and, motioning Teresa to remain behind, groped his way into the dark room and towards his desk with its lamp. Oddly enough, it felt very chilly indeed and he shivered involuntarily. Had there been an electrical failure? He stopped, perplexed. The hairs on the nape of his neck were rising and his heart thumped as alarm spread through his nervous system. He was possessed by the horrible suspicion that there was someone else in the room.

A second later, he uttered a shriek of fright as his being felt blasted by wave upon icy wave of frenzied, malignant and devouring hatred. Cold bones grasped his testicles through his clothes and squeezed them to pulp as Markby screeched out his agony – and his ears rang with the gleeful howling of Sandra Lang.

He died with his face contorted in a rictus of shock, as if he was in the stinking embrace of a fiend who was dragging him down to Hell.

26

Robert opened his front door in response to the bell and reeled back as Mike, Georgina and Vickie burst through the entrance and halted, bewildered by his surroundings. For a few seconds, he regarded them with a surprised frown, then his features swiftly composed themselves.

'What's the meaning of this?' he asked coldly.

'Darling . . .' Vickie pleaded.

'What's got into you?' demanded Mike.

'That's none of your business any longer,' Robert returned. 'You've been fired from the Company. You're not invited here. You forced your way in. Kindly leave.'

'Robert, are you sure that's really such a very good idea?' Georgina enquired concernedly.

'Yes,' said Robert, 'please go away . . .' his eyes caught sight of something she was wearing. His mouth dropped open and he blinked stupidly.

'Robert . . . ?' Vickie came in anxiously as he swayed unsteadily, his stare still fixed upon Georgina.

'Robert?' Mike took his arm and Robert made no resistance, while his head rocked groggily. Georgina took two steps towards him and he moaned and sagged against the wall. Vickie rushed forward to catch his other arm as Robert's legs gave under him. Georgina sprang to Vickie's assistance. The ankh she wore brushed against his head. Robert yelped as though he'd been burned and as it touched his temple once again, jerked in a convulsion as though an electric shock had stunned him – and slumped unconscious in the arms of his friends.

'He's out cold . . .' Mike gazed bemusedly at the others. 'Here, let's get him to a sofa.'

'What's *happening?*' Vickie cried despairingly as they carried the unconscious Robert into the living room.

'The ankh,' Georgina murmured and switched off the TV.

'What?' Mike queried as he set Robert down.

'The ankh was what did it,' Georgina responded. 'The ankh I'm wearing.' She held up the solid, chunky object, which was suspended from her neck by a slim chain of stainless steel. 'It belonged to Cliff Mitchell. As I told you, Mike, I went to visit him in prison ten days ago. I felt one should, really. He seemed so pleased that someone had come. Today,' she looked down at the ankh, 'this came from his sister along with a letter from Cliff. He said he wanted me to have it as a good luck charm.'

'Oh my God,' breathed Vickie, 'I remember Robert telling me how Cliff wore it because it meant life and he believed in life – and the Chairman sent orders that he had to remove it . . .'

'What are you *saying?*' Mike demanded as Robert groaned and shook his head.

Vickie knelt by him. Robert stirred again and his eyelids fluttered open. Vickie took his hand while the others watched expectantly. Robert's eyes widened in surprise and once again he shook his head.

'What's happening?' he asked faintly. 'Where am I?' His answer was an awkward silence. 'Where is this? How did I get here? What are you doing here? What's going on?'

'Are we all going mad?' asked Mike. 'If there isn't some form of explanation soon, I shall flip my lid entirely.'

'Well, I can tell you what I remember.' Robert accepted a cigarette from Vickie, lit it, inhaled deeply, then prodded his skull with his fingers. 'God, it's so difficult . . . all right, I was in full control of my faculties until . . . until I saw Harriet Baker.' He related the events which had followed. 'Then I burst into the Chairman's office and freaked when I saw Harriet lying there dead and Mike crouching on the carpet,' he finished.

'Did Harriet have a gun in her hand?' Mike asked anxiously.

'I can't remember. I was too shocked to notice much. Then Savage took off his glasses. He has these extraordinary dark eyes which seemed to reach out and grip my will. That was when I looked at Harriet once more and saw the gun in her hand.'

'So you saw that too,' Mike commented. 'And yet I have a totally clear recollection of Harriet leaping at Savage and waving a knife, not a gun. *Savage* had the gun. He shot her – I *saw* it,' Mike insisted. 'Yet when he took off his glasses, I felt weak and nauseous and when I looked again, he no longer had a gun. It was in Harriet's hand.'

'Oh, God,' Robert groaned, 'it ended up back on his desk.' He explained how Savage had taken him over. 'It seemed as though my very soul was at stake,' he continued. 'Suddenly I saw the gun on Savage's desk. It was my only chance. I snatched it up and shot him.'

'You *shot* him?!' Vickie gasped. 'I don't understand.'

'Neither do I. I shot him in the stomach. I saw him slump unconscious. I was sure that he was dead. After that, my mind's a blank except for the moment when I tried to leave his office. He came to life again.'

'*What?*' Mike demanded incredulously. 'I mean, presumably he was just wounded and there was blood all over the place.'

'I can't remember,' Robert answered helplessly. 'After that, I can't remember anything at all.'

'You came home.' Vickie took up the thread and told a horrified Robert how he'd acted. 'Then you walked out.'

'Oh, God . . .' Robert moaned, 'what did Savage *do* to me?'

'I followed you here by taxi,' Vickie went on, 'but I didn't know what to do, so I phoned Mike and Georgina.'

'But what is this place?' Robert gestured at his surroundings. 'Why did I come here? What sort of being *is* Savage?'

'I don't understand,' Mike said wearily, 'but he seems to have some kind of hypnotic power. You must've imagined that you shot him. It's the only possible explanation.'

'Heaven knows,' Robert responded, then added: 'Where's Ian?'

'More bad news,' said Mike. 'I was talking to him on the phone just before I saw Savage and the line went dead. I've been calling him at home ever since I left the agency and there's no reply. I suppose I should call the police but so far they've been useless. They took my statement about Harriet and said they'd be in touch. At this rate, Savage is literally going to get away with murder.'

'Unless something's done,' said Vickie.

'Is he even a human being?' Georgina queried.

'How d'you mean?' Mike asked.

'Well, perhaps he's not,' Georgina suggested. 'Just think a moment. I admit it sounds crazy but . . . he *does* have incredible powers of hypnosis. Look at how he affected your perceptions, Mike, and look at what he did to Robert. He's totally evil – that's not in dispute. And what does he really do? He corrupts people and destroys them. He sucks the lives out of them and eats up their souls . . .'

'Christ,' Vickie murmured, 'that's what Nick Peters said.'

'I think,' said Georgina, 'that Savage may be a sort of vampire.'

'No,' Mike snorted, 'that's simply too ridiculous.'

'Not all vampires suck blood, Mike. Couldn't there exist beings who are *psychic* vampires and who devour the energy generated by human beings?'

'Yes,' said Vickie.

'Yes,' Robert echoed her.

'How else,' Georgina demanded, 'do you explain the effect of the ankh upon Robert?'

'Sorry?' Robert stared wildly at her. She responded by holding up the ankh. 'I'm not quite with you . . .' he muttered, then: 'Hey, that looks just like Cliff's ankh.'

'It is,' Georgina told him. 'And when you were – well, I suppose "possessed" would be the right word – you were dazed and weakened by the sight of it, you yelled in pain when it touched you and when that happened a second time, you blacked out. The ankh brought you back to normal and so now it doesn't bother you at all. What does that mean?' Georgina asked fiercely. 'What is an ankh? It's the Ancient Egyptian symbol of Life. It's also the Sign of the Cross with a loop – and traditionally, vampires are repelled by its holy power. Maybe that's why Savage ordered Cliff Mitchell to remove his.'

'What you're suggesting is making my head spin,' Mike commented. 'What I do know for certain is that Savage is wealthy, brilliant, powerful and evil. I don't think he'll rest,' Mike continued grimly, 'until he's destroyed us. In the end, it's either us or him.'

'What can we do?' Robert asked.

'Silver bullets?' Vickie put in. 'Aren't they supposed to work?'

'Yes – and then we get done for murder,' said Mike. 'Try telling a courtroom about vampires.'

'I've got an idea,' Georgina said. 'It might be our only hope. We've got to move fast and before Savage strikes. The alternative, quite simply, is getting destroyed.' And she proceeded to talk for nearly fifteen minutes, then answered objections, nearly all of which came from Mike. 'Well, have you any better ideas?' she finally demanded. 'Would you rather sit around quietly until it's your turn to follow Nick Peters into some hellish oblivion?'

'We could all follow him into a mental hospital for the

criminally insane, that's for sure,' Mike returned. 'Suppose you're wrong and he's not a "psychic vampire" at all?'

'Then it's all rather difficult, really,' said Georgina.

27

John Savage awoke, as was his custom, at two A.M. that morning, took a bath, drank one small cup of black coffee, entered his study and proceeded to work at various matters until the phone rang at eight A.M. He listened impassively, issued a series of orders, then replaced the receiver and made notes until eight-fifteen, when he left his house for the chauffeur-driven Mercedes which was waiting for him outside. This took him to Savage & Markby, where he entered the building in the normal way and took the lift up to the top floor, where a security guard was waiting.

The Chairman followed the ashen-faced guard into Markby's office, where the Vice-Chairman's corpse was in *rigor mortis*, its hands clamped on the cloth which covered its genitals. There was an expression of excruciating pain upon the face. Savage betrayed no visible reaction at all other than standing silently by the body for a few minutes. Eventually, he dismissed the guard, went into Room One, telephoned Laura and gave her the day off and pressed a button which rendered access to the top floor impossible unless he wished it.

The ensuing ten minutes were spent in Room Four, where he watched the recording of Markby and Teresa arriving in Laura's office the night before on Screen 3, listened to the screams when Markby entered his own office on Screen 2, witnessed Teresa's panic on Screen 3 and watched her flee to the lift.

Returning to Room One, he telephoned someone he addressed as Information. Information called back within the hour, whereupon Savage dialled another number and spoke to someone else he addressed as Arrangements.

'Coffee?' Georgina offered as Mike came into the breakfast room. He nodded and she poured. 'Here's some orange juice and toast. I can make you scrambled eggs if you like.'

'No, thanks, love,' he returned morosely. 'I'm worried about Robert. Did we do the right thing?'

'I just hope to God we did. There's no alternative, is there? Savage mustn't suspect a thing and the only way we can ensure that is if Robert carries on as if he's still entranced. That means staying at that flat in the horrible Barbican and carrying on going to work.'

'And probably encountering Savage again.'

'He's wearing the ankh beneath his shirt.'

'Suppose we're talking nonsense and it doesn't work?'

'Then we're up the metaphorical shit creek,' said Georgina, 'without the proverbial paddle.' She drank some coffee. 'I was thinking of going to church this morning.'

'Why not?' Mike shrugged. 'Maybe it's a good idea.'

'But I've decided not to go after all. It's evil that we're fighting,' for an instant her jaw jutted like that of her father, the Rear Admiral, 'and the Church has done so many things in its history which I consider evil.' She paused and looked thoughtful. 'Perhaps I'll just go for a walk in Holland Park.'

'I'll come with you.'

'Thanks, Mike,' she smiled, 'but I need to be alone. Oh – here's a letter for you.' She passed it over.

'That's Ian Sharpe's handwriting.' Mike tore the envelope open. Extracting a handwritten letter, he began reading it immediately then stopped, astounded by its contents. He frowned and made another attempt. By the end, he looked utterly nonplussed.

'What is it?' Georgina asked urgently.

'I thought I knew Ian Sharpe quite well. It appears I don't. Listen, I'll read it to you. No address. It's dated the day before yesterday. "Dear Mike, By the time you read this, Kandy will have died on us as intended and we'll be suffering the consequences. I will have broken off all contact with you and fled. For this, I apologize. All I can say in excuse is that I'm terrified.

'"Contrary to the impression I probably gave everyone at the agency, I've been watching developments for some time. I knew the truth about Kandy long before you broke it to me. I had also learned about the ruined lives of those who had dared leave Savage & Markby. So my escape was planned in secrecy and silence.

'"By the time you read this, I pray with every atom of my being that I will have got away for good. Ian Sharpe is dead – please burn this letter after reading it – and his successor has gone somewhere else. You see, Savage is not just some malefic megalomaniac. *Savage is not human*.

'"Do you think I'm paranoid? Have I blown my brains on too much cocaine? Think about my words, I beg you, for I like you very much and am frightened for your safety.

'"There was a time when I kept my personal and work lives completely separate. For a long time, the sole exception to this rule was sex. I belong to a mystical sect which holds sexual intercourse to be a great and holy sacrament. I love sex. I find God and the Goddess in union with woman. And also, worldly sod that I am, I can't resist a woman who tempts me, least of all when Savage has planted her there as forbidden fruit. Every woman I fucked at the Company was more than the woman I adored with my body: our act was a gesture of defiance at the Company whether she knew it or not: and our act was also the bringing of Light into Hell.

'"You probably think that I've become a raving nutter. That's one phrase for people like me who start reading about the occult in their teens and taking it seriously. Luckily, I soon grasped four basic commandments –

Know, Dare, Will and Be Silent. So I've carried on my private quest for life, love, liberty and light whilst pretending at work to be someone else. That's been quite enjoyable, for the most part. I can see why, in the films, Superman gets a kick out of being Clark Kent. Even you were fooled, Mike.

'"My quest has led me through many curious paths. I have enough experience of the occult to know that beneath ninety-five per cent of sheer lunacy, there is a noble and dazzling gem of truth. What, then, do my studies tell me about Savage? There are a number of possibilities, all of them related.

'"That Savage is a psychic vampire – as poor Nick Peters told me before he went under. He lives off the energy generated by frustrated human endeavour. Maybe that's why one can feel so void and exhausted after seeing him.

'"But maybe there's more to it than that. Orthodox Hindus believe that their great gods – Vishnu, Shiva or Krishna, himself a form of Vishnu – manifest as human beings in incarnation after incarnation. The Indians call them avatars and they help humanity towards enlightenment. A similar belief is found in Mahayana Buddhism. Humans who have achieved liberation from earthly life nevertheless choose to return as bodisvhattas, refusing Nirvana until every soul has attained it.

'"If gods do it, why not demons? If there are those who seek to liberate humanity for incarnation after incarnation, aren't there likely to be those beings which seek to entrap and enslave the human spirit?

'"Christians believe that God was once made manifest in human flesh. Perhaps the Devil does this also. Perhaps there are demons who stalk in the midst of man.

'"Or possibly – it was the doctrine of a sect to which I once belonged – there are beings among us, and they have always been among us, but they have sprung from a seed other than that of Adam. They are not animated by a human purpose. They are hostile to the human race. Their desire is to supersede us in evolution and make us their slaves.

'"Choose whichever theory or theories you prefer – then ponder what you can do against Savage and you will be tempted to despair. We have antagonized him. Therefore every fraction of his vast forces will be turned to the task of exacting his vengeance.

'"Whatever you do, whatever you may think, for the love of God heed my advice.

'"Never, ever look into his eyes.

'"Wear an ankh. It is the sacred symbol of Life which Christians later corrupted into the Cross, symbol of death, though the idea of resurrection still keeps it holy. Whatever manner of being Savage may be, he hates and fears that symbol and will shrink from it.

'"If Savage is, as I have suggested, a demon or related evil spirit, then there may be something one can do in the way of traditional Ceremonial Magick. Perhaps you think me mad merely for mentioning the subject – but hasn't your recent experience convinced you of how strange a place the world is? Medieval magicians claimed to know of gestures, weapons, and spells which can subdue the fiends of Hell. I commend the idea to your most sober attention. Ankh Books of Leeds may be able to assist you. They have often helped my researches in the past and know what they are doing.

'"No, I don't think I'm mad. I hope that's your view too. And if I were you, I'd be me and abandon a fight you're likely to lose – and lose horribly. I pray that Georgina will disappear with you – along with Robert and that girl of his I haven't met but who sounds damn good.

'"Call me a coward if you like, but I cannot face an agent of the Devil unless I am charged with that task by God. Nor do I understand how God works His Will. It is possible that at this time, He is failing us because we are failing Him.

'"I wish you all the luck in the world, mate.

'"Love to Georgina,

'"Love,

'"Ian."'

At eleven o'clock that morning, Sid Ingram obeyed a summons from the Chairman and entered Laura's office. She wasn't there but he went straight through into Markby's office, as instructed. The Vice-Chairman wasn't there either. Sid went through, as ordered, and as he opened the door which led to the hallway, bumped into Dennis Wilson, whose eyes were glazed but who nevertheless seemed possessed by joy. Sid watched Dennis stride away and past Markby's desk. The man was looking ten feet tall.

There was confusion on Sid's face when he stepped into the Chairman's corridor. After insulting Stanley Haynes and walking out, things had been terrible. Soon after he arrived at his empty house, Herbie Tyler had phoned to say that Harriet was dead. She'd shot herself in front of the Chairman.

Sid stayed in and got drunk. He cried and he wept and he stumbled around the room. Gloria did not return. Shortly after ten, he passed out – coming to the following morning in an empty house with a raging hangover. He sank into misery. A girl he had been growing to love was dead. The girl he had loved and still felt so much for had not bothered to come home. He had lost his job. Then the phone rang and it was Savage.

The Chairman expressed his colossal regrets over the tragedy of Harriet. He expressed further regrets about Sid's 'unfortunate misunderstanding with Stanley'. He was sure it could all be sorted out happily provided Sid came to see him in Room Two at eleven.

When Sid knocked on the door of Room Two, he was fearful despite the Chairman's soothing words. He'd never had a personal interview with Savage before. At least this wouldn't be taking place in Room Three.

'Hullo, Sid,' Savage said pleasantly. 'Come right in and sit down.' He paused and looked tormented by strain. 'Things really have been pretty terrible.' Sid nodded. 'Compared to the dreadful tragedy of your secretary, your own incident yesterday shrinks into insignificance. It all became a bit much for you, didn't it?' he said gently.

'Yes,' Sid answered, 'that's exactly it.'

'Very understandable.' Savage nodded sympathetically. 'The point is that however bad things get, one simply has to carry on. The fact is,' he continued slowly, 'that I'm only here two days a week – I have interests other than this Company – and that's why it's taken me so long to notice your genuine ability.' Sid sat up attentively. 'In view of your worth, I'm prepared to overlook your insulting behaviour.'

'I'm really sorry,' Sid assured the Chairman. 'I've been under such a tremendous strain, as you said . . .' He stopped himself from adding 'guv'nor'. 'And I can't tell you how much I appreciate . . . well, the way in which you're being so understanding about it all.'

'That's my job,' said Savage. 'Anyway, as far as I'm concerned, provided you're prepared to apologize to Stanley, there's nothing in the way of increasing your salary by three thousand pounds per annum and promoting you to Account Supervisor on Browning's, Joy, Minnie, Trafalgar, Toreador and Tom Spivey.'

'Thank you.' Sid smiled in delighted astonishment. 'Thank you very, very much indeed.'

'You deserve it,' said Savage. 'You've been maligned and misjudged. I hope my action constitutes some form of reparation.'

'Thank you, Mr Savage.' Now Sid understood why Dennis had looked so glad. 'Thank you once again.'

'Not at all,' said Savage, 'the pleasure is entirely mine.'

At one o'clock exactly, Savage left the building for his Mercedes and the chauffeur drove him to White's, where he'd been invited to lunch by a government Minister. The Chairman instructed the chauffeur to have the car waiting for him in precisely ninety minutes, and went into the club.

The chauffeur, whose name was Greg, parked the vehicle and sauntered off to a nearby pub. He was followed by a girl who wore a skimpy sweater, tight jeans and a blonde wig and who had been watching the limousine for most of the morning. He noticed her only when she entered the pub, bought herself a glass of white wine and sat down at a nearby table, where she extracted a cigarette and appeared in need of a light. Greg moved swiftly to her aid and as his lighter spat flame, made a few chatty remarks to which she responded well. He asked if he could join her. She seemed happy about that.

Greg sat at her table and discovered that the girl, who said her name was Marie, had a delightful personality in addition to her appetizing looks. She listened attentively to everything he said and made him feel intensely interesting. She laughed appreciatively at his every attempt at humour. She seemed fascinated by him and encouraged him to tell her all about his life, even down to the details of his daily routine. Greg knew he had to be discreet but saw no harm in talking generally about what he did, where he lived and the hours he kept, especially since she seemed to find it all so riveting. Though she seemed rather unintelligent, Greg decided, she was a lovely person with a great body who was behaving as though she really fancied him. Just before he told her that he had to get back to work, Greg asked her for a date and she agreed to see him in a few evenings' time. Greg went back to the Mercedes feeling extremely pleased with himself.

Vickie, who had taken the day off work, went home exhausted by the strain of her pretence.

At three o'clock, Robert was summoned to Room Two by Savage. As he proceeded to obey the summons, he felt acutely nervous and hoped that the ankh beneath his shirt would afford him some protection.

It had been hard to keep going today. Robert didn't want to do one scrap of work for Savage & Markby yet he had to pretend he was completely dedicated to the Company. People kept coming up and congratulating him on his promotion and he had to keep thanking them and smiling and nodding. Otherwise, the atmosphere in the agency was awful. Harriet's suicide and the Kandy catastrophe had left nearly everyone shocked and demoralized.

Taking a deep breath, Robert followed the Chairman's instructions and went straight through the empty offices of Laura and Markby to Room Two, where he knocked on the door.

'Come in.' Robert entered. 'Morning, Bob,' said Savage.

'Good morning, Mr Savage.' Robert gritted his teeth and tried to look keen but submissive.

'How're you feeling today?' Savage appeared to inspect him closely.

'Fine, thank you.'

'How's the flat?' Savage enquired.

'Excellent, thank you.'

'I'm glad,' said Savage. Casually and deliberately, his fingers flicked a gold pen off his desk and onto the floor. 'Pick that up.'

'Sorry?' Robert was startled.

'I said, pick that up, Bob.' The opaque panes regarded him steadily. Robert had no alternative other than to rise obediently, bend over submissively, pick up the pen as ordered and meekly return it to Savage. 'That's right,' said the Chairman. 'I wanted to see you because the police are coming shortly,' Savage continued. 'They'll be wanting to interview you again with regard to the tragedy of Harriet Baker.'

'I've already told them everything I know.' The presence of the Chairman was making Robert feel slightly sick. 'She shot herself.' Speaking those words nearly choked him. 'I saw her.'

'That's right,' said Savage, 'but there are one or two other points.'

At four o'clock, Mike had just arrived by express train at Leeds station. A taxi took him from there. He passed the impressive Queen's Hotel, the magnificent Victorian Town Hall, the commercial centre with its busy streets and banks – and all the while he was wondering if he had gone crazy. His fear increased in intensity as the taxi drove him through a wasteland of slag heaps with no sign of human habitation, then entered a section of the city dominated by old and dingy back-to-back terraced houses, which brought back memories of his own early life. There were grubby fish-and-chip shops and drab corner pubs.

Now it appeared as though he was entering a section inhabited principally by students. The streets remained mean and shabby but the shops were more individual. Mike noticed a Real Ale Co-operative, a number of colourful second-hand clothes shops, several record dealers – and The Ankh Bookshop, which was his destination. The cab halted, Mike paid the driver and then he entered the shop with his heart thumping.

The only person inside was a slim red-headed woman of roughly his own age. She had a thin, pale and sensitive face and was dressed ordinarily enough in a black sweater with blue jeans. Mike greeted her politely and looked quizzically at the shelves of occult and religious books, fantasy novels, jars of incense and curious ceremonial implements in glass cases. The unfamiliarity of the environment was making him feel acutely uncomfortable.

'Excuse me,' he began. 'I was recommended to come here by a customer who's a good friend of mine. I'm not sure if you recall Ian Sharpe . . .'

'Oh, I know Ian.' The woman smiled fondly. 'How is he?'

'Um – he's fine, thanks,' Mike returned awkwardly. 'Anyway, he thought you might be able to assist me.'

'I'll do my best.'

'Well, I'm very interested in Ceremonial Magick,' Mike blurted out. The sentence made him feel like a complete fool and he reddened. 'I'll be needing some equipment and a book.'

'What sort of stuff?' she replied as though he was just another customer.

'Um – Ian advised me to take your advice,' Mike told her. 'But it's particularly important that I have some ankhs. Four to be precise.'

'Invocation or evocation?'

'Sorry – what?'

'Are you invoking the gods or dealing with demons?' His ignorance appeared to puzzle her greatly. 'Because for the latter, we also do these, which some of our customers find useful.' She held up an ankh which had been wrought out of the hilt of a wickedly sharp steel dagger.

'That's exactly it,' said Mike. 'I'll take four of those.'

'They're thirty pounds each.'

'Fine.'

'Okay, I'll wrap them up for you,' she returned, clearly surprised by the sums he was prepared to spend. 'Anything else?'

'Er – yes. What book can you recommend that's good on controlling,' he swallowed, 'demons and evil spirits?'

'Oh,' she raised a knowing eyebrow, 'working with the Goetia, are you?'

'Yes, yes, the Goetia.' He coughed nervously.

'*The Key of Solomon*'s the classic work on that, of course, but I expect you've already got it.'

'I had it, naturally,' Mike lied, 'but it's been stolen. So I'm in need of another copy.'

'We've got it in a limited edition.' She held up a volume bound in white kid-skin. 'But it's forty pounds, I'm afraid.'

'Fine. That should see me right, shouldn't it?'

'That depends on the nature of your work,' said the woman. 'D'you mind my asking . . . well,' she frowned, 'you don't look the type who's involved in the occult. Mind you, Ian didn't either. I assume you're familiar with all the precautions because, quite honestly, what you're doing sounds like pretty high-powered stuff.'

'You could say that,' Mike answered as his temples throbbed with an intolerable ache of unreality.

'I'm sorry we have to keep asking you these questions, sir,' Detective-Sergeant Dexter apologized to Robert. 'Only we do have to make absolutely sure we've got everything right. There's just one last thing I don't quite understand.' He consulted his notebook. 'You say that you witnessed the suicide of Harriet Baker. You tell us that you saw the deceased shoot herself through the head with a small, black pistol, right?'

'Yes, that's what I've said.' Robert stubbed out his cigarette. Would this nightmare of lies and corruption and deceit never end?

'So why,' asked Geale, 'has Mike Armstrong, your former Departmental Director, claimed that you were outside the office when the fatal shot was fired and that it was fired by no less a personage than Mr Savage?'

'I'm amazed,' said Robert. 'That's simply not true.'

'Why d'you think he's lying?' Geale queried.

'Heavens knows. I suppose,' Robert looked thoughtful, 'that he was so horrified when she shot herself that his mind couldn't handle it and started playing tricks on him.' Robert bit his lower lip.

'He'd just been sacked, hadn't he?' said Dexter.

'And after, I gather, an act of sabotage against the Company – am I right?' asked Geale.

'Yes.' Robert nodded.

'Would you agree,' Geale enquired, 'with the opinion of some of your colleagues, that Mike Armstrong has recently been acting rather strangely?'

'I think I would,' Robert replied slowly and forced himself towards the last lie the Chairman had prepared for him. 'These last few weeks . . .' he swallowed but his throat remained dry, 'Mike seemed to be going – well – a bit funny, really.'

At six o'clock, Simon Burns gazed contentedly around his Notting Hill bed-sit. No, he hadn't yet made it and his present home was hardly Buckingham Palace but he was finally realizing how enjoyable life could be. The room was spacious, it looked out onto gardens, the bed was comfortable, a roaring gas fire kept out the cold, there was a fridge and a couple of gas rings for cooking – really, he had everything he needed.

His days were his own and there was joy in that. Never again would he have to endure hateful Ronald Potter. And never again would he be tormented by his wife's incessant nagging.

True, there wasn't much money coming in but he drew the dole and the Department of Health and Social Security paid his rent and gave him Supplementary Benefit. Given that, and the smallish sum he'd managed to save out of his salary, he could survive quite happily for the present. After all, his needs were sparing and it wouldn't be long before the big money arrived.

He should've left his wife ages ago, Simon reflected. As it was, he'd never forget Chris's expression of open-mouthed astonishment when he announced that he was leaving. She couldn't believe that he'd found the strength to defy her and everybody else. She'd raged and stormed, then wept and pleaded but Simon had finally made up his mind. He'd grown into a man, he'd had enough of a woman who treated him like a naughty boy and he was leaving.

He'd stayed a night with Dennis, found a decent bed-sit remarkably quickly on the following day, sworn his friend and colleague to secrecy regarding its whereabouts, moved into his own home and re-organized his life. His adventure into independence had gone surprisingly well. And when Dennis had forwarded a letter from Chris, it had made him laugh.

'Darling Simon,' the letter began, 'I hope you're all right and I'm ever so worried about you. I feel I've sometimes been rotten to you, it's all my fault and I'm truly sorry. Please come back and I promise to make it up to you.

'There's something else that's good as well. The Company's being incredibly nice and understanding. Mr Savage himself rang yesterday – he's ever so nice and polite. He said they really rated you, that you'd been under tremendous pressure recently and that everyone wanted you back at the Company. What a fantastic agency Savage & Markby is! *Please* see sense and go back to them. You've got such a great future there and even the Chairman's taking an interest in you.

'And please come back to the loving arms of your one and only princess – remember how you used to call me that? I'll do everything for you, I promise, and you can write as much as you like – until the day when you have the bestseller you deserve. Come back and be kissed.

'Lots of Love.

'Chrissie.

'XXX.'

Simon had pinned that communication on the wall – next to a giant nudie poster – and in large red letters he'd scrawled on it the word: 'BOLLOCKS!'

Oh yes, he'd bucked the System all right and was going all out to buck it some more. A week after walking out of the agency, he'd written a ten page outline of *Tentacles* and sent it to another paperback publisher. Two days ago, a letter had arrived expressing much interest in the project and inviting him to lunch tomorrow with the Associate Editorial Director, no less. Naturally he'd bring along the finished manuscript – his days had been devoted to a critical scrutiny of its contents, perception of its faults and feverish revision and rewriting.

Perhaps the initial advance would be modest but he knew the book would explode its way to bestseller status. Then he would approach the great James Herbert as an equal and thank him warmly for the inspiration and influence which had helped him to chase his dream, defy the world and achieve his ambition. He would be up there with Stephen King and Harold Robbins, Frederick Forsyth and Jeffrey Archer, Judith Krantz and Jackie Collins. Russell Harty and Michael Parkinson would have him on TV and ask him all about his life and work and what he normally had for breakfast. Women would swan up to him at fashionable parties, hang upon his every word and offer their bodies in tribute to his genius.

True, there wasn't a woman in his life right now but these were early days yet. The instant that he made his first big score, Simon knew exactly what he'd do. He would return in triumph to Savage & Markby, swagger along the corridors, snub Ronald Potter, take Dennis for a slap-up lunch and then it would be time to dazzle Fiona Spencer-Wingate. He'd drive her to dinner in his new black Porsche and screw her back at his penthouse. God, how he fancied Fiona! She'd slapped his face when he was nothing – but in the future she would sigh for a suck of his stiff prick.

Simon regarded the typescript of *Tentacles* with proud anticipation. He'd worked hard today and felt he deserved a break. Checking his wallet, he discovered that he had enough for several pints of good beer at that pleasant pub he'd recently discovered. That'd be a real pleasure – and there was no one to scold him whatever time he came back. His time was his own. He'd fired all his bosses.

Putting on a coat, Simon went out into the dark, lamp-lit street. There was a chill wind but he found it refreshing. He walked with the assurance of a man who respects himself and thought of what he would tell the publisher tomorrow. He became so entranced by an imaginary dialogue that he paid virtually no attention to his surroundings. It came as a very sudden and unpleasant shock when two men seized him from behind and threw him into the back-seat of a saloon car with smoked glass windows. The blindfold was over his eyes before Simon's numbed brain had time to take note of faces and the muzzle of a gun was pressed into his ear.

'Don't move,' a voice hissed. 'Just be a good boy and don't move.' The order was unnecessary. Simon was already frozen by terror. 'Hands behind your back,' the voice whispered and Simon obeyed. There was a click of handcuffs around his wrists. Another *snap!* and his ankles were similarly fettered. He went into an involuntary fit of trembling as a hand snaked into his coat pocket and extracted his room keys. ''Ere.'

'Thanks,' another grunted and a car door opened and closed. The engine started up and the vehicle moved off.

'Open yer mouth,' the whisper came again. A petrified Simon complied with the request and was promptly gagged with a thick cloth. The journey continued. Simon began to perspire freely with the stinking sweat of fear.

His bewildered brain whirled with terror. He prayed silently and fervently for just an ounce of the courage and resourcefulness his hero had displayed in his novel while his bowels churned with the acids of anxiety.

The car stopped. Doors opened. Strong hands gripped him, hauled him out into the cold night air and carried him bodily into another interior. As he was set down in a hard chair, he had never felt so weak, so frightened or so completely helpless. A light was switched on. Doors were shut behind him. Cans were opened and poured but nobody spoke. Simon pleaded silently for his safety.

At length, there was the roar of a motor-cycle drawing up outside. Its engine spluttered and died and the silence was followed by a knock. A door was opened, there was a heavy tread of boots coming in and the door was shut yet again.

'Got it?' came the whisper.

'Yeah,' a coarse voice replied. 'No problem. It was on his desk.'

'Nice one. Okay, let's get on with it.' The blindfold was whipped away from Simon's face.

He blinked confusedly and fearfully. It seemed he sat inside a lorry of the type that's used for furniture removals. Three big men regarded him, though black silk masks hid their faces. A coal brazier glowed several feet away. Above it, one of the masked men held the only copy of *Tentacles*. Seconds later, he dropped the typescript onto the red-hot coals.

No! Simon tried to scream but the gag reduced his protest to a series of squeaks. *Don't do that, do anything but that. Hit me, beat me, do anything you like but don't do that. That's me you're burning there – that's my life's work – please no and no and no, no, no, no, – NO!!!*

His body writhed in speechless torment. He lost his balance and crashed to the hard floor where he lay bound and helpless, with tears streaming from his eyes as he sobbed.

'Crying shame,' said the burner and shrugged as the flames consumed Simon's masterpiece and left only ashes. Simon curled up in the foetal position as the last scrap of fiction was devoured.

The men picked him up and put him back in his seat. Once more the blindfold robbed him of sight. The lorry's engine started up and the vehicle moved off. Simon no longer cared where he was going. All his hopes for the future had perished in the flames.

Yet as the journey continued, Simon perceived one last faint ray of hope. Perhaps these men didn't mean to kill or maim him. Perhaps they would let him off with a hiding and he would have to promise them he'd never write again. He'd swear to anything just to get away – and then he'd run and hide somewhere. He'd find a place where they would never find him. He could remember nearly all of *Tentacles*. He would write it all over again – if only he lived. *Dear God, I want to live*, he prayed. *Please*.

Who had sent these men? Why did they want to destroy his writing? What would they do to him now? The lorry halted with its engine still running. To his astonishment, shears cut through his coat until it could be pulled away from his body. Then fingers undid his belt, pulled down the zip of his jeans and tugged the garment down to his ankles. His underpants followed. Simon shook with fear. A door opened and he was once more lifted up bodily, carried through the cold and set down on a hard surface. A doorbell rang and footsteps retreated hastily. He could hear the lorry draw away as another door opened. Somebody gasped and someone else went: 'Shush!'

He found himself propelled forward and inside. The chain on his fettered ankles forced him to take tiny, mincing steps. A door closed. The blindfold was removed – and Simon very nearly died on the spot.

'Surprise!' cried Chris – and Angie and Yvonne, two married friends and neighbours, shrieked with laughter.

For he was standing in the marital living-room, his mouth gagged, his hands manacled behind his back, his ankles chained together, with his trousers and underpants around his ankles while three women pointed at him and howled with gleeful mirth.

'So the wanderer returns,' Chris remarked with a sneer. A flash-bulb popped and she captured his shame on an Instamatic camera.

'More!' demanded Angie and toasted the captive with a glass of wine. 'I want a souvenir too!'

'And me,' squealed Yvonne. The camera flashed and clicked several times. 'Look, he's gone red as a beetroot.'

'Who's a silly little boy, then?' Chris taunted her husband. Simon wished the earth would open up and swallow him. His cheeks glowed with his humiliation as his defeated eyes stared helplessly down at the carpet. His penis had shrunk to the size of an acorn nestling between two hazelnuts. 'See,' his wife declared proudly, 'I told you he'd be back.'

'And I reckon he's learned his lesson,' said Yvonne. The girls exploded into high-pitched giggles.

'Serve 'im right too,' said Angie. 'He's a right disgrace walking out on his wife like that. Who does he think he is?'

'We can see what he is now,' said Chris, 'and he's staying like that till he's sorry. I've got the keys,' she held them up teasingly in front of Simon's face, 'and he can stand there until I'm ready for him to apologize in front of all of us.'

'I 'ope it's back to work for him on Monday,' Angie put in. 'You must've had enough of his scribbling rubbish.'

'His Company's been unbelievable,' Chris told her. 'They want him back just so long as he behaves himself.' She shot a scornful glance at her shamed and silent husband. 'Hear that, Simon?' The doorbell rang. 'Oh, I know who *that* is,' Chris said cheerfully. 'Someone at the agency had a really good idea, you just wait. 'Scuse.'

Simon wilted beneath the withering contempt of Angie

and Yvonne and wished he was dead. His wife answered the door.

'Chrissie!' a voice exclaimed and Simon almost expired there and then. 'Simply super to see you and sorry I'm late. Oooh! I say! *What* a sight!' exclaimed Fiona Spencer-Wingate and emitted a peal of laughter which finally destroyed what was left of Simon's spirit. 'How funny!' she squealed. 'It's the funniest sight I've seen in ages! And to think that, come Monday, he's my new boss.' Fiona swept into the room flaunting her fur coat. 'How appropriate,' she sniggered, 'and quite right too. As *your* boss is always saying, Simon,' Fiona told him sweetly, 'don't buck the System.'

28

On the following morning, which was a Friday, John Savage was once again working in Room One at Savage & Markby. To all outward appearances, he was satisfied with the course of events, despite the fact that Markby's sudden disappearance had been reported in the media and doings at Savage & Markby had become the talk of the town. A murder, a manslaughter, a suicide and now a mysterious disappearance – this was all too good for the media to miss. Clients were becoming increasingly jittery. There were rumours that many would depart in the wake of Kandy.

The Chairman had spent much time in dispensing reassurance. Brian Bishop, Chris Faye, Stanley Haynes and Tony Westbury had all been to see him too – and they'd expressed great anxiety. But all had left the office with their nerves soothed by the tranquil confidence of Savage. He'd admitted that the agency was facing the greatest crisis in its history and that its billings might even drop below twenty million as a temporary consequence – but Directors' salaries and perks were safe and the Chairman would look after them, investing his own private wealth if need be.

Nevertheless, any businessman in Savage's position would have been shaken by the phone-call which abruptly interrupted his labours.

'Doris,' the voice announced down the line. 'Peter's gone.'

'Oh, yes?' Savage seemed unruffled, as though he'd been expecting the news for some time. 'When?'

'I went to his bedroom this morning, Mr Savage, and

there was Jackson, lying in his bed and dead as a doornail. It wasn't . . .' the voice faltered momentarily, 'it wasn't a pretty sight, I can tell you. Davina and me, we brought him whisky all the time last night, just like you said, and he went and choked to death on his sick.'

'Good work,' said Savage. 'Thank you. There'll be a car for you both outside the back entrance in roughly twenty minutes and it'll take you to a hotel. Stay there. You'll get the cash tomorrow, plus a bonus.'

'Thank you, Mr Savage.'

'Then it's time you had a free holiday.'

'Oh, *thank* you, Mr Savage.'

'I'll call you tomorrow,' said the Chairman and broke the connection. After a moment's thought, he called another number. 'Hello, Removals. Yes, I need some goods transported from the usual place to the usual place. Now.'

Robert emerged from the barber's with a short-back-and-sides. Crossing the road, he headed for an outfitters recommended by Georgina as stocking every kind of uniform for servants and flunkies.

As Savage's chauffeur had mentioned to Vickie, he usually visited his local betting shop at around mid-day. On leaving the bookmaker, he strolled slowly back towards the Company car park in a section of the basement, taking the shortest route, which was via a narrow alleyway. He failed to notice the powerfully built man in working overalls who was walking behind him and had no reason to expect the cosh blow to his right temple which sent him sprawling to the ground, unconscious.

Mike thanked the juvenile gangs of the mean streets where he'd grown up for training which had finally proved useful in later life. Slipping the cosh back into the deep pocket of his overalls, he glanced around to see if anyone was watching. No one was. He produced a quarter bottle of scotch and poured the liquor over the chauffeur's face and hair. Then he hauled the unconscious man who looked and smelled like a drunk to his feet and carried him the short distance to the deserted Company car park. It didn't take long to whip the keys out of the chauffeur's pocket, open up the boot of the Mercedes, gag the man with a thick cloth, fetter his wrists and ankles with bicycle chains and shove the victim into the boot, after which he slammed it shut.

John Savage entered the car park at one o'clock precisely and, as was his habit, opened the limousine door for himself and climbed into the back. There was no reason for him to inspect the chauffeur closely. All he saw was the usual man in the usual place. He was about to close the door when Mike leapt into the limousine and placed a dagger across the Chairman's throat, holding the hilt so that the ankh tilted upwards.

Savage flinched.

'Don't move or I'll cut your throat,' Mike snapped. His free hand slammed the car door. In the front seat, Robert pressed the button which locked it.

'Have you gone insane?' Savage demanded hoarsely.

'Shut up,' Mike growled and pressed the blade's keen edge against the taut skin stretched over the Chairman's jugular vein. Robert started the engine. Savage's left hand came up to adjust his glasses. 'Don't move.'

'You're crazy,' Savage returned.

In answer, Mike touched the Chairman's chin with the ankh. Savage's head was thrown back against the leather seat as though he'd been jolted by an electric shock. The arm he'd raised dropped limply to his thigh.

'Behave yourself,' said Mike.

The limousine moved out of the car park, up a concrete slope and into the street. Its smoked glass windows hid Savage and his companions from public view.

* * *

It was Les Smith's fifth day in the Creative Department at Savage & Markby. His job was that of Visualizer and he was thoroughly enjoying the experience. Although he was wary of Ronald Potter, recently promoted to Assistant Creative Director and visibly proud of the fact, he was being shown the ropes by Dennis Wilson, who seemed a really great guy. On Monday, Les would be joined by the copywriter, Simon Burns. Apparently, there'd been some trouble and Simon had been suffering from severe nervous strain but that was all over now and Les was looking forward to meeting his colleague. Monday would also bring a new secretary in the delectable shape of Fiona Spencer-Wingate, who seemed to adore Dennis and who sniggered secretively whenever Simon's name was mentioned. So far, Fiona had behaved rather haughtily towards Les but he was convinced he'd have a chance with her in the future.

'Les – a quick word before lunch,' said Dennis, who'd just breezed cheerfully into the room. Les sat up attentively. 'Hope you're settling in all right.' Dennis adjusted his tinted glasses and Les nodded eagerly. 'As you know, from Monday I'm your Creative Group Head. Just one word of advice.' Dennis sat down opposite his junior and regarded him patronizingly. 'Don't make the same mistake as an old associate of mine. There's something here,' he explained, 'which exists for your benefit. If you've got any sense, you'll appreciate that. Otherwise, quite honestly, you won't get nowhere. We call it the System.' Dennis once more adjusted his glasses. 'And don't buck the System, okay?'

The Mercedes cruised into the garage of Georgina's house. Robert switched off the engine, left the car and closed the garage door.

'Move,' Mike ordered Savage. 'If you try anything funny, I'll hurt you again.' Savage, who appeared to be suffering from weakness in his limbs, complied with the instruction and clambered out of the car. Mike followed, staying close to the Chairman and keeping the blade across the latter's throat. Robert opened up the door which led to the kitchen and they passed through the room to a flight of stairs, which they descended. Again Robert opened a door and Mike shoved Savage into a bare and windowless cellar which contained nothing except a bunk, a naked, burning light bulb and, hanging from a peg in the wall, Cliff Mitchell's ankh.

'What,' the Chairman shrank away from the object and his voice was faint, 'is the meaning of this?'

'You'll see,' said Mike.

'Well, well,' Colin Miller chuckled in Conference Room One that afternoon, 'it's a right shame Mike's gone so suddenly but aside from that, everything's coming up roses, eh? Tony's on the Board, Charles is up to Account Director and for Supervisor, it's Sid – and it's a pleasure to meet you, Sid. Where's young Robert?'

'Bob's away sick, unfortunately,' Tony Westbury answered. 'He should be back on Monday.'

'Well, I must say I'm pleased that all of you have done so well.' Colin's eyes twinkled behind his spectacles. 'Because come Monday, I'm joining me own Board as the new Marketing Director.' There was a chorus of congratulations. 'Tim here's moving up to succeed me as Group Product Manager.' Tim beamed smugly. 'So it's congratulations all round and why don't we celebrate with a brandy, eh?'

'Good idea,' said Tony.

'And since it's me last time here at the agency for quite a while, how about another look at the *other* agency reel?'

'Why not?' Tony answered. 'It's been improved since you last saw it.'

Sid Ingram sat back happily as brandy was poured.

Things had definitely improved since his talk with the Chairman. There'd been the awkward matter of apologizing to Stanley Haynes but the bald Financial Director had been surprisingly nice about it all. Then last night, Gloria had been waiting for him when he came home. She'd got drunk with a girl friend the night before, she explained, and had ended up staying the night. She was sorry about that but she'd come home early today and made a special dinner. When he told her about his salary increase and promotion, she hugged him and it was just like old times. After a delicious meal, there was bed and sex for several hours.

Today Sid had woken up feeling in love and glad to be alive, though there remained a lingering sadness over Harriet and he doubted if that would ever disappear entirely. Still, now it was time for brandy and the legendary *other* agency reel, which he'd never seen before. That couldn't be bad.

Tony pressed a button. A panel in the front wall slid back to reveal a video screen. Another button caused blinds to slide down and cover the windows, plunging the room into darkness. The screen came to life to show a full-busted woman who was sucking a man's cock.

'*Phew!*' Colin whistled and leaned forward eagerly. 'Rum stuff!' He couldn't see the colour drain from Sid's face. He didn't see the Supervisor sit up in total horror.

For the woman sucking a cock was Gloria. After sucking it, Sid's wife mounted the cock and fucked it for a time. Then she pulled up her skirt to show she wasn't wearing any knickers and masturbated with a vibrator. Her next action was to lie across a man's knee and have her voluptuous bottom spanked. Colin breathed heavily and called pointedly for more brandy.

Sid watched dazedly as Gloria was sodomized then gang-banged in a group orgy. After a frozen close-up of his wife's wet vagina, the film died away.

'What a cunt!' declared Colin as the blinds slid up and the room was filled with sunshine. 'And she had a nice fat bum. *Four* cock-stands,' he informed them proudly, 'and all of 'em were winners.'

Sid resisted the urge to vomit. Tony and Charles were regarding him curiously.

'I'm sure I've seen the girl somewhere before,' said Charles.

'She looked,' Tony gazed knowingly at Sid, 'just a little bit like your wife.'

'He's frightened of the ankh.' Mike swallowed a shot of brandy. 'I don't understand it but he's scared of that symbol, just as Ian said.'

'When we locked the cellar door,' Robert came in, 'he'd retreated to a corner.'

'So perhaps,' Georgina was watering a potted plant, 'we're all talking sense after all.'

'God knows,' Mike sighed. 'In the eyes of the Law, we're now criminals and lunatics.' He put his glass down on the living-room table. 'I'd better go and compound our crimes by taking care of the car and the chauffeur.'

'I'll just get this bloody uniform off,' Robert said, 'and then I'll be right with you.'

'How long's this nightmare going to last?' Vickie demanded anxiously. 'I know it sounds absurd, given what we're doing, but if I keep taking days off work, somebody's going to get suspicious.'

'I know how you feel.' Georgina rubbed her tired eyes.

'At the rate we're going,' Mike burst out bitterly, 'we might just as well bump him off and get it over and done with.'

'We can't do that, darling,' Georgina told him resignedly. 'We just can't.'

'He said we were crazy,' Robert murmured. 'Right now I'm beginning to wonder.'

'You're not the only one,' Georgina returned. 'But what else can we do? If he's some sort of vampire, I'm praying that he'll perish now that he's deprived of victims. And if he's something even worse, I suppose the ankh will make him show his true colours.'

'And then?' Vickie queried nervously.

'Then there'll be all hell to pay,' said Robert.

No one was watching an hour later when a black Mercedes limousine skidded to a halt in a deserted country lane in Surrey. This was fortunate, for an observer would have seen Mike emerge from the car, pull a nylon stocking over his head, open up the boot, haul out the bound chauffeur and heave him into a copse by the side of the road. For the second time that day, a cosh thudded against a skull and rendered a man unconscious. Mike's gloved hands unlocked the chains and removed them.

Returning to the car, Mike drove on slowly for a few miles and was relieved to see Georgina's Morgan in his rear view mirror several minutes later. He stopped the Mercedes and climbed out. Robert drew up in the Morgan and opened the door for Mike.

'Refreshments,' said Georgina as she entered the cellar with a glass of water and a plate of sandwiches. A dagger with an ankh as its hilt was suspended from her neck by a slim steel chain and she took care to keep her eyes lowered.

'What are you doing?' the prisoner enquired calmly. He had seated himself on the floor in the corner furthest from the ankh hanging on the wall and had also removed his glasses. 'I don't understand how you can do this to me.'

'I think you know the answer to that.' Georgina placed the plate and the glass in the centre of the room and retreated in the direction of the door.

'No, I don't, I'm afraid,' Savage responded. 'I'm completely bewildered. All I can see is that I've been kidnapped by a group of lunatics. Have you lost all powers of reason?'

'No.' Georgina halted. 'Quite the contrary.'

'You astound me, Georgina.' She stiffened at the mention of her name. 'I've always thought of you as a rational, decent and intelligent person. Yet here you are engaging in a bizarre act of – well, I can only call it terrorism. Are you completely mad?'

'No.'

'Then why are you doing this?'

'I've already answered that.'

'You know,' Savage commented evenly, 'you're not making any kind of sense at all. It's anyone's guess what the police will make of your statements – they should be here shortly, by the way. One would think you were in quite enough trouble with them already.'

Georgina did not reply. Her instincts were screaming for her to depart from an evil presence yet her reason suggested that the prisoner was right. Her throat felt constricted and it was almost impossible to speak.

'Do you really want to bring shame and disgrace upon your family?' Savage continued with maddening tranquillity. 'Do I *look* like a monster?'

Georgina's eyes flicked upwards automatically but she caught herself just in time and returned her gaze to her shoes.

'Enough of this nonsense,' Savage insisted. 'Kindly release me.'

'No.'

'No? Why not?'

'I'm going,' said Georgina and backed away.

'You're going insane,' Savage stated.

She stumbled from the cellar, slammed the door and locked it, sagged exhaustedly against the wall and wondered if he was right.

* * *

Ian Sharpe left the plane which had just landed at the airport at Perth, Western Australia, where he would enter the country as Don Ashley. He'd shaved his head, his jowls were graced by the black stubble of an incipient beard, his eyes were shaded by dark glasses and a silver ankh was chained around his neck. His heart beat with gratitude for the cousin who'd suggested his move here and who'd set up the meeting with the Managing Director of Carling James Robertson (Advertising) when the latter had visited London nine weeks ago. As a result, Ian would be joining that company as its Creative Director.

He was aware that life in Perth would be very far removed – in more ways than the merely geographical – from that of London. It was why he had come here. But, as he strode briskly towards Immigration and Customs, he couldn't help wondering if he'd ever stop feeling paranoid about the malevolence and powers of Savage.

'Could we please be rational for a moment?' Savage requested when Mike entered the cellar with more water and some biscuits. Mike didn't answer. Keeping his eyes lowered, he placed the victuals by those which Georgina had brought earlier and which the prisoner had left untouched. 'I'm amazed at you, Mike,' Savage continued. He was still seated on the floor in the corner furthest from the ankh. 'I always thought of you as being a sensible, hard-headed sort of person.'

'I am.' Mike backed away.

'First Assault and then False Imprisonment,' Savage retorted, 'quite aside from Theft of a car and whatever you've done to my poor chauffeur. Kidnapping too,' he murmured. 'What's sensible about that?'

'You said,' Mike reached the door, 'that you'd enjoy destroying me bit by bit. I'm just making sure you can't – which sounds sensible enough to me.'

'But you'll be caught,' Savage replied matter-of-factly.

'And that'll be the end of you – and Georgina. For the sake of her life as well as your own, I urge you to be reasonable.'

'Like you?'

'Yes. After all, we're both businessmen. We don't like one another, I admit that, but it doesn't mean we can't do a deal that's of benefit to us both. Face it, Mike, if the police aren't here today, they'll be here tomorrow. It's hardly in your best interests to ruin your future along with that of Georgina.'

'I'm not listening,' Mike muttered.

'Pity,' said Savage, 'because I'm about to offer you one million pounds.'

'You can stuff your tricks.'

'Tricks?' Savage protested innocently. 'You're not thinking clearly. If you agree to let me go, I'll let you have a million pounds in cash and you can make your own life from there. We'll call it quits and I swear I shan't bother you ever again.'

'You're a murderer.' Mike couldn't prevent his voice from quavering. 'Go to hell.'

'I'll see you there first,' Savage returned as the cellar door slammed.

Sid Ingram, who had stumbled from the agency the instant that the Browning's meeting had ended, arrived home just before six. Every atom of his being throbbed with the shame and rage of a man reduced to the tiny and pitiful stature of a public cuckold. He'd phoned Gloria at her office but they'd told him that she hadn't been in today. There was violence in his heart as he burst into his empty house to find, not his wife, but the letter which turned his thoughts from murder to suicide.

Dear Sid, it read. *By now you will have seen the new version of what they call the* other *agency reel. You won't be seeing me again. You always said you wanted me to be happy. At last I am. Because of what I did, I'll never need to work again.*

I'm off to somewhere where it's sunshine all the time and I'll be living there with Terry, who was a co-star in the film you saw. You might remember him from the old days. He went inside a year before we got married. They let him out six months ago and I've seen a lot of him since then. I've always loved him but never could see a way in which we could be together. I thank my lucky stars now that certain people have made that possible.

Thank you very much for all you've done for me, Sid. I admit I've been a perfect bitch to you and I can't blame you if you hate me forever. You're a really nice guy and I'm sorry – but you should know by now that, in this world, nice guys finish last.

You've got a chance to get way ahead, though. Go back to the Company. There's a great future waiting for you there. Don't worry about the video. It'll only be shown to top level clients. I know you can't feel too pleased about that – but in this life, you have to take the rough with the smooth.

And I've been asked to tell you that if you don't return to Savage & Markby, the reel will be shown to any client who asks for it as well as in the Training Scheme and at the annual Summer Party. So you will go back to Savage & Markby, won't you, darling?

Goodbye, Sid, and thanks again for making my golden future possible.

Love

Gloria.

29

The man sat in the Vice-Chairman's office, stared dully at the notes he had made on the pad before him, frowned and scratched his head. He looked as unhappy as he felt, yet up until recently all had been going remarkably well. Last Friday morning, he thought he had reached the climax of his career and that had been made possible by the sudden and unexpected death of Hugh Vincent Markby.

The man wasn't sure just how Markby had died – Savage had been very cagey about that. Not that it mattered especially. Nothing was important when compared to the call he had received requesting him to see the Chairman, the ensuing talk which had made all his dreams a dazzling reality and the explanation which had made everything seem so terribly simple.

He had been chosen to succeed Markby. Savage had expressed his sorrow over 'poor Hugh's demise' but had added that the former Vice-Chairman had become just a little bit old-fashioned in his ways. 'You're here,' Savage had continued, 'because I need a deputy who's attuned to the mood of the Eighties.'

The man was only too happy to oblige. He was being offered everything he'd ever wanted. In his case, that meant power – for sex and food and wines and other luxuries really meant very little to him. Whereas Markby had gloated over the trappings of power, his successor thrived merely on its substance. Yes, there was a price to be paid but the newly appointed Vice-Chairman could barely bring himself to take it seriously. He thought that Savage had his quirks and eccentricities like all brilliant men and he was perfectly happy to humour the whims of the Chairman. Insofar as the man could feel joy, nothing could surpass his sense of exaltation at the moment of his promotion – and then the unthinkable had happened.

Savage had gone missing.

That was why the new Vice-Chairman scratched his head, frowned and stared at the notes before him with growing frustration and perplexity. '*Chairman – Room 1 – 5.00 – Friday . . .*' the words his secretary had written in his appointments book resolutely refused to offer him the slightest assistance. The plain facts were that Savage hadn't been there: that Laura had no idea where he might be: that repeated phone-calls to Savage's home had gone unanswered: that this behaviour was wholly uncharacteristic: and that Friday, Saturday, Sunday and Monday morning had come and gone without a word from the Chairman.

The man was worried. Naturally he had informed the police but they had so far discovered nothing. It was time for rather more drastic measures. Every possible lead had to be followed up and hunted down and perhaps the names to begin with were Oliver Dawes, Sid Ingram, Ian Sharpe and above all, Mike Armstrong. And, come to think of it, why was Robert Slade off sick again?

The new Vice-Chairman's fingers flicked through the little black book Savage had given him. His eyes narrowed as he reached for the phone and dialled a number listed simply as Investigations.

It was shortly after mid-day when Georgina went out to buy some necessary provisions. As she walked towards the shops, she couldn't help glancing anxiously around to see if she was being observed. Once again her situation struck her as incredible. She would not believe that it was so. It was something she would wake from, as she had woken from nightmares of Larry Cunningham's murderous assault upon her, for things did not really happen so. She could not believe it, she would not believe it. Maybe she had got into a book, into a tale which one read and shuddered at but didn't for one moment credit; all make-believe, it must be, and everything would be all right again. And then the truth came down on her like a heavy hammer and beat her down and held her down on the burning coals of her anxiety.

She bought her groceries mechanically and stepped outside the shop. It was a sunny day and passers-by were going about their ordinary business. For a moment, Georgina allowed herself to breathe deeply and to offer up a silent prayer that in the end all would be well. She looked thoughtfully across the street – and caught her breath. There, outside the little newsagent's opposite, were posters advertising today's papers: New Clue in Multimillionaire's Disappearance.

It was all she could do to prevent herself from breaking into a panic-stricken run. She walked home with her heart pounding furiously. It was as if she and her friends had found out and discovered, they alone of all people living, a new world of which no one before had ever dreamed, in which no one could believe if told the story of it. When she reached her house, she couldn't help slamming the front door behind her and bolting it against the outside world – then she dropped her shopping bag and sagged against the wall.

The doorbell rang.

Georgina started, gritted her teeth, ordered herself to keep calm and opened up reluctantly to reveal a nondescript middle-aged man in a shapeless grey suit.

'Miss Georgina Mainwaring?' he enquired politely.

'Yes . . . ?'

'You're the owner of this property?'

'Yes . . .'

'William Trevors, Value Added Tax Inspectorate,' said

the man and produced an official card. 'Well . . .' Georgina faltered, 'what's that got to do with me?'

'We understand there've been certain irregularities.'

'That's ridiculous,' Georgina retorted. 'I don't pay VAT.'

'Maybe that's the irregularity,' said the inspector. 'May I come in?'

'Why?' Georgina demanded.

'I'm sorry, Miss Mainwaring,' he inclined his head respectfully, 'but I'm only doing my job. My instructions are to enter and survey the premises and to ask you one or two questions – nothing to be frightened about – after which . . .'

'And I'm sorry too but I'm frightfully busy and I'm sure this is all some ghastly mistake. Tell your people to write me a letter.' She tried to close the door but the man's foot was in the way. 'If you don't mind . . .'

'I'm afraid,' returned the man, 'that I am fully entitled to enter whether it's convenient or not. The Law,' he pronounced the word reverently, 'gives me the power to do so. And it is my solemn duty to inform you that resistance to this legitimate demand is in fact a criminal offence.' His hand darted to his inside breast pocket and produced a crumpled copy of a Parliamentary statute. 'Must I quote you chapter and verse, Miss Mainwaring?'

As Robert placed a glass of water and a bowl of ravioli on the floor in the centre of the cellar, he noticed that the prisoner was still leaving his food untouched.

'You're making a terrible mistake,' said Savage. Robert warned himself to pay no attention to his words. 'You're the only person at the Company who has the potential to succeed me.' He glanced at Savage and stiffened in startled surprise. 'Which future do you prefer?' Savage continued quietly. 'Capture, trial and incarceration as a dangerous lunatic – or the fulfilment of your every desire as my right hand man?'

Robert wanted to move. He knew he had to move. Yet he stood quite still.

'Oh, yes, Robert, my right hand man. Markby's gone, you see. I need someone younger, someone with energy and new ideas. You'll never need to worry about money ever again,' Savage went on steadily. 'You'll have everything you want financially. You'll be an important figure. You can have as many women as you require in whatever way you require them. Perhaps you'd care to enter politics? I can arrange that. Fame? That can be done very easily. Power? Yes, that's what you really want, isn't it? Let me go – and I will give you power.'

'I'm not interested,' said Robert, 'in that sort of power,' but his tone sounded strangely unconvincing.

'Of course you are,' said Savage. 'Everybody is. It's just that it's become fashionable to deny the fact – isn't that true? Look at me.'

Robert did. The instant that his eyes met the dark, staring orbs of Savage, his senses shrieked out that he'd made a mistake – but he could not tear his gaze away. It was as though the room melted before his eyes and he looked out onto seductive visions in which his every fantasy was effortlessly fulfilled. He knew that if he stared a moment longer, he would be sucked into a vortex which would pervert his will beyond redemption. Sweat dripped from his brow as he clutched the ankh which hung from his neck and fought his way back to his own private vision of Vickie. He clung to his belief in liberty as though it was a piece of driftwood from a wrecked ship on a swelling, storm-tossed sea.

'Don't fight it,' whispered Savage. 'It is the way of the world.'

'Not my world,' Robert croaked, covering his eyes with his hands as he reeled back against the ankh on the wall.

Savage rose and took two steps towards him.

'*No!*' Robert screamed. He leaped blindly for the egress, staggered through the doorway, slammed the door shut, locked it and collapsed sobbing on the steps.

'You've just sealed your fate,' Savage called out from within the cellar. 'You're all crazy. This is criminal insanity. You'll never get away with this. The police'll be here soon.'

'Top floor, one bedroom, a bathroom and a storeroom,' said William Trevors, VAT inspector. 'First floor, two bedrooms, a bathroom and I suppose you would call it a second drawing room. Ground floor – kitchen, dining room, downstairs toilet and main drawing room, living room, sitting room, lounge – call it what you like, reception room, even – they're funny things, names.' He smiled.

'You might at least,' Georgina did not return his smile, 'have the decency to tell me what this is all about.'

'I'm just following my instructions,' said Mr Trevors. 'Just a cog in the machine, that's all I am, just a cog. Now that point of egress over there,' he regarded the door which led to steps and the cellar. 'What does that lead to, if I may ask?'

Georgina stiffened automatically, then ordered her tensed and knotted muscles to relax and said casually: 'Oh, that's just a damp old basement with a few bottles of wine in it.'

'May I see it, please?'

There was an awkward pause. Georgina's brain raced as anxiety constricted her chest like a clamp.

'No,' she said at last, 'you can't.' She wished to God that Mike hadn't gone out, that Vickie hadn't gone to work, that Robert wasn't downstairs in the cellar with Savage. 'I'm afraid that's just not possible.'

'Oh?' He raised a pained eyebrow. 'Why ever not?'

'Because I'm completely fed up with this absurd inquisition. It's an utterly unwarranted intrusion into my home and if the Law allows it, then the Law is a perfect disgrace. If you attempt to force an entry, I shall resist you as I would a common burglar and if you lay a finger on me, I shall sue you for assault. I've had enough. Kindly leave.'

'I'm sorry that's your attitude,' William Trevors replied calmly and ponderously, 'because the Law states . . .'

'I don't give a shit what the Law states,' Georgina snapped in total exasperation. 'And if you don't like it, you can stuff it. Get out!'

'Oh, God, what's the problem?' Robert had suddenly emerged through the doorway, his face white and drawn. He glanced wearily at the intruder. 'Who is this man?'

'William Trevors, Value Added Tax Inspectorate.' He appeared wholly unruffled. 'It appears, Miss Mainwaring (a) that my continued presence is not wanted here (b) that I am faced, in the course of attempting to perform my duties, with the threat of forcible ejection and (c) that you are defying the Law. Very well,' he coughed once and drily, 'I shall take my leave.' He strode self-importantly towards the front door. 'I shall see myself out, if you don't mind. And mark my words,' he opened the door then turned to face Georgina, 'you'll be hearing from us.'

Hours later, the four friends sat silently and miserably in the living room.

'How was he today?' Vickie spoke at last.

Robert shook his head and poured himself another whisky from the crystal decanter.

'I know how you feel,' muttered Mike. He put an arm around Georgina and gazed at her tenderly. Robert sank shakily into a chair and drank some more scotch. The spirit burned as it slid down his gullet and flowed into his empty stomach, imparting a warm glow to its walls. He relished the sensation but it still did little to assuage his anxiety. *This can't be right*, he reflected as he had done countless times today. *It's all insane. What the hell is happening to me?* His eyes roamed the room restlessly, avoiding those of his companions.

Finally, his lids closed wearily as his head lolled back – but his mind continued to creak on obsessively. How would the nightmare end? With the death of the prisoner, perhaps – that was possible – but in what manner and by what means? Or else there was the prospect of defeat, arrest and life-long suffering in a mental hospital. Which was more likely? He didn't know and didn't really dare think about it further.

Yet he wasn't one of the lucky ones who have complete control over their thoughts. His exhausted brain persisted in grinding out his recent past again and again and again – until he longed to cry out with the pain of it.

Dazed by shock and fatigue, his mind reeled before its contemplation of a horror that had blighted, scarred and broken lives – and souls, if they existed.

The new Vice-Chairman scrutinized his notes of the reports he had received. Oliver Dawes could be ruled out – he'd become a junkie and incapable of doing any harm to anyone other than himself. Something similar could be said of Sid Ingram, a broken man whose life would progress from one pub to another. However, Ian Sharpe seemed to have vanished as mysteriously as Savage – further investigation was urgent and imperative.

And of course there was Mike Armstrong, who was known to have moved in with Georgina Mainwaring. Could Ian Sharpe have taken refuge there too? According to the report, Georgina had seemed very ill at ease. She had refused to show a basement room to an agent posing as a legally empowered official – why? Then a young man had emerged from that very basement looking strained and exhausted – and the agent had written an exact description of Robert Slade.

There was no time to lose. According to Savage, Mike Armstrong was going mad. If he had infected others with his delusions there was no telling what might have taken place. It was essential to act promptly and for the present, legally. The man picked up the phone and dialled.

'Hello, police? Inspector Geale, please,' said Stanley Haynes.

30

The four friends sat morosely in Georgina's living room. Four days had passed since the incarceration of Savage. Now hour succeeded monotonous hour. There was nothing to do except wait. They had tried playing cards, board games, word games and telling stories but it was done without enthusiasm, even with resentment at the minimal concentration required. Down in the cellar, the prisoner still refused to eat and persisted in his attempts to baffle, compromise, split and dominate his captors. Outside the house, a manhunt went on – yet life continued as normal for most, as if to confirm that the captors had committed themselves to a gross and bizarre delusion.

Mike regarded his associates gloomily. Georgina was drinking her way through a bottle of claret. Vickie stared into space. Robert was reading *The Sun* for the third time that day. Otherwise there was silence, the subdued silence one hears in a betting shop just after the announced race result makes everyone a loser.

The police will have interviewed the chauffeur by now, thought Mike. *They'll be tracing the purchase of uniforms, discovering that Robert and Vickie weren't at work on Friday, asking anyone who noticed a black Mercedes to come forward . . . and meanwhile there's the comeback from the VAT people – if they were the VAT people.*

Suddenly he couldn't stand the silence any longer. He rose impatiently, strode towards the radio and switched it on.

'. . . police believe,' came the announcer's voice, 'that a new clue may enable them to solve the mysterious disappearance of company director John Savage. Foul play has not been ruled out . . .'

'Oh, shit,' sighed Georgina, 'turn that bloody thing off.'

At that moment, ten policemen were in the process of climbing into one car and one van parked outside New Scotland Yard.

'It fits,' said Dexter, who was sitting in the back seat of the Rover with Geale. 'Grudge against the Chairman, gone off his head, acting all peculiar – that's our Mr Armstrong. Let's face it,' he lit his pipe, 'it does fit.'

'Don't matter if it doesn't,' Geale muttered in answer. 'Fact is, we've got a search warrant. Let's go, lads,' he added to the driver.

'Here's your water,' Vickie said as she entered the cellar to see Savage standing at the end of the room with his head hanging limply from his shoulders. He appeared to be having difficulty in breathing. 'There,' she placed the glass in the centre of the room.

'I'm dying,' he moaned and all strength had left his voice. 'How can you do this to me? I appeal to your sanity and compassion.'

'You're evil,' Vickie retorted, 'and you have no compassion for anyone.'

'Evil?' Savage whimpered helplessly. 'No . . . no . . . I'm just a businessman, that's all.'

'I wish that was all you were.'

'But it is,' he whined. 'Please, I'm not the wicked man you take me for. Look at me – do I look like an evil being?'

Vickie looked at him and remembered she'd blundered just an instant too late. His eyes glowed with an inhuman intensity as his will fastened upon hers. She felt as though pincers of steel had reached out to squeeze her skull and mash her mind. All logical connections between her thoughts were banished from her head. She no longer knew what she was doing and her brain seemed to be melting in a furnace of confusion. Of course she had no right to imprison an innocent businessman. It had all been a mistake and she'd been such a fool to allow the others to talk her into it. All she could do now was make some form of reparation to the man she had wronged.

'Take off the ankh,' said Savage, 'and throw it in that corner.'

Vickie nodded dumbly. His voice seemed to come from very far away but it had an asserting and strangely reassuring quality to it now. She wanted to comply with whatever it commanded. Taking off the dagger with a hilt that was an ankh was the only possible course of action and she tossed it into a corner just as he'd ordered.

'Good,' said Savage, 'now the ankh on the wall.'

A police car and a police van skidded to a halt by a house just off Holland Park Avenue.

'Stay where you are till I call you,' Geale snapped into his police radio. 'We're going in easy. But when I call, just turn the ruddy place upside down!'

He stepped out of the car, the door of which had been opened smartly by his driver, and followed by Dexter and two uniformed men, strode purposefully towards the house's entrance.

'Vickie's been away a while,' Mike commented.

'Hadn't someone better go and check that everything's okay?' Georgina suggested.

'I'll go.' Robert rose wearily, left the room, crossed the hall, went down the stairs to the cellar whose door was ajar – and recoiled in shock as Savage came through.

The ankh, he thought and his hand darted for it as Savage smashed his skull into Robert's nose and rammed a knee into his testicles. Robert slumped groaning to the floor as Savage bounded up the stairs, ran into the hall and reached the front door at the instant when Georgina left her living room. A cry of astonishment erupted from her throat as she flung herself at Savage, ramming her ankh against his chest.

Savage shrieked with pain, staggered backwards and as Georgina came for him again, kicked her in the stomach. Georgina doubled up, her face bearing witness to her agony.

Savage had his hand upon the latch as Mike stormed into the hall.

'Right,' said Geale as he reached the front door. 'Let's see just what the hell is going on here.'

His fist thumped the door three times.

Mike tore the dagger from his neck and sprang at his foe. Savage's foot lashed out to thud against Mike's thigh and miss his groin by an inch.

Mike grabbed Savage by the hair, emitted a snarl of fury and loathing and, his face a mask of insensate hatred, drove the blade deep in between Savage's ribs and stabbed right through his heart.

The sound of a fist pounding on the front door echoed through the house.

Savage sank to his knees, blood bubbling onto the blade. Mike released the hilt of the dagger and stepped back, his eyes glazed with horror. Robert and Vickie crawled to the top of the cellar steps as Savage slumped upon the carpet, uttering the quiet and plaintive moans of a dying animal.

'You don't understand,' he gasped hoarsely. 'We . . . *we can run it all so much better* . . .'

'Police!' roared a voice from without. 'Open up!'

Georgina stared at Savage who was writhing on the floor. For an instant her vision blurred and then – then, to her disbelieving horror, Savage's face melted and changed as his body went into convulsions.

Before the glazed eyes and benumbed consciousness of his captors, Savage was transformed from one being to another – and another and another. They saw a Gestapo officer, a Nineteenth Century factory owner, an Eighteenth Century despot, a Puritan fanatic, a Spanish Inquisitor, a medieval Pope, a Hunnish chieftain, a Roman Emperor, a High Priest of Ancient Egypt – then an ape, an extinct mammal, a scaly reptile, a slimy amphibian, a saw-toothed fish, a mollusc – and then an unctuous oily substance which bubbled and boiled into a stinking pool of green, putrescent slime, like pus off a seeping boil.